VEGAS

one cop's journey

VEGAS
one cop's journey

a novel from the streets of sin city

Kim Thomas

Stephens Press
Las Vegas, Nevada

Editor: Edwin Silberstang
Designer: Christine Kosmicki

ISBN-10: 1-932173-48-X
ISBN-13: 978-1-932173-48-2

CIP Data Available

Stephens
Press LLC

A Stephens Media Group Company
Post Office Box 1600
Las Vegas, NV 89125-1600

www.stephenspress.com

Printed in Hong Kong

To A.D. Hopkins and Douglas Unger,
fine writers who believed I could do this.

… tonight the murderer is abroad
and the stranger is doped in the sailor's den…

— Alfred Hayes

The Imitation of Faust

The Clown

Becoming a law enforcement officer required an involved series of actions—psychological tests, background investigations, medical exams, and in between, the same stuff I hated most about my time in the military, which was a lot of waiting. While I progressed through each of the steps, I completed as many ride-alongs as I could. I went to the gym, where I lifted weights, ran, and talked with some of the cops I had met. Everything became about getting ready for the Academy. That part was easy. Exercising was something I'd done since I was sixteen.

For me, the ride-alongs were an opportunity to suck up, to get to know people who might help me get hired. I figured it wouldn't hurt to know a few names, which I would conveniently and not-too-subtly drop when I had my oral boards. In the true tradition of Vegas, I wasn't above using juice if it got me the job.

That's how I found myself in a black-and-white, wearing civilian clothes and listening to the pitfalls of being a cop. As I stared out the window at the passing streets, I thought about the ways my life had changed. Joey, a friend, and I were no longer roommates after he made up with his ex. The day he asked me to move out, I was only too happy. The lifestyle we had been living was killing me, but it didn't faze him at all. Joey had been able to go out after a day's work — every night — drink, smoke, then get up early the next morning, go to work and repeat the process. This was done each day on little or no sleep, and he managed to keep our boss happy, which made me believe the Army somehow physically altered and brainwashed its employees.

For me, it was all I could do to drag my sorry ass out of bed in the morning to make the plane, work all day, get home late in the afternoon, park in front of the TV for an hour until I could make an effort to pull on gym clothes, then drive the short distance to the track. Joey ran with me each night. No matter the pace I set, when we were done, he smoked a couple of cigarettes. Afterwards was the part where we ate, dressed, went to the bar, drank, played pool, and had considerably more success with the ladies, probably because we were in better shape. So, when his wife came back and I moved out, the drinking and partying stopped. My life settled into a routine of work, gym, movie or TV, and sleep. There was the occasional weekend bash, but that left a day or two so I had time to recover. I didn't have much contact with Joey as he was also getting ready for the tests to get into the Academy. Even though I was sure what he was doing was similar to my process, my life had entered a new phase.

■ ■ ■

Those were the things that were going through my mind as I watched the boring scenery — strip malls, stores, pedestrians, and traffic. It all looked the same as if I was in my own car, but I wasn't. I was in a black-and-white for two more hours. When that time was up, I was going home to my apartment filled with neat stacks of books, the TV, and the question of where life would take me if I didn't get this job. It wasn't like the test site job was going to disappear, but that I really *wanted* to be a cop. Since I'd moved out of Joey's place, I found an apartment by the University of Nevada, Las Vegas, called UNLV. The complex was close to the airport and downtown, a mile from the gym, and cheap. It amazed me how fast things went up here. A year before, there was nothing but empty lots and dirt roads. Now, in what seemed like two weeks, there was a fully landscaped shopping center with mature trees, green lawns, and a parking lot full of cars, making it look as if everything had been there forever.

"This is Union area. The valley's broken up into sectors and beats," Officer Pete Dix said. "Hey, she's cute. Want to stop her?"

He hadn't been real happy to get me at the start of shift, but things were working out. I didn't do any of the stupid things he spent the first hour telling me about, such as when one of his ride-alongs took the shotgun and ran after someone he thought was fleeing from a crime. It turned out the guy was trying to catch a bus. I was embarrassed by some of the stories and particularly intrigued with one in particular. It was the story of an untrained and unarmed ride-along who chased and tackled an armed robber. *"What could be going through that person's mind?"* I asked myself. *"Did they hire him? What would I do in the same position, even if I were in uniform?"*

What I really wanted was for him to get us into something exciting. In an hour or so, it would be end of shift. This day had to go in my book as one of the most boring ride-alongs I'd ever had. Up to that point, it consisted of stopping two cars driven by busty females, having lunch at Hooters, and taking several coffee breaks at local cafes that employed cute waitresses.

"Bored?" Pete asked. I guessed he heard the lack of enthusiasm in my voice. "Want to go in early?"

"No," I said. I tried putting some enthusiasm in my voice. "I love this stuff."

"Really?" He sounded like he couldn't imagine that. "Anyway, the sectors are named after the letters of the alphabet. Have you learned them yet?"

I nodded, but he was looking the other way. He went on as though I wasn't in the car. "We call the letters by their phonetic names. This means "A" is Adam, "B" is . . . "

"Hey, Pete," I broke in. "I was military. Alpha, Bravo, Charlie . . . "

"Yeah, like that, but we don't use the military ones. You'll have to learn a whole new terminology if you get hired. Now, where was I?" He slowed the black-and-white. "Oh, yeah, baby. That's what I'm talking about. Will you look at the ta-tas on her?"

I had to admit, I stared, too. It didn't take a detective to see she wasn't wearing a bra. When she'd disappeared from sight, he continued. "Where was . . . "

"The alphabet," I said. A vehicle, which would better be referred to as "a wreck," pulled up next to us. The occupants were three pimply-faced, hair-to-their-shoulders, drug-addicted-looking guys who were trying hard to appear innocent. When I looked down into the car, a Saturn, which I'd been told was one of the most stolen cars in Vegas, I saw the way they had their arms at their sides, were not talking to each other, and kept their eyes straight ahead like there wasn't a big black-and-white police car two feet away. This is exactly what I imagined criminals looked like. I eye-fucked the driver, which caused him to give me a nervous glance. This was the car stop we should have been making.

"Oh, yeah," Pete said. When I looked at him to see if he was scoping out these guys, he was staring out the window at a convertible. "Each sector usually has four beats. Imagine if Adam area was a box and you divided it into four smaller squares. You'd get Adam One, Adam Two, Adam Three and Adam Four. Get it?"

"Yeah. Uh, Pete . . . "

He continued, ignoring me. "The shifts are: one for graves, two for days, and three for swings. So a graveyard Adam unit that's responsible for beat one and two would be called One Adam Twelve, like in the old TV show. We're Two Union. So what do you suppose that means?"

I shifted my attention away from the car as it made an illegal left turn. If Pete saw, he wasn't letting on. "We're day shift, Union sector, but I don't know why there's no numbers after the U," I said.

"Fucking A right," he said, "and if you ask me, that's a reason to be pissed off." He slapped the steering wheel to make the point. "It means that I'm responsible for everything that happens in Union." What I knew from the last eight hours in Pete's car was that Union area consisted mostly of retail businesses, some apartment complexes, and a smattering of older residences. It was the type of mix that didn't make for a lot of crime. He'd told me that Friday afternoons, there were a few bank robberies. In the evenings, things picked up. I'd already made a decision from going on this ride along — I wouldn't be working day shift if I could help it.

"Well, I think you get the idea," he said.

An hour later, Pete drove down an alley. He stopped so we could talk to a couple of street people. They were sleeping off the previous night's excesses, so Pete had to kick their feet to get them up. He asked them all kinds of questions, which they answered. I learned that one of them was a diabetic. Pete made sure he had his medicine and reminded him that he had an appointment at the VA clinic on the tenth. The other one hadn't written to his daughter in a month. Pete said he was unhappy about that. He gave him a piece of paper and said he would be by the next day to get a letter, which he would mail.

"I don't know how people live like that," Pete said as we walked to the car. "In a few hours, they'll get hungry. That starts their same old routine." Pete explained when we were back inside. "They'll roam up and down this alley, eating the stuff the stores throw away."

For the next twenty minutes, we visited two other camp sites. I was amazed at the rapport he had with those people because he seemed like such a "lay-down." The only exception to that was one young guy who looked like he should have been working. Pete told me he'd arrested the guy at least a dozen times for petty larceny and drug paraphernalia. I watched the way Pete dealt with the man, which wasn't anything like the way he dealt with any of the others. With the other vagrants, Pete carefully made a point of being polite, civil, going out of his way to be friendly but not turning his back. He always kept a safe distance from anyone he dealt with, but with this man, before Pete even started speaking, he made the vagrant go to the front of the car where he patted him down. Pete kept his gun hand free and near his holster. He was brusque, sometimes borderline insulting. It became obvious he was trying to get the guy riled. At one point, Pete allowed himself to get close enough I thought the vagrant could have grabbed him. I could hear the insults because I was close. The whole time, Pete kept his voice down and smiled. It was weird.

"Did you see the way I did that?" he asked me after the vagrant walked away.

"Yes."

"If he'd hit me, I'd have kicked his ass."

"I bet," I said. We drove forward ten feet.

"Look up there." He pointed. I saw a camera.

"Whoever pulled that video would have seen me smiling, talking nice, and then this vagrant gets antsy on me. I'd been perfectly justified in whatever I did to him. That lesson might save you a trip to Internal Affairs someday." This was to be my first lesson in what would later become a whole way of life. It was about good and bad cops. It was about losing that innocent attitude I'd had from the first Academy. I hadn't done any ride-alongs then. One day I'd seen an ad in the paper, went and started the testing process, but that had not prepared me for what the street was all about. I knew something about how cops were supposed to be above the petty bounds that normal human beings spent their existence being governed by — like how sex or gambling or alcohol or drugs and a thousand other vices tempted them. It wasn't true. We felt the same pull from those temptations and sometimes we felt we were able to taste them without the same result. In the years that have gone by since I was in that first Academy, I knew that if a person was a stupid man and became anything else in life, whether it was a cop, soldier, or priest, then all he could become was a stupid cop, soldier, or priest. Putting on a uniform or wearing a badge didn't make people better than they were.

Finally, I had to ask, "What's up between you and that vagrant?"

"What?" he asked.

"Come on, Pete." The curiosity was killing me. Pete pointed a finger at the guy like it was a gun. He made a little "pow" sound.

"I want him gone, like dead. Prison-gone would be OK. That'd be a second-best case. Third would be California-gone. I'd settle for that if I had to, but dead or prison would be better. Crazy Mike is one of those people everyone's afraid of. He likes to work the corner of I-15 and Sahara."

"What do you mean, he 'works'?" I asked. "I thought you said he was a vagrant."

"He is," Pete replied. He pulled the car a few feet forward so we were in some shade. He took out a form. "At the end of every shift, you'll have to fill one of these out," he said.

"OK," I said.

Pete sighed. "I mean he *panhandles* that area. The word is he's violent. We think he might have killed three people for working what he considers *his area*, which is under the overpass."

"How could someone kill three people in this day and age?"

"Committing crime in those areas is different than committing crime out at The Lakes. People who live there . . ." He pointed at the cars going by at the end of the hot alley. " . . . trust the police. People who live here or next to railroad tracks, or have their lunch from a garbage can, don't. When someone gets killed in those places . . ." This time he pointed towards the distant, unseen railroad tracks. " . . . or here, might lay out for a week before the smell attracts a concerned citizen who then reports it. When you become a cop, you'll get your share of those calls."

I nodded. It was one of those things I wondered how I'd handle.

"It's getting towards quitting time," Pete said, putting the car in gear. "That means we'll start towards the station, but we can't go in yet. What I'll do is drive around within a few blocks of the stable until it's time. If you ever buy a house, remember, the safest places in the world are around police substations, especially when it gets to be shift change." He glanced at the instrument panel. "First, we'll head towards the gas pumps so I can top off the car for whoever gets it next."

As we pulled out into traffic, the radio emitted a sharp noise, which startled me. I looked at the MDT — the mobile data terminal with which patrol cars are equipped — to see if a message went with the noise. It was the first time that had happened all shift.

"Alert tone. Fuck! Please God, don't let it be my area," Pete said. Then he grinned, "Gets your attention, doesn't it? When you work graves, it'll wake you from a dead sleep."

The dispatcher announced a robbery had just occurred. She gave the location and the business name, which was a sewing store three blocks from where we were. Pete cursed under his breath.

"Here we go." He gunned the car, telling Dispatch we'd take the scene. She said the suspect was last seen northbound on foot. The afternoon traffic had increased, which meant it took us a couple of extra minutes to arrive. As we wheeled into the parking lot, Pete scanned the area before we headed for a spot several businesses down from where the robbery took place.

"The reason I'm parking over here is because sometimes the victims calling in are confused. I've walked in on these things and the bad guy was still inside. It'd be stupid to get killed because of laziness," Pete said. He looked at the group of women standing just inside the door. "Come on, but don't touch anything."

■ ■ ■

Once we were inside, Pete took control. He talked softly, which calmed the female employees. My estimation of Pete's abilities had been slowly rising since the alley.

"Who's the manager?" he asked. A little old woman, thin as a sign post, raised her hand. He took her gently by the arm and led her aside. Pete waved for me to follow.

"I'm the owner and manager. My name's Betty Lomox. Those five young women are my staff."

Pete let Mrs. Lomox describe the suspect — a black male who was maybe five-feet-five inches tall, heavy, with a muscular build that might have made him weigh two hundred pounds. She said he was twenty-four years old.

"How do you know that?" The woman was obviously surprised at Pete's question. "How can you know exactly how old he is when all the other things you've told me are estimates?"

"Because I can read, young man," Mrs. Lomox said, but before she cleared that up, she went on. "He looked like he was wearing a clown outfit."

"Clown outfit," Pete asked. When she saw the confused looks on our faces, she continued.

"It's as though someone drew a vertical line down his middle." She used her finger and drew an imaginary line from her throat to her groin. She then crossed herself with a horizontal one at her beltline. She indicated her upper right shoulder. "Red."

"Yellow." Left shoulder.

"Green." Right leg.

"Black." Left leg.

"And don't forget his cap," one of the girls called. "It's the same pattern."

Mrs. Lomox continued with a nod, "He'll stand out like a sore thumb."

"Hold on," Pete told her. He turned sideways, relaying the information via radio to the ATLing units.

"Officer," Mrs. Lomox continued. "He had a small silver gun and he took $333 from the register."

"What kind of gun?"

"I'm sorry. I don't know guns very well," she replied.

Pete pulled his semiautomatic pistol from the holster with his right hand, then removed a thirty-eight-caliber revolver from behind his ammo pouches with his left.

"Did it look like this one, Mrs. Lomox?" He held up the revolver. "Or this one?" Then the semiauto.

She indicated the semiautomatic, "Smaller though, and shiny, like it was made of silver."

Pete radioed the dispatcher to advise the units that the suspect was armed with a chrome semiautomatic pistol.

"Now, as to how I know exactly how old he is . . . come over here," Mrs. Lomox said. She showed us a full palm print on the glass counter.

"That's great. Are you a palm reader?"

She just stared at Pete.

"It was a joke," he said.

"He put his hand there," she said, then pointed at a sheet of paper on the counter, "That's an employment application."

"What?" Pete asked. "He filled it out?"

"Yes. Exactly." The expression on her face was serious. Her half glasses sat near the tip of her nose, reflecting the late afternoon sunlight that streamed through the plate glass window.

Pete lifted the paper by a corner. "I'll be damned," he muttered.

"Language, young man," she said. One of the girls tittered.

"Sorry, Ma'am. I've just never seen anyone do this."

"In that case, I understand."

I could see the application was fully filled out. The suspect had printed his name, address and all his physical information. Pete noted the address was an apartment complex three blocks from our location. He keyed his mike, directing a couple of units to the location.

"Was the guy high? You know, on drugs?" Pete asked no one in particular.

"Young man, I know what drugs are. I did my share in the sixties," she told us. "No. And he seemed such a nice, educated boy, too. He had no problems filling out the application before he robbed my store."

I actually caught the radio traffic as a unit advised both Pete and Dispatch that they had one in custody in front of the apartment complex. Pete asked Mrs. Lomox if she would mind doing a one-on-one to see if it was the same person. She agreed, getting in the car. As we drove to the location where the unit was holding the suspect, Mrs. Lomax fidgeted in the back of the car. I felt bad for her because it must have made her think people were looking at her as if she was the criminal. After we got there, she positively identified the man. Even I saw she could hardly fail to recognize him. That was because of his clothing. There might not have been another person on the entire West Coast wearing that outfit. The officers had found a chrome Jennings semi-auto handgun and $333 in the guy's pockets. After the one-on-one, a swing shift unit took Mrs. Lomox a distance away to get her statement. When Pete had a second, he took time to explain the reason.

"First, I want to finish the field interview and get the paperwork done without any distractions. I also don't want the suspect seeing she's the one who identified him."

The suspect, his hands cuffed behind his back, was placed in front of the patrol unit, where he waited patiently. The unloaded gun was laid on an evidence bag while an ID unit responded for photographs of the gun and money. As I stood at the side of the car's hood, Pete handed me the guy's ID.

"The information matches with that on the application perfectly. Notice anything else?"

I studied the card, then it hit me. "Hey! Today's his twenty-fourth birthday."

"According to these papers, he just got out of prison in California," Pete said. He tossed them in front of me. "Three weeks ago."

"That's weird," I said.

"Yeah, he hasn't been out long," Pete said as he filled in the boxes on the police reports. When he finished, Pete walked to the open passenger window. I heard him saying those familiar words I'd heard on TV so many times, "You have the right to remain silent . . . "

When Pete finished, he asked if the guy understood his rights. He nodded, but Pete had him say he understood. I stood to the side as Pete interviewed the man. The guy admitted everything that had happened at the store. When he finished confessing, Pete thanked him for being honest. We walked to another patrol vehicle, where Pete used the computer to pull up the guy's criminal history.

"See?" he pointed at the MDT screen. "His charge in California was robbery." He read through the guy's local rap sheet, then called the records bureau for the FBI record which reflects a subject's deeds in other states. "He did time in a first offender's camp."

"He must have wanted to go back to prison. Either that or he's a very dumb crook," I said.

"There's no figuring how some people think," Pete replied. "Hell! I probably understand him better than I do my girlfriend." Pete looked towards the car. "Still, when you've been incarcerated your whole life . . . first in Juve, then in prison . . . sometimes, it's hard to adjust to all the freedom society allows you on the outside. Maybe he went out and committed a stupid crime just so he could go back. The gun wasn't loaded. But it won't matter to his parole board. He's going back to prison for a long time."

I glanced to where the suspect sat, invisible behind the glare bouncing off the patrol car's windshield. I tried imagining a different car, one with another type of light on the top, a similar paint scheme, which had been copied by a local company. The suspect could have been just another man waiting in a cab for the driver to take him somewhere. There was a man who thought he had nothing to live for. At the time, I couldn't understand this attitude. Later, I was to realize people came to that conclusion for different reasons in their lives.

"Maybe, he thinks he's going home," I said.

■ ■ ■

Out of Options

My time in the Academy seemed like a blur. All these years later, there are parts that stand out in my mind — like the endless sessions of being yelled at, memorizing police codes and legal definitions, days and nights of shooting at the range, constant stress of worrying whether my gun was clean enough, pants and shirt adequately ironed so the creases would pass inspection, or whether each morning I had painfully shaved off the top layer of facial skin to get to the hairs underneath. During the whole ordeal, most of the time I either stayed home or went to a small cafe, studying until it was time for bed. There were changes in many aspects of my life. I stopped reading for pleasure and started reading simply to become technically proficient in policing. Reading was only one of the ways to stay competitive with my fellow recruits, because extra studying equated to higher scores on the weekly exams, which pushed me up on the lists the staff kept. The interior of my apartment suffered because I had no time to clean. It became a haven for pizza boxes, empty Coke cans, and clothes that I wore based on how bad they smelled. I started religiously watching *Cops*, analyzing what those other officers did on calls.

The first week of the Academy, my girlfriend, Sally, started giving me problems. She accused me of ignoring her, which was true. I barely had time to clean my apartment and I had even less time for myself. If I wasn't polishing shoes, cleaning guns, or reading the next class's assignments, then I was in class, sleeping, or eating. These are the things that involved my life, and often there was no room in them for her. By the end of my first month in the Academy, she threatened first to stop coming over, then to stop seeing me at all. I was able to say one thing, though, the fights all this generated relieved a lot of stress. After the first couple, I developed two rules. First, there would and could be no physical contact, no matter what the provocation. Second, we were only allowed to argue in a certain place, which was the car. The last thing I needed was to get into a domestic dispute with her that resulted in someone calling the police and them showing up. The Academy staff had made it clear that any of us caught up in such a situation would be quickly terminated and by situation, they included any of our personal problems that affected our jobs and came to their attention.

That time passed quickly and seems blurred today, but the things that stuck in my mind, like those things from when I was a child and went to elementary school, were the way the days went by. The week started with Monday's first inspection. While the staff looked at our uniforms, shoes, and personal grooming, they tested us on definitions and four hundred codes. Anything could result in an infraction — a missed string hanging hidden in an armpit; a Hi-Tech boot scuffed on the run from the locker room to inspection pad; or a microscopic carbon particle that had slipped into some inaccessible spot in a handgun. The TAC officers — Metro's version of the Marine Corps drill intructors — were experts at finding and exploiting these infractions, resulting in us having to write officer's reports — or do push-ups or grinders. Of the three, I preferred the grinders. Running the perimeter of the parking lot was a lot easier than researching policy or law for a many-page, time consuming OR that ate up an entire evenings. Although I could do the push-ups, there was always the possibility they might smudge the front of the uniform if I accidentally touched the ground. If that happened, the TACs spent the rest of the day focusing on that bit of dirt, making the recruit miserable in an effort to piss him off.

Tuesdays were reserved for lectures, such as how to handle domestic violence, forgery crimes, or what to do if you got shot. Wednesday was spent at the range — learning to shoot people before they shot you by training to be tactical. It was our favorite day because the staff didn't bother anyone unless we started to drift into horseplay. On Thursday, we went back to the classroom, rehashing the problems we were subjected to the day before while acting out practical problems. It was also a day when everyone drank lots of coffee and, sometimes, stood in the back of the room to keep awake. Then there was Friday, the end of the week, the start of the weekend, and another tick on the calendar towards graduation, but even that day with its promise of the weekend off contained the notion that the whole business was going to start again on Monday.

A workweek like that made a relationship a hard affair to sustain. The staff insisted on one hundred percent attention, which meant putting aside wife, kids, girl- or boyfriend, and any other problems someone had or made. This was the training — to get us so we focused on that one mistake out there that was going to get a cop or some citizen killed and, thus, deprive the Department of its investment or promote a civil lawsuit. The training made us unlikely to make that mistake, and in the process, I got to watch as some of the other recruits' relationships disintegrated under the stress this life brought.

■ ■ ■

Things went on this way for four and one-half months and then it was over. I stood as a member of a graduation ceremony on the Cashman Convention Center stage. It was my last hour as a quasi-civilian and a recruit. After the speeches and awards, our names were read off. We approached the sheriff, who stood next to a table that held our training certificates and badges. He picked each item up, handed it to us, shook our hands, and sent us out to the streets where we'd be cops.

The badges were special. Each was stamped with a serial number that matched that on the hat piece. When I retired, they'd give both to me, like one of those gold watches other industries awarded their employees for years of service. It was that ceremony, a condensed tribute to the months of hard work, that made us each a police officer I. That rank meant we were on probation for the next year. Probation meant the Department could fire us for just about anything — such as getting angry and cussing out some citizen or blowing a knee out in a foot pursuit. But none of that was in our minds on that day. Only the glow of basking in the pride of our families and friends, of our new freedom from the Academy staff, and knowing we had successfully completed one bitch of a training course. We thought we were invincible, both physically and mentally. Before we left that phase of our life, each of us was furnished with a copy of our reporting orders which stated the shift we would work and what station we were assigned to. Besides this, there is that last happy picture of Sally and me together. She wore a blue dress and I was in my full uniform, that gold badge pinned to the chest. Her arms were around me, her head on my shoulder, a glint in her eye. Little did I know that she had watched the whole process and her thoughts were, *If that idiot can do it, so can I,* which is what she told me a year later when she also tested for Metro and made it.

That night, I sat in my small apartment. The orders read that I was assigned to Northeast Area Command, or NEAC for short, and that I was on swing shift, starting at 1500 hours the following day. I looked at them over and over as they lay on the coffee table with a pile of old pizza boxes underneath. That reporting time, even though it wasn't the 0600 hours some of my classmates had gotten, was the reason I wasn't out celebrating like everyone else. I wanted to make the best impression I could with whoever was going to be my first field training officer or FTO. With an early night in mind, I had ordered my usual staple — pizza, which was half finished in the top box of the stack — turned on the TV and tuned in to *Cops,* and changed into the Academy sweats and t-shirt.

My life surrounded me like a swarm of bees. On the floor at my feet was my policy manual, opened to some things I thought I'd need to know on the following day. The apartment was messy and the sound of the neighborhood drifted through the open bedroom window. Summer was here and it was hot out. During commercials, I thumbed through the manual, stopping at different pages, and read words that seemed so familiar I felt I'd written them. There was gear all over the living room floor. A uniform hung on the closet door. I had gone over it thirty times, cutting and burning loose strings, checking buttons, and rearranging the badge, nametags, and pocket contents.

As twelve o'clock approached, I was wide awake. I had wanted to get to bed early, but I was anxious about what the following day would bring. By one a.m., I was sorry I hadn't taken Sally up on her offer to come over. It might have been the time I fixed things between us. They were bad. Prior to her coming to the graduation ceremony, I hadn't seen or spoken to her in a couple of weeks.

Finally I turned the TV off and went to lie in the bedroom darkness. In spite of the heat, I left the window open so the noise of the neighborhood continued to surround me with its strange comfort. There was the sound of music from the nightclub the university students visited, a speeding car, and far off in the distance, the crack I recognized as a pistol shot. These were all things I would be handling tomorrow. With that at the forefront of my thoughts, I looked at the door where my uniform hung. Its color was indistinct, but I knew it to be tan. The shape might have been any shirt and pants. The difference was that when I put it on, I was Superman, but lying there in bed that night, I was still Clark Kent. I wondered about that. Who would I be wearing that uniform? For the last four and one-half months I had trained to find out. Tomorrow was going to bring the first proof of what I had just asked and as I lay there, I imagined all kinds of things that could happen. Finally, late, late that night, I fell asleep.

At 1520 hours the next day I was doing what I had only imagined. I was sitting in a black-and-white, watching downtown Las Vegas go by. The radio filled the car with the sound of dispatchers telling cops where to go and officers reporting back. My FTO drove. He had explained to me right off that I wasn't going to be allowed to operate the vehicle for at least a few weeks. He said this was because we were going to work on one task at a time, starting with the simplest, which was monitoring the area's radio traffic. What I was supposed to be alert to was the dispatcher notifying us of a call. This meant that I had to recognize our unit designator or call sign, then acknowledge the dispatcher. On top of that, we had sister units, which were other members of my squad. I was expected to know where they were and what they were doing at all times. To that end, Sam, my FTO asked me constant questions, such as where units were doing car stops, what were the dispositions of the calls that had been cleared, and what calls were pending. The first couple of times he asked, I was embarrassed because I hadn't been able to answer them correctly. That caused me to pay more attention to what the dispatcher said, which meant I paid less attention to what was going on outside. Right then, there was just too much going on.

"What do you want to eat today?" he asked suddenly, breaking what little concentration I had left. Lunch was the last thing on my mind because I was excited enough just to be out on the street.

"What choices do we have?" I asked.

"The downtown casinos, a couple of fast food places," Sam said. "That's about it in our area. The Strip is the place to work if you're a gourmet."

"I'm not."

"Spaghetti," he said. "I feel like spaghetti."

"OK." I was up for anything.

"I want you to get used to routines. In this job, there aren't a lot of them, so it's important to make up a few. Helps keep you sane, especially as long as you're in field training."

I was to be in this phase of FTP, or field training program, for about three weeks. Then I would move on to another phase. In the military, there was OJT, or on-the-job-training, which in Metro was FTP. This was the modern police department's method of getting old, smart cops to teach fresh, out-of-the-academy rookies how to be effective. It also weeded out those who finished the Academy but were never meant to be on the street. I hoped I wasn't one of those. That was what I was thinking about as we turned south off Stewart Avenue onto Sixth Street. The El Cortez Hotel was to our left and the west side of Sixth was filled with old motels that had turned into poor people's apartments. As we approached the Crest View Motel, the radio came to life.

"Three Adam Thirty-four, copy a four oh five Z," the dispatcher radioed. I knew a 405Z was a suicide call, the "Z" part telling me it was an attempt so far. As she gave the location, the sharp sound of a gunshot could be heard because I had the window down a little. An open window was one of the things that Sam insisted on even though it was over a hundred degrees outside. The sound had been acute, causing me to duck my head. I almost wished the glass was up just in case the shot was meant for us and that made the memory of my first getting inside the car come back to me. The FTO had been in the car while I checked the trunk, then when I sat in the passenger seat, I had rolled the window up. Next, I adjusted the air conditioning so the heat my t-shirt and bulletproof vest trapped didn't cook me alive. Sam had shaken his head.

"That stays down," he said, pointing at the window glass. "At least part way. Your job is to hear people if they need help. The window being up means you can't do your job. They're not paying you to be comfortable."

That lesson was suddenly hammered home.

"You going to tell Dispatch we have possible gunfire?" Sam asked.

Damn it, I thought as I reached for the radio microphone. Before I could wrap my hand around the plastic, the dispatcher came on and gave the location of the attempt suicide call. We were right outside. A second later, a woman, wearing the name of the hotel on a tag pinned to her shirt, ran up to the car.

"There's a man with a gun inside room 211," she said.

"Let me guess," Sam said. "He's threatening to kill himself."

"Yes," she breathed. "Joey, our security guard, is up there trying to talk him into opening the door."

"Jesus!" Sam said. He threw the car in park. We both jumped out, running in the direction she pointed. At the same time I wondered what I'd gotten myself into even as I thought this was the coolest thing.

Room 211 was at the top of a set of stairs. It was obvious which one it was by the crowd standing outside. I couldn't help thinking that if whoever was in the room started shooting, one of the people stupidly standing there was apt to take a round.

"Come on," Sam said as he made an approach.

The security guard was working at the door by slamming his shoulder into it. He had it open a couple of inches. The reason I knew he was the guard was that he wore a blue shirt with the name of a company I had never heard of embroidered on patches that were sewn on the sleeves. There was also a tin badge that was very fake-looking pinned over his left breast. For that matter, he was fake-looking, too. He had to be sixty or seventy years old, five-feet-four, and 120 pounds.

"Sir! Get back," Sam called. As I came up, I was able to look through the crack, seeing someone in the room had pushed a dresser in front of the door to keep people out. The way it was wedged in there, it was amazing that the security guard had forced the door as much as he had.

"I said get back," Sam said. The guard didn't even look back, but put himself in position to slam his fragile-looking shoulder against the wood again.

I took Sam's cue and told the other people to clear out. One old lady put her hands on her hips and gave me a look. Her appearance made me think she could pass for the guard's wife or sister.

"Who you telling to get out of here? We live in this place," she said.

For a second, her refusing to comply with my lawful order had me stymied and caused me to hesitate. While I pondered options, Sam stepped up and tapped the security guard on the shoulder. The guard turned with an angry look on his face. When he saw it was the police, he nodded apologetically. He opened his mouth to say something. Sam held a hand up to stop him and looked at the woman.

"How'd you like to be living down at the city jail?" he asked.

She stepped back. "Since you put it that way, I guess I could see things just as well from the end of the hall," she replied mildly.

"Thought you might feel that way," Sam said.

"There was a gunshot from in there," the old guard said.

Sam made a show of looking at the man's belt where there was no gun. "And you were thinking about doing . . . " He hesitated to make his point. " . . . what? That is, when you got in there?"

"I just wanted to make sure everyone in the room was OK," the guard said.

"Everyone?" I asked.

The lady with the nametag stepped forward. It read, "Marge From Texas," in big letters. She smiled self-consciously. "Manager and owner."

This was getting surreal. Here we were on an active crime scene and people were introducing themselves, wanting to play spectator, and do things that we should be the only ones doing.

"OK," I said. "How many people in the room?"

"Ma'am," Sam said. "Can you talk to me over there? I don't want whoever's in there to start shooting and get one of you." The whole crowd shifted away from us nervously.

Marge went with them, then called to Sam. "As far as the record says, there's only one person registered in there."

Sam grunted as he came close to the gap the security guard had opened. I moved up so I was beside him. For the first time, I noticed Sam had drawn his weapon. Now it was my turn to be self-conscious as I released the catch on my holster and took mine out.

"Sound off from in the room," Sam yelled through the opening. I could hear something coming from inside, but I couldn't be sure exactly what it was. "Cover me," Sam said softly.

I lifted the gun and pointed it at the door. I didn't know what I was covering him from, but I did know how to make it look like I knew what I was doing. Sam stepped back, then threw his two hundred plus pounds forward. He hit the door with his left shoulder, gun hand back so he could shoot if it was necessary. The dresser slid back far enough that Sam was able to duck down and slip inside. I went in after him. The room was gloomy, but bright enough to see that the occupant had pushed the bed against the wall. He had then taken the mattress and leaned it so it formed a tent-like space, consisting of wall, box spring, and mattress. There was a pair of feet sticking out of the end closest to us. The feet looked like they were dancing. Sam moved to the side of the bed. I stayed by the feet, but not in the line of fire.

"Come out," Sam yelled. "Come out and show your hands."

Nothing happened. Sam pointed at the structure. I kept my gun trained where I figured the body attached to the feet would be. He slide-stepped forward, grabbed a handful of material near the center of the mattress and pulled. As soon as it tipped towards Sam, I saw the man lying on his back. He was naked except for a pair of boxer shorts, and the revolver in his right hand. Blood gurgled from the sides of his mouth, streamed in two rivulets down his cheeks from the corner of his eyes and out of his ears and into his hair. His feet were doing what one of the instructors in the Academy had referred to as "the chicken." Sam reached for the gun.

"Keep him covered," he muttered. I had to shake my head to bring my attention back to what we were doing there. Sam got his hand on the cylinder and pulled, but the hold was a death grip. Ignoring everything above his neck, this guy looked normal. I couldn't help wondering if he would sit up and start talking to us. That was when a hand fell on my shoulder. My heart leapt to my throat and I almost pulled the trigger. My neck cracked as my head swiveled.

"Jesus!" I breathed. "Sarg!"

"Easy, Cam," Sergeant Carver said. "It's only me."

"Let the fucking gun go," Sam said. He pulled harder. The man's finger was in the trigger housing. I think all of us were worried he was going to spasm and crank off a shot. Finally, Sam got the gun away from him.

"Control, This is Six Sixteen," Carver said. "Roll medical. Tell them we have a male subject with a gunshot wound to the head."

Sam jerked the curtains open, letting in sunlight. Now that we had the gun, I couldn't take my eyes off the man. Each time he breathed out, a blood spume shot up, splattering everything around his face like he'd turned into a human whale.

"Still alive," Carver said. There was a light note to his words, which made him sound amused. Off in the distance, I grew aware of a siren approaching. It had the warbling noise ambulances or fire trucks made, which was different than patrol cars. I decided to clear the doorway, making it easier for them to get in. The guy was slowly turning gray. I wasn't positive what was going to happen, but I had a good idea. As I pushed the dresser away, I noted there were things laid out in what had been neat patterns until we had forced entry. Those items included a wallet, jewelry, money, and a bunch of papers. When I got the dresser back to the side of the door, I saw his suicide note.

To whom it may concern:

I want my jewelry to go to my daughter, Nelly. The last I knew, she was in · Lubbock, Texas. Use the money to help pay for my funeral. I don't want people thinking I was a coward. I just wanted them to know that I was out of options and decided this was the best way to deal with everything.

Joe

When I glanced up, I became aware that Sam was looking over my shoulder. "That's the way it is with most people who do this," Sam said.

"What?" I asked.

"Laying things out so there's no doubt about what gets done with them." He pointed at the once neat order of the man's possessions. "I once had a call at this lady's house after she killed herself. She had sticky notes on everything, telling us which relatives got what. By the way, if this is a homicide, you've just put your fingerprints on evidence." I dropped the note. I heard the squeal of brakes outside. Sergeant Carver stood by the window, looking out.

"Medical's here," he said. A minute later, two firemen came through the door. One of them went to the man on the bed. He did the things I'd come to expect medical people to do — looking at the pupils and checking the pulse at the wrist.

"One hundred two and coming down," the fireman said to the air. He set the man's hand on the bed, then muttered something to his partner I didn't catch. They did the weirdest thing. They started chanting under their breath. I couldn't make out what they said, so I moved closer.

The words were, "Die, motherfucker, die, motherfucker, die . . . "

The first one through the door had been carrying a huge, red medical bag on his back. He took it off, looking as if he'd suddenly turned into a mime going through a slow motion act. Once it was on the floor, they unzipped pockets, removed equipment, and laid things out. Even in this they worked slowly, which wasn't what I expected. The chanting was eerie.

"Hey," said the paramedic who had first checked him. He looked at me so I knew who he was talking to. "You know his name?"

"No."

"Why don't you look in that wallet?" he said.

Before I reached for it, I took rubber gloves from my pocket. I only had to be told once. The patient arched as if he was suddenly in pain. He took a deep breath. Then he just stopped. The body relaxed like nothing I'd ever seen, settling back to the mattress. I'd never been around a human being dying before. I kept looking, waiting for him to let the breath out. He didn't.

"Thank God," the other paramedic said.

"What's up with you guys?" I asked. They looked at me like they didn't know what I was talking about. "The chanting . . . "

Instead of answering, the paramedic who'd taken the vitals said, "I'm pronouncing him." He started packing things back in the bag, keeping his head down. He made it look as if he wasn't speaking to anyone. "Call the coroner."

I guess, in a way, I thought there should be more to it—like they would start doing something — one of them jump on him and start compressions or bring out the paddles, but there was no movement in that direction.

"OK," Carver replied. He took out the cell phone, then let Dispatch know so she could log the time of death, and when the call-outs were made.

"Why aren't they saving him?" I asked. The second fireman took me aside. His partner finished putting equipment away.

"If this guy had lived with that gunshot wound, he'd just be a vegetable, which would be someone's problem — like the county or his family, if he had one. They, or us, would be paying to keep the body alive. That means one less bed for people who need it. Get it?"

I nodded and they left the room. I turned back to the bed. It was kind of weird looking at the corpse. It had gone from being a flesh-and-blood person to being a big chunk of meat.

"We'll be at the car," Carver said. He and Sam walked out, leaving me alone with the body. I knew how calls like this were supposed to be handled and this wasn't it. They were trying to freak me out. I didn't care. It was like the new badge on my chest made me impervious to normal fear. I stared at the man and thought about his note. There he was — alone. That was the way he died — probably with a family that didn't know where he was and with none of them around him. He'd spent his last minutes on the earth being attended by strangers who had no idea of what he was about — such as whether he might have been a veteran hero or if he had been a cop when he was younger or if there was a daughter, a girlfriend or a wife. I couldn't help wondering what his woman was like and what he was like to have chosen that person. I shuddered. Anyone, including me, could end up someday on a bed with a gun that had just put a hole in our head. For just a second, I wished I could run time backwards, hold his hand as he died — give him one last bit of human contact. Of course, there was no way I could because not only would my FTO and boss have thought me crazy, but my guess was that I'd have been looking for a new job after we were out of there.

Thirty-five minutes later, with just a couple of cursory checks by Sam or Sergeant Carver, the assistant coroner showed up. He was an older man, who dressed sloppily. The silver fringe of hair around his head needed cutting. I thought he looked like someone's chain-smoking doctor grandfather. To heighten the effect, he came through the door with the typical black bag. When he had set the satchel on the floor next to the bed, he took out a pair of rubber gloves. As he pulled them on, he studied the man.

"See him do it?"

"No," I said. "We heard it, didn't see it. We did see him die."

"You'll be lending me a hand. That comes from your sarg."

"Sure." I felt some trepidation at that pronouncement, but I decided I wasn't showing it no matter what. The coroner opened the bag and took out a wooden tongue depressor. He climbed up on the bed, kneeling beside the body. As I watched, he forced the mouth open with his fingers, then stuck the depressor in.

"You have a flashlight?"

"Yes, sir," I said.

"Shine it in his mouth."

At first, I tried to do that from where I was, but he ordered me closer. I moved up so I knelt next to him. He opened the mouth wider and I shone the light in. There was nothing but blood. He turned the head sideways so it spilled out. When he brought the head back to the upright position, he used the depressor to get the tongue out of the way.

"See where the bullet went?" he asked. I nodded as I saw the hole. Next, he grabbed the body by the shoulder and hip. He pulled, but the corpse was heavy. "Help me," he ordered.

I took out a second pair of rubber gloves and pulled them on. Then I hooked the leg just under the buttock. It took some doing but we rolled the body over on its stomach. He worked his fingers through the hair. "No exit wound. See that?"

"Yes, sir." With the man on his stomach, a pool of blood was spreading as it drained from his mouth and throat. I moved a knee to keep it from getting on me.

"We need to do one more thing. We need to sit him up."

I helped roll the body. This time we worked to get the legs off the bed. Then we each took an arm and pulled him to a sitting position. While I held both wrists to keep him from falling sideways, the head lolled. The coroner opened each eyelid. The blast had forced the eyeballs out of the sockets slightly. Blood oozed from the mouth, but it was congealing. It looked like spaghetti. That brought up the thought of lunch, which sent a lurch through my digestive tract. For the first time, I imagined I could be sick.

"OK," he said. "Let him go."

I gently let the body back. It was like he was a drunk friend.

"Let me teach you something about killing yourself," the coroner said. He pulled off his gloves and signed a form. "Just in case you ever decide to do it this way." He tossed the gloves at a corner. "If you stick the gun in your mouth and you close your lips around it like this . . . " He stuck his index finger in his mouth and puckered his lips, then removed it so he could talk. "Then you pull the trigger, the blast can't escape. The bullet loses a lot of velocity. It goes up into the skull and ricochets around. Chances are, it isn't going to kill you. Hence . . . " he pointed at the victim. "There is the fear, at least for us in the medical profession, that you'll live. On the other hand, you do this . . . " He stuck his other finger in his mouth, gripped it with his teeth, and made like he was smiling, and again removed it. "You pull the trigger, the blast escapes from the sides. The bullet goes through the spinal cord, cutting it. Nine out of ten times, the subject dies instantaneously. No pain, no fuss." He picked up another form and began filling it out. "This man was an amateur."

"I'll keep that in mind," I said, sarcastically.

"Good," he said still not looking at me. "Now call for the on-duty mortuary crew."

I went out into the hallway and used my radio to make the call. When I had an estimated time of arrival, I went back into the room. The coroner had pulled up a chair. He had his feet on the bed next to the deceased and was reading a paperback.

"Twenty minutes," I said.

"Thanks, rookie." For the first time, he looked at me, then smiled. "Officer."

I liked the sound of that word. "You're welcome, sir."

"You did good," he said, letting his eyes drop back to what he read. "Most likely, you won't be doing any of that ever again. Your sarg said you're new and asked me to see what you're made of. I'll tell him you passed. Send him up and I'll be seeing you around."

"Thanks, again" I said. At the stairs, I glanced back at the room. I could still hear the chant, "die, motherfucker, die," in my head. I didn't think I was ever going to forget it. When I got to the car, I told Sergeant Carver the coroner was waiting for him. He told us to go four eighty-two.

"Spaghetti?" Sam asked.

I shook my head. Sam didn't argue.

■ ■ ■

A Merry Chase . . .

indy nights in Las Vegas were the worst — traffic accidents happened, the usual bad guys hid out from the weather, and burglar alarms went off, meaning all there was to do was drive around. The police normally ignored those alarm calls and they especially avoided responding to them on windy nights. Contract security officers, whose companies provided the alarm systems, handled the initial responses. If something was happening when they arrived, like they found a broken window, an open door, or the lights on where none should be, they had their dispatch call our dispatch and we showed up and did the dangerous stuff. Incidents where crooks actually still were present during a burglary alarm were so rare, it just didn't make sense for us to be the first to arrive.

As I drove on the nearly deserted streets, I thought about the windstorm that rocked the car with a gust so hard I was forced to work at keeping us in our lane of travel. It seemed to lift the desert right off the ground and suspend it in space. The dust was so thick that if I cracked the window, the alkali caused us both to start coughing. It also worked its way into everything, including my underwear. That was what caused quite a few of the accidents I was sick of seeing. On the last one, I had stood outside a construction site, filling a page of my notebook with scribbles I hoped I'd be able to read once I got back in the car, where I'd finish writing the accident report. The whole time, loose sand streamed off a tall pile that shortened noticeably by the time I finished writing. When I slipped back into the car, I knew where all that sand had ended up because my balls itched something fierce, causing me to constantly squirm.

In the future, this shift would stay in my memory, causing me to hate wind storms. Partly, that feeling was caused by the driving habits of Las Vegans in comparison with all those people from back East or the California coast. Normally, the tourists drove like idiots but they were actually dong better in this weather, as much as I didn't like to admit it, than people who lived in Vegas their whole lives. That was something I couldn't figure — how it was that when the weather sucked — when it rained or we had a near-hurricane-speed windstorm or on those once-in-a-decade snow days — they drove so much better. Just a Vegas mystery, I decided.

The gusts were mainly forty to fifty miles an hour, although the dispatcher sent a message over the computer saying they had reached eighty in a few locations. Trees were being blown over, power lines snapping, and to make matters really interesting, drivers just couldn't seem to help running into each other, causing multi-vehicle accidents. The easiest accident we'd handled involved three cars, and the worst, five. Luckily, the injuries in all of them were minor. That didn't alter the fact that each vehicle involved in an accident required a separate section on the report. Those sections were divided into sub-sections that required information on everything from their insurance policy, the occupant's personal information, to any complaints of injury. Then there were other sections that required a detailed diagram showing the direction of travel and final resting-point of all the cars. Finally, I had to write citations for those at fault. Traffic accidents were a cop's worst nightmare, unless he worked traffic, which meant it was just another part of the job.

There was one weird thing that happened that night, which was that I experienced the rarest of circumstances. I met quite a few people who had actually been born in Vegas. It amazed me, because there was this myth that everyone in Vegas was from somewhere else. As if people didn't actually get born here. Those of us who lived here for any length of time knew that wasn't technically true, that people had to be born in

Las Vegas, but it didn't keep us from being surprised when someone said they were.

"I love the wind," Dave said. I glanced over. He had the seat so far back, all he needed was a blanket and pillow. Dave's eyes were closed, his face slack, like he'd been drifting in and out of sleep and was already heading back. Even in the tan uniform, Dave Stieber did not look like a cop. He was overweight. His gut stretched the uniform buttons until I thought they'd pop if he took a deep breath. He owned an investment company on the side, which was extremely profitable. When I came to work, it was in jeans and t-shirts. I drove a beater jeep. Dave arrived in three-piece suits that made him look like a banker. He drove a six month old, shiny black Mercedes-Benz. He was the epitome of what other cops wanted to be — successful.

"Gee," I remarked, "I didn't hear you say that a couple hours ago." I referred to his remark that he loved the wind.

"A couple of hours ago, we had a couple of hours to go. We're almost off. Don't take any calls," he warned. I had to admit the wind either had an up side or down side, depending on how one looked at things. The up side for Dave was that not many crimes had occurred. The down side for me was that I was bored. While I thought about that, a five-foot tumbleweed blew across the road. It was definitely not something I wanted to get run over by if I was walking. That fine sand followed the bush across the road in sheets that looked like water. From how quiet the night had been where calls for service were concerned, I knew that even criminals didn't want to be out in this shit. They probably stayed in to watch TV.

Maybe I should have been doing the same, but I was in the last stages of the first phase of field training. Each phase, two in all, lasted nine weeks, and each was completed at different substations. That was the way things worked for my particular training program. They changed with each Academy because the program constantly evolved, changing phase durations as different administrations decided on the needs of the Department. Each phase was divided between three FTOs. This was supposed to make it hard for any individual FTO's habits, especially the bad ones, to rub off on a trainee. Currently, there were two phases, but rumor had it, plans were in the works to extend the program. What new recruits learned was that Las Vegas was divided into four Area Commands — Northwest, Southwest, Southeast, and Northeast. Rumors were going around that there would soon be a South Central Area Command, which was to be the Las Vegas Strip corridor, and another called Downtown Area Command, which would encompass Fremont Street. At some point in the past, the administration established the area command boundaries by using main streets, which were considered natural barriers. For the north/south division, they designated Charleston. The city planners had already made it the zero line. As an example, one block north was one hundred North Charleston and one block south was one hundred South Charleston. Main Street was the original zero block for the east/west addresses, then Interstate 15 was built, which took over because it was a more difficult barrier to cross.

Officially, the commands were called by their initials, so Southwest was SWAC. Demographics, population and crime rates further separated the areas. My current assignment was NEAC. I expected my next assignment, which would be my last phase, to be SWAC. The changes were supposed to expose me to new experiences with different groups of people and types of crime.

Northeast had the trailer parks and junkyards, which attracted the white trailer trash. Northwest was a rural area, much like Southwest, but it also contained The Side, a neighborhood which was nearly all black. The area commands divided the valley into geographic units that the police could manage. This was a concept the police took from the military, just like the rest of what we did. This meant I reported to a sergeant who reported to a lieutenant who reported to a captain. After that, things kind of got weird. The captain reported to a deputy chief who reported to the undersheriff who reported to the sheriff. What was weird about Vegas police was that we were technically a county sheriff's office. But, instead of an SO, we operated like a city police department. As a police department, I should have reported to a police chief, but I didn't. My boss was a sheriff. A long time before, when the city police and the county S.O. merged, the powers that be decided to keep the mayor or the county commission from controlling the purse strings. The Department was structured so that the sheriff reported to no one and state law was established so that the Department's budget was autonomous. Later, when bipartisan politics went the way it did, state law became nearly impossible to change. This made the office one of the most independent and powerful in the state. For those who doubted this, all anyone had to do was look at the race for sheriff and governor. One or two people might run for governor, whereas a dozen candidates always ran for sheriff.

■ ■ ■

Outside, the wind seemed to get worse, as though that was possible. More sand hung in the air, obscuring the details of the neighborhoods, including those indicators I used for direction. Generally, I knew where I was. Specifically, I was at a loss until I turned a corner and an old tree came in sight. Since I'd grown up in Vegas, I had an advantage over many of my fellow trainees. One of my best friends, John Hernandez, who had been a Vegas cop for the past ten years, grew up in this neighborhood. By the glow of the streetlights, I saw the old residences made of cinderblock. The lawns were of dead-looking Bermuda grass that was shaded by big elm and cottonwood trees. Each species of tree was being attacked by its own species of parasite which caused the branches to die, making them look like they were waving giant skeleton arms at us as I drove by. I knew that those branches were dangerous. All it would take was a good gust and one of them could come crashing down.

I had a lot of memories associated with this neighborhood. During the summers of my younger years, John and I went to his house to drink lemonade after a day of throwing a football or Frisbee down at the green playing fields of Rancho High School. Being young, we didn't mind the summer's brutal heat. At that time, this was one of the best middle class neighborhoods in Vegas. Now as I studied the houses, I saw what always was true — time changed things. Most of the older residents had moved to the new stucco homes in other parts of the valley, places like Summerlin or Green Valley. They rented these old homes to new families, mainly black or Hispanic. Those that had stayed were the elderly who either didn't want to move or couldn't because of their fixed incomes.

"I'm going to start drifting towards the station," I said. Normally, a comment like that earned a trainee low marks for the day, but if I knew Dave, and I did, I probably raised my score by at least a point. When the most you scored for a shift was five, which required a trainee to do everything perfect, losing a point meant a lot.

"That sounds wonderful to me," he said, yawning. I accelerated towards the next intersection. The gusts seemed to pick up even more like they were going to blow the car home. The wind struck the passenger side, causing the car to swerve abruptly. Dave turned his head. He cracked a baleful eye at me.

"Sorry. It's brutal out there," I muttered.

"Don't . . . and I mean . . . Don't . . . get us in a four oh one."

I grinned, knowing what he meant. If I hit something or it hit us, it would be a cluster fuck. Our supervisor, the risk manager, ID, and the watch commander would show up and if I knew them, they wouldn't be a happy group standing out in this wind, getting sand in their underwear while they listened to some trainee's lame excuses for what had happened. If that were to occur, it might be easier to dismiss that trainee rather than to promote him to PO II, which was my one desire.

I slowed, thinking of what the Academy staff stressed whenever they talked about cars and driving — "Arrive Alive." I'd heard that so many times I might as well have it tattooed on my ass. The dispatcher interrupted my reverie by broadcasting another burglary alarm call.

That was nothing new because those calls had been coming out approximately one every thirty minutes. With the wind picking up in the last hour, there had been a huge surge in burglary calls — one every five or ten minutes. The area units were quietly ignoring the radio traffic. This call was different in that the address she indicated was about two blocks from where we were.

"We're driving in that direction," I pointed out as I coasted up to a stop sign.

"So?" Dave said.

"It's a shoe store." On the opposite corner, the street sign was oscillating so fast, I thought it would snap its screws and fly off like a helicopter.

"I know what it is."

"I wanna take the call."

"Are you out of your freaking mind? It's almost time to head for the corral. Besides, we'll have to get out and be in this stuff. Turn here." He jerked his head to the right, indicating the way back to the station. Without another look, he settled back, closing his eyes and scrunching deeper into the seat. *Like your fat ass can get any more comfortable*, I thought.

"Come on," I wheedled. "It'll give you something to put on the activity report for tonight besides all those damn accidents."

He sighed, raised his head and looked at me. I saw the reluctance in his eyes.

"The sarg isn't going to like me coming in without anything significant again," I said as I looked out the driver's side window. .

"OK, but let's make this quick," he said. I grinned at how well I knew how to play his game. "You can wipe that grin off your face, mister."

Damn, I thought. I'd forgotten the windshield glass was like a mirror. I tried covering my smugness with a logical reason, "Besides, I haven't been on too many perimeter checks."

"Don't push it," he yawned, popping the seat lever so it came fully upright. "I've already said yes so let's make this quick."

I thought this might be a good opportunity to get some experience and maybe add a little excitement to what had been an otherwise boring three weeks. Dave wasn't the most motivated FTO I'd had. He was close to retirement, which meant he needed to get as much money out of the Department as he could. His yearly base salary determined the level of income he would enjoy after retirement. With people like him, close to retirement, the Department tried to create situations where they drew those extra percentages that kicked their base pay up. What he didn't want was to get shot and not enjoy any of what he had coming. A gung-ho rookie like me could be just the thing that made that happen. I advised Dispatch that we were en route to the call.

She acknowledged, letting a little surprise seep into her normally emotionless voice. When I first started, I thought they gave the women who worked Dispatch drugs to keep them that calm.

"Even she thinks this is stupid," Dave muttered.

We pulled into the parking lot. There were a lot of lights, but half were out. The rest that did work had been replaced with those sodium bulbs that gave off that sickly yellow glow that was swallowed by the dust. The store was dark, but I thought I saw movement inside. Parked in front was an older model Chevy Monte Carlo. The car was painted a primer gray, lowered, and had the windows tinted so dark, it was impossible to see inside. It was a typical hoopty, the low-riding kind that blacks and Mexicans liked. At twelve o'clock midnight, it didn't look like it belonged there.

As soon as I lit it up with the side spot, the driver started to back out from in front of the store. Dave hit the redheads, giving the siren a quick toot. I switched on the takedowns and overheads, putting three hundred thousand candlepower on the car. It was like the sun just came up. The Chevy stopped as I angled the black-and-white around and behind it so we had cover from the doors when we opened them. I was happy, knowing I'd performed the perfect car stop, one less thing to get dinged for when I was graded later on. I kicked open the door, grabbed the microphone, flipped the switch from radio to PA, then stood so I had cover from the driver door. I could hear the rumble of straight pipes coming from the suspect vehicle's engine.

"Driver! Turn off the vehicle." My voice boomed around the parking lot. Even the wind couldn't compete with the big speaker in the grill. The hoopty's engine cut off. The cessation of that sound was eerie, leaving only the sound of the wind. I adjusted my spotlight, aiming for the driver-side mirror. This put a focused light beam into the driver's eyes, and helped light the inside of the car. Dave did the same with the one on his side. Now that things were under a little more control, I advised Dispatch of what we were doing, ending with the license plate number.

Now that I had all the light on the car, there were the silhouettes of two heads that could be seen through the back window. The hair, bushy Afros, made me believe the car was occupied by a couple of blacks.

"Ready?" Dave asked.

I nodded. With our guns unsnapped and our hands on the butts, Dave and I moved up on foot. When we reached the point where we both stood just behind the occupants, I leaned toward the driver window. The glass was up. I knocked with a knuckle.

"Helllloooo," I muttered. The driver rolled the window down.

"Can I axe why you stoppin' us?" he said.

"Good evening, sir," I replied. It was my canned speech, taught by the Academy staff and guaranteed to keep an FTO off my back. "Can I see your license, registration and proof of insurance?" I thought, *When I'm on my own, this is going to change to something like, "What the fuck are you doing here, asshole?"* That was always a good ice breaker I'd seen more seasoned officers use when a situation reeked of JDLR or just doesn't look right. Before I could go on with the spiel, Dave cut in.

"Get the fuck out of the car, now! I want to see hands and don't be fucking around!" The doors opened and they climbed from the car. I had to admit they played it cool, keeping up with the pissed-off innocence. Dave looked at them both.

"I know you," he said. He pointed towards the front of the patrol car. "Take your happy asses up there."

I backed to a position by the front driver's quarter panel, trying to keep my eyes on both at once. Dave called to the passenger, "Who owns this piece of shit?"

"Issa homey's," he replied.

"Homey's?" Dave asked. "What's this *homey's* name?"

I took that as my cue. "What's your friend's name?"

They looked like juveniles, maybe brothers. Both were skinny, under 150, and of the same height, five-feet-eight, I guessed. Faces dotted with darker spots — pimples and birth moles, their faces framed by hair in longish 'fros, which was strange, because this had been out of fashion for years. The clothing was typical street punks' — baggy pants that sagged until the crotches were even with their knees, no belts so their underwear would have showed if it wasn't for the oversize shirts with the tails out, and 49er team jackets. The tennis shoes must have set them back a couple hundred each. As I looked them over, I decided I couldn't pick a better outfit to hide a weapon in. *Dress like a banger, must be a banger,* I thought. The passenger shrugged.

"Does that mean that you don't know? Or you don't intend telling me?" I asked. I wanted to get him to talk, slip up with some information I could use to look good when Dave got back to our car. My experience so far with gang bangers was that information stayed in their heads like a dam with a crack. The idea was to make the thing leak, then it might pour out. I pointed to where I wanted the driver to stand so that I could start a frisk on him.

"We be not knowin' whoda cah. He jus up da cah so we get some smokes at da store." All that came out so quickly I couldn't understand what was said until I thought about it for a second. I went to a bad school, but I never bothered learning "Ghetto speak." I was a white kid who went to Rancho, a mostly black and Hispanic high school, to get an education. I finished, received my diploma, unlike many others in my class. My intention was to get a job, a life, and move to suburbia. Coming from a low-income school, I got to see my share of people whose only intention was to milk the Great American Welfare System. Those people would be happy to stay in North Las Vegas, vacation in places like Compton or East LA every once in while, and sit on the stoop or watch TV to pass the time. These two guys epitomized that whole scene. So, as soon as they started that slang thing, I sensed trouble. To head it off, I jumped in with the usual cop stuff that went with a car stop.

"Where's your ID?" I pointed both my voice and a finger at the driver. I wanted to be careful. Whenever a new Academy came out, the street element, which was the politically correct phrase we were supposed to use for the crooks, knew it. The trainees were expected by their FTOs to arrest people, jack them up, and show that we could do the job. This meant we made mistakes. It was those mistakes that allowed the crooks to fuck with us. They wanted to make us look foolish and we knew the

FTOs would allow it up to a point, then they would step in and take back control. I didn't want to let things get to that point where Dave or any other FTO had to step in. Not only didn't I want to look foolish, but I also didn't want the word to get around that I couldn't handle my business. Being polite wasn't going to get me far, so I decided to get into the act — the act of being a hard ass.

"Ain't got any," he said.

"Where were you going?"

"About."

"About where?" He shrugged. "What were you doing here? At this closed store?"

"Nothin."

While I talked, I moved to a position behind the two.

"Any police contact in the past?"

"Nah," they said in unison. I hadn't given either one an instruction so far, yet they both "assumed the position," which was that both of them put their hands on the car hood, spread their feet, and leaned forward. It was funny how getting in front of a squad car gives some people away.

"Where'd you learn to do that?" I asked.

"What?" the driver asked.

"Prone out like that. Maybe you been watching too much *Cops* on TV?" Dave was still at the car, so I knew my six o'clock was safe. I guessed he was checking for the vehicle registration in the usual places — the visor, glove box or the center console. A quick glance over my shoulder showed him leaning into the car, a knee on the seat and a foot on the ground.

"Clasp your hands behind your neck," I said. Again, I directed my voice so the driver knew I was talking to him. I intended patting him first because he was making me nervous. He didn't do as I asked, so I thought he hadn't heard me. "Lock your hands behind your head."

"Is I being arrested?" he asked.

"If I don't get some hands up where I told you."

"Hey," Dave called. I looked back again. He held up a small pistol. Now, I knew I needed to be careful. In the Academy, they taught, "Where there's one gun, there's two guns." This changed everything. It was my first call where an illegal gun was found. That had me paranoid, which was not necessarily bad. Paranoia had kept more than one cop alive.

What didn't help was when Dave decided to call out, "Gun!"

Maybe, he didn't realize I'd both heard him and seen it. The driver's head turned towards the passenger's. It was like they were on the same wavelength. I heard the single word, but didn't know what it meant until it was too late.

"Break!" the driver said.

And they were gone.

Chases. When someone runs, cops turn into the equivalent of human blood hounds. We chased people even when it made no sense to be doing that. When I was older and had chased many, many people, I came to realize that I had discovered things about life. One of those was that sometimes we caught what we pursued, and when we did, that old adage came into play: "Be careful what you wish for, you might get it."

As the passenger ran east, I noticed a traffic cop sitting on his bike across the street. I hadn't even seen or heard him pull up, but I guess that wasn't so strange with the wind blowing like it was. What amazed me though was that he was on his bike. I knew that when the weather was bad, they went to the substations and checked out cars. The motor cops were on the same schedule as us. That meant it was too early for him to go in also, so he must have decided to check out my call and kill a few minutes. As I turned my attention to the driver, I caught the traffic cop's leg lifting over the seat of his bike.

Later that night, Dave would tell me how the big motor-cop, Charlie Cruz, got off his bike and chased the passenger. Charlie was a huge man, an inch shy of seven feet. When he rode, he hunched his back into a big "C," giving the impression he was much smaller. Several times I backed him on car stops. I loved watching the startled look on some speeder's face when he saw Charlie step off his bike, fill the mirror as he walked to the car, then seeing him bend nearly in half to get his face by the driver's. It was funny as shit. What must have been funnier was seeing Charlie try to chase that nimble kid in those huge, Herman Munster boots the traffic cops wore. Those black boots might look like something

Adolph Hitler issued to his best Storm Troopers, but they had a practical purpose. The length protected the rider's legs from flying debris kicked up by cars. The cops spent money having an extra layer of leather added to the soles, which people thought was intended to make them look taller. That wasn't it. In the summer, the pavement got hot, sometimes as much as a 165 degrees. Standing out on that stuff for any length of time meant the heat penetrated through thin layers of leather into the feet. That was uncomfortable, which translated to irritable, which was bad for a motorist who was already having a bad day and, maybe, decided taking it out on the cop would make things better. They were not the best things to be wearing when chasing a tennis shoe clad teenager during a sixty mph windstorm. It didn't take the kid long to lose Charlie.

■ ■ ■

While all this was going on, I had other problems. I was on my suspect. The front end of the black-and-white was parked towards north, which meant the two suspects faced south. Next to the store, which was west of our cruiser, was an undeveloped lot. The surface had this moon-like look because northbound wind had scoured all the loose dirt away. That was the direction the suspect took. Each time his foot hit the ground, a cloud of dust whipped right into my eyes. In the pale light from distant streetlights, I saw a block wall coming up. The kid went over it like he was a blowing leaf. In spite of his head start and being unable to keep my eyes on him, I was close. I vaulted the wall smoothly, hitting the ground with less than three feet of distance between us. As I made a lunge to grab him, the eight-hundred-dollar Omega watch came undone. My feet hit the ground at the same time as the watch. This left me with a decision — leave the watch and catch the suspect or get the watch and possibly lose him. I chose the watch. When it was safely in my pocket, the kid's lead was substantial, almost all the way across the yard. For the first time, I called into the radio.

"Control, Two Baker Thirty-four, foot pursuit." I followed that with a direction of travel and suspect description. She gave me a code red. It was strange running through the sleeping neighborhood a little after midnight, which led me to think about the sleeping souls around me, how they were oblivious to the drama unfolding just on the other side of their thin walls. The illumination from the streetlights created a crazy scene. The blowing sand muted the light and gave the air this stained-with-blood look. To make it even crazier, the whipping tree branches caused the shadows to dance. When I lost track of the suspect, I had to search those shadows to make sure I wasn't running into an ambush. The constant movement screwed with my sense of perception, causing me to feel as if there were more than the two of us in this chase. Not only was the light playing tricks on me, but any noise we made seemed to get blown away like everything else that was loose.

I had to admit the kid was in shape, and to make things more interesting, he was a good runner. First, he stayed to the streets, where I slowly gained on him. I was straight out of the Academy, which meant I still retained the benefits of all those forced PT runs that were part of the daily regimen. When he realized I was going to catch him if this kept up, he changed strategies. The first indication of this was when he cut right, straight between two houses, then over a block wall. That definitely made things harder.

"Control, Two Baker Thirty-four, huff, huff, southbound, huff, huff, Webb and North Street, huff, huff." If anyone listening on the radio had a doubt about what was happening, they would soon lose it when they heard the distinctive sound of heavy breathing. The "huffing" worked better than the alert tones the dispatcher activated to indicate a code red on the radio channel. She was doing her part and I had to do mine, which was making sure I updated my direction of travel and tried anticipating the suspect's actions. I knew a lot of people were listening. Doing well or screwing up might create a reputation that would last a whole career.

In the distance, I heard units responding. If huffing on the radio was the sound of a cop chasing someone, then the wail of sirens and the roar of souped-up cruiser engines coming closer was that of help arriving. I knew I wasn't the only one hearing it, though. The suspect looked right and left, searching for an escape route. After we hopped the next wall we were back to the center of a road. I no longer had a clue where we were. I needed a street sign to get a bearing and to let my help know where to find us. I took my eyes off him to look at house numbers. My intent was to radio an address as soon as I had a street to go with it. When I turned my attention back to him, it was just in time to see him heading into a dark carport. It was one of those structures that extended from the side of the house on my left and was open to the right. Along the open side was a wooden fence. At the end of the drive was a locked storage shed and a tall, wooden gate — six feet tall.

Between the top of the gate and the roof of the carport was a space about a foot and one-half high. *Great!* I thought. *He's made a mistake. Right into a trap.* His only escape looked to be back toward me and that wasn't going to happen. I figured he had to stop or turn but he kept running, never slowing for a second. Just when I thought he'd crash into the wood, he leapt. It was then that I realized the other option, which was the gap between the roof and the top of the gate. It was like watching a rabbit disappear down a hole. I plainly saw there was no way on this side of Heaven I would fit through the hole — not with a gun belt covered with equipment. I also knew it would take time to find the gate latch in the dark. So, I did what any self-respecting rookie cop would; I booted the gate. What happened wasn't what I expected. Instead of it springing open, the whole thing, the latch on the left and the hinges on the right, gave equally, causing the whole panel to fly away from me. For an instant, I thought the homeowner might have propped it in place to give people the impression that the gate was secure. The suspect had landed on the other side, regained his balance, and was just getting ready to resume his flight when the gate hit him. Surprisingly, it didn't floor him. Instead, the gate slammed into him, acting the same way a giant tennis racket might if his body were the ball. He was actually given a boost.

The backyard was all dirt. In the center was a dead tree devoid of bark. In front of us was another block wall, only this time, slightly over four feet tall. There were rods of rebar steel sticking out the top. If I'd had time to think about it, I might have guessed the owner intended adding another course in the future. I was right behind the suspect. I mean two feet. I thought I could make a final lunge and grab him when he slowed to get over the wall. Again, he did something unexpected. He sprang — like a human gazelle. His body sailed up into the air. For an instant, he looked like Mercury in that old florist ad — his right foot was perched on the top block, the left one was in trail, and his arms were held in a runner's position. All he had to do was swing the left foot through, sail to the ground, and keep running.

I was close, although below him. I leapt. I placed my right hand on top of the wall, kicked my right foot into its center, and threw my left leg out to the side. All I had to do was use my momentum to lift me into the air, clear the wall, and I'd be on the other side with him. As I started the process, I looked up. His left foot was right by my face. I reached out and caught his ankle.

In order for him to land safely, he needed the foot I held. In order for me to land safely, I needed the hand I held his foot with. We were wedded, like a tug and a boat. We went over together. Crash!

On the other side, there was another yard. It was dirt also, which extended a few feet before a concrete slab began. I hit the dirt. He hit the concrete. We both landed on our heads. The impact stunned me. I thought of cereal, Lucky Stars, to be exact. Little points of light danced before my eyes and I heard voices. As I stood, the suspect did the same. He faced me, staggering back. I took a tentative step towards him, reaching for my gun.

Since then, I have always told people to look at cops carefully some time — to notice what holds all the stuff that they carry in and on their person in place. It is gravity. When a cop is placed upside down, for even an instant, all that stuff falls out or off. That was why I discovered I didn't have a gun where it was supposed to be. For that matter, there was nothing where it was supposed to be. This included my ammo magazines, flashlight, side-handle baton, and the loose change that was deep in my front pocket. About the only thing that hadn't fallen out was my watch, which, when I thought about it, was the reason I was still chasing this fool.

We stood three feet apart, both dazed, breathing hard, and wearing the same stupid look. He was bigger and I didn't want to fight him. I wanted my gun. As I bent to feel around for it, he ran.

"Stop, motherfucker," I yelled. He didn't and I truly didn't expect him to. I took one step in his direction, then stopped. Common sense reared its ugly head. The yard was dark without the street's light. I didn't have my flashlight or a radio. I didn't have a gun, but he might. I knew I'd be foolish to continue chasing him. I knelt and ran my fingers across the ground. The first thing I found was my flashlight, which I used to find everything else. I noticed there were dark spots on the lighter colored soil. Rubbing some between my fingers, I discovered it was blood. As I stood, getting my breath and deciding what to say on the radio, I saw there was a small puddle forming by my left foot. For the first time, I felt warm liquid dripping from the tips of my left-hand fingers. I bent my arm so I could see where it was coming from. There was a two-inch gash below my elbow. I realized I must have caught the point of one of the rebars sticking out of the wall. The radio was being insistent, asking questions about where I was, if I was code four. I put it to my mouth and told the dispatcher I was OK.

"Your location?" she asked.

"No idea. In a backyard," I said. The radio traffic said cops were everywhere. As I talked, one of them heard me and came into the backyard.

"Where'd he go?" he asked.

I pointed. My head and arm were starting to hurt. My heartbeat slowed now that the adrenaline had worn off.

"You OK?"

I nodded. The cop took off in the direction I had pointed. He gave the dispatcher the information as to where I was. I made my way to the front of the house. Once I was out on the street, I saw a bunch of patrol cars parked near an intersection. I walked towards them. The fun felt like it was over. When I got to the cars, Dave waited for me.

"You OK?" I held my arm up. There was a lot of blood. He advised Dispatch to roll medical. It only took a minute for them to arrive, so I guessed the paramedics were monitoring the police channel as the foot pursuit progressed. One of them sat me down and started cleaning the cut with water.

"I can't close this. It's going to need stitches," he said. It hurt as he applied a gauze bandage. "The bleeding's stopped, but the first time you bend this arm, it'll start again."

I wasn't paying much attention to him. The radio traffic detailed the progress of the search for the suspect. There were two canine units and a whole lot of cops set up on a perimeter. It seemed as though only a minute passed before one of the dogs caught him hiding under a pile of loose auto parts a couple of yards over from where I last saw him. Five minutes later, two cops led the kid up the street to us.

"I'll take him," Dave called as he went to meet them. He took one look at the blood on his face, then brought him straight to the ambulance. The paramedic examined the bloody knot on the top of his head.

"He'll live," he said. "Doesn't look like he'll need stitches."

"What about him?" Dave asked, pointing at me.

"Him? Are you asking me if he'll live?" The paramedic grinned. "I'm not sure. I mean, he'll need stitches," he replied.

"I know you," Dave said, looking at the caught kid carefully in the door light. "Leroy Brown. That's right, ain't it?"

"That be me, Porkie."

Dave slapped him in the head with the flat of his hand, causing him to flinch. "Watch your mouth. I thought you were still in Elko. When did you get out, Leroy?"

The juvenile suspect mumbled something. Dave slapped him again. The paramedic turned his back and cleaned up the stuff he'd used to fix me, then went to the front of the ambulance. Through the windshield, I saw him talking to a female officer. I glanced around the side of the ambulance nervously. The lieutenant and sergeants stood talking.

"I can't hear you," Dave said. "You need some shit knocked out of your smart ass?"

"No, sir," Leroy said, letting his head sink.

"How old are you, now?"

"Fifteen."

"And already a criminal," Dave said. "We need to talk. Come over to my office so I can have a word as to who your friend might be." He gripped an elbow in his hand. I guessed from the way the kid grimaced, Dave was applying a lot of pressure. They moved towards our cruiser. When they neared the front of the unit's passenger side, Dave gave the boy a little shove. The corner of the car caught Leroy in the groin, doubling him over. I heard the wind go out of him. Dave slid him across the hood until he was almost on the windshield, then pulled him so his torso was suspended in the air. He let go.

"Mutherfucker!" The word cut through the wind as Leroy crashed to the ground.

"You got to be careful," Dave said. He bent, roughly jerking him to his feet. Our sergeant and the Ell Tee glanced over, turned away, then continued talking. I felt as though I were watching one of those movies where you know bad things are going to happen.

Dave dusted Leroy off. The action was more like chopping the dirt from his clothes and body. When Leroy looked like he was going to cry out, Dave whispered in his ear. Leroy clamped his mouth shut. When Dave had Leroy by the side of the car, he gripped the door handle with his left hand and Leroy with his right. Dave opened the door. He brought Leroy and the door together like a man hitting a tambourine. That knocked the wind out of him.

"Watch what you're doing or you might get hurt," Dave's voice sounded full of concern. He shoved the sagging Leroy inside. We were taught to place a hand on the suspect's head to insure they missed the roof. Dave didn't do this. Leroy hit the car with the side of his head. That caused him to cry out. I cringed. When Leroy was in, Dave slammed the door, and went around to the other side. He grinned at me over the top of the car. It was an evil smile. Then he climbed in. I went back to the ambulance where I could watch. The figures were hunched towards each other, like two people having a very intense conversation. Dave's hands were animated and I saw he did most of the talking. Every now and then, I saw the kid jerk as though a cattle prod were being used on him. There was this little part of me that wanted to intervene, get in there and stop whatever was happening. The problem was that a bigger part of me wanted bad things to happen to the kid. I was in this for the ride, the whole ride, no matter where it took me. From the way the other cops stood with their backs to the car, it was obvious I wasn't the only one. It seemed that Dave was in the car for a long time. Finally, he finished. He stepped from the car.

"I'm done with him," Dave called. "Can we get someone to book him in Juve while I take my partner to the hospital?" Two cops came over. They took Leroy out. I saw the tear tracks on his face.

"Buck up, pussy," one said. "You thought you were bad back at the store."

Dave pointed to the passenger side of our unit, then walked over to speak to the Ell Tee. When he was done, he came back to drive me to the emergency room. I told myself I was going to keep quiet, but as I thought about what I'd seen at the car, I had to say something.

"Weren't you a little rough on him?" I asked.

"Think so?" he asked. We were at an intersection where the traffic signals were out. I thought about an answer to that.

"Yes," I said.

"While you were chasing Leroy, I had a unit check the store. Any idea what they're doing there?"

"No." I suddenly felt guilty that I might have missed some key radio traffic.

"The owner's going to need more stitches than you are. As a matter of fact, he'll be lucky if he isn't a tad less smart when and if he comes out of the coma."

"If?" I asked.

"Yeah. If. One of those boys hit him pretty hard with something."

"I didn't know."

"Right," he said. "Did you think I'd act like that back there for something minor?"

I didn't know what to say, so I kept quiet.

"It's important to gather all the facts in any circumstance," Dave said. "That's the difference between a good cop and a bad one."

The next day, when I got to work, seven new stitches had been added to my already extensive collection. As I dressed, Steve, one of the other rookies, came into the locker room.

"Ell Tee wants to see you in his office as soon as you're dressed."

"Sure," I said. I pulled on my gun belt, checked myself in the mirror, and headed for his office. When I turned the corner, I saw the other black male juvenile who ran from us the night before. He sat in handcuffs, in a plastic chair outside the lieutenant's office. Without saying anything to him, I knocked on the door, even though it was open.

"Come in, Cam." It seemed like he never looked up from whatever paperwork he was doing.

"Sir. You wanted me, Ell Tee."

"How you feeling? You need some time off?"

"No, sir. I'm fine. I can do my job."

"Good. But don't just say that because you think it's what I want to hear." It was then that he looked at me. His eyes swept across my uniform like he was inspecting me, then came to rest on the bandage around my arm. It was a very critical look that made me nervous.

"No, sir!" I put a lot of gung-ho in the words. He smiled. That must have been what he wanted. He leaned back, locking his hand behind his head.

"How is it, really?"

"Hurts, a little. Throbs actually. I took a couple of aspirin before I left for work. I'm good."

The night before the doc had said he'd give me a couple of days off. I told him no. Dave said he'd have taken it. I told him I didn't want people thinking I was a slacker.

"You did a good job out there last night. I'm going to make sure your sergeant puts a little something in your file about it," the lieutenant said.

"Thank you, sir."

"You understand it won't be a commendation."

"Yes, sir."

"A critical. It'll help if you have problems later. OK?"

"Problems, sir?"

"Well, Dave mentioned you weren't too happy about the way someone may have been treated."

"Oh, no, sir! I think he misunderstood me. I had no problem with anything." I held my arm up. "It was my blood spilled, sir. I'll have a talk with my FTO. I don't want anyone thinking I can't do what needs to be done."

"Maybe there was a misunderstanding then. I'll let you fix it." I didn't like being in his office without Dave. "When your FTO gets in . . . " He nodded towards the hall. "Take him to Juve. He's already confessed."

"OK, sir." He looked down at some papers. I knew I'd been dismissed. Still, this whole thing had me worried. As I turned, he called, "Close the door."

After I did, I unhooked the suspect from his chair. I took him down the hall away from the offices.

"What's your name?" I asked. The kid looked like his friend — too young and innocent. That was if you ignored his eyes.

"My name Tommy."

"Tommy?" I asked. He nodded.

"Leroy call me last night. He say Officer Dave tell him I better come in here or else," the boy said.

"Or else what?" I wasn't really sure I wanted to know what options Dave might have given him.

Tommy shrugged. "I'm here. All that matters, I guess."

"That's true. We'll take you down as soon as Officer Stieber gets here." We went to the briefing room, where I sat him in a chair next to me. He put his head on the table and went right to sleep. When Dave arrived, I was just finishing the booking paperwork. He poked Tommy in the shoulder, and after the boy's head lifted, he simply nodded to him. We waited while Dave dressed, then we took the kid to the juvenile facility. In those days, I liked Juve booking. It was quick and easy. When we were back in the car, Dave turned towards me.

"So, here's the rest of the story. Several weeks ago, I'm not sure when, these two shitheads decide to rob that shoe store. During the robbery, the owner recognizes them. When they realize they're made, they tell him if he says anything to the police, they'll return and kill him. Samuel, the owner, isn't one to be intimidated. As soon as the police get there, he tells them who did it."

"There were juvenile warrants out for those two in a day. They were free a week, then they got picked up. They were given hearing dates and let go. When their court date comes, Samuel shows up. He testifies against them and they're bound over. The holdup on their sentencing was the state trying to certify them as adults. In case you don't know this, that determines which court deals with them, whether District or Juvenile. District will get them another trial and possibly state prison. Juvenile court will guarantee a stay in a facility like Elko. The problem with juvenile court is that their records will ultimately be expunged when they turn eighteen. Their parents hired an attorney to fight against them being certified. So they're out on appeal, awaiting the outcome of that decision. Where Samuel's concerned, I'm not sure if they intended to kill him or intimidate him. Either way, that man's in sad shape. What'd the doc say last night?"

"He released me to duty, just told me to go easy on the arm."

"Good! You ready?"

"Yes," I said.

"We got things to do. I need to teach you about being a cop."

"I have a few things to learn," I replied. I wondered if there was going to come a time when I'd be able to slide someone across the hood of a squad car the way Dave had. My problem was that I felt sorry for those kids, for the way they'd turned out, and what they'd think of the police when they were released. Maybe there should have been another break for them.

■ ■ ■

Radio Silence and the Human Blood Hound . . .

After taking Tommy to Juve, Dave and I were dispatched to a perimeter position for an in-progress foot pursuit. With my elbow feeling like a piece of chopped meat, I wanted to take it easy, so I wasn't unhappy about the perimeter assignment. The chase took place inside a Federal housing project. Dispatch gave us a perimeter position on the southwest corner of the imaginary box. What they taught in the Academy, and what we were doing, was parking at the intersection of two streets. That way, we, as one unit, could cover two directions at once. There were two other units doing the same thing for three other corners, which normally didn't make sense, but in this case — did.

What was outside the box was a neighborhood consisting of older tract homes. They looked like the one my parents had moved into after my father left the military. He served for thirty years, the last five at the same base in Kansas. During those last years, all he talked about was getting out and finding a little place where no one was going to order him to pack and leave. For some reason, my parents liked Vegas. When my father retired, they bought a place at the south end of town. He started immediately fixing it up the way he wanted.

One day, my mother took a glass of ice tea out to him. He was sitting against a tree in the backyard, eyes open, head canted to the side as if he'd seen something that surprised him. The doctor said it was a massive heart attack. They took him back to Detroit and buried him across from his father, whom he barely spoke to his whole life.

For a while, my mother lived in the house. Then one day, she decided she liked California. She sold the place and moved into a small apartment by the beach. Each month, she received a check from Uncle Snoopy, as my father preferred to call the government. Strangely enough, her Social Security was more than enough for her to live on. The rest she hoarded away, spending little bits and pieces on my sister when she needed something.

They were the two who talked, being the atypical close mother-daughter relationship. My relationship with my mother was atypical, too. She didn't like me. She hadn't liked my father ever since she found out he'd slept around while he was overseas. How can a mother not like her child? All I could guess was that she transferred her anger for him to me. It wasn't something I let bother me much anymore. Time passed, things changed. That might, too.

It wasn't only my mother's dislike that made me similar to my father. I also had worked for Uncle Snoopy. First, there was the Air Force job, then the other for the civilian company that contracted for the Air Force. The difference between my father and me was that I only wanted to work for the government for a short time, not the full twenty years, which garnered a person a retirement. That was because I knew things and had seen things — wonderfully strange things from that time Joey and I spent in the secret places Up North. That was stuff I might never be able to talk about.

People had no idea. If it was only aliens, all of us could live with it, but there were other questions, like: How about when Uncle Snoopy insisted on building places where people could be warehoused? Kept alive with little pensions or food stamps and made to think they were doing well because they weren't starving? That was what Federal sponsored housing complexes were all about. From the outside, they looked nice and clean. There were lots of trees and grassy space between the duplex units.

Whenever we were near one of these places, Dave liked to disperse little bits of information and statistics that he had memorized directly from Federal studies. Those papers said those spaces allowed low income children room to play. He didn't care what the studies said because he knew what the truth was. Those spaces were really there so we could chase those people's children, who were nothing but drug dealers, thieves, and killers, by driving our cars between the units at high rates of speed.

When we first took our position, Dave remarked, "The only good thing about this particular project is that it makes for an easy perimeter." He pointed out how the curve in US 95 made a natural barrier along the entire north and east sides of the complex. "If he goes that way, he'll get smooshed."

After we parked, I pulled the call up on the MDT screen. It told the pursuit started when an officer stopped a black male juvenile for selling rock cocaine. After the stop, the officer directed the kid to the front of the unit, just as I had done the night before with the two from my car stop. Instead of doing what he was told, the kid bailed — again the same scenario as mine from the night before. I was beginning to realize that half the battle to becoming a good cop was realizing that people were predictable. If you saw something once, you could guess it was going to happen for the same reason every time. The trick was to know when it was the same and different — if that made sense.

If all he'd done was run, he'd probably have left the cop wondering if the kid was selling drugs. What dispelled any doubt was that the kid chucked his dope, leaving the ground littered with little white pieces of rock cocaine. Actual evidence made him worth chasing.

Catching him was the thing that was proving hard. Normally, that would have been simple. The ground unit would place a call for an air unit and have them see where he went. When dispatch said they weren't available, Dave made the usual remark.

"Probably off polishing their rotor blades or doing whatever else helicopter pilots do," he muttered. Even as a new cop, I knew they rarely flew, which meant they rarely caught anybody. Besides that, it was hot outside. From my days of flying to work, I also knew that heat affected lift on an airship. It sure affected ground cops. When the pursuit first started, Dispatch asked for area units to clear non-essential calls and help with the perimeter. Almost no one did. Cops hate being on perimeter, especially when it's hot outside. The reason we were here was because I didn't catch the fact that there was a pursuit going on. We had come out of the Juve with me gabbing and not paying attention. As soon as we were in the car, I cleared us.

"No, don't," Dave yelled as my finger hit the button. Before I could figure out why he yelled, the dispatcher assigned us to the call. We were stuck on the pursuit, which pretty much meant we'd be sitting around and waiting on the off-chance that the shithead came our way. In my limited experience, I was quickly starting to understand the bad guys rarely ran right into a unit. Still, I liked foot pursuits and that was a good thing because for as long as I was a street cop there were certain things I knew I'd better get used to — chasing people, chasing people in stolen cars, or chasing cars that had people in them that had done other bad things. It was a good thing I liked the excitement of chasing someone and the chance of catching him. I liked dragging some sixteen- or seventeen-year-old punk to my car, knowing I was the one in better shape. Dave didn't like any of this, but there were reasons — such as the gut hanging over his belt like a soft growth and the cigarettes often seen dangling from his lips. Dave was so anti-pursuit, he didn't even like it when other cops chased people. That was obvious from the aggrieved look on his face as we listened to the pursuit's progress. The cop who did the chasing was doing a great job broadcasting information. I knew what the kid wore, what he looked like, and that he was in sight. As I listened, I angled the car across the intersection, nosing us towards the corner. Dave hit the "arrived" button, muttering imprecations at the computer.

"I thought they couldn't hear us over that," I said. He gave me a blank look. I pointed at the computer. "Talking . . . you know . . . there's no mike." Still nothing, so I gave up. It was a dumb joke that would probably result in me getting even lower scores on my nightly eval than I knew he was going to give me for putting us here in the first place. I had to push aside the fear of getting low scores. I knew it was a throwback to the early days of field training. With this cycle about done, I was starting to get the idea that I stood a chance of becoming a cop. At this point, I would have to do something really stupid to get non-confirmed status. Still, whenever I thought about getting low scores, it was always with the past knowledge of how we'd get to the station and I would think I'd had a great day, then my FTO would show me my evaluation log with scores so low they made me feel like I was single-handedly responsible for the jump in crime in the Vegas Valley and, maybe, in the whole world.

What made it worse was that if my FTO didn't feel like explaining them, then that was the end of it. When I first started in the program, I tried to approach things logically. If I screwed up, I'd try to get things explained so I knew what was expected of me. I figured if I understood, I could fix my mistakes. That wasn't the way things worked, though. If he gave me low scores and I asked why, I'd get a blank look as if it should be obvious. If I got into a discussion that ended in an argument, I never won. Worse, arguing meant I was given homework, in the form of a paper supported by NRS or policy. A bad argument could mean the start on that road to non-confirmed status, which translated to being fired. It was a game we trainees called the Great Mystery, part of which was figuring out why one FTO wanted things a certain way, but the next one didn't. I thought they should have given us an Academy class on *How to Navigate the Personality Quirks of FTOs*. Of course, that didn't make sense either, because it would have been an art class instead of anything practical.

"I know the cop chasing the kid," Dave said.

Oh, I thought, *he's worried about his friend.* "I'm sorry. I didn't mean to sound like I was making light of a serious situation." I guessed a little humility might put me back in Dave's good graces.

"I didn't say he was a friend of mine," he said as he settled even further back in the seat. "I said I know him. What I mean is, he knows better than to get into a foot pursuit right after I've eaten."

I turned away, pointing my face down the street I was supposed to be watching. Dave was in a really pissed off mood. I wasn't sure if he was joking and I didn't want to make a mistake by laughing if he wasn't and not laughing if he was. I studied the middle class houses with all the stuff middle class people liked to collect. There were lots of older cars, some motor homes, hedges and green lawns. At the end of the street, I saw the project quads.

"I'd hate to live in those places," I remarked, wanting to be back on safe ground.

"Shitholes," he replied. "Every last one of them ought to be torn down. They look plain. It's the way the government wants them."

Shit, I thought, *I should have kept my mouth shut.*

"The feds," he continued, taking a deep breath so he could get started, "force them on communities with the promise of money. They always make the people who have to live near them unhappy. Us cops hear the logic from those ivory tower idiots, which is that all poor people really need to rise above their poverty is seeing the way wealthier people live. Instead, they should be thinking it's more like putting a bunch of cows close to hungry lions. Or, if that picture's too hard for them, in my humble opinion, maybe they should try putting one of those places near million dollar homes."

Wow! I thought. *He actually has an opinion and it sucks.* While he talked, the radio traffic became sporadic, so I figured the cop had either lost or was losing the kid. As with anything, this had its good side, which I really considered a bad side. If the cop lost the kid, we'd be able to do something else, like head to the station so Dave could use the toilet. If, on the other hand, the cop actually chased him to us, I might catch him. I knew that wasn't likely, but I could hope. What played in our favor was that the neighborhood was all white and the kid was black. The chances were good that he hadn't gotten out of the box, so I figured it wouldn't be long before some "concerned citizen" called in that they had a juvenile either hiding or running through a backyard.

I grinned at that thought. In front of me was a typical yard and in that yard was a typical dog — a big Doberman pinscher that watched us through a metal gate. It didn't take a lot of imagination to see he was as pissed off as Dave was, but for different reasons. He wanted a piece of somebody and I would have done as well as a running black kid. After we first arrived, he'd barked a lot. When that had no effect, he settled in to wait us out, which was really a matter of me watching him watching us. That went on for a long time. Then, the MDT beeped, I looked down to see another call for the area come on screen, which was going to have to hold. When I raised my head back to the yard, I was surprised to see the dog's head turned towards something behind him.

The dog ran off like he had suddenly lost interest in us — not something a dog like that does. That definitely got my attention. It seemed less than a second later that the kid came towards us, running along the top of the wall. He was looking back the way he'd come. I figured he must have been hopping fences in the process of working his way westward. The best thing was he hadn't seen us. That was when he dropped in the yard, which meant he hadn't seen the dog, either. I imagined the terror he'd feel when he came face to face with that monster.

■ ■ ■

After I put the car in park, we kicked the doors open so we could get out quickly. To make sure the doors stayed that way — open, we kept a foot on the door panel. That prevented the wind from blowing them closed or if we needed to close them, we could just give them a push against the hinges and they would spring back. Having a foot in the door served another purpose, which was that I just about already had a foot on the ground, which further meant I could use the procedure to exit the car like a launched missile.

That put me in position to reach the back gate in time to see the dog lunge at the kid's crotch. I never imagined a human being could leap back so quickly, almost having his dick bit off. The wall at his back, which he hit, producing a nice thump that carried across the twenty feet between us, was his problem. That wall was his trap, like a mouse's. The dog's was the spring-loaded wire about to come straight over the top and make short work of the situation. It wasn't working and if it wasn't so serious, I'd have cracked up. I saw the way the dog was looking and what was about to happen was definitely going to be ugly. As he lunged again, the kid grabbed a rake that was leaning against the wall. He took a swing. The handle caught the poor pooch in the side, spoiling its aim, and sending it sprawling. That gave the kid enough time to vault over the wall.

I pushed the gate open and charged through, expecting to see a dead dog. He wasn't, but he was pissed and looking to take it out on someone. We looked at each other.

"Nice doggie," I called. He wasn't that either and, to prove it, he showed me a bunch of very sharp teeth set in a snout that reminded me of certain animals that belonged behind bars in zoos. As I leapt for the top of the wall, those same teeth barely missed my ass. I hit the ground on the other side in time to see the kid launch himself at the top of the opposite wall. Just before he was over, he balanced precariously in preparation for dropping out of my sight.

"Stop. Police!" I yelled, which was about as futile as trying to arrest gravity.

"Fuck you," he replied as he dropped.

My radio emitted the sound of Dave's voice telling Dispatch that I was now the one in foot pursuit. She came back sounding very confused.

"Last unit, is that Two George Twelve in pursuit?"

"Negative, Control," he told her and even I could detect the weariness in his voice. I could imagine what he was thinking, which would have a lot to do with discussions later on about chasing people when your FTO has just eaten. I thought I could salvage some points by doing something I should have already done, which was tell her where I was going.

What happened next concerned the radio I carried, which was referred to as a brick. It was big and heavy, measuring an inch and one-half thick by three and one-half inches wide by fourteen inches from the tip of the antenna to the base. A brick was stored in this ingenious metal holder, which clipped over the top of the leather gun belt. There were newer, lighter radios, which didn't require holders, but they were never issued to rookies. One of the first jobs I had each day was to go to the equipment room and sign out a car and two hand-held radios. From experience, I asked for a brick and a new radio. The old guy working there suspiciously asked who was getting the new radio. I never could figure out how he could be suspicious — of course, it went to Dave. Could he even imagine a rookie would carry a better radio than an FTO? That was one of those things a trainee just knew, like God help that trainee if the air conditioner in the car didn't work perfectly because that trainee didn't get to work early enough to secure a really good car before all the cops that weren't rookies got to work.

I ran to the wall, sprang, and cleared it. I hit the ground in time to see the kid go over the wall on the opposite side of the yard. It had to be almost one hundred degrees, which was normally a cool Vegas day. The operative word, "cool," was relative, especially if you were wearing a uniform that consisted of a tan short-sleeved cotton shirt over a bullet-proof vest that was worn over an undershirt, all of which was tucked into wool pants that covered a pair of Hi-Tech boots. Those same pants that were held up by an under-belt were attached to a gun belt that had fifteen pounds of equipment stored in various configurations. This was considered proper attire for a cop but it wasn't what anyone with a sane mind would consider proper attire for physical exertion — gym shorts and tank tops met that criterion.

Still, I ran, leapt, and caught the top of the next wall, which was just in time to see him disappear over the wall on the opposite side of the yard. I was beginning to understand why the George unit lost him. And throughout all of this, I was tugging on that brick, which wasn't coming out. That was what I discovered then, but there was something else which I wasn't to discover until later. It was stuck. For a fraction of a second, I actually thought about stopping to rectify the situation, but I knew if I did, I'd lose him. Thinking back to the night before, someone might think I had learned. All I would admit to later was I felt God was testing me — first with my watch and now with my radio. It was little things like that which caused rookies to ask why the hell we weren't selling insurance.

■ ■ ■

We kept running and I started closing. Sometimes, I landed in a yard while he was still in it instead of already over in the next one. *This has to end*, I thought. It did, but only the wall-climbing part. We popped out of a side yard, then after a few steps, onto a street. I was happy to see his breathing was coming as hard as mine. Once we moved to the pavement, the time it took to close on him quickened. I readied myself for the push, which would send him sprawling. In cop shows, they tackled people. That was stupid and it wasn't the way it's done in real life. There was too much chance of me getting hurt. What I'd been taught was to get within arm's reach and shove the suspect from behind. That created an effect like running down a hill and having the body get ahead of the feet, which resulted in a crash.

The kid looked over his shoulder, realizing he was about to lose this race. I grinned.

"You better run," I huffed. It must have occurred to him that he'd been doing better in the yards, so he made a sharp left, straight between two houses, heading for another fence. I groaned, feeling as if I was having deja vu. In front of us was a four-foot-high fence. The slats were made from six-inch-wide, wormy cedar boards that had been nailed vertically to a couple of two-by-fours. He went straight over. My intention was to do the same. When I placed both hands on the top, then leapt into the air, I felt like I'd been torn in two. As I dropped back to the ground, I saw the handle of my baton had managed to fit perfectly into one of the knotholes. The baton is carried in a ring on the gun belt. As I jumped, the ring acted like an anchor, stopping my body from rising into the air. That was what made me think I'd tried to rip myself in half. Angrily, I jerked the baton from the hole. I stepped back, intending to jump the fence now that I was clear of getting hung up again. The kid had stopped about twenty feet away. Maybe, he thought I'd given up.

"Fuck you," he called. He gave me the finger, which added insult to injury. That really pissed me off. I cocked my arm back, the baton, called a PR-24, held like a tomahawk. The tool was twenty-four inches long, hence the number in its name, and an inch and one-half in diameter. It had a small handle near one end. Normally, one held the small handle, then spun the tool so the long end hit the suspect. Done correctly, the end traveled at 790 feet per second and, considering that a forty-five-caliber bullet travels at eight hundred feet per second and is only as big as your thumb, was intended to do some serious damage. Using the PR-24 like a tomahawk was not prescribed in any manual as an approved method of self-defense. All I thought about was his finger — no other consequences, so I threw it and as soon as it left my hand, I regretted the act. It flew straight towards the kid's head. I guess it probably was a good thing I wasn't raised on a reservation. It missed, but not by much. The look on his face was sheer fear. I bet mine was the same when I thought it was going to connect. If it had hit him, I'd be explaining a bad injury or death.

As it was, the PR-24 landed thirty feet past him. He turned and ran straight for the baton as I went over the fence. When I landed, I started for him. He bent over and picked it up. I thought I was going to have to shoot him. That was something that stayed in your head forever. As he straightened, now holding the PR-24, I drew my gun. Before I drew a bead, he slung my baton in the opposite direction from me, then headed towards the back wall. I had no choice except to stop and retrieve my baton. It would have been hard explaining to everyone where it was if I showed up without it.

The whole time, I kept trying to get my stuck radio out of the holder. The chatter told me that people were racing all over the place trying to find us. When I got over this wall, I saw he'd gained a long fifty feet. The air was heavy and quiet from the heat with only the sound of the occasional cicada breaking in. That loud noise was punctuated with the slap of our shoes as we ran across different surfaces, the constant huffing as we forced heated air into our bodies, and my radio. It seemed like the whole universe was a tunnel that contained only the two of us. The chase passed through long stretches of flat yard, turned corners of houses or sheds, then more wall to be climbed. Once in a while, he glanced back at me. I saw his fear. After what must have been ten houses, we popped back out onto another residential street. In front of me, in the distance was Mount Charleston, so I knew we were westbound. I was fatigued to the point I wanted to quit, just let him go but I wasn't going to do it. My shirt felt like I'd taken a shower in it. Sweat ran off my forehead and into my eyes. I swiped a hand across my face so often I felt like a car windshield wiper in one of those downpours where water fell faster than the device worked. I kept hoping a black-and-white would appear so someone else could catch him.

Just when I decided to call it quits, a vehicle turned the corner. It wasn't what I wanted, which was a black-and-white. Instead, it was one of those monster pickup trucks with a lift kit that pushed the full-size body high in the air. When I saw trucks like these, it was easy imagining the driver needing a ladder to get in or out. There were ten KC lights that lined on a bar across the top; a winch; giant, forty-four-inch all-terrain tires; and a gun rack in the back window. The vehicle had redneck written all over it.

The driver saw the black kid running from me. He must have thought it was his civic duty to help. He opened the door, stepped from the cab, and started my way. The problem was, the truck was still moving down the street. It was true it was traveling at a snail's pace, but it was big. There were cars down both sides of the street, which made it like a juggernaut bent on destruction.

The kid never saw anything in front of him because he was looking back at me. What I expected was for the driver to tackle him. Instead, as he got within two feet of the kid, he threw one of those huge, hooking haymaker punches. It caught the kid square in the nose, putting him right on his butt. I could tell the guy wanted to finish what he started, but his truck needed his attention. So, he decided to abandon me and rescue the neighbor's car. *If it was mine*, I thought. *I'd be worried about increasing my insurance rates, too.*

It looked like a great punch, but it wasn't. As the shock wore off, the kid jumped to his feet. I thought he might give up, but he didn't. Instead, he kept running. I had closed to within fifteen feet, though. Each time his foot hit the ground, he left a wet footprint where sweat squished out. That alone made me think the chase was coming to an end, which was good. I wasn't feeling all that great. I just wanted this finished. The world had this fuzzy look to it. The kid didn't look good, either. The punch left one of those scraped-flesh wounds, welling little bloody droplets that mixed with the sweat running down his face. We'd run at least a half-mile, climbing fences most of the way. I saw him looking sideways, knowing he was thinking of starting that again. I didn't have more fences in me. The whole race had come down to a simple contest of wills, not only between him and me but with myself. The whole chase had become a matter of one foot in front of the other. I had to keep telling myself just to go one more second, then one more after that.

So, when I saw him veer for a fence, I figured it was do or die. I put on the last burst of speed I felt I'd be able to muster. He must have heard me coming because he just stopped. We were in the front yard of a corner house. I drew my gun and pointed it at him.

"Get . . . *puff, huff* . . . on . . . *groan* . . . the . . . *puff, puff* . . . ground, fuck-er . . . *Wheeze, puff* . . . or . . . *wheeze* . . . I'll . . . *hack* . . . shoot . . . *wheeze, wheeze* . . . you . . . *puff* . . . by . . . *groan* . . . God!" He stood there looking at me but doing nothing. I felt like I had spoken in a foreign language.

"Fuck you, you ain't gonna shoot me," he wheezed back.

He was right. As much as I wanted to shoot him, I couldn't. It was a threat that sometimes worked. This time, it wasn't going to. Still, I had to try because I was too tired to do much of anything else, like wrestle with him.

"Get down, asshole."

"No! Don't be calling me an asshole."

While we were having this slow motion conversation, I knew I needed to do something before he recovered any more than he had. I felt lethargic, as if I needed to lie down and sleep. I stepped forward and booted him in the stomach as hard as I could. Normally, that would have floored someone. Instead, he settled to the ground. It was slow motion, too, like a leaf falling from a tree. *Jeez, that kick should have killed him*, I thought. He gagged, then tried standing. Before he could, I used my foot to push him prone on the grass. He didn't resist. I knelt, placing my knee in the center of his back. It was difficult, but I finally cuffed him. When it was done, I rolled off to the side and stared up through tree branches. They seemed to chop the deep blue sky into slices. I wanted to close my eyes and pretend I was ten years old, lying by the side of my favorite fishing hole, waiting for a perch to grab the bait and bend the pole.

Just as my eyes started closing, the noise of my radio roused me. A voice insistently repeated my call sign. I tried pulling the radio from the holder, feeling it slip in my sweaty hands. It was still stuck. With a tremendous effort, I climbed to my feet. The world spun. I had to reach a hand out to the rough bark of a diseased elm to steady myself. Even after sucking deep breaths for a minute, I couldn't get enough strength to give the radio a good hard tug. Then it occurred to me that I had no idea where I was even if I could tell someone. I turned to look at a street sign, which at least told me that.

I decided to rest longer, then tackle the chore of working the radio loose. I leaned forward, resting my forehead against the rough bark. From far away, I heard the sound of people running. It seemed like years before Dave stood with his hand on my shoulder.

"Are you OK?"

I nodded. I wasn't but I wanted him to think I was. Especially with the Ell Tee's words still in my thoughts. I desperately wanted to be on the same playing field with people like Dave, no matter what I thought of his physique or his stupid attitudes. I opened my eyes in time to see two other cops grab the prisoner, lifting him from the ground. They weren't gentle, and when he struggled, one of them elbowed him in a way anyone watching would have a hard time noticing. The kid gasped, then sagged.

"Get up, you piece of shit, before I drag you by your nappy-assed head to the morgue," the officer who had just hit him ordered. I could have cared less if he'd taken his gun out and shot the kid between the eyes.

"What happened to your radio traffic," Dave asked.

Without saying a word, I tried to tug the radio from the holder. He watched, then tried it himself. Instantly, his anger was forgotten.

"Are you okay? Really?"

I couldn't nod because a wave of dizziness swept over me. I teetered like I was going to crash to the ground. I managed to say, "No."

"Control, we need Medical," Dave told his nice new radio. He gave her our location. I was searching around in my thoughts for police things to say. Nothing was coming to mind. Finally, I managed to ask, "How did you find me?"

He pointed at the ground. I saw bright red splatters that seemed to glow against the white surface of the sidewalk. They trailed off as far as I could see. I glanced at the kid, thinking it must be his. Dave took me by the wrist and lifted my arm. When I looked, the skin was ripped open. The stitches from the night before hung there. Blood gathered, then fell in slow motion. I watched it hit a blade of grass, another bit splatter some dirt. Dave pulled a kerchief from his shirt pocket and tied it tightly around the wound. After he pushed me to a sitting position, he went to an arriving unit. The Sarg climbed from the car, then asked Dave in a loud voice why I hadn't been on the radio. I heard the same anger that had been in Dave's voice. An explanation quickly calmed him so that when he finally came over, it was with a pat on my shoulder and a few words of what a good job I did.

"Both of you take an EO" he finished.

"Both of us?" Dave asked. He beamed at me. I wanted the paramedics to look at me, then let me go back to work.

"Sarg?" I asked.

"Yeah, Cam?"

"Can Dave sign me off on foot pursuits so I never have to do another?"

He laughed. "I wish it were that easy."

"I'll take him over to the firehouse," Dave said. "I think my buddy can take care of those stitches. That way, we're not stuck at the hospital all afternoon."

An hour later, Dave led me from the substation to my car. He told me to follow him. On the way to Jerry's Nugget, a casino noted for good food at affordable prices, I called Sally. Her phone wasn't on. This was the third time that week. I wondered what was going on. I wanted to tell someone about my chase and the funny thing was I wanted it to be her. What is it about needing to let other people know when we do exciting things? About wanting them to understand why I'd done what I had? Since she wasn't there, I settled for a $2.99 cent steak dinner, Dave telling me stories from when he was fifty pounds lighter and ten years younger, and me picturing him that way — young, fast, and full of enthusiasm for the job. It was a hard picture to hold.

"Eat," he said, ordering another steak for both of us. "If you're going to chase people, you need energy."

■ ■ ■

The Desk Sergeant Job . . .

The Las Vegas City Hall used to be located in NEAC, but things were changing due to the way Vegas was growing. The valley's increasing population required a new area command be carved out of the old ones. This area was to be called the Downtown Area Command or DTAC for short. That meant that City Hall, the nine-story and three-story tower complex, now housed the mayor's and sheriff's offices, business licensing, the city jail, police records, and the detective bureau. This last was referred to as the bureau. The local cops loved calling it that because it forever confused poor FBI agents, who figured they had dibs on that name.

Between the buildings was a round area, which was sometimes used for demonstrations and special events. That area was called The Plaza. The level of the City Hall complex it occupied was called the plaza level. The Plaza had a police post called the plaza desk, which was manned by an officer referred to as the desk sergeant. No sergeant had ever worked there for more than a few minutes, but, for some reason, people thought one should. That was another throwback to the old city police department days. The cop who got stuck behind the counter was some poor commissioned schmuck, assigned light duty for an injury or being disciplined for an infraction. When neither one of those was available, the job was assigned and rotated through the regular patrol officers. It was a vile, thankless job that kept a cop off the street, which made it hated by just about anyone who had ever been so assigned. It was known as a job to be avoided and, up to that point, one I had been lucky enough never to be assigned. Therefore, it was inevitable that, sooner or later, I'd have to work the desk. That time finally came in the worst way. My sergeant informed me that my FTO, Ked, was to be promoted to sergeant the next week and had opted to take time off. As Sergeant Crawly was short FTOs, he told me to report to the desk until he could find me a new trainer.

"By myself," I asked.

The Sarg nodded. "You will be the desk sergeant, but don't let it go to your head."

Now, that was funny. *Go to my head?* I was petrified. No one threw a trainee into a slot like that without a senior officer to guide them.

"All you have to do is give the citizens *some* advice," Crawly said. "Listen to their complaints if they so desire, and make arrangements if anyone wants to file a report. In order to do that, you determine if there's been an actual crime."

"So, I'm to be a report taker?"

"No, the records girls do that. After you determine the crime, they'll write 'em up. Just go there and gauge the level of the world's insanity," Crawly said. When he glanced up and saw the look on my face, he stopped writing. He put his hand on my shoulder, kind of fatherly-like. "Don't worry. It'll be fun."

All my life, when people told me not to worry, I worried. I also didn't like being told it was going to be fun. It wasn't like I hadn't heard the desk stories. I had. As a matter of fact, I'd heard some that scared the bejesus out of me. There was the one about the vagrant who shit in the lobby, or the one about the criminally insane woman who came in naked with a knife and started cutting herself, and, my all time favorite, the off-his-medication outpatient who doused himself with gas, then tried to bum a cigarette and light up. All of those people had long ago discovered that this was the one place where they could go and someone might actually listen to them. Some cops, mostly those who had so much seniority they never had to work the desk again, said crazy people could sense a new officer on the desk. It was like the word spread magically or telepathically and they descended on the desk with one intent — to educate new officers in the more esoteric ways of their insane world. What worried me was that, as bad as any incident was that had ever happened on the desk, there could be one waiting with my name on it that would be considered the worst ever. To make matters worse, I might screw it up so badly my career would be over. All I could think about was my father saying that sometimes embarrassment was worse than death. True, I could lose my life in an incident behind the desk, but then I'd be dead. I couldn't care what people said if I was dead.

"Oh yeah, and make sure you answer the phones."

"The phones?" I asked.

"The whole Department sends anything different . . . "

"You mean weird . . . "

"Try not to interrupt me," Crawly said. "I need to be able to say I gave you this speech."

"You mean warned me," I muttered.

"Yeah, well . . . anyway . . . as I was saying, sends anything different, as in, no one else knows how to deal with it. You'll find lists of numbers on the counter. There are also books that explain the services certain organizations provide."

"I'm to be a glorified social worker?"

"Go!" he said. "It'll be fun. You'll see."

Now he sounded like my mother. She used to take me along when she spent time with her sister. While they sat and had coffee or shopped, I was put in the care of my older cousins. Every time we went, she said that would be fun, too. After being tortured by my cousins, I guessed the difference between her idea of fun and mine existed in different universes. Their idea of torture wasn't anything like pulling out my fingernails. That would have left marks. Instead, they held me and tickled me until I peed my pants or stuck snow cones down the front of my shirt, telling our moms that I'd been careless. My Aunt Frieda gave her boys a look like she didn't believe a word they said but it didn't stop them from doing mean things to me or me from being given over to them. So, it wasn't surprising that I couldn't help feeling the same dread as I walked out of his office, checked out a car, and drove to my new assignment. When I got there, the officer I was to replace gave me a look of pure relief and pointed at a bank of flashing buttons on the phone.

"See those lights?"

"Yeah," I said.

"They're all people waiting for you to explain whatever it is they need. Good bye and good luck." He left, almost running.

For the next twenty minutes, I was so busy there wasn't time for fear or doubt. When I had time to take a deep breath, I felt this strange confidence had come over me. It was as though the calls had made me smarter. The first one came from a citizen who said a marked unit had directed him to call me. I couldn't even understand what the man wanted until I had him repeat his question slowly three times. He had an accent that made his mouth sound like it was full of marbles. Once I understood that he wanted to report the neighbor's dogs for barking, I pushed the hold button. I said to the two records girls, Nadine and Beatrice, who were assigned to take the reports after I determined if a crime had been committed. "Now, does that make sense?"

Nadine rolled her eyes at my rhetorical comment, but she was game, "Does what make sense?"

"Just because I'm working here doesn't mean that I've suddenly become smarter than those guys out there. Most of them have way more time on the job than I do. What makes them think I know what to do any better than they do?"

"They are smarter than you," Nadine said. "They just dumped that call on you and you'll have to handle it. That's smart."

Once I was able to get rid of the guy, the next three calls were situations I knew how to handle, like the lady whose husband was complaining of chest pains. "Hang up, ma'am. Call nine one one." After that first hour, I discovered something that was simply amazing. You could dump a lot of shit on the poor fool working this counter. I decided that, in the future, if someone asked me something I didn't know how to do, I was going to do the same thing to whoever worked here. I'd do it on the off chance that I'd catch one of the assholes who were doing it to me.

This is how my time passed, so that after a couple of hours, I realized that when I first took the job, what looked overwhelming was really very simple. To remain efficient, I had to keep sanity on my side of the counter and the nuts on the other. When Nadine or Beatrice was in the area, I asked a lot of questions. They either answered them or simply pointed at the lists and books so I could look up the information on my own. After a while, other strange things began happening. I knew the answers to many of those weird questions as though the knowledge was hidden in some secret place in my brain I never knew existed — like where the closest shelter that provided a free meal was or if there was a Catholic church on the Strip. There were other things I discovered, too. Having to deal with crazy people made my brain extra creative. During the down time, I caught myself reading the pamphlets left by the various agencies. It surprised me to discover what some of them did, which was give people coats and gloves in the winter or free legal advice if the police beat them. Armed with those tidbits of knowledge, I knew how to find help in places I never guessed existed. Best of all, this was stuff that would have taken a long time to learn if all I did was drive around in a patrol car.

For some reason, things quieted down and I grew bored. I opened a drawer. At first, I thought I'd discovered the wastebasket but after a few minutes of pulling pieces of paper out and reading them, I saw that I'd discovered the treasure trove of esoteric information, such as direct phone numbers for charitable organizations, off-site addresses I wouldn't have found otherwise, and the names of the representatives who ran programs for many of those organizations for which I'd only been able to find automated phone numbers. This treasure trove was as rare as if I'd found gold. I felt like an explorer who comes to a new land only to find other explorers were there before him. I was pissed, but after I thought about everything, I got out the notebook Department policy required me to carry, and filled the covers with these numbers and names.

But that was only part of the desk's education. The rest came in the form of the nuts who came in off the street, like the first one. He wore regular clothes, tucked in shirt, clean pants, and a baseball cap. What set those people apart was what they thought the police could do for them. That astounded me. In my first hour, one lady wanted me to tell her where she could get a wiretap on her husband's phone because he was cheating on her. When I told her that cheating wasn't against the law, she pulled an old edition of the Nevada Revised Statutes from her purse. She showed me that, in fact, it was against the law to cheat on your spouse. I was lucky on that one. When I inspected the book, I saw the date was from twenty years before. I recommended she find a little more recent edition before she came back to argue her case. After a few hours, I realized that woman was one of the more pedestrian nuts. At least she was clean enough for me not to have to breathe through an open mouth.

By the time the shift was half over, I'd dealt with so many crazy people that I developed a little game. I applied what I'd told the last crazy person to the next. It amazed me how well this worked. When Nadine came back, I asked her if she noticed the same thing. She gave me a direct look as she brushed back her blond hair. She had this way of gazing directly into my eyes, which I'd noticed the crazy people also did. With them, it was as though they were either trying to get away with something or simply didn't care what effect their craziness had on anyone. With her, it was sexy.

"So," I started. "Do you like this job?"

Nadine stopped what she was doing, which was filling out the burglary report from the last victim I'd sent her. The items taken filled ten pages, all of which had to be entered in the computer.

"You wouldn't be flirting with me, would you? If you are, then let me nip that in the bud. My boyfriend is a lieutenant." She held out her left hand then spun what I thought was a plain silver band until I saw the stone.

"I thought . . . " I stopped. "Three-carats? Platinum setting? I didn't see it . . . "

"I know." She nodded her head towards a man standing outside the door talking to himself. "I'm always afraid one of them will try to pry it off my finger. My boyfriend's a very jealous man. He doesn't have to be, but he knows how cops are. I've had more offers on this desk just from the cops working back here than you can imagine."

"Wait. I wasn't trying anything . . ." Actually, I was.

"Didn't a little birdie tell me your girlfriend tested?" Nadine asked.

"Yes," I replied. I felt guilty, like a citizen who was busted doing something he normally wouldn't. Maybe even if things had been right between us, if she wasn't engaged, it still wouldn't have worked out. After all, she looked like my ex-girlfriend. "Yeah. She is. That's why I'm not hitting on you. I have a girlfriend. I'm making conversation."

"Uh-huh," Nadine said. She set the pen down, then sighed. "OK. Maybe I have you wrong, but if I don't, then we now understand each other." She turned the ring so the stone disappeared. When she dropped the hand, her tone changed. "What's scary is when you think those answers make sense, like they've been in the back of your head all along." She gave me that direct look, right in the eye, the one that started me on the path of thinking she might be interested in me. "Let me give you a word of advice. Be careful not to like it up here too much; there's word they're thinking of quasi-permanently assigning someone this job."

I tried not looking startled. There was a thought that hadn't crossed my mind. Not the one about liking the desk job. That was starting to happen. I'd actually caught myself thinking it wasn't so bad. The fact that I could be assigned here permanently hadn't occurred to me. She grinned wickedly, then went back to taking reports.

Just when I started getting hungry, which meant it was lunchtime, another cop joined me.

"Hey, Nadine," he called across the lobby, "You still dating that fool?"

She raised a hand laconically. "Hey, Jerry. You still around and still working with that asshole, my ex?"

"Yep and yes," the cop said. Jerry came to the counter and leaned on it, eyeing her appreciatively. I felt as though another dog had come into my territory. "I am and he *is* still an asshole."

"I know, but at least he's stuck paying off my car."

"So I hear, fifty times a day." He turned from her and stuck a hand at me. "I'm Jerry."

"So I gathered."

"Maybe your new FTO. I've been assigned to help you here." From the tone of his voice, I knew he wasn't happy, and an unhappy trainer was the worst thing a trainee could get. Unhappiness translated into low scores. Jerry continued, "Sarg says it's a good thing he found me. Throwing a new officer on the desk without someone experienced might cause him to quit. Probably be flipping burgers tomorrow. So, here I am."

What about an unhappy trainee, I thought. After all, I had the idea that the sarg had left me here so long without supervision because he trusted me, not because he was having trouble finding a babysitter.

"Oh, so you've worked here before," I asked.

"Never," Jerry replied. "Can't be any worse than Ida area, though. Have you eaten?"

"Where would I get something to eat?" I looked around innocently, then went back to helping a lady decide whether she was the victim of a rape or a poor choice in the man she willingly took home, who then had stood her up the next night. The phone rang and Jerry took the call. After a second, he slammed the receiver down.

"There's something not right with some people in this world," he said, looking at the instrument like I would a snake. "A lot of these calls should be routed straight to the mental health center instead of to us. That was an old man asking if there was a law about black people moving into his neighborhood. He wanted a police report taken so that he could press charges against the realtor who sold the house across the street from him to a black couple."

The phone rang again. I looked at Jerry. He was closest. As he answered it, he made a face. "Same guy," he mouthed. He listened for a moment, then hung up. By the time the man called back the third time, I offered to take the call. I knew from experience that if the situation wasn't dealt with, the caller would probably show up. It rang and I reached for the receiver, "Yes'm." I let the caller talk for a minute, then yelled, "What? I be black. I be cummin' down yonder to kick ya'lls prejudice ass." The phone went dead. I grinned at him.

"That is the worst nigga accent I have ever heard," he said.

"It worked, didn't it?"

"In a pathetic, white boy way."

"You're black. Teach me."

"Wat ya'll think? Ma mama raised me up to talk dat way? Ah isa college-edge-you-cated man."

"You don't do it well, either," I said. That broke the ice between the two of us. He grinned. The phone rang and Jerry grabbed it, listened for a minute. I watched his brow knit, sure it was the same caller.

"What? Your FTO told you to call with that shit? Who the fuck . . . " Jerry yelled. He took a deep breath. "Put him on."

"Hey, boss," I said. "Why don't you let me take that? I've already had a few."

"No. This is bullshit," Jerry said, not even bothering to put his hand over the mouthpiece. He went back to the conversation. "Get your FTO and tell him I want to talk to him." A second went by. "Who is this? Pete? Man, you tell your trainee to call here with a question you don't know again and I'll come out there and kick your ass!" He slammed the phone down. When he saw the look on my face, he explained, "Friend of mine. Don't try getting out of work like that until you're off probation. That was actually soon-to-be Sergeant Keesler. He just got promoted but doesn't sew his stripes on till Saturday. Petie was my roommate in the Academy." He picked up two pencils and acted like he was playing drums. "Bet he'll call back in a minute." He kept playing as if he didn't have a care in the world. I stood there not saying anything. "They got some guy in the field they're sick of dealing with, so he had his trainee pass the buck. Next time, he can pass that shit off on someone else."

After a couple of minutes when his buddy didn't call, Jerry called Dispatch. He asked to be put through to Keesler's cell. "Hey, Petie, this is Jerry. When you're done dealing with that fool, bring us some food. We're starving here."

As he hung up, a man came in. He wore a hound's tooth jacket and brown slacks, and looked to be six feet tall and 110 pounds. If I were to see Sherlock Holmes in the flesh, this would have been him. He explained that the government was bombarding him with X-rays, which was making him act like someone else. *Here*, I thought, *is one of those people who will be happier in some facility where he can play with people who are just like him.* His kind wasn't dangerous but they were a pain in the ass, not to mention they sucked up public services like dry dirt in a desert rainstorm.

"Who're you acting like?" Jerry asked. His face became suddenly attentive.

"The guy down the street."

"Didn't I see this on TV or in a movie," I interrupted.

Instead of laughing, Jerry glared at me. He turned his attention back to the man and asked him to continue. He listened carefully.

"I'm acting like the guy down the street. That's because I took a sip from his Coke. I didn't mean to. It was just that I was thirsty."

"What else?" Jerry asked. The man went on at great length, describing all his ailments. When he finished, Jerry said, "Take a TV antenna. The rabbit-ear type. If you don't have one, a coat hanger will work almost as well, until you can find one." He held two fingers up at angles. "You know what I mean?" The man nodded. He was seriously focused, a study in concentration. "Wrap the antenna with tin foil, then wrap tin foil around the top of your head. Don't let anyone see you do this or they'll report it." I was amazed he was able to keep a straight face the whole time.

"You mean to the police," the man asked.

"No, to the government scientists. This is secret stuff I'm talking about. If they get an idea of the amount of material you used, they'll change the frequencies and defeat the whole process. You have to stay inside with the blinds down for a couple of hours, then when you go out, act normal. While you're in the house, if someone knocks, take it off, hide it behind the couch or under a chair. Follow me?"

The man nodded.

"The important thing is to act normal. As a matter of fact, act normal any time you're around people. Only wear this thing when you're alone. The antenna will redirect the X-rays back where they're being beamed from. The effects will last two days after the device is removed. OK?"

"Thank you. Thank *you!*" The man reached across the desk and shook Jerry's hand. "You're the best cop I've ever talked to. Most of them thought I was crazy." As he turned to leave, Jerry looked down at his hand.

"Do we have any of that anti-bacterial gel back here?" he asked.

When the guy was outside, I sat down. "I think I saw that episode on TV."

"Yeah. You might have. Always wanted to do that."

"I hate to break this to you, but I was here first. I'm supposed to be in training, so I'm the one supposed to be getting to do the cool stuff. You had your time."

Jerry shrugged. He extended his hand like he was going to give it to me. "Remember who gets the ones on their eval and who gives the ones. I'm going to find a restroom and cut this hand off. Hold the fort."

While Jerry was gone, a vagrant came in. "I . . . I . . . I'b-b-b g-g-g-ot a wa-wa-wa-rrant."

It took me a minute to understand what he was saying.

"You got ID," I asked.

"No-o-o-o."

Jerry came back. He watched me grow frustrated trying to figure out who the guy was. I had him repeat his name several times, but I couldn't understand what he was saying. If I had to guess his original nationality, it would have been Eastern European. His skin was swarthy and I could see his hair had been black when he was younger. Just when I thought of giving up, Nadine stepped forward and shoved a pencil and paper at him.

"Try to be smarter than they are," she said to me. "Can you write?"

The guy nodded.

"Then write your information down for me, sir."

"Go over there," Jerry pointed at a seat. "Cool off, take your time and let us know when you're done."

"Jeez," I muttered. "I feel stupid."

"You should," Jerry laughed.

"So did he when I taught him that trick," Nadine said, smiling sweetly at Jerry. She went back to her station.

After the man sat in one of the lobby's hard plastic chairs, Jerry came over to where I stood. He dropped his voice so only I could hear. "Let me tell you a story. It's almost a legend. This tale takes place on one of those cold winter nights in Vegas. The wind was blowing, and the chill factor must have made it all of twenty degrees. A vagrant came in and said he needed to be arrested. The officer working this desk asked why. Now pay attention, here comes the important part. In the old days, cops on the desk assumed if a vagrant came in here when it was cold out, all they wanted was to get upstairs to that nice warm jail." He stopped to glance at the man as he laboriously penciled the paper. He continued. "So, while the guy was hemming and hawing, the cop lost patience and threw the guy out. I mean threw, like physically grabbed and just tossed him right out there on the cement. Ah, the good old days," Jerry acted like he was wiping a tear.

"Anyway, the guy came back in. Now, he was a little afraid, so he stood in the door and tried to explain he had a murder warrant. The cop chased him off. Literally. Two days later, homicide caught the guy playing cards at the Horseshoe. They were amazed because they had been looking all over town for the guy and there he was, sitting there like he didn't have a care in the world. When the homicide dicks got him to the bureau, they asked him why he wasn't hiding out. After all, he had a murder warrant hanging over his head. He told them he figured the charges must've been dropped. He went on to say he tried to turn himself in at the Plaza desk, but the cop threw him out. They asked when this was, not really believing the guy. He gave them the exact day. They checked, just for shits and grins. They found out who it was and called him in. When they showed the cop the mug shot, he said 'Yeah, he was in. I threw the bum out. Figured he wanted to go to jail to get warm."

"When the brass heard the story, they gave the copper a week, no pay. He was able to afford that. What was harder was the hit his reputation took. You can tell that because I'm telling you the story, even though it took place long ago. I can tell you his name but I won't. The fact is, if you really want to know, there are plenty of people who will."

I nodded. Jerry timed the story perfectly. The vagrant was back with the note. He had scribbled his information, name, date of birth, and social security number in large block letters that reminded me of something my first-grade nephew might write. Jerry typed everything into the computer and found him. He showed me the guy's priors, which were all vagrant-type crimes. There were several for petit larceny, one for defrauding an innkeeper, and pages of loitering, which was no longer a crime. There were no wants though. When Jerry told him that, he wasn't happy.

"Go on back to your hooch. Get out of here," Jerry said.

"I can't. It's too hot out there," he stuttered. "Besides, the city bulldozed it a few days before." As he talked, he reached inside his shirt and started scratching his skin furiously. *Lice*, I thought. He also began to sweat. The air in the room filled with the stench of vagrant, which can't be described. It was a smell that once a person has been introduced to it, can never be forgotten.

"Go to the shelter."

"I can't. I don't like the rules I have to follow to stay there. I can't drink. There ain't no smoking. And if you say words like 'shit' or 'fuck', you get yelled at."

Jerry narrowed his eyes at the guy. Some people would have taken a hint, but not that guy. "So, that's what it's about. Well, tough shit. Hit the bricks. The jail's not a hotel. It's for people who need to be there. Go stay with a buddy. You must know someone with a room."

"I don't. I don't know anybody. I need to be in jail. It's cool. I need to be cool."

The two of them looked at each other. I could see Jerry was out of suggestions and patience. "Get out, 'cause if I come over this counter . . ." Jerry yelled, leaving the rest unfinished. This brought a smile to Nadine's face, who sat in a corner reading a novel.

"I love a forceful man," she called. The vagrant left.

"I'd bet we haven't seen the end of him," I muttered.

"We better," Jerry relied.

I watched him standing out on the hot Plaza. His mouth moved and he threw evil looks our way. I answered the phone and, when I next looked up, he was gone.

About twenty minutes passed, then he was back.

"I thought I told you to go," Jerry sighed. "You're gonna make me do something I don't wanna."

"Then do it," the man said. "You better put me in jail or else."

"Or else what?" Jerry's tone went flat, the emotion dropping like a stone off a bridge.

The vagrant reached into the layers of smelly clothing. Both our hands dropped to our gun butts. He pulled a four-inch knife out and held it threateningly. Before the man could blink, he was looking down the barrels of two semiautomatic handguns. He really wasn't much of a threat on the other side of a four-foot counter, which he'd have to climb. Where knives are concerned, we have a policy referred to as the twenty-one-foot rule. That meant when a man threatened one of us and was within twenty-one feet, he was fair game and we could kill him. That was because studies had shown a person has the ability to cover that distance before the average cop, even with training, can draw and fire a weapon before being cut or stabbed. The counter probably precluded the rule.

The problem was Nadine, who sat within ten feet of the man. She sat quietly, trying to make herself invisible. I glanced at her, willing her to get up and move out of the line of fire. I didn't want to say anything, because, up to this point, the crazy on the other side of the counter hadn't thought of her. It was as though she read my mind, rising slowly, quietly making her way around the plants on either side of the door. My hand tightened around the gun's grip, ready to take a shot in case the man made the least threatening move in her direction. The vagrant realized his mistake. Jerry ordered him to drop the knife on the counter and back away from it. When he did, I snatched the knife, throwing it on the desk behind us.

"That'll be impounded for safekeeping. Now get the hell out of here. The shelter's that way."

"N-n-n-o! I did a bad thing. You have to arrest me."

"N-n-n-o!" Jerry mimicked. "I don't have to arrest you." He pointed towards the door with the barrel of his gun. "Go, before I beat sparks off your dumb ass." As he bolted through the door, we holstered our weapons. "Can you believe some people?"

I knew it was a rhetorical question as I reached to answer the phone, which hadn't stopped ringing the whole time. Nadine fanned her face with an exaggerated motion.

"I thought you guys were going to shoot me."

"How much you think your ex would give me if I had?" Jerry asked. She stuck out her tongue at him. An hour later, I pointed towards the glass where we watched two patrol guys dragging what looked like a bundle of clothes across the Plaza. When a face looked up, I tapped Jerry on the shoulder.

"Hey, isn't that the vagrant . . . " Before I could finish, Jerry went around the counter to talk to the cops. When he came back, he told me the guy found a brick and tossed it through a window down at the Golden Nugget Casino. It was a small window, valued under $250, which made his crime a misdemeanor.

"So, he gets his wish granted, anyway. A few days inside with three hots and a cot, clean clothes and sheets . . . provided free by the citizens of the city," I said.

"Yep. He was determined, I'll say that for him," Jerry said, grinning.

"Maybe we should have arrested him," I replied, troubled by the lack of response on our part.

"Maybe. Sometimes, you have to give people the benefit of doubt, though. Besides, you can't read people's minds and you can't arrest them for thinking about committing a crime."

"And sometimes, it's all about ego."

Jerry laughed. "Yep. I'm the man. But let me tell you what we might have had him for with the knife. Assault. He threatened us with it, right?"

"I guess."

"No, you don't guess. You know. That's what people expect of you, to know the law. How would it have looked if two of Metro's finest, protected by vests, armed with handguns, carrying lots of bullets, had been assaulted across a counter by a sixty-year-old man with a knife? Do you know the difference between assault and battery?"

"Yes. Assault is the threat of harm. Battery is the harm."

"Exactly. So, this guy comes in and threatens us. First, if you tried to tell a judge that, he might laugh. He might even have to do something about it for appearance's sake. It would be a waste of the court's time, though. That would make things worse. If I were that judge, I would remember an officer who wasted my time. Then, every time you were in my court, I'd think about you being assaulted by that old guy. How're you ever gonna be taken seriously again?"

"I see," I replied. These were the things that made this job harder than it looked.

As Jerry finished, Nadine stuck her head back in. "Is it safe in here?"

"Yeah. What's up?"

"We got a four forty over in records," she said.

"What's the person wanted for," Jerry asked.

I knew people went into the police record's section for various reasons, including updating their addresses for convicted felon status, work card or criminal history checks, or picking up copies of reports. The clerks checked their "wants" while they waited for whatever they came in for. If they had a warrant, one of the cops was asked to come over and arrest the perp. If the warrant was for county, a transport unit was called, which was really just a black-and-white. On the other hand, if the person had a city warrant, the arrestee was walked upstairs to the jail.

It was funny to see the look on a person's face when he discovered that a warrant had been issued ten or fifteen years before and was still active. In many cases, the person claimed he didn't remember getting it and I'm sure he didn't. The good thing was that officers had a lot of discretion whether they made an arrest on a warrant or not. Some cops took everybody, even if the bail amount was a hundred bucks. Others set limits based on all kinds of parameters, such as whether the guy was a dirtbag, what time lunch was scheduled, or whether they might need that warrant at a later time when the guy needed to go for something else, being drunk or an asshole. The nice thing about warrants was that they were like diamonds. They were forever. It never failed that a warrant always seemed to pop up when someone could least afford it, like when that killer new job started the next day or he was in a hurry to get to the first date with that special somebody he'd been waiting to meet his whole life.

Jerry motioned for me to follow him across the Plaza to records. When we were in the lobby, we saw a biker-looking guy waiting at the counter. I guessed the guy to be in his late forties or early fifties. He had the Willie Nelson look, long hair, craggy face. He wore the typical cut-off, blue jean jacket, black heavy metal t-shirt, ragged jeans, and motorcycle boots. Lying on the counter was a brain bucket. Whenever I saw those guys, I always thought they looked like they came off some assembly line.

"Can we talk to you a sec?" Jerry asked.

"Sure, officer. Did I do something wrong?"

"I don't know, yet. A warrant popped up under your name."

"What?"

"Do you have ID?" Jerry asked. Nadine held it up, along with a criminal history printout. Jerry took both so he could examine them. As he looked at the ID, he kept it so he didn't have to take his eyes off the man. "What's the warrant for? And how much?" The question was directed at Nadine.

"Starting a parked car. One hundred dollars," she said.

Jerry glanced at her. "Is that a joke? An actual crime?"

"Obviously," she replied. When she saw the looks on our faces, she went on, "Hey, I didn't write him. It says traffic on the reports, so it's one of theirs. My job is to tell you guys I've got a four forty. I did. Now it's up to you to do whatever you do." With that she turned and stalked away. "Wait here," he told the guy. We moved several feet away.

Jerry glanced at me, "Don't start liking her. Next thing you know, you might start thinking she'd make the perfect wife. I worked with her last husband. He says it's a miracle he didn't put a round in her. If that happened, you'd be in world of do-do."

"Dang," I replied mockingly, but I watched her walk away appreciatively, "It might be too late."

Jerry turned his attention back to the guy. "I'm going to give you a chance to get this taken care of. I don't even know what this law is, starting a parked car. If you don't get it taken care of, you're going to get stopped by the wrong cop and you'll end up in jail."

"Thanks. I don't even remember getting it," the guy replied. The way Jerry eyed him, it was obvious he didn't believe him. As we turned to leave, the guy called after us. He lifted a newspaper, then pulled a huge forty-five caliber Colt from a gun case. "I came in to get this registered. Will there be a problem with me doing that now?"

That was the scary part of working the desk. Citizens brought guns in that needed registration. Like this man, they just pulled these things out of thin air, causing the kind of fear and anxiety that led to stress. That, in turn, created all the medical problems. Insurance company figures showed cops died on the average of five years after they retired. I felt it, at that moment, as I looked at his hand-held elephant gun. I wondered if he was one of those people who didn't even know how to use it. At least I wasn't looking down the barrel. I'd heard a story from Sam, one of the other people from my Academy. He'd gone to a house on a burglary call. When he finished taking the report, the old woman asked if she could get some advice. She went in back and returned with a big revolver. It looked like something a lawman a hundred years ago might have carried.

"Young man, can you tell me if this is loaded?"

Sam said he almost shit himself when he turned and saw the thing pointed right at him in her shaky old hand. Luckily, this wasn't one of those. I couldn't help thinking that if this guy had been the vagrant, someone might not be alive right then.

"Would you mind setting that down," Jerry told him.

Part of our job, especially when people did stupid things, was teaching them a lesson. I wondered how Jerry would handle something like that, or if he even would. Maybe, he would progress right to the ass-whupping.

"Only register it?" Jerry picked the gun up. He expertly flipped the cylinder open, checking to see if it was loaded.

"I thought both register it and see what it'd take to get a CCW," the biker replied.

"Hmmm. CCW. So you want to carry concealed? Did you tell her you were in here for that," Jerry asked.

"Yep. Sure did. She said to leave it right here under the paper after I showed her it was unloaded and assured her I didn't bring in any bullets. She said after I talked to you, I was to take it out and show you it was unloaded."

"She did, did she?"

The man nodded.

"See?" Jerry kept his eyes on the man but I could tell the next words were for me. "That woman's pure evil."

Still, when he glanced across the lobby, I couldn't help noticing the way he looked at her. I thought how someone like Nadine was rare. She handled the tense situations with the vagrant and the knife-wielding vagrant well. She was the type of companion a cop wanted. I couldn't help comparing Sally to her. There was much they had much in common, yet I chose to pretend they didn't. Just as I pretended other things weren't what they were. That was a failing in me, something I either ignored or needed to come to terms with. Later, much later, I was to realize that in those moments when I wanted the grass to be greener than it could be, to live in a better Eden than the one I already lived in, I lost my chances. I just threw them away by doing the same thing a lot of cops did, which was to allow dissent and disaster into my life.

■ ■ ■

Yes, No, and Maybe . . .

When I came into the station, early as usual, Sally sat polishing her boots. She was still dressed in civilian clothes. She had her fine blond hair in a couple of buns on the sides of her head. I knew she wore it this way to keep from having it grabbed in a fight. When it was down, it hung to the middle of her back. Every time I saw her, my heart did this little lurch thing. It was as though some part of my subconscious was reminding my body how stupid I was. I'd pushed the rift between us until the day she called me and said she wasn't going to see me anymore. I remembered thinking, *She'll be back. She always came back.* Then a month later, a friend of mine called to say she had moved in with a NEAC sergeant. When that happened, I ran out of choices. For a while, I was bitter. I sometimes saw her when I was down at the Academy, where they conducted in-service training. She ignored me. It was all I could do to act like the pain wasn't there. It was. I knew it was and I'm sure a few people who knew me well enough did, too — like my sister.

"Throw away that stupid pride of yours and fight for her," Brenda said one day when she came over to check up on me. The first thing she did was go to my dresser and make sure I had clean underwear. Then she visited the refrigerator.

"I could give a fuck less," I snarled.

"Hey!" she said. "You should keep some fresh fruit in here." She started dropping shriveled brown things in the trash. "Don't bite my head off. I didn't treat her like shit. It wasn't me that ignored her."

"Fuck you." I intended the words to have more fire than they did.

"This is what I get. Abuse."

Still, she came and I felt better just knowing someone shared my pain on a level other than that of my partners. That was the funniest part of the job. On TV, two cops in a car were always portrayed as close. I wondered how that could be, then when I started riding with a person who was my equal, instead of someone who was grading me, I found out. There was this thing that happened when you counted on someone to totally have your back. Little things came out in conversation. Pieces of advice were traded, and quirks of personality became the basis for friendships. The guys in the car with me became as much my friends as was possible. My problem was with the degree it was possible. I still felt as though I was hiding out, not letting too many people in. That had always been my way.

Sally was two weeks fresh out of the Academy. She had started the testing process while I was still in my Academy, then started her Academy while I was in field training, and now was completing field training while I was getting ready to go off probation. It sucked that we had been assigned to the same station, but that was the way life worked for me. I wasn't sure I could deal with both the job and my feelings for her while I was doing my work. When we were out on calls together, I secretly harbored a wish for things to go wrong so she'd get dinged. Then, I felt guilty. Through the grapevine, I heard her FTO was awfully impressed with her, which was evident because he had her driving already. It had taken me almost into my third cycle of first phase before I was allowed to drive. The word was that many of the other trainees from her Academy were jealous, too. That was especially true when they saw her from the passenger seats where they were still sitting. When I was in the locker room, someone said, "It's what happens when your boyfriend is up for Ell Tee." I thought it was bullshit, but I didn't come to her defense. *Maybe*, I thought, *I feel guilty of that, too.*

"What up, girl? Ain't you supposed to be on the street?"

"Nothing and no," she replied. I waited for her head to come up and her to look at me. She just kept polishing her boots. I picked one up, which caused her to raise her head.

"Want me to help?" I asked. She shook her head. I thought she looked haggard, the way she did when things weren't going right. The boot looked fine, the toe so shiny I saw myself in it. I'd heard things — little inklings.

One night when we were drinking in the same bar, another cop I'd ridden with came over and sat next to me. He watched the game on the TV that was fixed over the bar. His eyes never left the screen while he talked. "Ever notice the silences when she's at the bar with him? How about the mean looks they give each other?" he asked. "I have a friend who's a dispatcher. She said she peeked at some of their AMs. She's reporting thinly veiled threats. Someone in the know might consider it an opportunity." AMs were the administrative messages sent on the department computer system. He gave me a punch that was supposed to be reassuring. *Good,* I thought. *She's having problems.*

■ ■ ■

I heard Sergeant Windsor, her boyfriend, out in the hall. She took the boot and started to work on the toe. What I knew was that he arranged her first ride-along. I would have taken a line at a local sports book that he also must have been thinking about what else he could arrange.

I remembered the day she called and said she needed to talk to me. I sensed the tone from her voice. My guts clenched up. She said she wanted to meet me at Sunset Park to talk, but I pushed until she told me over the phone she was breaking up with me. We ended up at the park anyway. When I got there, I thought I could talk her out of it. She met me by some picnic tables. It was one of those sorry-ass February evenings, filled with unexpected gusts that came from different directions. They cut right through my jeans, found those little places where I wasn't covered well. *What a perfect day for bad news,* I thought — cold breezes, crunchy yellow grass underfoot and dead-looking leafless trees. It was like the end of summer was the end of the world. She told me about being unhappy and how she'd been thinking of breaking things off. It was funny how I'd been thinking the same but now that I had the opportunity, I suddenly didn't want things to end between us. We talked, argued, and cried for hours, long past the time when I was so cold I was miserable. In the end, she said she had to go, he was waiting. So, in spite of everything, it ended. And here we were, with all of that still between us, and all the other things — the vacations together, the lovemaking, the fights — the whole life of five years in the making and breaking.

"None of my business, but if you want to talk," I told her.

"Nothing to talk about. I'm waiting for my FTO to get back from a doctor's appointment."

"Oh."

"Don't believe what you might be hearing about me and Dan. We're not breaking up."

"You're not?" She shook her head. I felt stupid.

"I'm going to get dressed," she said. I watched her get up and leave. I couldn't help staring at that ass. There was a time it all belonged to me, but I had let it go. That only made me feel more morose. I went into the men's locker room and dressed out. I was at the key room before her. There were only two sets of keys left. I knew which was the better car, so I made sure I took it. The other one needed freon, which meant the air conditioner barely worked. Her FTO, John, was a creature of comfort. He would ding her for not beating me to the key.

When I came out, my partner, Jerry, was waiting for me in the briefing room. I looked at the garbage can by the door. A bong stuck out. Someone hadn't wanted to impound the shit, so they dumped it in the garbage. That was a major policy violation. I bet there wasn't one of us that hadn't done that. I know I had. Sometimes I checked my car and found things under the seat or in the trunk. They might have been put there by a suspect on the way to jail or forgotten by the last cop who drove. If I felt charitable, I might throw them in a bag and hide them until the next shift, but only if the thing looked important — like it might be for a court case that would go down the tubes.

While I waited for Jerry to finish what he was doing, I opened the small notebook I was required to carry. Inside, I had lots of small pieces of paper. I started reading some and when I decided which were useless,

I crumpled them up. When the notebook was better organized, I took the trash over to the can. I saw a Playboy magazine under the bong. The cover said the centerfold girl was from Vegas. I dug it out and checked to see if it was someone I knew. But it wasn't.

We were getting a late start because Jerry had a meeting with the Ell Tee on a project he had planned. Up until a couple months before, Jerry had been my FTO. Since I passed the solo portion of FTP, I now mainly rode alone, but Jerry had mentioned he needed an extra body. That worked well for the station, which was short cars because so many were in the shop. I knew a little of the project he planned. It was going to involve walking some desert areas by the vagrant camps, counting how many people lived in the bushes. He wanted to have a plot made of those areas by the crime analysis section, then check on the trends. It seemed obvious that crime would be higher, but the brass wasn't going to go on gut feelings. They wanted the hard numbers before they allowed us to spend time doing something with the homeless.

I threw him the extra set of keys. Jerry attached them to a keeper on his belt. "You drive. I want to relax today. Try not to get us into anything before chow."

"Okey dokey." I was happy. He was senior and could have opted to drive. As we left the parking lot, I watched Sally come out to face the wrecks left in the yard.

We had been out an hour, handling small calls — a 911 disconnect, a four thirty-eight or broken down car that had traffic stalled, and a lady who wanted to complain that a corner pay phone was being used by drug dealers. There was an hour left before we went to lunch. By the time we were finished, Jerry figured the temperature would have dropped enough that we could start checking the vagrant camps. The dispatcher came on, assigning a unit just leaving the jail to a nearby call. I ran it up on the MDT. It looked like a combative vagrant, who was supposedly destroying a convenience store.

"We're a two-man. Let's take this," I said. Before I could get the mike out of the holder, John's voice came on and told the dispatcher they'd be en route.

"We'll go," Jerry said. "Just don't put us on it. I don't want to get tied up in anything so we're late for lunch. Besides, aren't you still mad at her?" Jerry adjusted the seat forward so he was sitting.

"What's there to be mad about?"

"Some sergeant took my woman, I'd be pissed. She looks good. What is she, five-foot-three?"

"Five-two," I said. "How about we talk about something else?" I thought I shouldn't have recommended we go on the call.

"Must weigh about a buck ten," he said. "I like the way she puts her hair in those things on the sides of her head. Looks like twisty bread."

"Hey, Jerry, are you trying to piss me off?" I asked. "He can have her. Other birds on the horizon."

"No. I'm not. I wanted to make sure what your attitude is. Just keep it in check. I think you two should stay away from each other. I don't need to watch my back and yours, too. Especially this evening when we're out hiking through the countryside."

"I got my own shit," I muttered.

"Good," he said. "Keep it that way."

I didn't like being told what to do and, technically, Jerry was no longer my trainer. He was my partner, although senior. My problem was I still was in the mode of thinking of him as my trainer. When he made a suggestion or got on my case for the way I handled something, I caught myself feeling I was being given a low score. There was also the business of being uncomfortable with someone wanting to be involved in my personal affairs, even when what he said was right. His life might depend on me.

To get my mind off my feelings and back on business, I thought about how many calls in IDA area involved vags or, for the more politically correct, the residentially challenged. In three months of working IDA, I'd handled my share of poor, mentally ill, and legitimately needy people. Those people we called Four Twenty One A or, if they were really, really crazy, Four Twenty One Triple A. We also handled the other kind of vags, too. These people were criminal, lazy, and shiftless. The one thing

I quickly learned was that neither could be taken for granted. If a cop let his guard down, even for a second, he could be hurt or killed.

When we got to the call's location, I pulled up at the opposite corner from where John and Sally had parked. The store's exterior looked calm, but that didn't matter. If something wasn't wrong, we wouldn't be here. We climbed out, stopping to listen and look around. I didn't see anyone, so I thought they might be inside or around the corner. When I was away from the engine noise, I heard voices towards the front of the store. If we had put ourselves out on the call, I would have asked John or Sally by radio where they were. Since we *weren't there*, I couldn't do that without Dispatch knowing. Jerry and I quickly crossed in front of the store's plate glass windows. This was a danger zone. If the source of the call was inside and had some type of weapon that didn't get mentioned when the call was made, he would have one or both of us. The inside of the store looked empty.

If John and Sally were out of sight, I knew there had to be a reason. John was a good cop and a good trainer. He gave his trainees time to evaluate calls — take their time figuring out what to do. He wasn't like some trainers who thought the trainee should be in action mode as soon as they made their appearance. I'd seen trainees hesitate before jumping into things, then really get reamed. That created a lot of stress, which some FTOs felt taught a trainee to operate in a typical gone-to-shit environment. Whenever I saw an FTO like that, I thought about Ed. He was one of the people from my Academy — a guy who had been a cop for fifteen years with another department. Ed's FTO encouraged his trainee's to practice that manner of response. It started Ed on a downward spiral. He couldn't get out of it. The three-year FTO, who I'd worked with and thought couldn't find his ass with both hands, claimed Ed didn't know what the fuck he was doing. After a month, Ed was allowed to resign before he was fired.

As I rounded the corner, I saw the owner, Sally, and John holding a little powwow. The MDT said the disturbance was inside the store and the suspect was supposed to be a regular. The way they were standing there, I thought everything was code four, meaning it had been taken care of.

"Is he H?" I asked.

"No. He's still inside," Sally said. "At least, Mr. Sanchez thinks he's still inside." Sally's tone was confident. She acted like she did this all the time, which sparked a tinge of irritation. The owner looked unhappy. He was Mexican. He was also short, fat, and impatient. I knew Jerry despised Mexicans. He'd grown up in The Side, and they'd been encroaching on his neighborhood. He claimed they were turning it into a shithole. The couple of times I'd been there, it looked like that had started long before any Mexicans even thought about moving into those neighborhoods.

"Go een there and get heem out of my store," Sanchez ordered.

"We don't rush into things we're not sure of," John replied. "Tell us exactly what's going on." Jerry told me a couple of days before that he thought the guy sold dope out of the store, but he'd never been able to catch him. Just rumors.

"Heee crazy," the man yelled.

"Mr. Sanchez, will you calm down? What do you mean "crazy," Sally cut in.

"Go een and see," Sanchez said. He waved his arms, looking like a tree caught in a windstorm. "You better get een there and save mi' property," he threatened.

That wasn't the way to get a bunch of cops to do your bidding. I saw John and Jerry's faces tighten.

"What's his name?"

"How the chinga should I know that, eseee? He go in my store to buy beer. Food, sometimes. He steal things when he got no money. But you police never come when I call. You could give sheet about me and my business. Today, he no have money, so he steal."

"What's he doing right now?" Sally asked. She was trying to keep the ball in her court.

The man threw his hands in the air and walked away. There was a crash from inside the store. Without waiting for us, Mr. Sanchez rushed inside. There it was. We had no choice. In a line, we started towards the door. As soon as John opened it, the owner ran out past us. One by one, we rolled around the frame, keeping close to the walls, then fanned across the floor. Bottles of something orange exploded like bombs against the counter and displays. Our guns were out and we stayed low. Whoever he was, he hadn't seen us, because the bottles weren't aimed. The store was a mess. There was food from ripped bags, spilled liquids that made the floor slippery, and something else.

"Oh, my God," I called. "What is that stench?"

"Shhhh," Sally replied.

What the fuck? She's telling me to be quiet, I thought. As we rounded the corner of a display located back by the coolers, I saw who we were looking for. I could tell right off he was going to be a "no" person. It was a thing taught in the Academy. I remembered the lecture that classified citizen contacts into three different categories. The first category was the "yes" person. These people would comply with requests and demands willingly, because they were regular people, citizens who normally obeyed the law and respected the police. The second category was the "maybe" person. These people would comply reluctantly to commands or requests. They had to be watched, ordered about politely, and controlled at all times; otherwise they could be a safety threat to us or themselves. Everything that got done with "maybe" people had to be explained. The secret to "maybe" people was to find their carrot or stick. The next category was the "no" people. They were the ones we hated. Sometimes, "no" people started as "maybe" people. Either the cop or the circumstance turned them. Other times, people were in that category before the police arrived. When dealing with "no" people, the best a cop could hope for was non-compliance with commands because a "no" person knew they'd done something wrong, had nothing to lose, and didn't intend to pay any consequences.

In my way of thinking, that was what happened with Rodney King. He was a classic "no" person. The cops saw it right off and made the mistake of going to batons. The whole incident had looked bad on video. What they should have done was dog-piled his ass and while he was on the bottom of the pile, threw him the beating he deserved. With a whole bunch of cops on him, all it would have looked like was another unruly man being taken into custody. Happened all the time.

"Stinks," John muttered. He took an exaggerated sniff. "Smells like napalm . . . ugh . . . wrong movie, I mean, vagrant."

"Funny," Jerry said. "Henry, come on over here."

I couldn't tell what race the man standing before us was. I guessed black. Part of the problem was the layers of clothing he wore — more than anyone I'd ever seen in the middle of summertime. Then, whatever skin was exposed was literally black from dirt and too much sun. He was filthy. If I'd dug him up, he couldn't have been dirtier. His hair looked like a rat's nest. It fell over his face and I could see nothing but a couple of eyes that looked like they were made of molten lava.

John grinned. "I should have figured. Didn't he do this over at the store on Decatur and Tropicana last month?"

"Heard something about that," Jerry said. "He still got warrants?"

"Betcha," John said. I guessed both senior officers knew Henry well. If I also guessed about the warrants, they knew he had them. They'd probably allowed them to sit. It was an unspoken agreement amongst the area cops to let people's warrant sit, in case that person became a problem that needed to go to jail — as Henry did now. Even without the warrants, Henry had plenty he could go for.

"What you waiting for, officer?" John asked. I stepped forward, but Jerry stuck a hand in my chest. "Let her," he said. "Training."

I nodded, moving to a position so I could jump in if I had to.

"It's hot out, Henry," Sally called. "Let's go sit in my car."

"Look eet my merchandise," Sanchez called from behind us. He was extremely agitated. "I'll kick your ass, puto."

He shook his fist at Henry, who tossed aside a bottle he'd been holding. I noticed it once contained Thunderbird. I didn't even know they still made that shit. When I was a kid, we drank that and Boone's Farm. It was all we could afford. Henry picked up another, pulled his arm back like he was going to chuck it.

"Don't," Jerry warned, pointing his gun. "I ain't getting that shit all over my uniform. I just got it outta the cleaners."

Sanchez moved so he was partially behind John. "He have no money to pay. He drink wine from bottle, then leave it een cooler. Theese is against law. I have sign on wall." He pointed, but we didn't look. "I ask heem pay. He say, he no drink from bottle. Someone else must leave eet there. He start fight with me. Look at mi tienda. He trash este store."

John turned towards Sanchez. "Get out. Don't come back until I tell you."

Sanchez looked like he was going to argue. The look on John's face even intimidated me. I heard Sanchez muttering that it was his store.

Henry stood there, glowering. Sally stepped out into the open, keeping her gun down at her side. Henry raised his head so those scary eyes were on her. He looked like he might try staring her down.

"The alcohol's making him bold," Jerry muttered.

"Put the gun away," I called. "Use the man-in-the-can or your baton."

John turned and glared at me.

"I'd keep my mouth shut and let him run his trainee," Jerry said.

I shrugged. "Just thought I'd help."

"Don't. She's got to learn."

"Henry, can we go out to my car?" Sally holstered her weapon. She unsnapped her Capstun. She shook it behind her leg. This was supposed to mix the oleo capsicum evenly throughout the carrier. The store was hot, the air still. *Maybe*, I thought, *mentioning the Capstun wasn't the best idea.*

"Henry. We need to go outside." She moved closer. He didn't reply, instead he just stood there shaking his head. In the still air, his smell was becoming cloying. For the first time, I noticed he had on a silk scarf. It was oriental in design — birds of paradise, orchid-looking flowers and Chinese cuneiform symbols.

"Great. He doesn't want to leave his new-found home," she muttered. "Maybe Jose can charge him rent."

It was then he decided to make noise. If it was talking, I couldn't make it out. It sounded like babbling in another language.

"I think he's saying he ain't going to jail," Jerry said.

Sally looked at Jerry and John, who looked right back. I watched her expression start out unsure, then change to determination. She was going to have to prove herself. That was how things worked in field training.

"No one ever said police work was easy," she said. They grinned. "But, you did say it was going to be fun some of the time."

"Can we get to it? We're gonna be on lunch here pretty quick," Jerry called.

She gave him a dirty look, then directed her full attention to Henry, "Sir, you're under arrest. Please turn around and place your hands behind your back."

Nothing but more incomprehensible sounds came from his mouth. I thought he looked like one of those Holy Rollers. All he had to do was raise his eyes to heaven and dance with his arms out to the sides.

"Henry, will you please turn around and put your hands behind your back for me?" It was a nice ploy, changing her voice and trying for the sugar. Heck, she'd worked it on me enough. I was gratified to see all she received was a glare in return. The whole thing was starting to be fun.

"Don't like women pigs," he said.

"Wow! He does speak English," I called.

His face took on that far-away look — the one that said bad things, like a fight, were coming. While he looked at me, Sally sidled closer. I recognized the strategy. I think it was called trying-to-sneak-up-while-keeping-gun-side-away. As she reached to take him by the sleeve, he lifted his shirts, stuck both arms down his baggy pants, and squatted.

"Stand up," Sally ordered. "That's not keeping you from going."

Now, she was angry. Henry was bigger than her. It was the quintessential problem with women officers — most men were bigger, stronger, and faster. It was the reason the Department didn't hire many women as officers. Not only was he bigger, but he had that buffed look — wiry and thin. Vagrants got it from a no-nonsense diet, which consisted mainly of what they gleaned from garbage cans. Throw in cheap alcohol, bad drugs, lots of walking from place to place, and that was enough to keep anyone from getting fat. If what I saw developing was going to turn into a slugfest between those two, I'd put my money on Henry. But, if it became a debate, Sally had him hands down.

She reached to jerk him to his feet. Personally, I'd have pushed him over, then jumped on him. I couldn't help thinking it was too bad I'd been told to keep my mouth shut. Just as her hand touched his sleeve, Henry stood. When he pulled both hands from his pants, she stepped back, startled. Without thinking, I aimed my gun at him. I saw the other guys had, too. In the Academy, they taught you to watch the hands. Eyes might — and they stressed might — tell you what a man would do, but his hands were where the harm came from. In Henry's case, his cupped hands were filled, but not with harm in the conventional sense. They contained an unbelievably foul measure of human excrement. He raised them towards the ceiling, then spread the entire load from the top of his head to his knees.

"Jesus Christ, Henry," John yelled. He stared at Henry like a flying saucer had appeared and he was leaving in it. Sally's look was one of pure horror. I would have thrown up, except for the shocked expression on her face. I started snorting, then I couldn't help it. I howled. Jerry caught it from me and it spread to John. Between breaths, John finally yelled, "What're you waiting for? Get him."

And she did. I don't know if I could have. A normal human being would never accept such a command without some pretty strong incentive. But then again, she wasn't a normal person. She was a person in field training. Those people existed for the moment, in tiny spans of time where everything they did was evaluated and might determine the direction their lives took. She was a person who got to that speck of time after having spent the last year trying to get hired, then spent every working moment and some off-time trying to not blow her chance at being a cop. All of that made obeying her FTO's command one of the most powerful emotional and psychological motivators that a person might be given. That was because Academy and field training were modeled on military concepts developed in basic training. They depended on peer pressure, the desire to excel, to earn respect, and a fear of failure.

Without any other conscious thought other than to keep her gun, she jumped Henry. I watched as the can of Capstun rolled across the floor. Sally's left hand disappeared behind her back only to reappear with her handcuffs. When she tried to hook a wrist, the fight was on. Not punches and kicks, but a whole bunch of wrestling. I started forward, but John touched my arm.

"See how she does, first," he said. "If she gets in trouble, we'll help."

Every once in a while, John or Jerry used their feet to control some of Henry's movements. I noticed they were careful that only the soles of their feet made contact. John got a foot on a wrist and she was able to get the handcuff on. She used an ignition twist, a technique where the edge of the cuff was ground into the bone, to flip him. He screamed at the pain and she grunted as she leveraged him onto his belly. Henry tried to flail at her with his other arm. That was when she caught it. It took her a few seconds, but finally, we heard the click. She rolled off, out of breath and covered in human crap.

When the huffing slowed, the retching started. Sally rose to one elbow and slimy fluid dripped from her mouth. She ran for the front of the store. I followed her out, turning away as she puked against the wall. Each time I thought she was done, the smell hit her and she started in again. After a while, she slumped against the store's wall. I guessed there was nothing else left in her.

"Good job," I said.

"Fuck you, Cam. You could have helped."

"No, I coo . . ."

"You thought it was funny."

"Well, you got to admit . . . " I started.

"You're an asshole. You've always been an asshole."

"You're right about that, I guess." The hot August sun quickly dried the shit stuck to her uniform so that it flaked off her. It made her look like she was molting. When we went back inside, the prisoner was sitting quietly. At the sight of him, I saw her go pale as one of her hands settled across her stomach.

"Done?" Jerry asked. The two FTOs stood together, calmly watching her. Our clean uniforms were a sharp contrast to the store's interior and Sally's exterior. She squared her shoulders.

"Yeah," she said. She reached for Henry. She turned her head slightly, ignoring the fact she grabbed an arm covered in shit. As she jerked him to his feet, he moaned. "Our car or theirs?" She glanced at me.

"Ain't putting that shit in my car," Jerry said. He laughed.

Without waiting, she took Henry outside. She stood him in front of the patrol car like he was a giant Ken doll someone had found at the dump.

"Stay," she ordered. He did. She patted her belt like she'd lost something. John threw her the set of car keys that must have come unclipped from her belt.

"You might need this, too." Her can of Capstun followed.

"I'm riding with them." He pointed at us. "We'll meet you at the jail."

Sally nodded, then went to the trunk where she took out two yellow emergency blankets. One she threw on the hood and the other she unwrapped. She flipped out the blade of her Spyderco tactical knife, then sliced a hole in the blanket. She draped it over Henry's head like a poncho. He seemed quite pleased with the result. She cut the other blanket into strips, which she used to tie the poncho around his body. While she did this, John went to our trunk and got another one out.

"This one's for you. Try not to get any stuff on my seat. Don't wreck the car. The Ell Tee will have my ass for not being in there with you."

"Then ride with me," she said.

"Are you kidding?" he asked "I'd throw up."

Right then, Mr. Sanchez ran over. "I press charges," he yelled.

"Later," John said. "We'll come back later. Take the reports, get statements, do whatever else."

"No, now," Mr. Sanchez demanded. He took a deep breath and tried to make his body larger, like he could be more imposing to a bunch of guys with guns who wore bulletproof vests. John's next look made him go back in the store.

"He's lucky we ain't in Mexico," John muttered. "I'd throw that asshole a beating for sure."

Jerry drove while John rode shotgun, which put me in back. We were already inside the jail when she got there. The first correction officer who reached her took one whiff of the two of them and groaned. He waved a couple more people over in case Henry decided to get squirrelly. As they went about the business of booking him, they grumbled as much about her as they did Henry. One of the female C.O.s finally looked at Sally, who stood to the side looking a little pale.

"Honey," she said. "You smell like shit. Come with me." She took her back to the inmate showers, where they gave Sally a clean set of orange clothing. The CO told her she could bring them back later, washed, of course.

"Come on, Henry. Let's go take a shower," a big officer said.

"No, I like the way I smells," Henry mumbled.

"This is going to get ugly," Jerry said. "He's going to fail booking."

"Let's wait," I said. Just for fun, I wanted to stick around to see if anything could be done to make Henry a "yes" person.

■ ■ ■

House Call . . .

F inally, I couldn't stand my apartment anymore. The place was filled
with memories, many of which I was making worse than they had
been. I took off for a day and went house shopping. The first one
I found I took. It was on a quiet street in Henderson, which was the city
south and east of Las Vegas. Henderson was actually the largest city in
Nevada. It included of a lot of undeveloped desert.

The house had been built in the early fifties, but it was nice. That was
because the owner had gone in and totally remodeled it from the roof
down. It was a two bedroom, which meant I had room for my books since
I wasn't going to have a roommate. The backyard was small, planted in
grass, with a huge tree that shaded the whole yard. On summer nights,
if I didn't turn on the porch light, it was black out there. For the first
two weeks, all my possessions remained packed in boxes. They might
have stayed that way for a long time except that Brenda came over one
day while I was at work. When I came in that night, tired to the point of
distraction, I discovered the place had become a home. On the kitchen
counter she had left a note saying Mom was going to be in town for a
week and I was expected to show up for dinner at least for a couple of
nights. I grimaced, thinking of that fight announcer's famous call, *Let's
get ready to rumble.*

A week later, on what was my mother's first day in town. I thought it
would be good to get things out of the way. Brenda called to say they would
meet me at the Klondike Casino coffee shop. This was a small casino on
the south end of Las Vegas Boulevard. My mother liked the place after

she stopped in to gamble one night. A woman, who sat down next to her, Helen, turned out to be the owner. They hit it off and whenever she came to town, she ate in the coffee shop, sometimes took a room, and always gambled in the small casino. The Klondike was Old Vegas, the way things used to be. A lot of tourists knew the place without actually knowing it because the famous "Welcome to Las Vegas" sign was out front. The sign was planted in the middle of the dirt median, a dangerous place where people stopped to have their pictures taken.

The Klondike was like the sign. It was old fashioned, designed in a time when people thought atomic bombs were just another way to move a lot of dirt, when light bulbs were good enough to advertise things, and cars were simply carbureted. There was none of the stuff that made the new Sin City image so appealing, like sexy women with their underwear around their ankles, multi-colored bright neon, smooth circus acts from France, or the fancy slot machines with celebrity pictures. Vegas in those days was just a place to go and be made to feel comfortable.

Jerry and I had just left the jail when I suggested driving down Fremont instead of going straight to the freeway to get back to where we were supposed to be patrolling. On that night, we had IDA area. Jerry was in a good mood. We'd caught a man who'd robbed half a dozen bars in Southwest and he thought the chances were good that we might get a commendation. Normally, he wouldn't even humor me with the suggestion we drive down Fremont Street, which was way off our area, but things were slow. As we drove east, I thought of how I liked Fremont because I'd started off being a cop there.

Jerry drove. He was one of those cops who took his time getting places. His theory was that if we arrived last, the call stood a good chance of being solved by those who got there first. I figured we'd go east, turn north on Eastern, then hit U.S. 95 and head back to where we belonged. As we cruised that old section of town, I stared at the old motels and hotels. They looked like shit. Even the new convenience store, which was less than a year old, looked bad. The strip malls were filled with stores struggling to stay in business. The only one that was doing great was the gun store. I knew from past experience that everything along the street had been robbed, including the gun store. The fool who'd tried that left in the coroner's van, some of his brains still at the scene. The motels had slipped from renting monthly, to daily, to hourly. If that wasn't a boost to prostitution, I couldn't think what was. All their live-in clientele was poor, with a large percentage being almost-invisible illegals. Those people worked hard, filled jobs no one else wanted — like house cleaning, gardening, or manual labor. They were good people who only wanted to get on their feet and run straight into the American Dream. Their problem was the bad people. They came out at night — sold drugs, robbed, whored, and pimped. They were the little predators — like weasels or foxes — while we were the big predators, wolves or mountain lions that lived to catch the smaller prey.

In daylight, Fremont Street looked like any other run-down neighborhood. In the morning, while kids waited at bus stops, groups of parents stood over them like sheep dogs. In the afternoon, the same buses dropped the kids off. They were taken home where they played in the dirt courtyards of the motel apartment complexes or the lots where businesses once stood. We were the sheepdogs then. For the most past, bad things didn't happen until late afternoon.

As we passed Eighth Street, I remembered an incident in training when I'd stopped a girl for looking like a ho. What attracted my attention was the way she walked. Her hips swayed with an exaggerated swing. She obviously practiced it as a form of advertisement — intended to bring bees to the honey, as they said on the street. As I talked to her, I tried to keep my eyes off her ample body sheathed in Spandex. Mike, my FTO at the time, let me do the all the talking. When I finished, I wished the woman a good day.

Before I turned to go, Mike stepped forward. He stuck his nine-millimeter in her face, taking the safety off with a click. Her eyes were huge. Without being told, she put her hands up. He tapped the material of her tights. I saw the huge kitchen knife. When he pulled the material away from her body, it slid down the outside of her thigh and fell to the ground. Mike put his foot on it without looking, then kicked it so I could pick it up. I stood there like I'd been lightning-struck. That was a "one" day on the old evaluation.

"Man, I can't believe what I know now," I said, keeping my eyes on the street.

"Yeah. Experience is strange," Jerry agreed. "One day you're innocent and dumb, then you start getting smart. The problem is what goes with the loss of innocence."

"Like?"

"By the way, that was a good spot earlier," Jerry said. I noticed he didn't answer the question. "Eighty feet and you see the gun under his shirt. I was impressed."

I didn't want to tell him that I was as impressed that I had spotted the gun on the robber, too. He hadn't looked like a thief, but a man walking away from a bar. I knew I was going to have a hard time dictating the report where I explained what made me look at him, but I had all shift to come up with something.

While we were stopped at Fremont and Fifteenth, I watched two guys getting ready to do a drug deal. They were so focused on each other, they hadn't seen us. What made the transaction stand out was that the guy who seemed to be selling was white. The blacks traditionally made the open sales on the street corners. Mexicans, who mainly sold heroin, used the pay phones, which were all over the place, to do their business. As I studied the dealer, I noted he looked in good shape. Catching him would be fun, so I reached for the door handle.

"Don't even think about it," Jerry said.

"Come on. It'll be a challenge."

"No. And I mean it. We don't know this area. I'm not chasing after you and making a fool of myself on the radio. Let it go."

"Jerry, I used to work Fremont. I know it."

"No, Cam. I'm the one who'll have to call the pursuit." He was right.

"OK," I muttered, but I opened the door, anyway. As I stepped out, I yelled, "Hey! You better not be selling drugs."

The white guy had his hand in his pocket. He looked over. I noticed something on his throat even at that distance. At first, my thought was birthmark, but then I reconsidered. It had to be part of a tattoo that just showed. For a second, our eyes met. There was no fear in them. The black guy ran. That caused the white guy to look away, which set him running. It wasn't the panicked sprint of the buyer, but a leisurely jog, much as if he was late for the bus. *I'll remember you*, I thought. *We'll meet again*. I climbed back in the car.

"See. I told you he was selling."

"Who isn't? We need to get back. I don't like our area being unattended."

Po-leazz, I thought. IDA was the slowest area in the valley. That meant it always seemed like we weren't working while we patrolled that area. There were times when we went an entire shift with nothing — not a form to turn in, a ticket, or the ability to say we handled something. We turned north on Eastern and stopped for the light that would put us on US 95. The dispatcher came on the radio and gave us a hot-prowl burglary call. I sat up straight, feeling the little rush that came with a call that promised to be exciting. Jerry hit the switches for the emergency equipment. He put the cruiser in the number one lane. This is where NRS said we should be driving if we were rolling code. Still, it scared me to death the way people drove when an emergency vehicle got behind them. The law said they were supposed to pull to the right, but that hardly happened. One guy actually stopped dead in the lane. Just when Jerry started to switch lanes, the other driver decided to move to the right. We came close to being broadsided.

I loved crimes in progress. They meant using good tactics and the possibility of being in the shit — like an ambush or shootout. Some cops lived for these things and others avoided them like a sharp stick in the eye. The funny thing was that Jerry was the avoid-them type. Normally, people like me despised people like Jerry. We looked at them as chicken-shits who should have been accountants. The reason I didn't feel that way about him was that I knew Jerry's history. He was a highly decorated cop, having been in two shootings where he killed two people. In the cop community, this was the equivalent of a military Medal of Honor winner. What irritated me was his experience made him cautious about his remaining time on Earth. That came out in things like his driving. There we were, rolling code, and my sister could have driven faster.

"Can we stop for McDonald's?" I asked. "After all, it's not like we're in a hurry."

"I'd like to get there alive," he replied.

"I'd like to get there while there's still a crime."

"Fuck you," he muttered as he slowed for another car. Once again, I caught myself thinking I would avoid partnering with him in the future. After we exited onto Blue Diamond Road, he cut the red lights and siren. I set my eyes on him.

"He'll hear us coming," Jerry said. I heard the defensiveness in his voice. That made me grin. He was senior, after all.

"Jesus Christ. We're at least five miles from the house. God! I should have driven." I needed to take deep breaths. I felt the adrenaline pumping me up.

"Three Ida," the dispatcher radioed. "Copy an AM" I hit the button and read the message out loud. It said the person reporting, a neighbor, said that he would meet us on the next street over from the actual location. He described the crook as a white male, six feet, thin, brown short hair, gray shirt and blue jeans. It went on to say that the PR had seen the suspect climb through the window of the victim's house. That residence was described as being behind his. The PR's friend was at work and he was sure it wasn't the owner he saw going through the window. That was all good info to know.

When we finally arrived, the PR stood in his front yard. He repeated the same information the dispatcher had already sent us. I wanted to yell, "We know that!" Jerry saw me getting impatient, so he gave me a look. I shut my mouth and started to edge away.

"See him come out yet?" Jerry asked. I saw him sweating slightly. *Jeez, he's afraid*, I thought.

"Nope. Still in there. I got the wife watching."

"How do you know he didn't go out the front?"

"Bars on all those doors and windows. I helped Dale install them. Ain't none on the back. Dale's been adding them a little at a time. You know. As he gets the money."

"Let's go," I said.

Jerry pulled me aside. "Let's call and see if we can get backup."

"OK. You do that. I'll get in a position where I can watch," I said as I turned, drew my gun, and started towards the back of the PR's house. From the corner, I quick-peeked the wall. A window was open. I saw I was going to have to climb a wall, which was going to put me in plain view of anyone looking out the open window. If he had a gun, I was dog meat. As I considered the best way to get into the yard, I felt Jerry's presence at my back. That made me happy. The best way was just going over. I pointed, he nodded; I went first while he covered me.

For a second, I considered what I knew to be a fact: I was getting a reputation for stunts like this. I'd heard people referring to me as a loose cannon. What I knew was that if I was to have a reputation that could be misconstrued, then I should have something to balance it. Other cops developed something in the way of a wicked sense of humor they used to defuse their reputations. My problem was that I could be cruel and funny, but, for some reason, I never knew where the limits should be. That meant I often took things further than they needed to go, which pissed people off. Because of that lack on my part, I simply didn't bother joking around or defending myself. Instead, I did my job and let the consequences be what they might.

Those consequences included Jerry quietly complaining to Sergeant Dodd about the things I did. Dodd was a pussy, more worried about his stripes than his people. What I had going was Lieutenant Giles. He liked me and had already intervened on my behalf a couple of times, like when my old FTO complained I wasn't doing enough car stops and the time I forgot a t-shirt and a temp FTO wanted to write me up. The Ell Tee told him to let me wear a black shirt I had, suggesting that I cut the neck out of it so it wouldn't show above my vest. What I learned was to keep things in balance, the lieutenant on one side and anything bad the sergeant might do on the other.

Once Jerry was over the wall, we made our approach quickly. I wanted to be flush to the wall in case the shitbird inside had a gun. If he started shooting, I hoped he was either a bad shot or he chose Jerry first. It might be cruel, but I was sure Jerry thought the same thing. I took the east side of the window, waiting while Jerry ducked under and took the other side. He touched a finger to where the lock was broken. I nodded. I pointed two fingers at my eyes, then one at the dark hole. He nodded.

I quick-peeked the interior. This was something taught in the Academy. The idea was for me to clear my mind, pop my head into view, and duck back. My brain was supposed to have absorbed the impression of what was happening where I'd looked. The cop was supposed to sort out the impressions and repeat it if an image needed to be built up. This time, with my head safe, the impression was of a dark room, ransacked drawers, no bodies. As usual, whenever I did the technique, I didn't trust myself. So I just popped my head in and stared at the room. As luck would have it, just when I popped up, the crook walked by the bedroom door. Either the motion or my face in the hole caught his attention, causing him to stop. We stared at each other.

"Fuck me," he said, then disappeared from the doorway.

"Stop! Police!" I screamed. Like a snake, I went through the window.

Jerry also screamed, "Stop!" I got stuck half way through the window. It took me a second to realize he was yelling at me because he had me by the pants leg.

"Shit, Jerry. Let me go," I shouted. I was dangling a foot off the ground. If the bad guy came back with a knife or gun, I was dead. I kicked the other leg and hit Jerry in the head. He dropped me. I landed in a heap, hitting my head on the corner of the bed.

The window was sixteen inches high and four feet long. If I were bigger, I wouldn't have made it through. Jerry definitely wasn't coming in that way. I had to give him credit. He tried.

"Cam," he hissed. "Stop right there." As I stood up, I lurched into a dresser. A lamp fell and shattered. I gave the dresser a shove and the stuff on the top — knickknacks, ashtray, coins, and papers also fell. I charged across the room, kicking a chair out of the way. It also broke. When I came around the corner into a hall, I saw the guy looking back at me. I went in full foot-pursuit mode.

"You better stop," I yelled. He ran faster. "Motherfucker, I'm going to kick your ass when I catch you." As he put on a burst of speed, it occurred to me that maybe that wasn't the smartest thing to yell. We ran down the hallway into the living room. The bad guy grabbed things as he ran — like lamps, furniture, pillows, and pictures. He tossed them in my path in an attempt to slow or trip me. The more he did this, the madder I got. All I could think was how he was in for a royal ass-kicking when I caught him.

He dodged around the coffee table. By then, I was like a heat-seeking missile. I wasn't going to zigzag or change my path to avoid things. It was going to be straight for the target. I put my foot right through the tabletop's thin panels. All I wanted was to get close enough to tackle him. Just when I thought I had my chance, he left the living room for the dining room. I snagged a piece of his clothing, which spun him slightly. That caused us both to careen into the dining room table. The weight of two bodies crashing into it broke a leg off, tilted the top, and spilled a bowl of waxed fruit across the floor. I gave the guy's body a hard shove. He bounced from the flat surface like a tennis ball off a racket. I dove and missed him, slamming into the wood top. The other three legs snapped off. I felt the breath explode from my lungs but I still had his shirttail. The cloth ripped, leaving me holding the whole garment. He made it to the kitchen with me back in pursuit. I heard a heavy booming noise, which shook the wall, making pictures dance. Jerry called my name.

As I made to tackle him again, he swung open the refrigerator door. This time, I looked like the tennis ball. I bounced back a couple of feet. Food flew off the shelves, landing everywhere. Bottles shattered and half-opened cans spilled their contents across cupboards and counters. Blood-red catsup sprayed across my face and uniform when he stepped on the bottle. That blinded me for a moment. He opened a cabinet and started throwing china plates at me. They exploded with loud pops that sounded like gunshots.

I ducked and charged forward, sliding more than moving across the slippery floor. He saw the plates weren't having the desired effect, so he ran again. The kitchen had a door at either end. We went in one, we went out the other, putting us back in the living room, then back inside the hallway. As I followed, the sight of all the destruction almost stopped me. The place looked like we'd done a search warrant on it.

He ran past the room where the two of us made our entry, then straight into what had to be the master bedroom. As we entered, I got a solid grip on the guy's naked shoulder. In spite of the sweat, I managed to sink my fingers into flesh. He screamed, spinning in my grip. The left hook caught me on the side of the head. It hurt. I punched back, getting a glancing blow off his chin. The next punch caught me square in the nose. My eyes filled with tears. I slammed two punches into his face. The fight settled into blows and grunts when something solid connected. I knew I should back off and go to baton, Capstun, or gun but I was mad. Twice we came close enough to start wrestling, which caused us to stumble into things. They broke and crashed to the floor — an antique lamp, an ashtray full of change, a small color TV. What I *wanted* was to get him on the ground and stomp the shit out of him. The problem was we were pretty evenly matched.

There was a huge crash that seemed to come from a long way off. What I didn't know was that when Jerry heard the sound of breaking china and bottles, he thought I was being shot at. First, he called "shots fired" into the radio. The dispatcher immediately sent out a four forty-four. This was the highest priority the police have, meaning an officer was in serious trouble. The call went out to everyone in the valley, which included Highway Patrol, school police, military police, city marshals, Taxicab Authority — everybody. Next, Jerry moved from the window, which he was incapable of climbing through to the back door. What he didn't know was that it led into the garage, not the house. He started slamming his shoulder into it. He only stopped long enough when he heard the cries and thumps. Because he thought the guy was finishing me off, he stepped about ten feet back from the door and took a run at the panel like a bull going for a matador. Without even flinching, he crashed into the solid-core door. The owner had put extra money into having the doorframe screwed into the framing. All the hits Jerry made before this final attempt had caused things to loosen inside the wall.

That last hit, backed by the momentum the run had added, was the last straw. To say, "The door gave way" would have been an understatement. When the dust cleared, a jagged hole was left in the place of the wall. Jerry picked himself up from the entire section that lay on the ground. It consisted of about two feet of stucco wall from all the way around the door and doorjamb. More graphically, it looked like a car had driven through the back of the house. The hole in the house was a mess of ripped stucco, trailing lathe, and broken electrical wiring, which may or may not have been hot. The neighbor, who had called the burglary in, watched as Jerry ran inside, disappearing as screams drifted out. He, of course, called 911 again to report that possibly two cops were being killed inside the house. When the dispatcher put that out, literally every cop car in Vegas started in the direction of the call. The air filled with wailing sirens.

■ ■ ■

Meanwhile, I was in an earnest knock-down-drag-out fight. We traded punches like a couple of amateur welterweights. My back was to the door, so my first indication that we were no longer alone was when an arm reached past me and grabbed the suspect by the throat. His body was jerked towards me, which knocked me down. Jerry practically stepped on me as he pushed the suspect farther into the room. He started slamming him into the dresser. I heard the wood crack. Once should have been enough. With the fourth thud, I struggled to my feet.

"Enough. Jerry, that's enough." The guy looked like a child's rag doll. Jerry dropped him. I felt my nose, seeing the hand come away all red. I looked at the apparently unconscious bad guy and kicked him in the ribs. When there was no reaction, I took out a pair of cuffs, flipped him on his stomach, and pulled his arms behind his back. The radio was going crazy with units putting themselves en route or arriving. Neither one of us had been on the radio for a few minutes. I pulled the pack-set out to let Dispatch know we were OK and we had one in custody. Jerry told her to have medical en route. We each grabbed one of the suspect's arms to drag him outside. When we were in the evening light, I saw the neighbor, cordless phone in hand.

"I called Dale," he said. We gave him blank looks. "The owner. He's on his way."

"Oh, yeah. Good. We'll need to get a report."

"Is that him?" the neighbor asked.

We stood looking at the neighbor. Neither one of us blinked. I guess we looked like a couple of lizards. Sergeant Dodd came around the corner at a run. He was a big man who no longer was made for running. The uniform shirt had come out of his pants, so it barely covered his belly. He'd stop wearing his vest because it might not have done any good with huge gaps where the side panels no longer protected his ribs. Besides, all the blubber made him sweat profusely and the vest only trapped more heat.

"You guys OK?" he wheezed.

"Yeah, Sarg," Jerry said. "Can I talk to you for a minute?"

A second later, I heard, "It's my house." Then a man appeared, pushing at another officer I didn't recognize. He jingled a set of house keys at us.

"Let him come, Steve," Dodd called to the officer whose job it was to secure the perimeter. Dodd turned to me.

"Anyone else in there, Cam?"

I shrugged. "Don't think so. Me and the suspect were in the house but not the garage."

"From the look of things," Dodd said, peering through the gaping hole in the wall. "Someone came in the garage. Is that how he got in?"

"Not exactly," Jerry said. The look on his face was sheepish.

"Steve," Dodd said, "Take a couple of guys and make sure there's no one else in there. Then let him go in and look to see what's been disturbed."

Jerry and the Sarg went over in a corner while I watched the paramedics bring the suspect around. The first indication he was still with us was a groan. One of the paramedics was a female. I couldn't help thinking she was pretty. She had red hair and green eyes, a combination that was sure to catch my attention. I'd try and get her name later. The other paramedic came over.

"Better let me see if that thing's broken."

"Cam, can I talk to you a second?" Dodd asked. after I'd been checked out.

"Sure."

"Did Jerry ask you to wait for backup?"

"He mentioned it."

"Then why didn't you wait?"

"We didn't even know what was going on. I wanted to make sure before I started units coming all the way out here."

"What if he had a gun? You could have been hurt."

"What, Sarg? I should wait for another cop to get here and let him get hurt? I thought this was our job. To protect and serve and, maybe, once in a while, to put our lives on the line for the citizens."

"Don't give me that shit. I'll . . . "

"Good job, Cam." We both turned to find Lieutenant Giles standing behind us. I wasn't sure what he'd heard but I was glad to see him. I was mad, and if things had gone on, who knew what trouble my big mouth might have gotten me into. "Sergeant Dodd, haven't we been having a series of burglaries in the area?"

"Yes, sir." Dodd's voice became tentative, as if it suddenly occurred to him.

"I bet this is the guy that's been doing them all. Look at him! He's a dead ringer or haven't you been reading the bulletins?"

"Oh. Yes, sir! I do read them and I think you might be right."

"That's two in one day for these guys. First the robber and now this serial burglar. I expect commendation paperwork on my desk by tomorrow afternoon."

"Yes, sir. I'll get right on that," Dodd said, "but, before I take care of that, I need to finish taking care of this problem I have."

"I don't see any problem here, Sergeant. You think you better get started with what I want done?"

Dodd gave me a look I didn't like, then left without another word. The Ell Tee walked over to me.

"Son, you're going to have problems. You make enemies like Dodd, sooner or later, they'll come back to haunt you."

"Sir, my daddy says if a man pays you, you owe him a day's work. That's the work ethic he wanted me to have. He said if that man gave me shit, shovel it. I think if I hold to that, I'll be alright."

"If you were digging ditches, that'd work," he said. He wiped a hand across his face, then sighed. "It ain't going to be an easy life for you. Let's see what we have inside."

The place looked like a major storm just finished blowing through. As we walked from room to room with the victim, Giles whistled. I expected a major butt-chewing from either the Ell Tee or the owner.

"I can't believe he did this to my house."

"Well, yeah. Kinda," I said. Giles looked at me and I closed my mouth.

"You guys are great," the owner said. He looked at Dodd and Giles. "Is there some kind of medal you can put these guys in for?"

"Ahhh. I had no idea," the Ell Tee said as he looked around. For a second it was as if the Ell Tee was in a trance, then he shook himself. "Unfortunately, we don't give medals. We're happy to serve the public and that's all the thanks we need, sir."

"No. Really. I think they deserve something. Your guys have done a wonderful job. I want to see they get something for this."

"You don't need to worry," Giles replied, dryly. "I'll make sure they get something."

That day, I realized honesty wasn't always the best policy — letting people have their perceptions of events was sometimes enough. They were going to create what they wanted from any given incident. I finished going through the house, looking at what I had done with the help of the bad guy. It was pretty fucking amazing what two people can destroy.

Afterwards, I went outside. I stood next to the curb as the ambulance left. The red-headed paramedic was in the passenger seat. She turned her face, and our eyes met. As corny as it sounds, it felt as though a spark of something jumped between us. I shook my head, trying to dispel the feeling as illusionary, but it wouldn't go away.

Before I could think about it any more, my radio came alive. Jerry asked me to come back to our car. When I got there, I bent so I could look in the glass. My reflection showed the abrasions and bruising. I fingered the marks. They were all the medals I needed. I grinned at the reflection. Once again, I'd been tested, and once again, I'd passed.

■ ■ ■

Don't Step in the Evidence . . .

I liked graveyard. It kept me away from people like Dodd. What I didn't like was missing my gym workouts. That was my time, my place to go where I could burn off the stress from the job. I loved going there either pissed or depressed, feeling the slow process of overcoming whatever troubled me. The sound of slamming weights, the lifting of the metal on the very edges of what I knew were my abilities, was enough to make me better. I also loved when I could use what I took from the gym — the physical stamina, which stood me in good stead in those moments when I chased and caught some young, fast dope dealer or had to fight a bigger opponent. When I won those fights, survived the encounters until my backup arrived and kicked the suspect's ass, it was confirmation that I was working for God — with just a little help.

My new sergeant was cool. He spent a lot of time hanging out at The Peppermill Restaurant on The Strip. I'd heard through the grapevine he was trying to convince the night manager that she really wanted to be his next wife. He showed up on calls only if he really had to and, on those rare occasions when he did come out, he stayed out of our way. His method of supervising caused me to develop my philosophy of supervisors. There were three types: One kind had confidence in people and let them do their jobs; the next type was so inept, they stayed away from anything that smacked of a problem so they never looked stupid or had a chance to be called to task for anything; and the third type was a micromanager — always meddling by making people fill in all the boxes or getting in the way or ordering people to do what they would have already done. I'd take a trusting boss or the inept one over a meddlesome asshole any day.

Getting used to graves took me a while. The first night I was on shift, I was dispatched to a burglary call. It started when the victim came home and discovered the burglary, but the suspect was already gone. The complex was located behind the Hard Rock Casino on Paradise Road. While I used a flashlight to check for fingerprints on the windows, a man in a black trench coat walked up behind me. I turned. My expression must have been as startled as his. Little alarm bells went off in my head, but I ignored them. If I'd been more experienced, I might have listened to the things in my head and wondered why someone would be surprised to see a cop near the front door of an apartment. I would have also spent a little time wondering why someone would be wearing a coat like that in the middle of a Vegas summer night; after all, the temperature was near a hundred.

A second later, I was back in the apartment, listening to the owner tell me the stuff that was taken.

"Can you believe he took my black leather trench coat? What would someone do with a thing like that this time of year?"

"Was it long? Like down to here?" I used my hand to indicate a place below my knees.

"Yeah. I guess." By the time he said, "Yeah," I was back out the front door, running down the walkways where I could see the farthest through the complex. I radioed for available units to set a perimeter. The dispatcher informed me there were no available units and that I was on my own. The man got away, and to make matters worse, at the end of shift, while I sat in debriefing, the whole squad, all five of them, made fun of me.

"Control, I need a unit at the south side of the complex," William said into his cupped hand, reproducing the hollow noise the radio made.

"Oh!" David cut in with, "And, while you're at it, can you put one on the north side, one on the east. No, Control. Make that two on the east."

They practically rolled out of their chairs, they laughed so hard. After I dressed out, the sarg called me into his office. "I think you got the point," he said.

"Yes," I told him. "I don't think anyone needs to rub it in anymore that it already was." I tried to keep my voice light, but some of the embarrassment leaked through.

"Just to make sure, Cam," he said. "You're it out there. Be creative and stay alive. Don't make me have to come out of that nice air-conditioned place I like. There'll be nights where you'll have to handle a robbery by yourself. Get smart. Understand?"

"I do."

"And Cam."

"Yeah, Sarg?"

"Next time, get in your car and drive around in circles real fast. That'll give you a perimeter."

"Funny," I said sarcastically. He couldn't help it, I guess.

The next night, just after midnight, I got a call concerning an inn east of McCarran International Airport. This was actually Nora sector, which wasn't my area, but the Nora units were slammed. There were times when this happened. Most cops were unhappy when it did, because it meant either working with cops they didn't know or going into unfamiliar areas. Things like apartment complexes or certain businesses had quirks, almost like personalities, that were known only to those who worked them all the time. There might be a robbery alarm that went off every couple of days or a way to make an approach that was safer or even a manager that had to be dealt with because he was politically connected with someone important in the community.

When I read the computer screen, it said two PRs had called in. The first PR said he'd heard a screaming woman. The second, who wanted to remain anonymous, reported a woman being beaten. The only other information was that the location was somewhere in the middle on the south side of the complex. That wasn't a lot to go on, but sometimes, that was all we got. I knew the place was a daily/weekly, which meant the rooms would be mainly leased by locals who couldn't afford the monthly rent on a regular apartment and tourists who wouldn't know about the locals. It was my experience that when tourists knew people lived in motels, they avoided renting rooms at such places.

I was in a single-man unit. That meant Dispatch would be trying to get me someone else for a backup, which depended on a unit clearing from chow or another incident. With this type of call, I could wait or just go in — either way, it was my choice. What concerned me was that if I waited, certain people would dog me bad for being chicken shit. That was something I decided long ago I was never going to have a problem with — that no one I worked with would ever think I was a shirker or coward. And that was why I rolled across the motel's driveway with my windows down and the headlights off.

Outside, the night was quiet except for the sound of passing cars on the parallel streets — Paradise and Swenson. I stopped twenty feet in, where I could see all the way from one end of the complex to the other. Nothing seemed out of place, so I decided to park and make a foot reconnaissance. With this type of call, we usually found nothing. The whole process usually involved looking around while driving through, and when I was sure nothing was out of the ordinary, clear with the code for "unable to locate." Going in on foot was something a lot of cops wouldn't do, but I hated missing something I couldn't see from inside the car.

I parked near the southwest corner of the complex, behind a screen of bushes. From there, I walked east, keeping close to the buildings. This was a tactical approach, something taught in the Academy through role playing and later perfected in field training by actual use. I still remembered my FTO, Sam, making sure I never screwed up after the first time. He took me aside and quietly talked to me. The call had been a guy with a gun. Luckily, we arrived after another unit had already arrested the man and took the gun away from him.

"You parked right in front of the house. Didn't they teach you any better? What would happen if we'd been first? I'll tell you, he'd stuck that rifle out the window and shot us both. Not only am I pissed because I'm dead, but some poor SWAT fucker has to come down here and try to get our bodies back. Then maybe he gets shot, too. There are two dead people pissed at you." I thought he was kidding until I saw the look on Sam's face. I remembered the traces of the fear in Sam's eyes, which made him ugly-mad and, at that time, wondering why.

Now, I knew. You only get so many chances on the street before something bad happens. A cop who said he'd never been in a shooting or fight or bad situation in his entire career was a lay-down who hid from what the job was all about, because no one is ever that lucky.

As I made my way through the shadows, Dispatch came on with an update. I had my radio turned way down, so I had to stop to hear. The anonymous caller must have felt guilty. Dispatch said he called back with an approximate room number. I glanced at the doors and saw I needed to keep moving east. The motel was a two-story building. The front was a sequence of alternating doors and windows. The second floor walkway, which extended out over the first story as a concrete landing, was shadowed by a meager awning. This was meant to prevent sunlight or rain from either getting in the rooms or bothering the customers. For the tourist, it was one of those places designed as simply a cheap place to sleep while waiting to catch a missed flight. To the renter, it would represent sinking pretty near the bottom of the barrel. The place had a bare minimum of motel comfort — no pool or restaurant. The lobby was tiny, a model of efficiency, like the room, which contained only a bed and bathroom. If someone stuck his head out, they would easily see me coming. This I didn't like. My advantage was the darkness. All the street and parking lights were that low-sodium kind that barely put out any illumination.

The people who lived here wouldn't be model citizens, either. That was probably the reason neither PR had provided a name, contact phone number, or more of a description of the events or any suspect involved. If it was discovered they had, they might have to worry about the state of their tires or, more important, their health. Loaded as I was with this new information, I moved a little more quickly. My radio squawked the information that a unit was clearing. The dispatcher sent him my way. I checked for the thirtieth time to make sure my gun holster was unsnapped — nervous habit. As I got to what I considered closer to the room, even though I still didn't see the number sequence it should be in, I rested my hand on the butt. *Just in case*, I thought.

As I walked, I kept checking the numbers on the doors. They were all screwed up, jumping from the single digits to the five hundred series. The caller had said the room number was 110 or the room just to the right. As I walked, I heard voices coming through the walls. It was sometimes televisions, sometimes people, and sometimes a voice I wasn't sure was either. Once, I heard the sound of the headboard banging the wall and a woman's moans. That I could hear them so easily made me conscious of the thinness of the single-paned windows, the construction of the walls and doors. I also knew they could hear me if I wasn't careful. What kept coming to mind was how it was that a woman had been screaming and there wasn't a crowd outside. Every other time I had been out on one of these there were people standing around, only too happy to see the police so they could either point at things or hope we would fuck up and they could bear witness. I wondered if any of these people would even care if someone had been killed close to where they were.

"One Paul Thirty-four. One Nora," the other officer radioed. "What's your status?"

"One Nora, I haven't found anything yet."

"Paul Thirty-four, I'll be arriving in a few."

"Copy!" I un-keyed the mike. "Damn!"

I wanted to solve this before the Nora unit arrived. The officer arriving was more senior and when he got there, he'd be technically the boss on the call. As I passed the breezeway, I saw that I was in front of 112, which meant the next room should be 111. The one after that was the one I wanted. I hurried past the door, watching the other to see if someone came out. As I glanced at the number, I stopped. It was 110. If the bad guy opened the door, he could have shot me. *What happened to 111?* I stepped away from the building to get a better look at things. With a wider perspective, I saw the second floor was all odd numbers and the first floor even ones.

It was then I noticed the concrete. There were two lines of shiny footprints leading from the door to where I stood. They looked like someone had taken a can of black paint and followed me to where I stood. I knew it was going to look stupid, but I had to lift a boot and stare at the bottom, like it was going to change what I already knew. The print pattern matched that of my soles.

"Were you deliberately trying to ruin the crime scene?" Without thinking, I turned my Mag-Lite on the speaker. The other officer's hand went up, covering his eyes.

"Jesus," I said. "You scared the fuck out of me. You trying to get shot?" I felt like my heart had jumped out of my chest and landed in my mouth.

"Oh, great," he replied. "There goes my night vision."

"Sorry," I muttered. I dropped the beam out of his eyes, but it was still centered on his body.

"Are you going to spotlight me until someone shoots me? If that's the plan, I promise not to tell anyone how you handled this."

I switched the light off.

"I don't know you," he said, walking over to the door of room 110. "My name's Steve. Steve Dozier. I just came out of Laughlin." I watched him squat by the evidence, playing the beam of his light across. "Blood. And a lot of it. Shall we knock and find out what happened?"

"Think it's a four twenty?" I asked. I'd never had my own homicide scene. I'd been on a few, like the one a couple weeks before where a couple of dope dealers had shot it out. That had been a bitch. I stood over the murder weapon for three hours until the crime scene people came and took it away.

"Let's not jump to conclusions," he said. He pointed at the door. Steve waited for me to take a position on the other side, then knocked.

"Who's there?" The female voice was faint, sounding as though it were coming from another room altogether. In a motel like this — thin walls and all, it wouldn't have surprised me.

"Police," Steve called.

"Everything's fine."

"Come to the door."

"Everything's fine," she repeated, louder this time.

"Ma'am, open the door, now," he said.

"OK, give me a minute. I'm in the bathroom."

"God," I muttered, "She sure is making it seem like a homicide, isn't she? What'll the detectives think when they see the mess I've made of their scene? I'm a little worried about that, you know?"

"My concern, if I had one, would be for the victim. He could be inside, dead or hurt. If there is one," Steve said. He pointed down. "If we get in, try not to track up the carpet."

I had my body pressed against the wall. As far as I was concerned, reality would come when someone started shooting through the walls. The vest would take the body hits but even my hard skull might not stop a headshot. Steve had his gun out but it was down by his side. He had that experienced-officer manner, relaxed but vigilant. Stories of people screwing up crime scenes kept popping into my thoughts. Cops were funny. In many cases, they were more afraid of appearing stupid in front of their peers than they were of getting hurt. Steve rapped again, "Come on, lady. Open up. We don't have all night."

The light leaking through chinks in the blinds went out. I tensed, and Steve brought his gun up. There was no further noise.

"Open up or we're kicking the door in," Steve called.

"Jesus. I told you I was fine. I wish you'd go away," the woman's voice came from inches away.

"We can't leave. Just open the door, please. Now!"

The locks cycled and a face appeared at the crack. I could see the chain that kept the door from opening further was attached.

"Quit goofing around. Unhook it," Steve pointed at the chain with his gun.

Reluctantly, she did as he ordered. When it was open, she stood so we could see only partway in.

"What do you want?" she asked.

"I want you to get out of our way and tell me where he is," Steve said.

"Who?" I was a little confused until I saw her face and the thin trickle of blood that still leaked from her left nostril. Gently, Steve pushed the door open. He took her by the arm and tugged her towards us. When she was out, he placed her a few feet behind him. He reached into the apartment and turned on the light next to the door. With the added illumination, I now saw her nose was broken — not just broken, but mashed. I didn't think there was going to be a way to make it look like anything except what a boxer might have, unless she had a lot of money for a good plastic surgeon. I quick-peeked the apartment. From what I saw inside, that didn't seem likely.

"God," I said.

"Check the place. Be careful," Steve told me. I moved forward. He stepped behind me, but stopped. I knew he was keeping an eye on her as he covered me. As I moved inside, I saw her raise a rag, blood-soaked, and full of ice. She winced as she applied it to her nose.

"Control, Three Nora Thirty-four, roll medical to room 110. Tell them it looks like a broken nose," Steve radioed. Without taking his eyes off me or the place I was heading — the bathroom and closet, he asked, "What's your name?"

I could tell people had been living there for a while. The apartment was full of biker stuff: t-shirts, helmets, saddle bags, and at least one Harley-Davidson motorcycle lying in pieces all over the place. As I moved towards the walk-in closet and bathroom, I quickly checked the kitchen and beside the bed.

When I had jerked the shower curtain aside and saw no one there, I called, "Clear!" I came back into the living room. Steve had her sitting on the end of the bed.

"What's your name, again?" I asked.

"Rena," she replied. "Rena Lester." She looked at Steve. "I don't know where Charlie's gone."

"Did he do that to your face, Rena?" She began to cry softly. Steve found a clean towel and handed it to her.

"I don't want him arrested, again. He's already been twice. He got out of jail a month ago for this. The judge gave Charlie counseling. He also said he's running out of patience with my old man's shit. He said he was going to send him to prison the next time. Charlie won't make it there and . . . " she hesitated. "I love him. What would I do without him?"

"Same old story, different day," I muttered. I hated domestics. They were like those algebra equations that had an unpredictable variable — where the answer seemed like it could be anything. I knew the stories of how one party or the other, and sometimes both, turned on the cops. You expected that from the men who beat them up, but it was the women who really got my goat. That was because, one minute, we thought we were the knights in shining armor, coming to save the damsel in distress, and, the next, we were shooting her for trying to stick a knife in us. Before I got started on my usual tirade, Steve gave me a look that made me shut my mouth. I was miffed. Technically, I was the first officer on scene. He was the backup. This should have been my call and already he had put himself in charge. Still, I decided not to argue, not wanting to push my luck with the seniority issue.

"What happened tonight?" he asked.

"He had his *Avoiding Violence* counseling. It's part of that *Impulse Control* class. You know the one? He has to pay for it after the judge stipulated it," Rena said. I watched her dab at the blood. I couldn't believe that much liquid could still be leaking out of her. She should have been white as a fish's belly. The two towels were both saturated. "The class is taught by a psychologist. Charlie hates the guy's guts."

She hesitated, as if she talked too much.

"You're doing good," Steve said. "Tell me the rest."

For the first time, I really looked at her. She had to be thirty and, if it wasn't for the swelling, I saw she'd be pretty. I noticed a picture over her shoulder. It was an older guy, bearded, thinning hair to his shoulders. He looked to be late fifties, early sixties.

"Who's that? Your father?"

Rena glanced back, then shook her head. "That's not my father. That's Charlie." There was this stupid tone to her voice. It was love. I was disgusted. Steve cleared his throat. That brought her back to the conversation. "I hate those classes. Things were OK before he had to go. He'd slap me now and then but nothing serious. It was always my fault.

I'd say something stupid, like he was spending too much of my money or I liked him better when he was working. I always regretted it afterwards."

"I'll bet," I muttered.

Steve glared at me this time. "Can you get her another towel and then go see where that ambulance is? That nose should have stopped bleeding by now. I'm a little worried about it."

Jeez, I thought. *What am I now? His flunky?*

Still, I left. In the bathroom, I found another towel, then got ice from the freezer. Just as I got to the door, the ambulance pulled into the parking lot. The driver turned off the siren. It filled the parking lot with red and blue light. If that didn't wake a few people up, I didn't know what would. "They're here," I told them.

"Since he's been going to the shrink," Rena continued, "who most times pisses him off, he comes home and takes it out on me."

"Why stay?" Steve's voice was totally neutral. His patience impressed me. I'd have been yelling at her, already. She needed a shaking to get her brain working again. I just couldn't understand people like her. No one would ever lay a hand on me like that if I were a woman. I'd watched Mandy, a friend of my sister, go through this for years. The guy she lived with beat her. He beat her kids, the dog, and even the car once. One day, Mandy's father had enough of taking his daughter to the emergency room. He went over there and beat the living shit out of the guy, then before his daughter came home, he waited while the boyfriend packed his bags and left. I wondered if Mandy would ever forgive her father.

"So what happened tonight?" Steve asked. The paramedics came in — a male and female. I knew the female from the burglary call in IDA area. As the female paramedic inspected Rena's nose, she pulled on a pair of gloves. I couldn't help noticing she filled her uniform pants rather nicely.

"How *you* doing?" I asked. She gave me a look as though I was some kind of fungus. I grinned. She moved the woman's head.

"This is bad. It's broken." She tilted the victim's head. "What's your name?" she asked.

"Rena," Steve said. "I have all her information here." He showed her his notebook.

"Rena, I'm Karri May. You need to go in. When it finishes swelling, you won't be able to breathe," she said. "Does this hurt?" She touched it near the bridge.

"Ugh." Rena flinched. Karri May started doing medical things with ice packs and tape as I watched.

"Finish telling me what happened," Steve prodded.

"Tonight, Charlie came home. He seemed calm. Said he'd been forced to discuss his violent tendencies in front of the whole class. I could see he was upset, so I got him a shot and a beer. They got in a big argument," she said.

"They?"

"Him and the shrink. So, the security people were called. Before they got there, he left. Charlie thought that was pretty funny. He finished the drinks quick. I made him a Jack and Coke. He sat right there telling me about the argument. The more he talked, the madder he got. I tried to take his mind off things, but he didn't want to let it go. Before I knew it, he just got up and backhanded me." She bowed her head so that her hair fell around her face, like a curtain. She sobbed for a second, little drops falling on her t-shirt. They weren't tears. Karri May waited for her to get her composure.

"I'm sorry. He wasn't thinking. He didn't mean to do this," Rena continued.

"How many times did he hit you?"

"Only once. Hard. The others didn't hurt much."

"I think both your eyes are going to be black tomorrow," Steve said. Karri May nodded.

"I got dark glasses. They'll hardly show."

"Do you know where he might be?" Steve said.

"And would you even tell us?" I asked.

"Mr. Sensitivity," Karri May muttered.

"Nope. I mean . . . " Rena hesitated. We could see her thinking before she answered. "I don't know where he'd go. He knows the laws. Four hours. That's how long he has to stay away."

That's right, I thought. It meant we had to make the arrest within four hours and, if we didn't, a warrant had to be issued through the court system. I saw Rena had no desire for us to get him. Why should we care, either? I knew that if I told that story later, all the cops who heard it would think, *Let the bitch get the shit kicked out of her if she wasn't going to cooperate. Screw her and the shrinks who said she couldn't help herself.* The problem was — it wasn't about her. It was about us being hunters. We wanted to catch him and when we didn't, it was a failure on our part. The trick was to get her to give up enough info to set us on Charlie's path.

"I won't press charges against him," Rena said.

"He won't stop doing this," Steve argued. That was logic and it wasn't going to work. It never did.

"Come on. We're wasting our time. One of these nights, we'll be carting her body out of here," I said.

"No, you won't. He won't do this again. I just need to quit antagonizing him."

"Can you go get me the paperwork?" Steve asked me. I hesitated, thinking I didn't like to be ordered out in front of Karri May. "Please?"

I sighed. "Sure."

"Do you want to go to the hospital?" Karri May asked.

"No. I'll be alright."

"You need to go," Karri May said. "I'm going to get another ice pack. This officer is going to talk to you. You can change your mind." Karri May said on her way out.

I hurried to catch up. A fire department rescue unit had arrived. I waited while she talked to the rescue crew. She wanted them to help her convince the woman that going to the hospital was in her best interest. I bet it wasn't going to happen. As I looked at her, I kept thinking about when I saw Karri May at the burglary. I also thought about Sally. We were still seeing each other — tentatively. Her problems with her boyfriend, the sergeant, hadn't gotten better. We weren't at the messy stage where sex was happening. There had been several times I'd met her in the same park where she broke up with me. We talked for hours, comfortably, as only two people who have known each other for as long as we had could. Still, I was having my doubts — about whether I wanted to be with her; about whether I could make it work again, and even about whether I really wanted to spend any more time with her. Then there was the other side of the coin. Sometimes, I was sure it was only a matter of not wanting to be alone.

"Dating anyone?" I asked Karri May when she was done. I don't know where the breath to make the words came from. She gave me a blank look. I changed gears. "Listen, I'm sure you know how many of these calls I get. It's always the same. I'm not the bad guy here. I just don't have any patience with that stuff."

"Do you have any idea how many of those I get?" Karri May asked.

"Probably all of them from all of us cops."

"That's right. Let me ask you a question," she said. Before I could nod, she continued, "Do you have patience with anything? The woman's in love and there's no explaining love. What would you do if you were in her shoes?"

"I wouldn't be letting some asshole beat the piss out of me. I also wouldn't be beating the shit out of someone. That's not the way things are supposed to work. It's the same with people shooting each other or beating their kids or drinking and driving." I thought I'd gotten to her with that.

"I'm not interested in dating a cop. You guys are assholes. Always playing around. You're about as trustworthy as rattlesnakes."

"Experience, huh? Must have been bad."

"Something like that. I have work to do," she said. With that, she turned to go back to her unit.

"Will you have dinner with me?" When she turned, she had an incredulous look on her face.

"Are you always like this?" she asked.

"No. It's you." I stopped because it wasn't coming out right. "Look. I've seen you before and I wanted to talk to you then. I know I came across as a jerk in there, but that isn't me. Just give me a chance and you'll see."

She shook her head, then turned to go back to the ambulance. I stood watching her climb in. The light went out, casting her as a silhouette. I turned away.

"Hey!" Karri May's voice reached out to me, barely heard over the sound of the big diesel engine moving the vehicle forward. "Here's my number. One chance; don't waste it."

I hurried forward, catching the slip from her fingers as she was swept away. I went to my car and gathered the forms I needed. As I walked back into the apartment, I stepped in the blood again. "Motherfucker," I said. "How many times do I have to do that before I learn?"

Early the next morning, an hour after shift, I stood at the bedroom window watching the world wake up. The guy who lived next door to my house cursed his lawnmower as he pulled the starter cord over and over; kids lined up for the school bus, their young mothers looking on like old hens; and two people jogged by. All this made me remember it was my Thursday and the world's Friday. One more day and I would have my regular days off, or RDO. I intended going to bed soon. I held the slip of paper, which, up until a few hours ago, worried me more than its minuscule weight should have. The whole time I was driving — before I'd stopped at a 7-11 and stepped from my car, I kept wanting to touch it, but I was more afraid to — in case I dislodged it and it fell out. I might open the door and it would blow away or disappear under the seat. Once I had the note in my hand, I both copied the number to my notebook, and placed the original in my wallet. It was strange how something so small could make a person happy. Yet — like that tiny mustard seed the Bible talked about — be able to grow into something so large, it changed everything around it.

"That's some bright sunshine," I muttered. I thought about calling the number on the paper, but decided that was for later. Right then, I was happy — happier than I wanted to admit. I glanced at the answering machine. The light flashed from the message I left saved in the memory.

It let out the feeling underneath that happiness. I had the thought that, sooner or later, I needed to tell Sally we needed to say our goodbyes — let things go. I pulled the cord on the blinds, shutting away the other light.

■ ■ ■

Let Sleeping Dogs Lie . . .

I wanted to turn around and look back, to see if there was a line somewhere back there in the street, dividing the world into "their side" and "our side." On their side, was the real world — middle class, safe, and relatively well off. On our side was something else, something that became apparent as I watched the houses slide by — getting poorer, more dilapidated, changing to primary colors. I wondered why some people, those people in those houses, chose to live the way they did. To say the houses around us were run down was like saying a totaled car could still be driven. Many of them showed boarded up windows, no paint, and dilapidated swamp coolers on the roofs, that made an awful racket when they worked. These people didn't know air conditioning except when they went to the grocery store to buy junk food with government-issued food stamps. Yet, for all that, I thought, *There are people living here.*

There weren't many areas in Las Vegas as run down as The Side. In the thirties, the hotels needed workers. Instead of using the readily abundant supply of Mexicans, they decided white people would rather be waited on by blacks. So they came up with a plan. In furtherance of it, the major properties sent recruiters to Louisiana. The recruiters cast hooks baited with talk of great jobs in Las Vegas and the black farmers took it. The farms they worked were still really plantations, but had come to be referred to as corporate farms. It wasn't hard getting them to leave. After all, those people, whether they were called sharecroppers or self-employed, were still poor, little better off than they had been a hundred years before.

So many blacks left the area that the landowners around Tallulah demanded the sheriff keep the bus from coming into the town. He did, but that didn't prevent the people leaving. They hiked whatever distance they had to go to meet it, even if it meant the middle of the night in the middle of nowhere. That kept the exodus going.

For some, Vegas was the Promised Land. They were given jobs that paid more money than they'd ever seen, which by any standards other than theirs, was not a lot. Others found coming to Vegas an opportunity of getting away from the fields, being clean, and having their children get a shot at a better life.

For many of the stronger men, the promise proved to be a deception. When they arrived in Las Vegas, they found there weren't many jobs. They were encouraged to go on to LA, where they were given work in the aluminum casting plants that made lawn furniture and garden articles, such as furniture and lights. It was hot work. Still, it paid better than the fields.

"How hot you think it gets inside those places?" I asked Dan. It was one of those scorcher days. The temperature was up and getting near to setting a century record.

"I worked this area when I was days. I've been in a lot of them. It's murder. I don't know how these people do it."

Even the yards looked like murder. They were dirt or dying Bermuda grass yards. Bermuda grass is hard to kill. What I saw out that car window made me think time had stood still here. It was the same as it had been before — the same houses, the same poverty, the same accents, and the old people wearing the same threadbare clothing. This was what these people had ended up with, which was little better than it had been fifty or sixty years before.

"What you thinking?" Dan asked. He wasn't my regular partner.

"Not much." It wasn't true. I was trying to keep my mind on the DPA or directed patrol activity I'd been assigned to. It was supposed to last a week. My sarg, at the Ell Tee's insistence, thought that by assigning me to a special squad, I might get out of the doldrums I'd been experiencing. Lately, I hadn't felt like doing anything but driving around in circles. I wasn't doing car or pedestrian stops. I barely handled the calls given to me. I was lethargic. Graves was feast or famine, which meant long periods of nothing until that one fucked-up call came along — the one where the shit hit the fan. Those long periods in between were part of my problem. They'd lasted a month.

Karri May was the other part. Things were getting serious, at least, with me. I found myself wanting to spend all the time I could with her.

The day before, the Sarg called me into the station. When I walked into the briefing room, I found a pile of my clothing dumped in the middle of the floor. There were gym clothes, dirty uniforms, and, yes, underwear. The stuff had come out of my truck, or actually, Sally's truck, which was gone. She was supposed to have sold the truck to me because she couldn't afford it. What brought it on was that I'd told her the night before in TP's Bar, which was a favorite cop hangout, that I wasn't going to be her boyfriend. This happened just after she and her friends came in. They were tying one on for being fresh out of field training. We were celebrating, too. Our celebration was for a big drug bust, six pounds of speed taken in a random car stop. Both of us stayed at opposite ends of the room, but, before long, we were shitfaced. Then she had me back in a corner, trying to trade spit with me. I was fending off her hands, which meant trying to keep her from undoing my fly. After a minute's resistance on my part, she pushed away, holding me at arm's length.

"What's wrong?" she asked.

"I've decided I don't want to see you anymore," I said.

"What?" Her eyes were suddenly wild. "Are you seeing someone else?"

"Kinda. I'm not sure," I started. I was unsure. I realized I didn't know what I had with Karri May. We'd been on four or five dates, which always ended with a chaste goodnight kiss.

"You fucking asshole! After I broke up with Donnie for you." She tried to push me over, but she was too drunk. The thought of a fight, a domestic between us, scared me, which had the effect of ruining my drunk. I didn't want to feel sober. That, added to the thought of all the shit I'd gone through when she dumped me the first time, and started making me mad. Heck, once, when I was in the Academy, I thought I was going to fail a critical test because we had a terrible shouting match just before I left that morning, which made me so crazy I couldn't think straight. With all that in my head, I pushed past her.

"Where are you going, you shit?" I heard her start crying. Three of her friends made a beeline for her, glaring at me as they went by. I went out to my truck, her truck, and drove to my sister's. I must have been sober. I remember feeling everything — the night's hot wind, the smell of diesel exhaust from a semi, and the sound of those big sprinklers irrigating a school's soccer field. Brenda gave me the couch for the night and never asked a word. I'd probably have lost the truck that night if I'd gone home. Instead, she waited until the next day. Then in the station, I grabbed a plastic bag from the janitor's closet. I gathered all my things and stuck them in my locker.

With all the shit going on, Lieutenant Giles thought sending me to another area command for a few days would take my mind off things. This how I ended up working William, or The Side, as it was called. I still remembered some of the streets from my civilian ride-along days. The one we drove brought back memories of a cop in a patrol unit chasing a crook, who was on foot. The bad guy was dressed all in red silk. He had just robbed the local liquor store with a gun. I was in another unit that had just arrived. The first unit was driving across the grass in the park. As it came abreast of the runner, the officer opened the driver's door. It caught the guy square in the ass and legs, flattening him.

My thoughts returned to when we'd first driven into the area. What I knew was that whenever any of us worked here, we always thought how the area should have been written off long ago. The houses were beyond ever being brought within compliance of any housing code. The parks were so crime-infested that if the parents sent their kids there, they would surely come back as drug dealers, crackheads, or car thieves. Every now and then, Dan started telling a story about some house we passed. He pointed at a small, pink one.

"I went there for a seventeen-year-old girl who stuck a butcher knife in her boyfriend. He was cheating on her. When we arrived, we couldn't find the victim," Dan turned left. He pointed. "The guy was standing right there. One of the old women pointed him out. He was calm as you could want — the knife handle was sticking right out of him. He fought to keep from going to the hospital. Almost caused a riot because people, thought we were arresting him."

Stories like that were daily occurrences in these neighborhoods. Dan had a million of them, hardly any with happy endings. I was hot and bored. The air conditioner was going full blast, but with the windows down so we could hear outside noises, our uniforms stuck to our bodies. It was late summer. Our shift had started two hours before and we had four or five hours of daylight left. That meant it was going to stay over 105 degrees for quite a while. I knew the temperature wouldn't fall much below a 100 even after the sun set. We drove slowly, trying to get a feel for the neighborhood.

"I'd rather be riding a bike," Dan said. Now there was a job I wanted to get to, but not out here. I wanted to be Strip bikes. The women were gorgeous and the hotel security officers handled the majority of the crime. They caught 'em, the bike cops cleaned 'em.

"Me too, buddy. I need to figure how to make one of the teams. The Strip sarg is a tough nut to crack."

"What you really mean is Sergeant Smith is an asshole," Dan said. "He was my FTO straight out of the Academy. Talk about a guy who's got 'little man syndrome.' Heads up." He pointed his chin at a group of young black juves standing on a corner. As we drove by, the kids eye-fucked us. They used the same chilled attitudes that were normally reserved for rival gang members. "Crips," he said.

"Yep." I already knew this from all the blue they wore. Dan lifted a hand off the steering wheel in a laconic greeting. They made no move to acknowledge us, barely concealing their hatred. Truth be told, we thought they were the scum of the earth. There was nothing good about them. They preyed on the innocents in their community. They killed each other, which was good riddance. If we had a choice, we'd put all the rival gangs in a place with a lot of guns and let them sort it out then lock the survivors up for life.

"They ain't up to any good. I bet we'd get a gun and dope if we jacked 'em," I hinted. Dan ignored me.

"We ain't chasing people in this heat."

"Don't matter," I said, not pushing things. "You know we'll be back here later."

As we turned a corner, Dan saw a banger he knew. The kid was walking straight for where the Crips were hanging. It was a small neighborhood. He was wearing red, so if he kept walking for the half block, then turned the corner, he'd be right where the other guys hung out. He'd either be running or shooting for his life. "That's Ghost. He's a West Coast Blood. I think I saw a warrant with his name on it. Check the hot sheet."

"Act like we don't see him," I suggested, sarcastically. I took the stapled pages from under the visor. "What's his real name?"

"Jeffery Franklin Wells," Dan said. He released his seat belt the same time I did. "He got his street name from some skin condition that lightened his skin when he first became a teenager. If you take a stab at running 'Ghost' in the police computer, you'd discover there are quite a few. It's a popular street name. Not only are light skinned blacks called that, but street people also call mopes, that have the ability to fade when we're looking for them, Ghost, too."

I scanned the pages until I came to his entry. "Yeah, I got him," I said. I read the entry to see what the warrants were for. "Says no bail."

"That's what I thought," Dan said.

I put the sheets back under the visor. "So? I take it his name comes from the skin thing?"

"He's fast, too," Dan let the seat back a little. "Jeffery was all-star track at Rancho in his senior year. He was a class in front of me. People thought he'd go to the Olympics."

"What happened?"

"Drugs. What else?"

The situation called for something more than a typical pedestrian stop. Dan radioed Dispatch that we had a possible 440, which was the code for wanted person, and that he'd probably run. Other units in the area asked to be put on the call. When he finished, he gave the big cruiser gas, causing it to surge forward. A lot of Chevy cruiser characteristics caused us to refer to them as Orcas — their color: black and white; the fat body with its Trident sub look, a shape I heard was based on that of a killer whale; and its slow, heavy start when the driver first got on the gas. I preferred a Ford over the Chevy, but Dan's station was short of Fords. The one thing the Chevy cars had in common with the Fords was that when they accelerated, they both produced a distinctive noise from the high performance engine. It was unique, known to both the cops and criminals. Dan aimed the car as if he intended to run Ghost down, which was a technique we were taught in the Academy. It was supposed to cause a suspect to freeze — like that deer in the headlights thing. Ghost heard us coming. When he turned to look over his shoulder, I saw the fear on his face. I'd bet at first he thought he was about to become another victim of a drive-by. I unsnapped my gun and grabbed the door handle. What I intended to do was, as soon as the car stopped, to hop out and be on him.

The brakes locked and the car came to a screaming stop. I was happy to see the technique had the desired effect — Ghost stood frozen, his eyes showing whites all the way around. Sometimes, this technique worried me. There was always the possibility the brakes might not work, or even if they did, the driver hadn't noticed the water or oil or antifreeze on the street. Either way, the suspect was going to get smeared. In those times when we discussed the possibility, the conversation always ended with someone reciting those magic words, "So sad, too bad, shouldn't be doing the crime."

At the last second, just when I judged the car to have slowed enough, I pulled the door handle. The car's momentum threw it forward. When the recoil from the spring hinge bounced the door back, my foot was in place, keeping it from closing on me. I dropped the foot to the street, let the same momentum catapult my body forward, straight out of the car. Everything was working exactly as I wanted. I was moving toward Ghost faster than he thought possible. His face changed from terror to relief. For a second, I was sure his life had flashed before his eyes.

It seemed like the technique had served its purpose, for he didn't run. I was already thinking ahead; once I had him on the front of the car, I'd use the relief he felt at being alive to get him admit to something we didn't know.

I should have known this was delusional thinking. Because what I couldn't know was that in the past other cops had used this technique on Ghost. And something else, too — something I didn't know and Ghost did. Ghost had heard the word on the street that the gang unit was looking for him. He knew this because the night before, he'd shot a rival banger — one of the Pinu Boys, over in North Town. His second of hesitation was over. He ran like a rabbit. I was his greyhound. The last thing I heard from the car was Dan telling Dispatch I was in foot pursuit.

I followed Ghost between two houses, towards the back yards. In that neighborhood, everything — the sides, the backs, and the dirt lots between, everything — looked just like the fronts. Some of those yards contained an occasional lifeless tree surrounded by junked cars, washing machines, or nondescript machinery. Others had tufts of dead grass in a lot of tan dirt that was baked harder than concrete. People just didn't have money to waste on water. What separated the yards were chain link fences — the three-foot-tall kind.

Ghost was tall, six-foot-three. Drugs had kept him lean and muscular. He didn't run with short chopping steps like I did, but with graceful, gazelle-like strides. He also wasn't carrying twenty-five pounds of shit — vest, gun belt, gun, radio, extra ammunition, baton, and Capstun — on his person. I found myself wishing I'd left the station dressed like Ghost. I didn't mean all that red Blood clothing, but those long baggy shorts, tennis shoes, and tank top. I could do without my underwear showing or the five pounds of gold jewelry.

When Ghost went over fences, it was in hurdler style, indicative of his former track training. As tall as he was, he could have stepped over the fences. To get over, I used a method that amounted to placing my left hand on top of the horizontal support pipe, swinging my legs and torso out to the side, and landing on both feet. My method cost me time, took more energy, and let the distance between us grow. My advantage was that I was in better shape physically. Being a veteran of many pursuits by this time, they seemed as if they took a long time, but seldom did. This one was less than a minute in duration so far. I huffed. I wanted Ghost to veer towards the alley, which would take us away from the fences. Once there, I bet I could not only keep up but start closing some of Ghost's lead. The alley's street access could be used to box him in with responding units, which I heard coming.

He veered, just as though my guardian angel was listening and making things happen in my favor. Ghost hurdled one last fence, landing on the junk-littered dirt road. Once we were in the alley, just as I thought, I closed on him. It was eerie the way there were only the sounds of running feet, heavy breathing, and voices coming out of the radio. All that amplified off the flat backs of the silent houses. Within the tinny radio noise, I recognized Dan's voice as he called the location and direction of the pursuit. When I realized that he was with me, if not in person then in spirit, the nagging feeling of being alone disappeared. I gave a quick glance left — that was how I knew Dan was able to call the pursuit. He was paralleling us. He could catch glimpses of the two of us running from between the houses. Since I didn't need to call our direction, I shifted all my attention to running. I was close, within a few feet. I gathered a big burst of energy that I intended to use to close the distance. I just needed to get within arm's reach, then I'd shove him so that he'd trip and get fucked up enough I wouldn't have to fight him. Before I was ready, Ghost glanced quickly over a shoulder. He saw how close I was. Fear flashed across his face.

"Damn," Ghost breathed.

"Stop, Jeffrey," I said. I hoped me saying his name and everything else — the sound of the arriving police cars, my persistence, and the fatigue I guessed he felt, would finish this. For the first time, I saw people were outside watching. It was one of those things that I never understood. How did they know? How *could* they know what was happening outside their houses? It didn't matter whether it was day or night, rainy or sunny.

They appeared. It was like they were telepathic. It never failed to give me the jeepers.

As I ran past an old house, the owner watched us. She was an eighty-year-old lady, wearing a threadbare dress that probably never saw a better day. In her hand was a beat-up broom, mostly long stick and almost no bristle. She looked to be eighty or ninety pounds and almost as short as the stick she held. She stood on the broken back stoop, craning her neck as we came in sight. When Ghost appeared, she started jumping up and down, shaking her hands, one holding the broom, as if she was at church.

"Run, Jeffery. Run! The poe-lease is gonna catch you, boy. Run faster!"

Ghost looked back. I saw the white of his eyes showing all around the pupils. Down at the end of the alley, a black-and-white skidded so that it blocked the exit. *There goes Ghost's path*, I thought. Dan opened the driver side door, stepped out, and leveled a Remington 870 shotgun across the roof. He racked a round into the chamber, which seemed the loudest sound I could imagine. The sight of that gun and the sound of the racking round scared the shit out of me. I couldn't help thinking that if Dan fired, I might catch some of the double-aught buckshot.

"Stop, Ghost," I tried yelling. What came out didn't sound like English.

"Get on the ground," Dan yelled. Ghost had no intention of giving up so easily. He must have known Dan wouldn't shoot. He veered once again, straight towards the backyards on our right. I moaned. I would have taken thirty to one odds there wasn't a drop of water left in me. Ghost leapt the three-foot fence, heading straight for the raised back stoop. I followed. Going over the fence by vaulting it lost me what position I'd gained.

Oh, oh, I thought. *He's running for the house.* I had visions of hostage situations. What I didn't see, at first, was the dog. When I did, I realized it was a massive, 150-pound, black and tan rottwieler. It had found itself a little shade under the cover over the stoop. The dog, which I was sure was a male, was happily asleep and oblivious to all the goings-on. I thought for sure that Ghost hadn't seen the dog. I thought he was in for a rude shock.

I didn't think Ghost would do what he did. As soon as he was close to the stoop, he didn't leap up and try to open the door. Instead, Ghost cut sharply to the right and, as he passed the dog, he reached out and slapped the monster between the ears.

It took literally a second for the cobwebs to fall away and the pain to register. As an unconscious reaction, the dog's body jerked partially to its feet. Ghost had ten feet on me, which meant the dog was also ten feet from me. As it opened its eyes — I will swear this to my dying day — I saw a look of pure evil radiate forth. It was one of those defining moments, the kind where a person saw most of their whole life as it passed before his eyes as though from a great height and, at the same time, where a white boy ran at a madder-than-hell dog who must have had no other thought than to eat that white boy. Crazy!

If I wasn't about to be killed, I might have empathized with the animal, even commiserated that some fool had violated him.

"That's him, boy. Sic him," Ghost yelled.

The animal came off the porch like a rocket. The only thing I thought was how I wished I still had my gun out, but when we started going over the fences, I had no choice but to holster it. As the dog came, I was like a man shifting gears — trying to throw that car in reverse. I spun on one foot, ran for the fence, and jumped. Later, Dan swore he saw the whole thing. He said I cleared the fence with over two feet between me and the top, twirled in mid air, drew my duty weapon, and landed, running backwards. He said there never was a karate movie that had a move in it that looked like that.

I wasn't going to shoot the dog unless it cleared the fence, too. To my relief, as soon as it saw the intruder safely outside its yard, it stopped. It wasn't the type of dog to waste breath barking, either. It growled a warning at me, then went back to its sliver of shade. My heart slammed against my rib cage. I let a hand fall to my groin to make sure I hadn't peed my pants. When I got back to the car, I heard the arriving units hadn't set a perimeter. Ghost was long gone.

"Wow! That was a sight," Dan said.

"I'll bet."

"Damn, partner," Dan grinned. "Ya almost had him."

"Yeah and he . . . " I pointed. " . . . almost had me. Let's go." I opened the passenger side door, feeling the cold blast from the air conditioner. Dan climbed in, picked the mike from the seat and told Dispatch we were clearing. "Where to?"

"Grocery store," I said.

"You mean a convenience store?"

"No. I mean a grocery store. I'm buying that pooch the biggest steak they have. If I ever chase anyone through his yard again, I want that dog to remember me as a good guy."

"I can see that," Dan said. I looked at the houses.

"Seems like a waste having a dog like that guard the place," I said.

"It does," he agreed.

"In this part of town," I continued, wanting to put my thoughts in words, like the granny on her porch yelling for Ghost, "The only part of the population we might have a positive impact on is the animals. The people are way beyond saving."

"Maybe," Dan said. He didn't sound like he agreed.

That night, I had dinner with Karri May. I took her to the Italian restaurant in the Liberace Plaza. It was one of my favorite places in town. After the waiter brought my spaghetti, I sat slumped in my chair, winding it around a fork.

"I had this call last night," she said. Something in her voice made me look at her. She seemed a little lost. I sat up and held the fork like I was going to actually eat. "It came out as a suicide attempt. This guy had taken a shotgun and put it under his chin."

"Pull the trigger?"

"Yes. He did."

"Messy?"

"Kinda. It pissed me off, though."

"Really?" I couldn't imagine her being anything but patient with a hurt person.

"Yeah. The doc on the phone had asked me to check his pupils, so I got on the radio." I was listening to her story, yet I still wasn't paying all that much attention. I lifted the fork and tasted the food. She held her hand over her mouth like she was talking into a mike. "Please be informed patient is in downstairs living room, eyeballs are in upstairs bedroom."

I stared for a second. I couldn't believe her. I snorted. The laughter started. Ten seconds later and I was choking. I thought I was going to have spaghetti coming out my nose. The people at the next table got up.

"I got him," she said. "I'm a nurse."

For some reason, that cracked me up even further. With a tremendous effort, I forced myself to stop, then guzzled some of my wine. When I could sit, I had to put the napkin over my mouth to keep from starting again.

"No way," I said. "That didn't happen."

"Sure did. I wish I could take credit for it, but I can't. Happened to Eddie. You think me telling it was funny, get him to tell it sometime. He'll kill you." She stopped for a second. "Have things been bad out there lately?"

"No worse than usual," I said.

"We see the same things. When you need to, you can talk to me."

"I know."

"No. You don't, because you haven't been. You've been distant lately. I had that with the last guy I was with."

"I'm sorry," I said.

"Don't be. We'll pretend you didn't have a clue I could be your friend and now you know."

I played with my wine glass before I went on. "Do you know I like you?" I asked. "I think about you all the time. Sometimes, too much."

"I suspected and, now, I know." She stopped to play with her glass. It was like I started something. "I like you, too," she said. She leaned across the table and kissed me. The people at the next table applauded. I was beaming like a fool. It was a kiss and it wasn't even the end of the night.

■ ■ ■

Kaaaa-Booom . . .

When I got back from the TDY, I was told there was a slot opening up on Strip bikes. I had wanted to work there for a long time. The Strip, Las Vegas Boulevard from the Sahara Hotel to Sunset Road, was one of the most sought-after assignments on patrol. The bike teams worked the geographic boundaries that included a block or two on either side of the Strip. They were a necessity, because on holidays, the weekends, and certain other nights, when concerts or fights came to town, the Strip turned into a parking lot. If a cop had the bad luck to turn onto the Boulevard, as it was also referred to, and get his unit stuck in traffic, it was going to be there for a while, even if the emergency equipment was used. There just wasn't anywhere for cars to go except the major cross streets and a few hotel entrances.

For three weeks, I waited anxiously for the slot to open. The station's rumor mill had several of us being picked. Before taking off each day, I'd stop in the bike sergeant's office and ask where I stood.

"It's between you and another guy," Sergeant Smith would tell me. "I'm pushing for you, but the Ell Tee has his favorite." When we sat in briefing, I'd stare at his guys wearing those yellow polo shirts and black cargo shorts. That uniform set them apart. They were all white, tall, and young. To a man they had blond or light brown hair, blue eyes, and looked like they were pressed from a mold. I looked like I might have come from the same factory with my blond hair, blue eyes, and muscular build, but I was short. It was as though the factory had run out of stuff to fill the mold, so out popped me — a shorter version.

One day, just after briefing, Stan, the one who was leaving bikes, pulled me aside. "Do you know what's going on?"

"With what?" I asked.

"The bike slot."

"It's supposed to be between me and someone else."

"Is that what Smith told you?"

"Yeah. Just a few minutes ago."

"He's lying," Stan said. He went on to explain that Sergeant Smith had been doing that for a while. Stan said Smith had his own ideas for the squad he was building and those ideas would have worked well in 1939 Germany. He pulled the shotgun from the car and ejected all the rounds, as we always did at the beginning of a shift to make sure it was loaded properly. As he started putting them back, he continued. "He's been trying to keep you off since day one. He's been telling the captain you're a loose cannon. The truth is, you don't fit the image he wants a bike officer to have."

"Shit!" I took a deep breath. This was disturbing information and I didn't know Stan's intention telling me this.

"Watch your back, Cam," Stan said. I thought of how the week before, he'd been chasing a guy on a bike. During the pursuit, Stan drove the marked unit through the open exit gates at a high rate of speed. I was already inside the complex and I could have picked the guy up and continued the pursuit, but Stan was never one to let someone else take his glory. There was the sound of four loud pops. I never understood how he missed the huge sign that said, *Danger! Wrong way. Severe tire damage will result* or if he just figured his tires were impervious to punctures.

Later that evening, I got a message on the car's computer that Smith had chosen another guy who was halfway down the list. Shortly after, the computer beeped every few minutes as people sent AMs back and forth. As I read them, it became clear that a war was brewing between Smith and the Ell Tee. At eleven thirty, Dispatch sent me to the station. When I walked in, Smith was waiting.

"Tomorrow, go to supply and draw bike uniforms," he said. "There's a forty-hour bike school starts Monday. You're in it. Only after you've passed will you fill the open slot." He did not sound like a happy man.

On the other hand, I was so excited I could have bounced out of there. What I didn't know was that Smith's war with the Ell Tee had been fought in the hours since the messages started. Smith had posted the new roster with the name of the man who was sixth down at the top. Lieutenant Giles walked in, ripped the sheet off the wall and called Smith into his office. People said there was a lot of shouting, most of it the Ell Tee's. When Smith left the office, I had the slot.

Later, if I'd looked at some of the things that happened during the bike school, I'd have understood how much he wanted me gone. That school wasn't about making me a better officer, but about getting me to quit, and go back to my regular squad. Smith was constantly on my ass, mainly trying either to discourage or bounce me. He made me ride the obstacle course over and over. He chose the bike I had to use, which had slicks. While I rode down the hill on sidewalks that were wet, he yelled at me. I wrecked. My knees looked like raw hamburger. No matter how hard I tried, I was always marginal. I had to ride between the poles at the Convention Center as slowly as possible and never touch one of them. He berated me because the other guys were able to go faster.

Then there were the stairs — everyone had to be able to ride down a set. I was last to go and for some reason, we ran out of time. I was told I'd be first the next morning, but the set we'd used the day before were closed. They took me to the ones by the baseball field. They were twice as high, and curved. The first three times, it was all I could do to keep from getting killed. I crashed, time after time. The only good thing was that each time I looked up — the Ell Tee was there. From that point on, Smith was careful. One of the guys took me aside and said Smith had made the lieutenant's shit list again. I asked around, but no one knew what had happened, so it stayed a mystery. Finally, I could say one thing about his fucking with me, the new guy, I was ending up a better bike officer than any of the others. With Smith, it didn't make any difference.

For me, the important thing was that I passed in the end. Graduation was held on Friday. I started Saturday afternoon.

It was two o'clock in the afternoon and we were on our way to the third call of the shift. It was a bomb threat at a Strip hotel. I was riding with Arnie, who was to be my regular partner. The day was hot and we weren't in a hurry to get there. Bike officers always rode in pairs. This was a policy designed by Smith because we didn't have a car body to protect us when we made car stops or pedestrian contacts.

Arnie was OK, but the man drove me crazy. The first call we responded to was a car accident. He insisted on filling every box on the report, even though it had nothing to do with what happened. What should have taken ten minutes took an hour.

"I can't believe Smith did this to me," he bitched. It had to be the eighth time I'd heard this. "I had shit to do and he gives me the FNG."

"Jesus, Arnie. Will you shut the fuck up?" I asked. Then feeling guilty, "Can you lay off? If I'd known you were going to complain so much, I'd have taken a unit out. Everybody had shit to do. You were the unlucky one and you got stuck with me. Suck it up."

"Well, my wife had tickets to a show tonight. I was promised an EO"

When I worked for other sergeants, Early Outs were usually given halfway through a shift, not ten minutes into one. While we were in the bike office down at the Convention Center, the guys on my new squad said Smith was good for time off. He carried people on shift by telling Dispatch they were doing something for him, like repairing bikes or scouting training locations. In this way, he kept them from being dispatched. His people went home or did personal business, which was called PBs. I was happy to hear this. Many times Karri May was given time off because other people wanted or needed to get hours to keep their paramedic certification. If that happened, I could ask for and, maybe, get the same hours off. The way things had been, I never seemed able to find enough time to be with her. Still, Smith's way of giving people time worried me.

"Isn't it a little risky letting people go home, but keeping them on? What if someone has a problem, like a car accident with their chippy?"

"Listen, asshole," Arnie said. "Be careful who hears you ask those questions. Smith takes care of us. You don't burn vacation or sick time with him. If you got a chippy, he makes sure your wife don't know. You need to learn to watch your mouth."

"You see anyone else here but us? I'm just asking how this works."

"Well, don't ask. I can see already you're going to be a problem."

I pulled my bike a little ahead of Arnie's. When my front tire was just in front, I cut in front of his, hitting my front brake. He applied his brakes, running into me. I almost laughed when he barely got both feet on the ground before he stopped.

"Fuck! You trying to wreck me?" he yelled. I gripped his handlebars, keeping him from moving. "I'm still new, but not that new. I know what it takes to do this job. I've been careful to work hard and learn how things go. The only problem you'll have with me is if you don't get my back. If that happens, I'll make sure you'll get what's coming to you. Got it?"

He jerked his bike from under my hands. Without looking back, he quickly peddled away. From then on, we rode in silence. The late afternoon heat beat the concrete, reflecting back at us. I felt the sweat dry before it could cool me, leaving a crust of salt on my skin. My first day and my face was red as a tomato, in spite of the ball cap. I thought about what was happening with the bomb threat at the casino. I'd been on these calls before when the bike units had been tied up with other things. Now that I knew the lay of the land, I wondered if they'd been off fucking around when I was covering their calls.

The call concerned some idiot losing money, getting angry and, afterwards, deciding to get even with a telephone and a fake bomb threat. Most of the time, we never had a clue who the perp was, but we did catch a few. Bomb calls were a constant with the casinos. They were bogus ninety-nine percent of the time. The problem was on that one occasion, when the call was for real, as it had been at Harrah's in Lake Tahoe. The hotel had been the recipient of a threat and, when no one took it seriously, had suffered extensive damage in the subsequent blast. The incident insured the police never ignored a call thereafter.

The manner in which such calls were received varied: notes, letters, e-mail, and the easiest method, telephonically. It happened so often there were procedures in place for handling all the communication methods. One set concerned a threat called into Metrocomm, the police dispatch center. There were rules that had to be followed by the call-taker so intel could be gathered and passed to the field units. Other procedures, the civilian ones, laid out the way calls were made directly to the hotels and handled by the arriving units. The hotel personnel, either security or the PBX operators, were specifically trained by corporate policy, which was often based on police procedure. Either way, the idea was to get as much information as possible.

That's part of the reason we were so pissed off. We were being sent without knowing anything. We didn't know if we were arriving on a suspected or actual device. We didn't even know what doors we were supposed to be at. That could make a big difference. For instance, if a guy was in the casino with something strapped to his body, we wanted to be there, not down at the security office. If there was an actual device or something that looked like it was one, the decisions about what was to be done shifted to the Federal Bureau of Alcohol, Tobacco, and Firearms, and the fire department bomb team. They would advise us how big an area they wanted cleared. If the caller gave no specific information to believe there was an actual device, the decisions fell on the casino or hotel as to whether they wanted to shut down and evacuate. The police might help search the premises, although many times, we simply stood by while security officers did that.

As soon as we got to the west doors, the chief of security, Jim Robinson, flanked by a couple of supervisors, approached. I knew he was a retired Metro homicide cop because I spent an hour in his upper floor office a few months back just listening to cop stories. Like a lot of old-time cops, his sense of humor was as dry as the desert. I was supposed to be investigating an alleged room burglary where a high roller claimed the maids took his Rolex and fifty large. Chief Robinson thought the call was bullshit. The night before, the guy lost a couple hundred thousand on the tables. His bet, and mine, too, was that the guy was trying to get a comp marker out of the casino so he could take his chances at getting even.

"I'm sure my dispatch told you what's up, Cam." I felt flattered he remembered me.

"Nope! Details were scarce in coming. Dispatch couldn't get anyone from your office on the line."

He pulled his lapel mike to his mouth, "One to Control." There was nothing on the air but static. "One to Control." Still nothing. "Larry, go down there and find out what's wrong. If she left her post, suspend her on the spot. I'll fire the bitch myself as soon as we get this in check."

Larry ran off. For the first time, I noticed there was a perimeter of blue-uniformed security officers standing around. They eyed the crowd like some crazy was going to rush them. I was reminded that many of the Vegas casinos had security staffs larger than eighty percent of the real police departments in America. All Chief Robinson's officers carried guns. His staff drove marked units and he had plainclothes investigators whose job it was to act in the same capacity as police detectives. Robinson told me the day I was in his office that he'd spent the last fifteen of his twenty-five years waking up with the dead and putting them to bed. A day had come when he'd had enough. He took the job as the hotel's security chief and never doubted his decision. I looked at the paunch he'd grown, the liver spots on his head, and the slight tremor in his hands, knowing that, when I retired, I was going to an island. I'd watch waves come in, one after another, endlessly, and, if I had a wife, she could grow as fat as she wanted.

"Perhaps you two can chitchat later," Arnie said. "Why're we here?" He pushed his bike in front of mine. I loved the look Robinson gave him. He turned his back and another supervisor who wore a nametag that said "Joe" stepped forward.

"We had a white male adult come inside," Joe said. "He went to a blackjack table, where he started playing. He's carrying a case...blue plastic," he used his hands to indicate something eight by twelve inches square. When he saw we had the idea, he held his finger and thumb apart an inch and a half. "This thick. There's clear plastic on the top.

Like a window. The dealer says he saw a watch with some coiled wire inside. We had surveillance put a camera on it after we figured out what was going on. There is a wire leading deeper into the case. The watch is resting on something gray and there seems to be lots of little pieces of metal imbedded in the gray stuff. When the dealer asked the guy what's up with the box, the guy tells him it's a bomb."

"Wow! An actual?" Arnie said.

Joe ignored him, looking at me. He continued, "The guy's still there. The dealer says he said when he loses all his money, he's going to set the thing off." Joe glanced at his boss, who nodded. "The way it started for us was that surveillance sees the dealer takes a hit when he's got twenty showing."

"What?" Arnie asked. Joe stopped and looked at Arnie. We both could see that Arnie didn't understand.

"Arnie, did you ever play twenty-one?" I said.

"No. I'm a Mormon. I wouldn't even go in these places except I have to for this job."

"Oh," Joe replied. "Well, the dealer should have stood. Instead, he busts. He pays the guy. Now, my people have seen cheating, but this is going a little far. Casey, the camera guy, watches the next hand. The dealer draws a blackjack and manages to split the ace and jack and bust both hands. Casey calls Fred, his boss, over, and they watch this go on hand after hand. The guy's pile of chips is growing. This is the first time they've seen blackjack played like this, so their interest is piqued, to say the least."

"That means they're interested," I cut in.

"I know what it means," Arnie said.

"Just checking."

Joe winked at me. "If you two need a minute, I can go away, then come back and finish the story. Oh, but then the casino might not be here."

"Sorry," I muttered, acting sorry. I winked back.

"They tell me later they are considering all kinds of scenarios where the guy is a friend of the dealer's and that the dealer is cheating for him, but this is all a little confusing. That's because no one has ever seen cheating like this. It's not the usual type."

"Usual?" I asked.

"You know, subtle and sophisticated types," Joe said.

"So, what happened next? Is the guy still in there?" Arnie asked.

"I'm getting there. The dealer loses and loses. He's sweating a storm. Surveillance calls the pit boss, Sam. They tell him he needs to check out his dealer on eighteen. He does. He's also astounded. And quite confused. Finally, Sam can't stand it any longer. He calls over another dealer, intending to replace the original guy. We have four of my officers ready to take both guys into custody. I'm wondering if the dealer is on drugs. He's sweating like a pig. When Sam taps the dealer on the shoulder, the guy almost comes out of his skin. Sam says the other dealer is to take over, but the customer shakes his head. He tells Sam that the original dealer is to stay. They start arguing, then the dealer leans over and whispers to Sam. You should have seen him. He turned white. Sam went to the phone and let us know what was happening and we called you."

"What're you doing now?" I asked.

"Well, Cam. You know we know what to do in cases like this. We turned off our radios and cell phones, just in case the thing can be radio activated. We don't want to get the guy upset. I had my people pull back. Several drinks were taken over to him."

"Did you think that's a good idea? What if he gets drunk and decides to set the thing off?"

"We didn't think of that," Joe said. "It shouldn't matter, he isn't drinking much anyway. All he seems to want is to gamble and win. We don't want a panic. Do you guys have any idea what you're going to do?"

"Seal the room. Keep people from going in."

"We did that. As a matter of fact, we're trying to get people to leave. I had a couple of officers go through and offer people free comps to the restaurants and shows. It cleared better than half the tourists out. Some people just won't leave no matter what we offer."

"Isn't that the main casino area?"

"Yes, it is. Now, you see what some of the problem is."

I did, too. There were a lot of people in there. They could keep people from going in, but short of announcing an evacuation, there was no way to get all the people out. Telling people they couldn't gamble was sure to attract attention. We might have a three-ring circus here soon if the media got wind of the goings on. That was a problem we didn't need to worry about, but the hotel did. If people thought they were unsafe, they'd check out and go elsewhere.

"What else have you done?" This time I asked Robinson.

"We've been sending dealers on breaks, getting them out of the way, too. I wish I could get all those people out of there, but..." the chief shrugged.

Joe, who had gone to check on the dispatcher, rushed up. "Hey, Chief. The guy's gathering his chips, like he's going to leave."

Arnie used the radio to call the sarg. I heard him say he would be with us in a minute.

"What was going on with Dispatch," Robinson asked Joe.

"She thought when you said no radio or phones, that meant her. She unplugged everything."

"She's fired just as soon as we get this under control." He switched channels on the radio, "One to Sky."

"Go ahead, One. This is Fred."

"What's he doing now?"

"He had the pit boss cash his chips in. Now he's asking for tokens. It looks like he moved to progressive slots." There's a pause. "The guy's made himself at home in front of a dollar machine."

Sergeant Smith pulled up in a black-and-white. He parked on the curb.

"Jesus," I muttered. The only thing else wrong he could have done was use the siren. He had Lenny, the most senior guy on the squad, in the car with him.

"What's going on?" Smith said. I watched Robinson take him by the elbow, leading him over to brief him. When they were done, Sergeant Smith came back to where we waited.

"Let's see what we've got," Smith said.

"We can go up to the surveillance room through that door," Robinson said. He pointed towards a set of double doors.

"No. I mean *see* what he's doing," Smith said. He pushed his glasses up onto his nose. "Like walk by the guy."

"Ohhh," the Chief hesitated a moment. "Are you sure that's a good idea?"

Without replying, Smith turned to Lenny. "Get the rest of the guys down here." He then waved at Arnie and me. "Let's go."

"In there? Sarg, we're in uniform," Arnie said.

"No shit. Is that what all that bright yellow is? Get your ass going, Arnie."

"I ain't going in there."

Smith stopped. "I didn't say I wanted you to go all the way in, just *to* where I can signal you in case I need you for something."

"Oh. You mean like right inside the door?"

"No. I mean right where I tell you to stop," Smith made his voice whiny like Arnie's. I didn't say anything. It was my first day, and I'd had nothing but problems with Smith and I didn't need more. But it was one really stupid idea.

We started inside. When we got through the doors, I saw there were still a lot of people in the casino. Smith walked to where a security officer stood. He said something to the guy, who pointed. I looked. The guy sat at a video poker machine. He carelessly fed tokens in with his left hand, then poked at the buttons, choosing the cards he wanted to keep. His eyes were fixed on the screen, oblivious to anything around him. His right hand sat protectively on top of the blue case, which he had sitting on his right leg. The sarg stared at him for a few seconds.

I heard something behind me and turned to see Chief Robinson at my elbow. He shrugged. "My casino. I figured I better be on the tape in here or I might be looking for another job."

When Smith came back to us, he crossed his arms, putting his chin in his palm. He stayed like that for a bit. We waited. I was fidgety, something I do when I'm worried. The guy could look up and see us, then what might he do?

"Here's what we're going to do," Smith started.

"Call SWAT," Arnie cut him off. I almost smiled at the hope I heard in his voice.

"No. We can deal with this," Smith said. He wasn't looking at either of us. If anything, his eyes had that thousand-yard stare I was used to with vagrant vets who'd been in Vietnam. I didn't like it. I liked Arnie's idea better. I'd heard stories about Smith and if half of them were true, the man shouldn't have been a cop. He looked at the two of us. "I say we can deal with this. First off, time is of the essence. The place is chock full of tourists and I don't want to start a panic."

"I like to hear that," Robinson said.

"Don't worry, Jimmy. I'll make sure you keep your cush-ass job."

"Maybe Lenny can come in and spell me. I ain't feeling too good," Arnie said. I glanced at him. He was really pale.

"Sarg," I said. "Maybe we better get someone in here that has some balls."

"Fuck you, Cam," Arnie said. "I didn't sign up to get my ass blown all over the place."

"Shut the fuck up, you two. You're in this till it's done, Arnie. What we're going to do is walk up behind the guy. You guys are going to grab his arms and I'm going to grab that box."

"What?" Arnie's eyes actually started jittering in his head. I thought that only happened in cartoons.

"When I have the case, I'm going to run. Jimmy," he said as he looked at the Chief, "have a couple of your guys hold those double doors open. I'm heading for that hall. That way, if this guy has some type of remote detonator, I might be able to get far enough away that it won't work. I intend to keep going until I'm in the parking lot. We'll have the bomb people come out and deal with it there. Your job is to make sure he doesn't get his hands on anything in his pockets or on that belt. Come here." Smith took us closer. "See? He has three or four beepers. One of those could be a remote."

My thought was that Smith was either out of his mind or trying to earn himself the department's coveted Medal of Honor. Maybe both.

It was true though that if you had that medal, you were pretty much guaranteed promotion. The rumor mill had Smith shooting for a slot on the lieutenant's list.

"That's a plan? Why don't you just shoot the guy?" Chief Robinson asked.

Smith ignored him. "Come on, people, we have a time critical situation here. What if this nut decides to detonate that thing? People are going to get hurt."

"Sarg, we don't know what that thing is," Arnie said.

"Doesn't matter. I want to get this over with."

Before the Ell Tee gets here, I thought. There was no way he'd put up with this crazy shit. But I wasn't complaining. I needed to fit in here. I wanted this bike slot.

"I'll be up in surveillance. I'll have them rolling tape," the Chief said. He went to where his supervisors waited. As we started moving, I felt conspicuous. After all, there weren't a bunch of other people wearing bright yellow shirts with guns on their hips. Still, he might not know we weren't regular security. Several people glanced our way as we moved through the area, but being Vegas, the craps and card games were more important. As I followed Smith, Arnie walked next to me.

Arnie caught my eye. "See you in Hell."

Oh, so now you're on my side, I thought.

"No, you won't," I replied. "I'm going to heaven. We work for God. Remember, fool?"

Smith planned our route to come up behind the guy. The slot machines made the little noises that were supposed to attract people, which masked our approach. I have to admit, it worked like he said it would. We came to within five feet of him and he never looked around. I had this urge, like when you're a kid, to start giggling.

Smith yelled, "NOW!"

The shout almost caused my heart to stop. Smith grabbed the case and I got the left arm. Arnie missed his target. As Smith started moving away, I saw a wire leading to the guy's wrist. I started to yell, but before I could make a sound, it popped off. The guy reached down, like he was going for something on his belt. I hit him in the side of the head as hard as I could. He was struggling, which pulled me off balance. The blow glanced off. Smith ran. I kept expecting to hear a boom. I didn't really care as long as he managed to get far enough away from us.

The blow was enough to let Arnie get the arm he'd missed. We jerked him to the floor, where the fight was on. I looked up in time to see Smith going through the double doors. There were three young security officers who were supposed to open the doors. They scattered like leaves in the wind at his approach. *Smart guys*, I thought.

Arnie couldn't get the guy's other arm under control. He managed to snag the guy's shirt near his bicep, which was not the best place. The guy flailed, hitting both of us. I got a knee on his hand and hit him again. It was like my punch had no effect. The guy didn't look all that tough.

"Stop resisting," I tried yelling. He got the arm loose and slapped me.

"Motherfucker!" I hit him twice. Both were hard, with the second splitting his eyebrow open. As I pulled back my fist, intending to throw a really good punch, Arnie tried punching him. The guy jerked me forward, so I got hit instead.

"Sorry," Arnie muttered. He yelled, "Stop resisting!"

I felt like saying I wasn't. The fight drew a crowd. I felt this concern about what people would say later, especially if the guy was really injured. I started giving a lot of verbal commands, in spite of the fact I was having a hard time breathing. But yelling at him only drove him into a frenzy. My patience was running out. I tried getting to the Capstun behind my back. Arnie hit him again. Then he missed again. This time he cracked me in the jaw so hard I saw stars. One more punch like that and I wasn't sure if I could stay conscious. It seemed like a million years had passed since Smith ran off. He should be in the parking lot by then, I figured.

John, another cop from our squad, pushed through the crowd. He ran up and leapt into the air. He came down with his knees in the middle of the guy's back, knocking me aside. I heard air rush out. Before I could get up, John wrapped an arm around the guy's neck and used a lateral vascular neck restraint technique.

"He's choking that poor man, dear," a lady said to her husband.

"*It's not a choke,*" I wanted to yell. "It's the *LVNR*." It looked like a chokehold, but really wasn't. The guy bucked, but finally, his eyes rolled up into his head and he stopped struggling. They got off of him so they could place him in handcuffs. By then, the rest of the bike team arrived. They heaved the guy to his feet and stripped everything off his belt and out of his pockets. As they removed the items, they threw them in a corner. I rolled to my stomach, then pushed to my knees. I touched my eye. I bet it was already turning black.

"Where were you guys a minute ago?" Arnie asked.

"Over there," someone said. "Waiting to see if you would go BOOM."

Several security officers collected the items that were thrown, depositing them into a plastic evidence bag. From what seemed like a mile away, we heard a cell ringing. I watched a security officer reach in and take it out. Before anyone could say anything, he answered it.

"It's his mother," he said, holding the phone towards me.

"Tell her we'll get back to her," I replied. As I got to my feet, the crowd began clapping. They probably thought we were filming a movie. It was then the pit boss called, "Show's over, folks. Place your bets. Place your bets." People drifted towards the tables. We dragged the guy to the double doors. When we arrived at the security office, I saw the case he had carried open on a table. Smith was in the room. We pushed the suspect in a chair, where he remained hunched over. He looked bad. Arnie looked accusingly at Smith.

"What?" Smith said. "I was running. It slipped out of my hands and broke open. Scared the shit out of me."

"I'll bet," I said. "Anyone call medical?" I asked. I used a finger to push the objects from the case around the table. The box had been filled with all kinds of funny looking things, like a wristband, wires, sockets, and wrenches. The whole lot had been embedded in gray foam, which was designed to keep them in their places. I knew what they were from my days in the military. This stuff was used to open electronic modules.

"Don't worry about it," Smith said as Karri May came in.

"I should have known this would involve you," she said. She glanced at my head, a look of concern about her eyes. I shook it, making me see more stars. "Him? He do that to you?" She asked. I shook my head. She tilted her head at the bad guy like she was considering not treating him.

"Nope. Guy barely hit me. This was caused by my partners." I pointed at my eye. "Perhaps I need some personal attention."

"I'll say. A shrink would be my guess."

I moved close so she was the only one who could hear. "I have to admit, even your smirk is cute."

"Unfortunately," she said, "he has to get looked at first."

"Good," I came back. "Then I'll think about letting you treat me."

"Letting me. I'll let that big burly partner have a go at you." She went to the guy and lifted his head.

"Perhaps you love birds can do this later," Smith said. "Anybody search him? I mean really search him?"

"Why? Were we supposed to?" John said.

"Funny. Where's his stuff?"

"I . . . need . . . my . . . inhaler," the suspect wheezed.

I pointed at the bag one of the security officers held. Karri May took it, fished out an inhaler. She read the label. When she finished, she said, "Asthma?"

He nodded. She put the plastic piece in his mouth and pressed. After a minute, the medicine worked.

"It was in my pocket," he said. "I was only trying to get it out when those cops tried to kill me. I think my ribs are broken." He started wheezing again. She gave him another blast. When he settled down, she turned to me.

"Want me to take a look at that eye?"

"Is there anything else you can do for me except tell me to put an icepack or steak on it? Speaking of steak, dinner tonight?"

"Sure. What time you getting off?" she asked. I glanced at Smith.

"Late," he said. Then he went across the room.

"He's an asshole, but he's still the boss," I whispered. As the words came out, I glanced at the video camera, hoping the audio didn't pick it up. She began gathering her things. I looked across the room where the sarg was on the phone.

The suspect called to Smith, "Why am I being arrested? What's this all about? Why was I abused, assaulted and battered?"

Smith took the phone from his ear, "Did you threaten to blow the place up?"

"Has he been Mirandized?" I asked. Without waiting for an answer, I pulled the card out and read the words to him. "Understand?" I asked.

He nodded. "I was only joking. There wasn't a bomb. Look! You can see it was just tools in the box. Jesus, I have a Ph.D. in computer engineering."

"That means you've taken a whole bunch of math, doesn't it?" Smith said.

"Of course." He said. He put a look of superiority on his face. "Do you think you can get a Ph.D. in engineering without math?"

"Don't know, don't care," Smith answered. "But in that case, what'd you think when the dealer split an ace and jack, then drew until he busted?" The guy eyed Smith for a second. "It's on video tape." Smith pointed at a camera.

"Hell," the guy said. "I thought that was the way they played in Vegas. Everyone knows anything goes here."

I left the two of them to argue so I could walk Karri May to the ambulance.

"We eat in an hour. If you want to join me, we'll be at the Barbary Coast. Chinese food tonight."

"No," she said. "You don't need any more problems with that man. Call me when you get off."

"OK." I watched her drive away.

"Nice chippy," Arnie said. I hadn't heard him come up behind me.

"Don't call her that," I said. Why was it that anything most of the guys on my squad said to me made me angry?

"Ewwww! Are we in love?"

"Grow up, dude." I turned to get my bike. I pushed the anger down inside, I wanted to bury it deep. In police work, all it took was a second's loss of control with one person and someone else got their ass kicked.

■ ■ ■

But Officer, It Was a Real Gun . . .

After three months on Smith's squad, things were no better. He gave me the shit details. When my new partner, Ryan, and I were first to arrive on a jumper call at Circus Circus, he sent us off to take care of calls for service. The rest of the squad set the perimeter and were portrayed on the evening news as heroes.

It wasn't that I wanted the accolades. I wanted the work. I was in the job for the excitement and variety. Those little instances where people did things out of the ordinary were the situations cops lived for.

Ryan was another of the lieutenant's additions to the squad. He was overweight, which made him slow. He smoked, which Smith hated more than anything else. That caused Smith to hound Ryan. I watched Smith make Ryan dump his pockets to show he had no cigarettes as if the man was a criminal. Smith ordered us not to be seen smoking in public. He also tried putting Ryan on a diet. When the Ell Tee found out, he put the quash on both the smoking ban and anything that had to do with personal appearance unless it affected the job or went against policy. He told Smith he'd have his stripes if the harassment didn't stop.

It was constant war between the two supervisors, not to mention Smith and Ryan. I didn't mind that I caught some of the flack, especially when it kept Smith off Ryan's back. Lieutenant Giles backed me when Smith got on my case in public. I hated Smith and there were times I couldn't let the feeling go. I would ride down the street obsessed with something he'd done, such as correcting a report I knew was fine. I mulled the incident over so much I'd miss a car making an illegal turn or some person whose demeanor cried out to be stopped for questioning. Ryan knew what was going on. He'd speed up, ride towards me until he slammed on his brakes, then put both hands on my handle bars just as he knew I'd done to Arnie. It was our little joke, intended to make me think. One day I was really pissed because Smith had given me a dressing down for not cleaning my bike before I went on the street.

"Dude, let it go. Don't let that fool make you like this," he said while looking me directly in the eyes. I'd do what he told me and off we'd go.

I liked being a bike cop. It took just a little craziness. The regular patrol officers drove around in air-conditioned comfort when it was 110 degrees outside. They also had all that metal and glass around them when things went to shit. If they needed to get somewhere fast, they stepped on the gas pedal. We pedaled.

It was one of those afternoons in early August. Ryan and I were at Wet N Wild. Every time I was there, I marveled at the vision of a man like Bill Bennett, the owner of the Sahara Hotel, who came up with the idea of a water park in the desert. I also marveled at string bikinis. Hanging out in places like that was part of what made bike patrol a sought after assignment. We were stationed near the front entrance. In our conspicuous uniforms, we attracted quite a few good looking women, who'd come up to flirt with us. Several dropped hints about where they might be found later that evening. Even when I wasn't interested, I enjoyed the attention.

"You know if Smith catches us here, he'll have our asses? We'll be taking pictures in front of the Stardust," Ryan said. The shift started with him spending a half hour in Smith's office, getting his quarterly performance review. When Ryan had come out, he hadn't looked happy and he wouldn't talk about what was said.

"Oh, yeah. Ruin it for me," I said. I laughed.

"What's so funny?"

"That fucking tourist, who took your gun. I wish I could get the tape to show you what your face looked like." I watched Ryan's hand drop to the triple retention holster he wore. It was new, not a scratch in the plastic yet. The incident I was laughing about had taken place one afternoon right after the junket busses pulled into the north parking lot of the Stardust Hotel. They were loaded with Asian people, who were in from LA, Pickpockets and bag thieves liked to converge on the area because they saw the Asians as easy marks. The Stardust management complained to Smith while he was in the chief's office. Smith was there to make a pitch for donated money, which he intended to use for new bike equipment.

Of course, the sarg saw this as a perfect opportunity to work out a deal. It usually took an hour for the Asian tourists to mill around, jabbering at each other in their singsong babble. All the while, the drivers unloaded luggage, stacked it in neat piles, and stood around as it was carried into the hotel. No one paid attention to what was going on right around them. The tourists stared up and down the street, pointing at the McDonalds or Riviera across the way, and taking pictures of each other. That was why the thieves thought it was heaven. Smith's deal with the chief was that a bike team, whoever he was pissed at, would put themselves on a directed patrol activity, or DPA, ride down to the Stardust, stand around in the sun, because there was no shade, and provide security until all the tourists were safely inside. The unlucky pair was almost always Ryan and me. To us, the worst part was having our pictures taken, which was the reason for Ryan's new holster.

Two days before, four young Chinese men had approached us, pantomiming that they wanted to get a photo. I nodded. Instead of standing next to the bikes, two hopped on the handlebars and one snatched Ryan's handgun from his holster. Before he could do anything, the guy pointed the gun at his friend and said, 'Pow!' The camera clicked. Thank God, he didn't pull the trigger. Ryan was stunned at first. When he finally got going, he snatched his gun back, then started screaming at the guys. They left with really sullen looks.

As I wiped the tears from my eyes, two blondes came up. They offered tentative "Hellos." There was the faintest hint of something foreign in their voices. Before I could continue the conversation to determine exactly from where that accent originated, the radio squawked.

"Bike Thirty Four, copy a four oh four a at the Excalibur. Possibly involving a four thirteen."

"Bike Thirty Four," I acknowledged the unknown trouble call, possibly involving a gun. "Sahara Hotel," I radioed. "Damn!" I said to Ryan. Smith will know what we're doing if he's monitoring the radio traffic." The 'damn' was also for all the cleavage pointing back at me.

"We got a call down the street," Ryan said. Five miles down the street, to be precise, and in the middle of one of the hottest days I could remember.

"I know what and where it is," I said. Turning back to the short blonde, "Are you going to be here long?" I could see Ryan was already thinking of her as his.

"In Las Vegas or here at the water park?" the taller one said. She had a German accent, and from what I saw, her ancestors must have been Vikings.

"The water park."

"Ja," she said. She smiled at Ryan. "We vell be here for four or five hours. I am Heidi. This is Dalka."

"Nice to meet you both. I'm Ryan. He's Cam. Let us handle this call, then we'll come looking for you," Ryan called as we rode off. I thought if it hadn't been for his review, he would have dumped the call on someone else.

Dispatch normally started another unit, so there were two teams, but this time everyone else was tied up. An experienced dispatcher was like gold. She could look at a call, figuring how long we had been on it or how long we should have been on it and if we should be clear. If she had calls backed up, she'd subtly remind the officers by asking if they were OK. If she sensed the call was going badly by the things the officers were asking her to do, she might ask a closer unit if they could clear and be en route before she was asked to do this. All this was especially important on a gun call because the officers might get so wrapped up they wouldn't think to ask until things had gone to shit.

Once we were on the street, we were able to make good time. The north end of the Strip consisted of the Sahara Hotel, a big empty desert lot across the street, and a closed hotel-casino complex directly south of Wet N Wild. It wasn't until we got to the Riviera that traffic started to cluster. On a cool, light-traffic evening, the bikes could cover the distance to the Excalibur in fifteen minutes or less. It being Friday afternoon and hot enough to fry eggs on the asphalt, it took us more time to get there, not to mention the miserable side. Friday afternoon meant bumper-to-bumper traffic because the tourists were pouring in for their weekend-getaway time.

But the call was a priority, especially on the Strip. The tourist industry was a fickle enterprise at best, having much to do with visitor dollars and who competed for them. The California and Utah Chambers of Commerce and those of the various regional cities, such as Laughlin, Anaheim, or San Diego, would love a situation where something bad happened in Vegas. The sympathy they would initially express would be real, but later, they would pay big bucks to have their advertising agencies slam Vegas' safety record. As far as we cops were concerned, that was only a small reason why we answered the calls. There was also our oath — to protect and serve. But the biggest part was just the fact that we could be in the shit, feeding that need for adrenaline.

■ ■ ■

At times I thought it was unfortunate that the protect-and-serve part had to apply even to Californians. I hated when I pulled them over for doing something stupid, such as stopping in a through lane because they weren't in the correct left turn lane. They didn't care how many cars they held up while the light cycled. When I presented the citation for signature, they would complain in their whiny voices, "In California, you can do that." There was nothing better than replying, "Last time I checked, we're still in Nevada. The People's Republic hasn't managed to annex us. Until then, this is *still* Nevada, where you can't do that." Then you thought the rest. *You could keep your dumb, happy ass back in California, you know, where your People's Republic politicians made the police into pussies.* I'd heard other cops say the things I thought, but to me, they weren't worth the beef.

By the time I notified Dispatch we'd arrived at the Excalibur, we were drenched. The ride felt good, so I made Ryan push hard. I knew, even without the festivities of the night before at TJ's Bar, which was a favorite cop hangout, he would be dying from all that blubber he had to peddle, a result of too many buffets and cigarettes.

Since I found out the other guys on the squad started making TJ's their hangout, I stopped going. Ryan, on the other hand, made a huge effort to go every night. He wanted to fit in. I'd decided I never would, and after a couple times of trying, I accepted this. When I needed a bar, I used another location where I could drink without the possibility of being involved in one of the bike team's incidents, like the time they got in a fight with a bunch of guys from another department. The lawsuit on that was still pending. Smith's personality dominated the bike team, making them think they were invincible or, at the least, protected.

I believed there was bad karma waiting. As an example, Lieutenant Giles was snooping around to verify the rumor that a couple of my off-duty partners had gotten drunk, gone to a McDonalds, stuck their guns out the car window and fired off all the rounds. I heard a story that afterwards, Smith, who was driving to a mandatory meeting, responded. I'd bet he intended having someone's job until he recognized it was his people. It was rumored that he had the arriving officer, a friend of his, load the idiots in the black-and-white and drive them home. He stayed long enough to assure the manager that everything was being handled, then followed in their car. Everyone at the scene thought the police were taking the two to jail. I heard that Smith's buddy, the officer who covered the thing up, was offered a slot on bikes for his complicity. It was the old, "You scratch my back, and I'll scratch yours."

Ryan still harbored the belief he would be part of their club; that they were going to let him in. He went to the bar, spent his money buying them drinks. The shits preyed on his generosity, rarely returning any of it in the form of a round for him. They put their arms around Ryan's shoulders and called him "brother" to his face, then talked shit behind his back. I constantly heard the badmouthing in the locker room until one day when I told Dave and Arnie I was sick of it. I told them I'd be happy to meet them out back. They sullenly walked away, then never said anything else where I heard it. Smith was no better. At night, he accepted Ryan's drinks, and the next day, while we sat in Squad briefings, he berated Ryan for being too fat. None of Ryan's "friends" came to his defense. Ryan was broke all the time and it wasn't unusual that I paid when we ate. His girlfriend, who raised his child, had to practically beg him for money.

"What are you trying to do? Kill me?" Ryan asked, as he came abreast of me.

"How many Jack and Cokes you have last night?" I returned.

At this point, he'd been thirty feet behind me until I called back, "Pussy! My sister rides better than that."

It was true. My sister had come out when the bike squad made a road trip out to the lake. She brought her mountain bike and led the guys through some desert trails that would have made a world-class race. John was the only one who had kept up, thinking he might actually beat her back to the road. When they were a half-mile from the pavement, she poured on the speed, actually took a fifteen-foot jump across a ravine. Her specially outfitted bike sailed across, landing on the other side with a smoothness that astounded John. He'd talked about it for days. He wanted to marry her. He'd been forced to ride down one side and up the other, taking a full minute. When John had gotten to the road, she was resting comfortably in the shade of a large piece of red sandstone.

"Took you long enough," she called. "Afraid of a little air?" The rest of the team finally caught up ten minutes later. When they joined the two, they claimed they hadn't even been trying to catch her, but go for a nice day's ride.

"One thing about these bikes," I said. "They can sure keep you in shape."

"Where can I puke?" Ryan gasped.

"You look good all pasty like that," I said as I searched the place we'd come into, the northeast parking lot, for security. I didn't see anything that looked like an incident scene. A suspicious, white Monte Carlo was leaving. If we weren't here for something else, I'd have chased it down and stopped it.

As we rode south, I saw three trucks with flashing yellow lights, two security bike officers, and a bunch of suits. Several security officers started waving madly as we rode on property. Half of them wore the same yellow-and-black uniforms as we did.

"Like I can't see that gaggle," I muttered. I put on speed.

"Slow down. You are trying to kill me, aren't you?" Ryan asked. When I was close, I hit the brakes and took my weight off the seat, letting the rear wheel come out. The bike came to an impressive stop, skidding within an inch of a supervisor. Ryan just rode right up and stopped.

"What's up?" he wheezed.

"Hi, you guys," the guy in the jacket said. He didn't even blink at my stunt. "I'm the duty supervisor." He stuck his hand out and I read the name "Mike Smiles" on his nametag.

"That's got to be tough." I pointed.

"Heard them all so don't even go there."

"I'll bet."

"Can we cut the chitchat and let me know why I just pedalled my ass all the way down to this end of the Strip?" Ryan's color was returning.

"We just had two LMJs in a white eighties Monte Carlo get in a beef with some drunk tourists from Canada. The driver pulled a gun and scared the bejesus out of them. The kids made them take their pants off and hand them over. As far as we can see, they were on property for about ten minutes. From the outside cameras, we can see them screwing with our guests. Surveillance says they just left. You must have passed it when you pulled in."

I glanced at Ryan. "Why no, I didn't," I said, sarcastically. "Damn!"

"So you did see it?"

I nodded. "It was very four twenty-five." I said, using the code for suspicious. "Did you notify our dispatch? Give an update with the vehicle description?" The question was directed at the security officers.

"Did one of you guys do that?" Mike turned to his people. "Did anyone do that?"

The officers started looking at everything but their bosses. One of them said, "Gee, boss. I guess we dropped the ball."

"Where are the victims?" I asked.

Several officers pointed toward a bunch of cowed guys wearing blankets around their waists and standing by a truck. Wrapped in the blankets, they looked as if they wore sarongs. I set my kickstand, then walked over to where they were. Ryan followed me. "Everybody OK?"

One of the guys opened his blanket and yelled, "They took our undies."

"Oh, for Jesus's sake. I didn't need to see that," Ryan said. "Can you describe the LMJs?"

"What's an LMJs?" a man in the back asked.

"Latin male juveniles," Ryan said. "That's what you told the security officers."

"Yeah, we got a very good look, for sure," the biggest tourist said. He stepped in front of the group, so I guessed he'd be the leader. He burped, filling the air with the odor of alcohol.

Ryan's hand flew to his mouth.

"I'll get the paperwork," he whispered. I'd never seen anyone turn white so fast in my whole life.

"We've already got everything started," Mike said. "Their voluntaries are done. All you need to do is decide on the crime and add your name."

As I questioned everyone, they became very excited. I couldn't help thinking this would be the highlight of their Vegas vacation. As Ryan finished the report, a security officer asked if we wanted something cold to drink brought out.

"Heck, yeah. I'll take a gallon of iced tea if that's OK," Ryan called.

The man jumped in a truck and drove away.

"Control to Bike Thirty-four," the dispatcher called.

I keyed my mike, "Go ahead, Control."

"Are you going to be long?" she asked.

"Just finishing a report," I radioed.

"We just got a call from Wet N Wild. We have a PR standing by. Two LMJs in a white Monte Carlo threatened a subject with a four thirteen." *You got to be kidding,* I thought. "I don't know if I got this right, but he says they're making the guy undress. Can you be en route?"

"Control, that call has to be related to this one. Security reports a vehicle matching that description left her ten ago and they took the victims' pants, and their underwear. Do you have a closer unit?"

"Negative, Thirty Four."

"Can you get a DTAC unit to respond?" I asked.

"I tried," she said. "They have a four thirteen call going, also." *Two gun calls in a few minutes. Just our luck.*

"Is the DTAC call related to ours?"

"Negative, Thirty Four. Their call is a barricaded subject."

"We'll be en route, Control."

Before the cold drinks arrived, we were peddling northbound. Ryan looked like death warmed over. Northbound was actually better than southbound on the Strip. It was downhill. We could keep a good pace as we negotiated between the long lines of cars. I never understood why people wanted to drive. They could have taken the access roads, parked at their hotels, then waited until evening when it was cooler to walk between the hotels. As we went, Dispatch let us know that several more people called to say they were witnessing the same thing. I knew Wet N Wild Security wouldn't get involved. They were unarmed. That was a decision the Sahara Hotel, which owned the property, had made to appease parents who didn't want their kids seeing guns. As we passed the Riviera, the dispatcher announced a partial California plate. Ryan asked in a wheezy voice if she would recall the PR and see if that person could get the rest of the numbers. After a minute, she came back to tell us the person reporting, who was still on the phone, said the rest was obscured with a rag.

Finally, we arrived and we had to be the two sorriest looking cops there ever were. Ryan was literally dripping sweat from his shoes. My hands were so slick, I had problems keeping a grip on the handlebars. I didn't like wearing gloves because it was hard holding a gun, but I swore I was going to buy a pair the next morning.

"There it is," I said. It was a white seventy-nine Monte Carlo. It was clean, lowered, tinted, and occupied.

"Control, Bike Thirty Four," I said. "We got that vehicle."

It was then I heard another bike unit ask to be put on the call. He had been much closer. It never failed, other cops never wanted to be on something that might require them to take a report, but they'd clear to work a call where they might get to shoot someone. Several patrol units cleared, too. They started our way. Now that there were actually suspects, cops were coming out of the woodwork. We made our approach, using the cars parked in the lot for concealment. Our bright yellow shirts were great on the street, keeping us from getting run over, but at times like this when we didn't want to be seen, they were a hindrance. What did help, though, were the two girls, wearing skimpy bikinis and leaning in the driver-side window.

When we'd gotten closer, we dumped our bikes. We didn't just let them crash to the ground, but set them down carefully. Something must have caught the girls' eyes, because they looked up. I saw it was the German girls. When they saw the guns, their eyes got big, then they started to smile.

"Heidi," I yelled as we continued towards the car. I was having a really bad feeling about what was going to happen. "Get away from the car." Ryan was a little ahead of me, but to my right. He had the passenger in his sights. The problem was, this side of the car was turned away so we couldn't see what the passenger was doing. If he got out, he had the whole car to hide behind. Ryan sought cover. I was happy to see he chose the front quarter panel with all the metal of the engine between him and his target. I prayed the driver didn't decide to take the girls hostage. *Run,* I thought.

As though they read my mind, they did. I saw the driver reach for the gearshift.

"Don't do it or I'll shoot," I yelled. "Keep your hands where I can see them." This was the hard part. In the next split second, a person might live or die. I had decisions to make, questions to ask myself, answers to resolve. Did I want to let the bad guys drive away? Could I shoot? What did policy say? *Ah, for the good old days,* I thought. *When the cops fired warning shots.*

"Police! Put your hands out the window," Ryan ordered. For a second, I saw their indecision. "Do not put your hands down or we will shoot," Ryan yelled again. There was a long pause, then we saw hands come out the windows. "Driver, throw the keys from the car."

One of the driver's hands disappeared. A second later, there was the chink of keys hitting the pavement. Before I could start the whole felony extraction process, two single-man units pulled into the parking lot. They drove right to the front of the suspect's car and blocked him in.

"Those stupid fuckers," Ryan said. "Now we got a cross fire."

"Control, Three Nora has the vehicle at gunpoint," the driver of one of the cars radioed. It was like we didn't exist anymore.

"All units," Dispatch said. "Code red this channel for Three Nora and the suspect vehicle."

"Let them have it," I said. I started making my way to the left, hearing Ryan follow me. Technically, we were primary and the stop was ours, but I wasn't going to hang in what started as a safe position for us, but was now very unsafe, with the possibility of getting shot by our own people. From a distance, we watched the regular patrol officers pull the driver out and handcuff him.

The passenger was next. He was thin. When they had him, I saw he wore a pair of shorts, flip flops, and a tank top. His head was shaved. I saw a tattoo. It ran up from his forearm across his bicep, over his shoulder, then up under the side of his neck. It continued under his jaw and covered the side of his face and scalp. It included his ear. I couldn't imagine how much pain that must have been when it was done. From where I stood, I saw the tattoo was extremely complicated, entailing women's faces, names in cursive letters, and the two masks, Happy and Sad, which the gang guys once told me represented the ups and downs of life. Getting caught by the police was definitely a downer.

Now that things were safe, we walked over. One of the patrol cops checked the plate. He discovered the car returned stolen in the system. While the arresting officers interviewed, Ryan and I tossed the car. I found a black gun between the seats. It was a water pistol, but it looked real. In the back seat were several large pairs of pants.

"This what you used to make those guys at the Excalibur get naked?" I pointed the gun at cops who took our call. They ducked as I pulled the trigger. It squirted them.

"Fucker! That wasn't funny, Cam," Joe Moss yelled.

"Oh," Ryan countered. "You guys didn't think anything of pointing real fucking guns at us a few minutes ago."

"Treat us like this," Joe said. "We're going to clear."

"You can't," Ryan said.

"Hello, Ryan." It was female and it was Heidi.

"Well," his partner, Marty, said. "Maybe we're being hasty."

"I'd say," I replied. "I think those are your cuffs. And if I remember correctly, you called the code red, which I think makes you primary." I turned to Ryan, "I think the rule is you catch 'em, you clean 'em."

"I do believe you're right," Ryan said. We high-fived.

Heidi came up to Ryan, "That was so brave."

"It were nothing. Let me get my bike and I'll tell you how I saved Cam's ass the other day."

"Holy moly. Will you look at those tans?" Marty said.

"I don't believe there are any tan lines under there," Joe replied.

"I'll let you know," Ryan called. "Have fun at jail."

I let Ryan walk the girls towards where our bikes were lying. I went to the squad car and picked up the booking forms. The sun was starting to go down, which meant it would be a little cooler. While I filled them out, I called Karri May on my cell.

"So, what are you going to do now?" Karri May asked.

"Paperwork. Wanna go get a beer when I get off?"

"Why don't you come over here? I picked up a movie at Blockbuster. I can make popcorn, we can snuggle," she suggested.

"Oh? Is that what they're calling it now?"

"I don't know who *they* are, but if you think that was an offer for something other than a warm, fully pajamaed body lying wrapped in your arms, you better stay where you are."

"I sense a challenge. I'll be right over when I get off. Do you need me to pick anything up on the way?"

"Yeah. Feminine hygiene products. I'm out." I listened to that buzz that comes on phones when no one is speaking. "Is something wrong." Her voice leaked innocence.

"There is no way," I said. Joe was filling out another form. I was afraid he was close enough to hear part or all of the conversation. Suddenly, I felt flustered. "No way. I'm not standing in a line with people watching as I wait for some clerk to ring those things up."

Joe grinned at me. I dropped my pen and moved a little ways off.

"Not even for me?" she asked.

I was quiet. She laughed. "I was kidding. I don't need them. I was just seeing how far I could go."

It was funny, but beneath the relief, there was almost a feeling that I'd just missed an opportunity. When I tried figuring out why, I discovered I could actually see myself standing in line as I paid for a bunch of groceries just so I could hide the tampons under the lettuce or hotdogs. It wasn't such a bad image.

"I'll be over when I get off. I'll try to push Smith for an EO. He kinda owes me and Ryan one," I said. I looked to where Ryan and Marty were talking to the two German girls who stood in the skimpiest bathing suits and not an ounce of modesty between them. My Catholic upbringing, as though it were a person, was knocking at the door. As I stared, I wondered what it was about us Americans that made us such prudes. I had to shake the feeling off. After all, with things I'd seen — raped children, violent beatings, and death in all its forms from the man who'd shot himself in the head to an old woman that died naked on the toilet, I had no room to impugn those who really were innocent. I walked over to them.

"Hey, Ryan. I want an EO tonight."

"You read my mind, partner," he replied.

Later that evening, I discovered something about my partner: When he wanted something bad enough, he could get it. He whined so hard, Smith sent us packing, disgust in his voice. We were out of there by nine and I was knocking on Karri May's door by ten. She fed me, we watched her movie, I ate popcorn, and she foiled my best advances until it was late and I fell asleep.

The next morning, I woke on her couch — alone. It was early and I thought I'd sneak out and make the gym since it was the start of my days off. When she was up, I'd call her and see if she wanted to get breakfast. I pulled on my shirt and shoes, then went to the bathroom to take a piss. After finishing, I glanced at the unshaven face in the mirror. Turning out the light, I started to leave. Two steps from the door, I went back and put the seat down. I quietly pushed the partly closed bedroom door, hoping it wouldn't squeak. It was a couple of months now and we still hadn't slept together, although the petting had gotten heavy, like the night before. For some reason, I wasn't in a hurry to have sex with her. I thought everything would happen when it was supposed to.

The curtains filtered the light, filling the room with a soft yellow glow. There was this magic that women did to spaces, the way they made a house a home. It was about little things — like pictures on the walls, knick knacks on shelves, and doilies under table lamps. It looked so simple, yet I could never get my place anywhere near this comfort level. My apartment was messy on the best day but sterile just the same. Right that second, it was cluttered with police and gym gear. The stuff was stacked on and under the coffee table, books and magazines were laid open and half read across the back of the couch, clean clothes were haphazardly folded on the end of the bed where I left them after they came out of the laundry, and other piles needed to see the inside of the washer. As I stared about, I realized here was the epitome of the female's wiles. It was a trap, lined in sheer comfort.

I went to the bed and moved the hair from her face so I could see her better. Her breathing changed, so I knew I'd awakened her. She opened her eyes, smiled as I leaned in and kissed her.

"Sleep OK?" I asked. She pulled on me until I was stretched out, then lifted the cover over both of us. I felt the warmth of her body envelope me, tension drain away like water leaking from something punctured. The desire to go to the gym left me. I was drowsy again, sliding down into sleep. She turned on her side, her back to me, then wiggled in closer, pushing against my groin until I was hard.

"Stop or bad things are going to happen," I murmured.

"Bad, huh?" she asked. She turned so she faced me, kissing me with a passion that dissolved my sleepiness. Her mouth was soft, wet, inviting.

"Well, not *bad* like that, but good." I tried scooting out before she became aware of what was happening down below. Instead, she tightened her arms around my neck and kissed me harder. I tensed up, resisting for a second, then gave up. As my hand slipped under her shirt and across her back to her breast, she moaned. I moved the hand down her stomach, feeling the result of all those sit-ups at the gym. I came to the elastic of the pajamas, fully expecting to be stopped as I had every other time I'd gotten that far. Instead, she sucked in her lower stomach, making room for my hand to go where I wanted it to. As I slipped my fingers into her, she moaned, arching, and writhing all at once. She pulled off the shirt I'd just put on.

That was the first time with her. It was what I'd wanted to happen, waited for all that time. I wanted it to be perfect, after a good dinner, a show we both liked — one of those magical nights that people built their lives around. Instead, it happened like that, early on a normal morning, in a normal neighborhood, after nothing special — just another day. But what could be more perfect than that? A typical day where two people came to understand they wanted to be with each other. It was as though the trap had sprung, the spring-loaded wire arced its way over the top, and Bam! The victim was caught. I had stepped right into it and I didn't care.

■ ■ ■

On The Beach . .

I had this theory about life, which I called The Three Ws. Each one stood for a thing — Who, Where, and What. They were the things that made life worth living. "Who" was supposed to be those people who loved us, but especially that one special person everyone needed. "What" was the thing we worked at, in other words our job or purpose. It was what we put our physical and mental efforts towards that made the society the good or bad place it was and, hopefully, a better place in the long run. It didn't matter what it was, whether a job or charity or cause. And finally, the "Where." It was that place we called home, where we went to feel safe from the world when it threatened to overcome us. For life to be perfect, all three needed to be there, exactly as we envisioned them to be. Most of the time, we were lucky to get two right, which left us striving to attain the third. When things were bad was when we only had one and they were downright shitty when we had none. During that period, I had two.

Karri May and I were happy. I spent a lot of time at her place, since I had the key to her home. We talked about moving in together. That would be a big step. I had the feeling it was a line that, once crossed over, would leave me with no option but to marry her. I knew she would say yes if I proposed. I was worried about those nagging doubts I felt. I had the "Who" and "Where." It was that third "W"—the "What" that was the problem. Smith and I were at odds almost all the time. It had gotten to the point where he didn't have to make things up to get me in trouble. I created them. The simple pedestrian stop had turned into a shouting match between a jaywalker and me. It ended with Ryan dragging the guy off the sidewalk, slamming him into the asphalt, and, with his knee on the back of the guy's neck, putting handcuffs on. They were way too tight and the guy's hands turned blue.

The term *on the beach* referred to the time a cop spent either suspended or waiting on a decision for a disciplinary action. Suspension was time off with no pay. Administrative leave was time off with pay but waiting for something bad to happen, like getting fired or demoted. What many cops did was scrounge together whatever money they could afford so they could make a trip to the beach, hence the term. After I was hired, I wanted to be one of those cops whose jacket was chock full of commendations. I envisioned that file to contain no complaints or suspended action reports. I might as well have wished for the tooth fairy to leave a new car under my pillow.

Part of my problem was my big mouth. I saw stupidity all around me and I couldn't help remarking on it, which meant other cops heard those comments and passed them on. The comments were added to or embellished, then, somewhere down the line, they reached the wrong ears, like Smith's or the captain's. The next thing I knew, I was called on the carpet.

The other part of my problem was being too outspoken. There were times I knew they were giving me an out, letting me deny the matter, but I just couldn't seem to keep myself from taking the opportunity. I'd admit I'd said it. The first time it happened, the captain simply stared at me.

"I don't know whether to admire you or kick your ass," he said. "I'm going to let Smith and Giles decide. Now, get the hell out of my office."

Saying bad things about other cops, even when it was true, was referred to as "disharmony." The first time was right after I said Smith was an idiot. I got a "critical." The second time it happened was when I said Dave and Arnie should have been security guards because they wouldn't know crime if it was happening to them. I got an "oral." It was a matter of time when a "written" or a "suspension" came my way.

It was the beginning of September, and it was hot. The extreme heat made people wish for fall to be here, the air filled with yellow, red, and gold leaves and pollution's yellow haze, which would contain the sweet smell of wood smoke. In my vest, t-shirt, and blouse, I wanted the crisp chill that made what I wore comfortable. There wasn't any breeze, so the stifling air seemed to hang around a body like a too-tight coat. On this day, the air in the car made me feel like I was suffocating. Ten minutes out of the station, the air conditioner produced a sorry-assed noise, then stopped working. I wished I were on my bike, but that wasn't going to be an option until Ryan got back from vacation in a couple of days. Smith's rule was that patrolling by bike was always a two-man function and no one would ride with me after the incident with Eddie, another of the guys on my squad.

The incident started with three juveniles in custody who thought shooting tourists along the Boulevard with frozen paint balls was funny. We had them in custody, but were having a problem determining who the actual shooter was. Eddie decided to apply a little persuasion. When I saw what he was doing, I could only consider it torture. First, he applied a wristlock. That was painful enough to bring the kid up to the balls of his feet. Eddie then grabbed a handful of hair just above the back of the neck and pulled him backwards. Leaning back like that had the effect of making the kid think he was going to fall over. Another effect was the kid could barely breathe — much less utter a sound. Between the two sensations, he started to panic, but the pain of an impending broken wrist kept the kid in place. Tears started running down his face. Maybe if it were only a second or two, I would have ignored it. After all, I saw the old woman who was transported after a paint ball gashed her face. What made me go over was when Eddie kept at it longer than I thought was necessary. That was over the line. Other cops, both people from my squad and some patrol guys, stood around, simply ignoring the whole thing. When I was close, I touched Eddie's sleeve.

"Put him down, Eddie," I said. "Now!"

I didn't want the other cops or suspects, people on the sidewalk, anyone else, for that matter, hearing. I couldn't help that the kid did. We were supposed to be showing a united front out here.

"Fuck off, Cam," Eddie said. He jerked his bicep away — the thing was as big as my thigh, though he was only an inch taller than me. Eddie was one of those people who drank like a fish then went to the gym and slammed more weight in one set of bench presses than I could lift in my entire workout. He had his hair cut in a high and tight. He should have been in the Army, humping a machine gun, belts of ammo, a case of grenades, and maybe a Hummer.

"Put him down or so help me God . . . " I hissed the words, still quietly. Eddie released the pressure.

"You'll what?" he asked. His voice took on a nasty tone.

"You want to fight me? We'll do it right here in the middle of this motherfucking street," I said. I let my voice get loud enough that everyone heard. He glanced at Arnie and Dave. I sensed fear, so I thought I better push it. "Well?"

Eddie shoved the kid at me. As I caught him, Eddie turned his back. The kid collapsed to the ground, drawing in a breath, then breaking into sobs.

"Get him," I told Arnie. I went after Eddie, taking him by the arm to lead him away. He shook me off. When we were in a position where no one could hear us unless we started yelling, I continued with the conversation. I didn't care about the anger he made no effort to hide. "I'm not going to IAB and lie for you, asshole."

"Who you calling an asshole?"

"You didn't want a piece of me back there and now you do?" I asked. It can be amazing what a little person can do with a bigger one if the bigger one thinks the little one is crazy. It was all about not showing fear.

"It wasn't your business," he said. His eyes were on my shoes.

"It was."

He kept his eyes on my shoes.

"We'll all answer for shit we don't stop that's wrong. Look at the street." I jerked my chin towards the sidewalk. There were the usual crowds — parents, kids, lovers, people with their heads up their asses. Cars passed in the next lane. "You think one of the hotels might have turned a camera this way?"

"So, what? Sarg'll take care of us."

"He might take care of you. He won't take care of me, but that don't matter 'cause I'm taking care of me right now," I said. "The way I'm doing it is I'm telling you, don't ever do that shit again when I'm around you. Understand?"

"Fuck you, fuck you, and fuck you!" He walked away. I didn't care.

That was that and now here I was, in a car — driving down The Strip with Smith gunning for me again. The bad part of being a bike officer in a car was that I got the shit jobs, jail transport, report taker, and general gofer for the rest of my squad. If the Sarg wanted hot coffee, I made the Starbucks run. When there was time, which was really never, he expected me to perform pedestrian and vehicle stops.

Normally, I only stopped people for two things — really excessive speeding and running stop signs. Both of those had happened at the same time, then to make it even sweeter, the guy turned out to be a lawyer. He wasn't just any lawyer, but the senior representative for the ACLU, or, as we liked to call it, the American Criminal Liberties Union. The downside was I knew the next day he'd be in some judge's chambers, whining and getting the ticket I wrote him fixed. Probably first thing in the morning, but, hey, screw him. At least I'd inconvenienced him. I couldn't help grinning as I replayed the stop. First, he started arguing. I thought I was in court. Then it finally came down to me writing, he talking, me telling him to sign, he saying he wouldn't, me telling him I'd yank his ass out of his car and take him to jail.

He said, "Is that so?"

I lunged inside, and he practically jumped into the passenger seat. He signed as fast as he could, then tossed the ticket book at me. I ripped his copy off and tossed it on the seat.

"Have a wonderful day, sir," I said

"You'll pay for that," he threatened.

I nodded at the pink copy. "So will you."

After I climbed back in the car, I watched the Porsche drive off.

"Control, Three Bike Thirty. I'm clear," I radioed.

"What's your disposition?" There was just a hint of irritation in her voice.

"B-Baker," I said. I drew the words out slowly and clearly. I knew better than to clear without a disposition code, but I also knew when I first pulled him over, I'd made a show of giving the guy's personalized plate over the air. After I stowed the ticket book, I read through the computer messages other units had sent me. Everyone was jealous that I'd stopped the guy. When I sent a reply that he refused to sign at first, the overwhelming consensus was that I should have thrown him in jail.

Before I'd gone far, the radio emitted an alert tone, then the Dispatcher radioed, "Bike Thirty. Can you be enroute to a Four Sixteen?" *Ah*, I thought, *happiness is always short lived.*

"Copy, Control," I replied. Fight calls used to be fun. They were a good excuse to roll code, all the lights-and-siren stuff. That was because they were considered a priority. Now that I was more seasoned and had my share of those kinds of calls, I'd changed my opinion. Half the time, when I arrived, the fight was over and everyone gone. Then there were the stupid situations when what people thought were fights were really something else, like verbal arguments. The ones where people actually threw punches were rare. With experience, I'd learned to drive slowly to the scene and keep the siren keyed so that it solved the problem by announcing my arrival.

Dispatch gave the location, which I recognized as being a block away. If this was any other Vegas street, I'd be able to look in the direction she told me and see the disturbance, but on the Boulevard, it was common for crowds of people to mill around.

As I started forward, using the yelp mode on the audio system, I heard another bike team clear and tell her to show them en route. They gave their starting location as the Mirage, which put them far away from where things were happening slightly north of the MGM. I guessed they'd been sitting in front of the volcano at the Mirage Casino. The water spilling off the artificial waterfalls formed a breeze and a fine mist. The breeze carried the mist towards the sidewalk. This acted like a huge swamp cooler, dropping the air temperature ten degrees or better. Another advantage was that people loved to stop and talk or have their picture taken with the cops. There were times I'd staked out that exact spot in the hope of getting a date from some tourist chick. I guessed that was what John and Arnie had been doing.

Before I arrived, the hesitant voice of a trainee came on the radio. He told Control they'd arrived on my call. The training units liked to spend time on the Strip. The FTOs said it was good for their rookies to get some exposure to high profile police work. The Strip, which is always filled with people, was one of those places where everything we did had the potential of being witnessed, if not recorded. An incident that wasn't handled properly could end up on a national news show. There was the time I'd been in the middle of Las Vegas Boulevard, conducting a felony car stop. The driver was considered armed and dangerous. The car was reported stolen. While I pointed my gun at the bad guy's prone body, yelling commands, tourists kept walking through my field of fire. The bad guy finally saw his opportunity and ran. He headed for a casino as I chased him. I'd seen the gun in his waistband, which meant he was fair game if I could have gotten a clear shot. With all the people, there wasn't any guarantee I wouldn't hit a tourist. Just as the guy went through the doors, a huge security officer cold cocked him. I later learned the surveillance technicians turned a camera on us when the stop started. They notified security, who stood by to offer assistance if things went south.

Situations like these were what the cops in patrol lived for. The problem was: Sergeant Smith didn't like regular patrol on the Strip, his territory. He called it poaching. The Department's game was "stats." Those numbers justified every unit in the police department's existence, from the bike teams to SWAT. That was typical of government; new enterprises were established by robbing from someone else's budgets. Bike detail was no different. When it was first started, patrol's budget was docked enough money to buy a car. That money went towards uniforms, training, and equipment. The patrol supervisors felt that the bike units were a waste of time and money. I think they hated seeing all the fun we had. Even after three years, many of the administrators believed we were having too good a time. They didn't think it was *adult* that grown men rode bikes, even though the numbers showed we were getting to calls faster than they could in the cars. To say cars moved expeditiously on the Strip was like saying LA didn't have traffic problems. In a car, it took me fifteen minutes to drive a block. I could walk faster.

As I pulled up, the air conditioner started working, but the air coming out was warm. For a second, I wanted to sit in front of the thing and let it dry the sweat on my face. Finally, I stepped outside. The air had only made it feel like it'd gotten hotter. Both my shirts were drenched before I'd walked ten feet. When that happened, I always worried. A wet vest doesn't stop bullets.

I pushed my way through the usual crowd. They watched two of Las Vegas' finest dragging a toothless old woman over to their car. She was five feet and one hundred pounds of kicking and screaming hell-fury. With her mouth open, it was easy to see the three teeth still in her head. Of course, I recognized her, even with all the blood on her face.

"Liz. Stop screaming, for the love of God," I said. I looked at the patrol guys in their summer uniforms. They were trying to keep body fluids at bay. I grinned. "You guys need me to call medical?"

"Nope. Already did it. Didn't I?" The last was aimed at his rookie and delivered in a sarcastic tone. Someone wasn't doing what he was supposed to. "You know her?"

I didn't recognize the FTO. "Yep. She's a frequent flier. Probably off her meds again."

"I'd say," the rookie added. His nametag was hanging by one pin over a ripped pocket.

Elizabeth was one of those people who should have been kept locked up in a mental asylum. She was released during the Reagan administration's challenge to the rights of such people, which said if they weren't dangerous, they had a right to their own brand of happiness. The courts deemed her sane and let her go. Now she was our problem — over and over.

My first time meeting her had been last winter. She approached me, claiming she was freezing. It was true the temperature had dropped that night, a freak weather condition because it was raining somewhere up north. I'd gone to a nearby casino and explained her predicament. I knew the casinos had a stash of clothing that came from luggage that was abandoned in the rooms, mostly from the guests skipping out after losing at the table. After a period of time, the items were turned over to local charities. The shift supervisor took me back and let me pick from what was there. I was surprised at what I found. There was a lot of high-end clothing — leather jackets, designer shirts and dresses.

"Wayne Newton's wife skip on you guys?"

"We don't have a clue. The ID on the room was fake. Maybe you guys popped her."

That happened. We sometimes took people to jail without them telling us where they stayed. In most cases, I wouldn't have let the hotel know we were taking them to jail anyway. It was the suspect's problem if he lost all his shit. I pulled a nice jacket from the pile and held it up. "Can I take this?" It must have cost four hundred bucks.

"Take what you want," he said

After gathering a couple of long shirts and a pair of pants, I went back to where Liz was begging. When I held the coat out, she grabbed it like it'd been hers all along. I offered her the rest, but it was the coat she was mainly interested in. I rode away feeling that I'd done a good thing for someone. An hour later, I was back at the corner. The two shirts and the pair of pants were on top of the garbage.

The next night, I was waiting for my partner to use the shitter in one of the Gold Key Shops. As I sipped an iced coffee, I noticed a vagrant wearing a coat that looked like the one I'd gotten Liz. Since the distance was about fifty feet, I couldn't be sure until I noticed the coat barely fit the guy. I got up to check and as I closed on him the thought that he might have jacked Liz, made me angry. When I was close to him, I called him to me. I should have figured he'd run, which, when he did, really pissed me off. We had a short foot pursuit, which I didn't even bother radioing in. When I caught up with him, I gave him a good push. He hit the ground rolling, then came to a stop on his stomach. His hands were curled across his chest. When I told him to put his hands behind his back, he wouldn't. There was no way I was getting on top of his sorry-ass lice-infested body to take him into custody.

"Put your hands behind your back," I warned. "Do it now." I had my gun on him. When he answered, his words came to me muffled. I kicked him, using the toe of my boot, on the nerve that runs along the outside of the thigh.

"Owww!" he howled.

"Show me some hands," I yelled. I waited a few seconds, then kicked him again. This time, I gave it all I had. He tried rolling away from me. This let the next kick catch him in the side, just below the ribs. There was a whoosh of air as he flipped. I saw the six-inch hunting knife then. The next kick was into the side of his head. After the eyes rolled upwards, his hand slipped to the side. The blade struck the concrete, making a ringing noise.

I huffed a couple of times, then keyed the radio. "Control, Bike Thirty-four. Foot pursuit with a possible Four Thirteen A." I gave it a minute as I listened to a whole bunch of units start clearing, then told Dispatch I had one in custody. I grabbed a wrist, keeping my gun on him in case he was faking. I pulled his body away from the weapon, flipping him back to his stomach. I holstered, slipped my cuffs on the wrist I held, caught the other, which I secured also. The whole time he was out.

"I can't leave you for a moment," Ryan wheezed as he came running up. "What's up with him?"

"Secure the knife," I said. "I wanted to have a word with him because it looks like he took Liz's coat."

"The new one?" Ryan asked. I nodded. He bent down and started slapping the unconscious man. "You piece of shit. Wake up."

After a second, the guy's eyes fluttered, then opened. He moaned when he saw us. I couldn't help noticing he was going to have a great shiner.

"Where'd you get this?" I pulled on the jacket's lapel.

"Lizzie gave it to me," He murmured.

"What?" I yelled. "You're a liar. I got her this jacket."

"No. I gave her my bottle of beer. She traded me. Even Steven." He sank back against the building.

"Where's Liz?"

"Fuck you, asshole. You kicked me," the man screamed. He started sobbing uncontrollably. It had to be DTs. One minute calm, the next he was totally irrational. We saw it a lot with the homeless. Ryan called for a paddy wagon. When I reached down to pull the guy to his feet, I couldn't help thinking it was a good thing the wind was blowing. Otherwise, I might have smelled him. As I thought of stripping the coat off, I realized he was a lesson in vagrants. Give them ugly things that are functional, and they'll keep them. Give them nice things and they'll turn them to shit.

"You taking the coat?" Ryan asked. "Maybe we can find her and give it back." The vag started sobbing, making big blubbery noises that got on my nerves.

"Shut the fuck up so we can think," Ryan said.

"Screw it. Let him have it," I said.

This was the first time since then that I'd seen Lizzie. As I watched her struggling with the new trainee, I glanced back in the direction from which she'd been dragged. I saw a young street thug, who looked out of place. When he saw me staring, his face took on an aggrieved look.

"Bring your happy ass over here," I said. There were a lot of tourists watching, so I added a slow "please." As he started towards me, I had the worst feeling I knew this guy. I hated when that happened.

"I know you," I said.

"I don't think so." There was something in his eyes, as if he was afraid I was right.

"What's your name?"

"Officer. She attacked me first," he said, changing the subject.

"That what I asked you?"

"No," I caught the sullen edge to his voice. I stepped in close and smiled. He was about four inches taller than me.

"Listen, you fuck. There better be a "sir" on the end of that "no." I spoke quietly so only he could hear. "Either that or I'll make sure you spend the night in jail."

While I talked, I continued to smile. It was those early lessons from my FTOs coming through. Then, speaking louder, I asked again, "Did I ask you that?" Before he could answer, I saw a slice of tattoo at his shirt collar. I hooked a finger in the cloth and pulled downwards. He had a lightning bolt that came up from his left pectoral muscle to the neck line, which was a good thing. He'd changed. The way his face looked, the effects of the meth, I'd have been hard pressed to know him otherwise. *Fremont Street. I saw you on Fremont Street a long time ago and . . . there was something else.* I remembered enough that I didn't need to say. I wanted my advantage if I needed it later.

"No, sir. My name is John Simone. They call me 'Eight Seven' on the street."

"Eight Seven?" I asked. "Why?"

"They just do," he said quietly.

"Well, if you don't mind, I'll call you 'John.' You don't mind that, do you, John?"

"No, sir. John'll be fine."

"What you been arrested for, John?"

"Stuff."

"John. In a second, I'm going to the car. I'm going to use the computer and run you up. If it doesn't say 'stuff' on the screen as the exact charge you were convicted for, I think I'll take you to jail and solve everybody's problems out here."

"I'm an ex-felon . . . " The last word trailed off.

"Spit it out," I said.

"Attempt murder, robbery, and some other stuff. I did my time, officer."

"Where?" I asked.

"California."

"And California's penal code for murder is?" I asked the question as if I was a detective solving a mystery.

"One eight seven, sir."

"Exactly." I finished getting what I needed to run him, which was his date of birth and social security number. I calculated he was thirty. I turned away, then looked back at him. "How much time?"

"Twelve long ones."

I whistled. "On an attempt? How come? Who'd you try to kill?"

He muttered something.

"What?"

"Cop." He looked me in the eye. "I tried to kill a cop. I did my time, though."

"Front of my car. No fucking around or I'll shoot you," I smiled again. I wanted him to wonder if I was going to, not whether I would — I think he'd already guessed that. There was this thing about people who tried hurting or killing us. It was as though there was this line and they'd stepped across. It was bad enough for someone to hurt another human being, but to go after a cop meant that a person wasn't afraid of anything.

This was my second time being around a man who was involved in hurting a cop. The other one had a warrant out of South Carolina for the murder of a police officer. While I waited for the Feds to show up because they were taking him, I tried to understand what was going on in his head. I wasn't allowed to talk to him, so all I could do was think. What I came up with was that when I was younger, I'd done my share of beating up my sister. It was something siblings everywhere did, so I knew about breaking the rules — even though they were simple rules made by my parents. I knew that secret feeling that went with it, the sense that I had done something wrong and I was going to pay a price and I didn't care. That was the best I could do to empathize with that other man and now John.

"What happened here," I asked.

"I was working," he said as he held a handful of flyers towards me. What he showed me was smut magazines. They were pamphlet-like advertisements for the strip clubs and escort services. The businesses used people who stood on the sidewalks handing the stuff to tourists. The things were filled with pictures of near naked-women who promised to do things that were borderline legal. For years, we'd tried to get the stuff off the Strip but the advertisers had learned the lessons bigger magazines, like *Playboy, Penthouse,* and *Hustler* had pioneered. The editors of those magazines discovered that if they included at least a political essay, if not an entire section, in every edition, the First Amendment protected them.

The Ninth Circuit Court was currently considering the case for the Vegas magazines. The case presented a couple of perplexing problems. First, was the way the magazines presented their political opinions. The editorials railed against a government that disallowed smut ads from being given away without at least a piece of political diatribe to legitimize their existence being placed in their pages. Talk about a circular argument. Secondly, people rarely thought about what was being protected. The pages were covered with ads for businesses we knew as outcall dance services, which were really scams and fronts for prostitution.

The prostitution services were few and far between because most of them had been investigated by vice and when their real purpose was proven, they were closed down. There were some purely private enterprises, which were harder to catch. This was because those businesses did an excellent job of screening their customers. They did this by referrals from people they knew. What the businesses didn't have to worry about were women. There were always girls willing to do the nasty for money and they had to be dealt with on an individual basis, which meant an appointment had to be set up, an unarmed cop sent in, and the act stopped just before it was consummated.

Other than prostitution, what most of the ads were about were the scams. That involved the ads promising that a girl would come to a guy's room and dance for "up to an hour." The customer was led to believe that "dancing" involved more than cavorting around the room in g-string underwear, or, to put it simpler, tourists thought the government was winking at illegal behavior. In actuality, the girls were only going to dance. Having been on those calls numerous times in the past, I knew what that meant. Some irate customer, after putting his money safely in the girl's hand, found out that "up to an hour" might only be a minute, which literally meant she'd get her money up front, let the guy get naked or down to his underwear, wiggle her ass for the minute, then scoot out the door before he caught her. Most men wouldn't give chase, especially in a state of near undress. As I went through that whole process, why John looked familiar suddenly popped into my head, but there was something else behind that story. I kept thinking about Fremont Street.

"I know where I know you from."

"I was waiting to see if you remembered," John said. He smiled.

"We've met twice."

I went over the other time in my head. I was on one of those calls where a customer called security, who then came and detained both the girl and John. They told me that, when they arrived, John was "explaining" to the customer what would happen if the guy called John's dancer girlfriend "ugly" one more time or if he continued trying to get his money back. After hearing the story from security, I was going to take John to jail for threats to life. It was then that John pointed out what a nice wedding band the customer was wearing. The guy turned white as a dead fish. John went on to remark how the lawyer for the company he worked for would get the guy's address off the police report after he went to jail. Of course, they'd have to subpoena the guy's wife, just to see what she thought about the whole thing. Maybe she'd have an opinion as to whether the dancer was ugly. That changed the victim's mind. He said the girl looked fine now that the alcohol was wearing off, which must have adversely affected his judgment. As a final shot, he insisted on the girl keeping the fee, which was the least he could do for causing everyone all the problems and, perhaps, he could even throw in another fifty and he was sorry for getting the police involved. I had to admire John's strategy. No victim, no crime.

"You were with that ugly woman at the Excalibur."

John grinned. "Man, you is right there. She was ugly as sin. She made me some money though. I remember you was fair to me, but that ain't the only time I saw you."

"It isn't?"

He shrugged. The fact that I had a feeling I knew him for more than that one call nagged at me even more. I thought how many people I had made contact with since I started working Patrol. After a while, people's faces seemed to blur into each other. By then, one of the things I knew about policing was that it often took a few contacts before a cop knew some person was going to become part of their life and I was having that feeling about John.

"Did you used to hang out downtown?" I asked because I knew it was time to use what I knew.

"When I first got to town."

"Maybe sell a little dope down there?"

"I lived in that area." His lips curled in a grin. "Funny. I remembered you, too…" He stared at my nametag. "…Officer Madden."

"And about the dealing?" I asked.

"I wouldn't say I sold dope."

Good answer, I thought. It was also one of those answers that told me I wasn't going to get much further with that line of questioning. "What happened?"

"With that stripper bitch?" he asked. I could see he was playing with me now, so I decided to bring the conversation back to where I controlled it.

"You know what I mean."

He gave me a blank look.

"You want to be treated stupid, then we'll play that game." I came closer and pointed. "I want to know what happened with Crazy Lizzie."

"I told you already, she attacked me."

"Yeah, you did say that." I had to wait a few seconds before I went on. He was pissing me off and if I wasn't careful, I could be the one in trouble if I let him push me too much. I took a breath. "Now I want to know the specifics. Why would Lizzie attack you?"

"For no reason whatsoever. Ask them if you don't believe me, Officer Madden." John pointed at several t-shirt vendors. "Ask them!" I rolled my eyes at the people he was pointing at. They were all involved in another one of those issues for which we had the courts to thank. The t-shirt tables were another great scam. First, a prospective entrepreneur acquired a load of t-shirts, a table or a bunch of tables, and a section of sidewalk. This was the same sidewalk that was already filled side-to-side with more bodies than the original designers had ever anticipated. Part of what pissed us cops off was that our job was to keep people on the sidewalk and out of the street. Those tables defeated that whole strategy by taking up so much room they created bottlenecks where whole slews of people were forced to step into the lanes of vehicular travel.

Walking in the street was dangerous. When people drive on the Strip, they aren't always looking where they're going, but at the hotel facades, other people, if they're guys, they look at women. We figured it was only a matter of time before someone was going to be scraped off the front of some tourist's car or a taxi. It was bad enough that sixty lives were lost along Las Vegas Boulevard from jaywalking every year without adding deaths or injuries that seemed preventable.

What kept the county from barring the t-shirt vendors was that they did the same thing as the smut peddlers, which was that they printed some political endorsement, such as: Save the Whales, Protect Battered Sea Slugs, or Wife Beaters Need Love, Too. They also donated a few cents from each sale to that cause. It didn't matter to the courts that those same charities were set up and operated by the owners of the tables.

A lot of people might ask, "Who cares?" Probably just those people who owned shops in the strip malls, the same ones who had to pay for things like rent, business licenses, and social security taxes on their employees. The tourists didn't care. They bought the t-shirts off the tables and got a great deal. First, there wasn't much difference between the shirts from the stores and those on the tables, except for the endorsements. The pictures on the fronts might be of the Las Vegas casinos, like the Luxor, MGM, or the Paris, or they might have logos of Coca-Cola, Nike, or Ford. The kicker was that, without overhead, the vendors could offer deals, like four or five shirts for twenty bucks, which the stores couldn't do without going out of business, which was happening anyway. So, between these two issues, we cops held the opinions that the Ninth Circuit judges had their heads so far up their asses they'd forgotten common sense.

The two cops were having a time with Liz. When I was a newbie, I'd have rushed over and gotten a piece of that. Now that I had more experience, I figured two strapping cops in full uniform ought to be able to handle a sixty year old woman. And if they couldn't, maybe it'd teach them to stay in their area. While struggling with Liz, the rookie keyed his mike. A second later, the dispatcher asked if they were code four. I had to smile because I knew it was Liz's screaming that caused her concern. The trainee missed the dispatcher's radio traffic.

"You gonna get that or do I have to do it, too?" the FTO asked. *Uh oh*, I thought. *Someone's getting low scores at the end of shift*. The trainee didn't move. I knew exactly what he was thinking.

"Get what?"

Before she started sending the cavalry, the FTO told her they were OK. There went any points the trainee might have salvaged.

I'd already guessed Liz was off her medications. If I remembered correctly, it was some shit like Thorazine. I knew mental health services gave her enough to get her through a month. But I also knew that was a mistake. She ended up selling it on the street. When she got her money from the street junkies, she used it to buy booze, which only exacerbated her condition. If they were smart, they'd make her go somewhere every day and dole it out to her. I pointed at a t-shirt vendor. When he looked at me, I yelled, "Come here." The expression on his face became extremely wary. Liz's yelling was suddenly muffled. When I looked over, she'd been placed in the back of their unit. She pushed her face up to the glass. Her head was really bleeding.

"What the fuck you do that for?" the FTO screamed.

"She was getting on my nerves," the trainee stammered.

"Do you have any idea what you just did?" The trainee shook his head. The FTO looked around and saw several people looking at him with concern on their faces. The trainee saw it, too.

"Move along, folks. Nothing to see here," he said. Hell, even I wanted to see what was going to happen next. He grabbed the kid by the sleeve and pulled him closer. "She's bleeding. Right?"

"Yes, sir."

"I told you not to call me 'sir.' You just put her in our car. Now there is blood all over the inside. Right?"

"Ohhhhh! Hazmat. I shouldn't have done that." The way the trainee's face lit up, I almost saw a bulb going on over his head. When they had her at the jail, they'd have to go to the hazmat area. Once there, the trainee was going to be in back of their car with a bucket of bleach and water. It was going to take him a bit of scrubbing in the back of that cruiser, especially after the blood dried.

"Go over there and help the bike officer." He pointed at me.

"Yes, sir." The FTO opened his mouth, then just shook his head and walked away. I heard him on the radio asking for medical. With the traffic the way it was, she might bleed out before they got there.

I turned to the trainee and held out my hand. "Cam. Take some breaths and don't worry about it. OK?"

He nodded. I turned to the vendor. "What'd you see?"

"Just tell them the truth, Joe," John said. His voice was quiet, kind of lifeless.

"Listen," I said, moving closer. "You open your motherfuckin' mouth one more time, I'll stick my boot in it. Then I'll book you for intimidating a witness. Got it?"

"I was just…" I gave him *the look*. For a second, I thought it would work — like a switch turning off, but then he must have decided he had a witness. "That crazy bitch attacked me." It was loud enough for Liz to hear. She screamed something from inside the car.

"Keep it down or I'll do you for disturbing the peace," I said. "John, you see these long stains under my arms?"

He glanced at my ribs, sullenly. "Yes," John muttered. When I looked in his eyes, I knew how he'd done what he did to spend all that time in prison. I decided to try another tack.

"I'm hot and tired. The easiest thing to do would be to haul her off to the hospital and you off to jail. Would you like to go to jail? Now, either calm down and let me get on with this — or else."

"She threw my literature in the street," he said, pointing. I turned in the direction he indicated.

"How the fuck can I tell what she threw and what the tourists have done?" I asked. "Look at that mess."

"Well, I didn't want to punch her because she's old," John said. "And crazy."

"And with your record, you could end up back in prison." I turned away before he could get another word in. I looked at the trainee, then pointed at the t-shirt vendor.

"Why don't you take him over there and get his story?" He took the man by the elbow and led him off a distance. I had my back to Simone as he continued talking.

"I didn't punch her. I pushed her instead but it was just to keep her off me. Look . . . " I turned around so he could show me his arm. There was a nice set of punctures, three to be exact. It looked like a weird vampire had gotten a hold on him. "She did this to me. When I pushed her, she tripped off the curb. I think she hit her head. That's how she got the cut."

"You expect me to believe that?" I asked.

I heard an air horn. The ambulance had arrived. When the back door opened, I saw Karri May.

"Stay here. Don't move. Don't talk, think, or anything else that you'd guess will piss me off. Are we clear, John?"

He nodded. I left him in front of my car. The FTO was on his cell with someone.

"Watch him, will you?" I called. He looked at me, but didn't acknowledge me.

"How's your day?" I asked Karri May at the back doors of the ambulance.

"Shitty. Yours?" She brought a hand up and fluffed her hair. "Notice something different?"

I had to look at her for a second for it to sink in. She started getting a hurt look. "Your hair. It looks redder."

"Highlights."

"Uggghh. I'm not good at noticing those things." Before I could finish making a total ass out of myself, she went to the car.

"Let's see what you've got." Karri May glanced in the back, where Lizzie was lying on her side. She grimaced. "Damn. It has to be this one. She's never easy to work on."

"Maybe you can give my trainee a hand while I get the vag out of the car?" the FTO asked as he stepped between us. *Wow! That was cock blocking big-time*, I thought. I didn't want to make an issue of it, so I grinned. Someone was about to get his lunch taken out if he thought he was going to make time with my woman. The funny thing was it wasn't me that would do it, either.

As soon as he opened the back door of his car, Lizzie started acting up. I shifted so I could keep an eye on things. Karri May stayed back so the FTO could bring Lizzie out. I motioned for the trainee to give his partner a hand. It didn't take more than ten seconds before they were trying to put a headlock on Lizzie. She was jerking all over the place, getting blood on both their uniforms. After the three ended up on the ground, Karri May talked to her in a soothing voice that reminded me of a mother trying to calm a child. Lizzie stopped struggling and it wasn't long before her head was being wrapped in enough bandages to make her look like an Arab.

When I moved back to John, he said, "Jesus, Officer Madden. Is she terminal?" From the way the tourists acted, they must have thought so, too. Many of them simply stood, staring like they were at a casino show. Karri May and her partner had Lizzie lie on the gurney while they worked on her. The rookie came back over, brushing at the blood that was drying on his uniform. I put him to work with John, filling out a voluntary statement. I headed back towards Karri May.

"Young man, did you see this?" A lady stepped in front of me. She handed me a pamphlet.

"Yes ma'am," I said. "They're pretty common."

"So, I see" She pointed at the ground. "That man gave this to my husband. Arrest him." She shifted her finger from the ground to John. "I'd be happy to swear out a complaint and press charges."

"Wish I could," I said. "Nothing better I'd like to do than take you up on that. Unfortunately, it's not a crime. Can you excuse me?" I started to step around her but she blocked me again.

"Why not?" she asked. The FTO was so busy helping Karri May he looked like he was all over her. I pointed at the trainee.

"He'll explain everything to you," I said.

"While I do that, can you read this," the trainee said. He held out the statement the t-shirt vendor had filled out while everyone was dealing with Lizzie.

"Later. I'm sure it's shit." The lady's mouth fell open. "Sorry, ma'am. Cop language."

"The guy says he needs to get back to his table," the trainee said. "He says people are stealing his stuff."

I sighed in an exaggerated manner, then took the statement and started reading it. As I suspected, it was shit. The t-shirt vender, claiming to be a disinterested third party, made the whole thing sound exactly the way John wanted the story to be told.

"Come here," I ordered. The witness walked over. I didn't think the sullen look had left his face since I first contacted him. "How is it that this looks like it was rehearsed, then signed?"

He shrugged. "That's my statement. Throw it out if you want but I ain't changin' a thing." I saw the look he threw John's way.

"I don't care. When you get subpoenaed, it's your ass on the witness stand. You perjure yourself and you spend the time in jail." I glanced towards the fence, where there must have been thirty smut peddlers lined up. All but one averted their eyes when they saw me looking.

I pointed at the one — a large black man. "Come here."

"Me?"

"Jesus. Is there another *you* I'm pointing at? Get over here," I said, then I added an exaggerated "*please.*"

He came like a tank. It wasn't until he was right in front of me that I saw how big he was. "Holy Cow! How much do you weigh?"

"Two seventy-five."

"Six three or four?"

"Six five."

"You afraid of him?" I asked, pointing at John.

"Phew. Ain't afraid of nobody."

"You like him?"

"Not especially." From the look on his face, I'd bet on it.

"You tell me what really happened?"

"Why should I?" he asked.

"Maybe, 'cause you want to be a good citizen, or maybe 'cause you really don't like him. What's it matter?" He shrugged. "You got a name?"

"People call me Joe, Big Joe." His collection of tattoos weren't nearly as artistic as John's, but then I could tell Joe's were done with one of those homemade tattoo outfits people made in the Joint. A prison guard told me how the inmates built their own motors out of wire and cardboard. They took a ballpoint pen, ground off the point, then inserted a needle so the ink could enter the flesh.

I pointed, "You the artist?"

"Yep."

"Where?"

"Folsom. Two years. Most of it in solitary."

"Now that we know each other so well, what happened?"

"Shithead white boy was talking shit to them dudes there. It was *fuck* this and *fuck* that. He was talking that shit loud. Crazy Lizzy yell for him to be stopping. She say her mama say the *fuck* word bad. She say she never to use the word. Fuckhead tell her to fuck off. She jump in his face."

"You fucking nigger, that's a lie. You gonna listen to his smack?" John asked, then started around the car. For once, the trainee did the right thing without being told. He stepped in John's way.

"Put some cuffs on him," I said before I turned my attention back to Big Joe, but keeping an eye on John in case the trainee needed help.

. "Then what?" I asked.

"She snatch his stuff. Throw it in the street. He not touch her. Not even a little pinky."

"See?" John yelled as the trainee put the cuffs on. He started to bring John over. I held a hand up in a gesture to stop him.

"Keep him there," I said. I didn't want the two of them too close. If Big Joe decided to go after John, we'd be obligated to keep him safe and, although, I would have liked to let Joe go at it, John's safety was our responsibility.

"He telling the truth," John said. "I never laid a finger on her. I tole you that."

"He cursin' her something fierce," Big Joe went on. " 'Fuck, fuck, fuck,' he say. Crazy bitch jump up and start slappin' that boy all on the face and head. He raise his arm up to protect his face, knock her in gutter. She bang head, bleed plenty."

So there it was. I guessed it was the closest thing to the truth I was going to get. Technically, I could take John to jail for starting it. What I wanted was to get to the ambulance. "Have him write it if he can."

"Can't." Joe dropped his eyes. "Can't read. Cain't work ah pen except'n to make mah mark."

"He'll do it for you. OK?" I pointed to the trainee.

He nodded. I headed for Liz and Karri May.

"So what's the prognosis, doc?" I asked her.

"Good, Cam," Karri May said.

"And what's mine. Maybe dinner?" the FTO quipped.

"You," I said, "ain't got a prognosis."

"Is that right?" he asked me, belligerently.

"I'm afraid it is," Karri May said. "Have you met my boyfriend?" She put an arm possessively across my shoulder. "Where you taking me tonight, honey?"

"Anywhere you want, sweetie." I grinned as only a man who has won a battle can.

"Is this for real?" the FTO asked. I nodded. "Lucky dog," he muttered.

"We'll discuss that dinner later," she said to me, then she turned to Lizzie who was lying quietly with a small cold pack taped over the top of a compress. Karri May lifted the dressing away, checking to see if the wound continued to bleed. When she was satisfied the seepage had stopped, she put a fresh compress on, then started winding another length of cotton swathing around Lizzie's head. When Karri May had enough to make Liz look like a Bedouin, she searched on her belt for scissors. She must have left them in the ambulance, so I pulled out my Spyderco knife. Expertly, I flicked the blade out and offered it to her. She shuddered.

"I hate those things," she said. "Every time I see one, I get the willies."

I was surprised. I couldn't think how many firemen and paramedics I'd seen carry knives. The company even made special versions for their line of work. She called to her driver, Chris, who was on the phone with his wife. He came over, still talking, looked at Lizzie and handed Karri May his scissors.

Once she had the cotton cut and held with small metal clips, she put things back in the medical bag. She said in a quiet voice so only the two of us could hear, "Ignore the bandages, you guys. I made it look worse than it is so she'd think I really fixed her up. She's doesn't even need stitches. What're you going to do with her?"

"Send her on her way," I said.

"No. You're going to take her to jail. I heard the witness," the FTO said.

"Wow!" I put a hand to my forehead, feigning as though I was thinking hard. "For a minute there, I thought I was standing on the Strip, which, by the way, I believe is Mary area. Bike territory, isn't it? Maybe we should call Sergeant Smith and see what he thinks. We can ask him about you being down here and jumping my call. We can ask him if he thinks his favorite vag should go to jail. Yeah, I like that idea," I let my finger settle on the radio microphone button.

"OK. OK," the FTO said, hurriedly. "You're an asshole, Madden." Since he'd looked at my nametag, I looked at his for the first time. It read A. Adams. "We're clearing. You're primary."

"Thank you, Officer A. Adams," I said, sarcastically. "And stay off my turf unless I kick out a four forty-four."

I watched as he went and got his trainee. They removed the cuffs from John and told him to park his ass on the fence until I was through with him. As far as I was concerned, this thing was close to being a wrap. Karri May went to the gurney and helped Liz off. I pointed to the open back door of my car.

"Lizzie, wait right there and we'll talk."

She nodded, then went to sit in the air conditioning. She looked at the ground as she walked, moving her head back and forth.

"What're you doing?" I asked her.

"Looking at my shadow. My head is huge," Liz said.

"Yeah, you look like a space alien," I said.

"My, Cam. You handle yourself so well," Karri May said. "Did you ever hear about this thing called diplomacy?"

"It's for pussies. I'm the straight-forward type of guy."

"Bull in the china shop," she said. "I see that in you."

"Hey, I can be as sensitive as the next guy."

"Oh. I'm sure. See ya later, alligator." Karri May gave me a peck on the cheek, bent, and picked up her bag.

"Now, that's an ass," John said. I turned to see him watching her. If it had been from FTO Adams, I'd agreed. But, from this piece of shit, it pissed me off.

I took a step closer and quietly told him, "I told you to stay over there, asshole."

"Officer Madden. You shouldn't call me an asshole in front of the lady." He stepped away from the fence. "What kind of chance would I have with her if she thought bad of me for letting you talk like that in front of her?" he said. The smile he made reminded me of something the wolf would have given Granny.

"Don't worry about the way he talks in front of me," Karri May said to him.

"You better get your ass on that fence or you'll be sorry," I said. I took a step forward. He retreated reluctantly. For just a fraction of a second, I saw a fleeting expression come over John's face as he looked past me to Karri May. The flicker in his eyes was a look I don't know if I could categorize — the closest thing I would attempt to say, if pressed, would be hatred. All I knew then was that I saw it, saw where it was directed, and chose to disregard it.

She pulled the oversize beeper out of the holder that was attached to an epaulet and glanced at the screen. "Baby choking on a chicken bone. Gotta go." She opened the back doors and threw the bag in, then climbed up. With a door in either hand, she looked me in the eye, then winked.

"Call me later and tell me where you want to go to dinner," I said.

She grinned, then pulled the doors shut. I was left in a cloud of diesel fumes. John stepped away from the fence again. He waved at the ambulance as it drove away.

■ ■ ■

To the Hoosgow

When I turned back to John, he saw my expression. He moved back to the fence, but he grinned at me. It was as if he'd changed — as though he thought we had something in common.

"You're free to go," I told him. "Don't let me see you again today,"

When he was on his way. I moved Liz into the passenger seat of my car. It was going to be hard getting in the right frame of mind to deal with her. I needed to get Liz's side of the story to finish writing the report. I wondered what universe that was going to come out of.

"What happened, Liz?" She saw John walking away.

"You better arrest him," she screamed.

"Lizzie!" I said forcefully. "Calm down."

Instead, she raised both legs and kicked my dashboard. Her foot slipped off and slammed into the windshield. I was amazed it didn't shatter or pop out. I caught her right wrist and hooked the cuff on it, then using what was called an ignition twist, I forced her forward. The dash kept her from struggling. It was unbelievable. I caught the second wrist on the first try and felt the other cuff go right on. I grabbed her coat and pulled until she was flush to the seatback. With my other hand, I trapped her knees, forcing her feet to the floorboards. When I had her in position, I slid the seat halfway forward, then tightened the seatbelt. I looked out the window and saw John had come back to see what was happening.

"Now you've done it," I told her. "You're going to jail."

I stepped out and closed the door. I turned to John. "I thought I made it clear it's your lucky day. Get going."

"Her going to jail makes my day," he said, giving me a grin I didn't like. I promised myself I'd deal with him sometime in the next few days. "Like I said, if I have to come back here . . . "

"You'll what?" he asked. Before I could reach him, he threaded his way though the crowd. I walked around the car and climbed in. The car was an oven. Liz was struggling with the seatbelt. "You're killing me," she sobbed.

"If you promise to behave, I'll loosen the seatbelt."

"I will. I promise." I reached across and pulled the belt to create a little slack.

"Where you taking me?" she asked.

"Downtown. Air conditioning, good food, nice nurse to give you some medication."

"We going to jail?"

I didn't want to say. "We're going for a ride."

"Where?" she asked.

"Down the Strip. Then downtown."

"Is John going to jail? Do you have him in another car?"

She'd heard what I'd done about John, but it sounded as if she'd already forgotten. I decided as long as she was calm, I'd keep my mouth shut. People could be funny when they were taken to jail. They could be calm as could be up until the point they saw the place and the reality set in, then they did stupid things. Once, when I was arriving at the jail at the same time as Joey and his FTO, I'd seen a man panic and start kicking the windshield out of their car. Or there was the time when another officer sat at a red light a block from the detention center and his arrestee opened the door, dove out, rolled to his feet, and ran off down the street. Another cop leaving the jail gave chase and tackled the man, causing the original arresting officer to sit at UMC for five hours while they sewed the guy's chin up. With people like Lizzie, there was no telling what might happen. She was supposed to be a paranoid schizophrenic, or something like that, and I wasn't about to start getting her upset. It could be like putting out a fire with gas.

For a couple of minutes, she was quiet. The air in the car was hot, with the fan doing about as good a job as the open window. The heavy Strip traffic made my progress slow. I figured in another five minutes, we might get to Flamingo, then I could cut west to I-15. From there it normally took a few minutes to get to county.

"So arrest me, Pig!" she said, suddenly. "I'll go to jail, but that son of a bitch better go, too. I'll cut off his balls when we get in the cell together."

"Lizzie, stop," I said in a soothing tone. "You're already arrested. Relax."

"Oh, I can't wait to get in there with him."

"They aren't going to put you in the same cell. They're going to give you one of your own."

The next thing I knew, she reached across and worked the electric window button. "Help! Help!" She screamed at people on the sidewalk, who turned to look. She wailed, "The police are kidnapping me."

I worked the master control causing the window to reverse direction. As soon as it was up, she pressed the switch and down it went. I tried activating the window locks to freeze the glass as it was in the all-the-way-up position, but as soon as I had the window up, she put it back down. At one point, she actually had her head out the window when the glass went up, catching her at the throat.

"Oh, great," I muttered. "People will think I'm killing her." I had to put the window down so I could pull her back in. Just when I had the window closed, I heard a funny noise — something I'd never heard a car make before. There was the smell of smoke. I figured either the air conditioning or the motor for the window had burned out. I reached over and grabbed a hunk of hair and jerked her head inside. She turned on me as if she was a bobcat, trying to get her teeth into any part of my body she could reach. I must have looked as though rats had gotten loose in the car.

When we reached the red light at Flamingo, I slammed the gear shifter into PARK. Using both hands, I grabbed handfuls of hair. I jerked her head upright, then let one hand go so I could tighten the seatbelt. When

I had the belt tight, I put an arm across her chest and pulled at the lever under the seat until it was as far forward as it would go. I was afraid I was going to have to get out and use a hobble on her, but the thought of trying to hook her feet in a rope loop made me nervous. The last time I used a hobble, the guy kicked me three times in the head before I trapped his feet. The device was great once it was on. The problem was getting it on, then pulling the feet towards the door. A knot was tied at the end of the rope, which was left outside after the door was closed. The knot trapped by the door was supposed to keep the suspect from kicking or moving.

Instead of going though all that, my intention was to pull over. I'd call a code five prisoner. Once Dispatch knew I needed help, she would request another unit to come across from Southwest Area Command, park his or her car at the meet, and ride in with me. With two of us in my car, I could drive and the other officer could control her. Before I could make the call, the light changed. People actually started honking their horns at me. I decided I better get out of the intersection. I put the car in DRIVE, accelerated through the light, and turned westbound on Flamingo Road. This way, I was off Las Vegas Boulevard and I could use a small dirt lot on the south side of Caesars Palace until Dispatch could get me help. With that plan in mind, I reached the lot. I reached for the mike as Lizzie started crying.

"I'll be good. I promise," she said between sobs. "Let me go. Please."

"I can't. Besides, you already said that once."

"I will," she said. "I promise, Mr. Policeman."

Her head was almost on the dashboard as she sobbed. She wasn't struggling anymore. I needed just a few more minutes and we'd be at county. Just to be safe, I radioed Dispatch that I was going to need help with her.

"Is she code five, Bike Thirty?" Dispatch asked.

"Negative. She was," I said. "She's code four for the moment."

"What's your ETA?"

"Ten-fifteen, depending on traffic. I'm at Flamingo and I-15, Control." I knew she'd have several large COs waiting when I came through the jail's sally port. I turned onto I-15, heading north. I was at the top of the on-ramp so I could see a distance. Traffic was heavy going northbound. The cars barely moved. I knew I'd miscalculated our arrival time. With construction at both the Spaghetti Bowl and the Sahara Avenue off-ramp, I might be sitting for a while. I thought about reversing and taking the Strip all the way to jail, but I was already on the on-ramp and with cars stacked behind me, it was going to be a pain in the ass backing up. As soon as I was on the freeway, I cut people off, using the police vehicle's ability to intimidate people into getting them to allow me to move across the lanes of travel until I was in the number one lane, or what would normally be the fast lane. At any other time, people would be doing seventy, in spite of the signs that indicated a fifty-five limit. When I first merged into the lane, I was doing ten. Within a few minutes, the cars had increased their speed to forty-five. The distance between vehicles was three or four feet. I wanted to stay over in the number one lane, which is by the cross-over wall. That was because lanes three and four, which were those closest to the emergency lane, would back up with people trying to get off at Sahara. Once I was past Sahara, I needed to cross back to lane four so I could exit on Charleston Boulevard.

With all the traffic it was going to take a while to get to the jail. While keeping my eyes on traffic, I reached for the microphone to tell Dispatch I was going to be delayed. Lizzie bent and sank what teeth she had left into my hand. The pain was instant and intense, causing me to involuntarily try to jerk my hand back. She was like a dog with a bone.

"Lizzie, let go," I yelled. When she wouldn't, I propped my knees under the steering wheel. With my left hand, I took the can of pepper spray out and hosed her down.

The policy manual suggested some procedures, recommended others, and clearly spelled those that were mandatory. Spraying Capstun in a vehicle that was sealed with the air conditioner running was one of those highly recommended to be avoided. Up to that point, I'd never given the reason much thought. Within seconds, I knew it — intimately. Vehicle air conditioning systems were designed to recycle the already-cool air within the cab. When the air was full of pepper spray, it recycled that, too. In other words, Lizzie got the main blast and I got the residual overspray — over and over and over again. Pepper spray, or Capstun, has a distinct flavor just before it has its effect. I'd heard it described differently by other cops, but to me, it tasted the same as if I were chewing wood. As soon as that taste filled my mouth, I knew what was coming next. That was because when we were in the Academy, a TAC officer made each of us stand and take a blast. The active ingredient, oleo capsicum, acted on the mucous membranes. That meant the eyes, nose, and back of the throat began to run. It was the body's attempt to protect itself. Furthermore, it also shut down breathing, which caused shortness of breath. Being an irritant, the spray worked best when people were hot and sweaty. Only a man who just made love in a bed of poison ivy could describe the itch.

Lizzie threw her head back and screamed, which let my hand go. That was only going to make things worse. All that space in her lungs she'd just evacuated would need refilling. Part of what filled it was going to be pepper spray. With my eyes swelling, I was having a hard time seeing. I tried getting to the window controls. That was when she started violently rocking her body sideways. Lizzie's head hit the steering wheel. The car swerved left. It struck the dividing wall. My head slammed into the driver's window, shattering the glass. The blow partially stunned me. I heard the squeal of brakes.

■ ■ ■

When things like that happened, the world sometimes seemed to go into slow motion. My eyes were tearing, but for an instant, I clearly saw the face of the driver to my right. She was looking at me, her eyes big. I would always think she gave me a pleading look —like, "Please, God! Let me get home tonight." There was the sound of a click. It took me a second to realize what it was. As I watched but could do nothing to stop her, Lizzie's hands, still in the cuffs, pushed the seat belt button. She then shifted, caught the door handle, and opened it. She looked like a woman falling off a building. Her eyes never left mine. I saw nothing crazy about her right then — just an old woman who wanted to live without the likes of me interfering in her life. I slammed on the brakes.

I felt the centripetal force as the rear end came around, pinning me to the door. She disappeared. The patrol unit bucked. Before mine stopped, the vehicle behind me slammed into the driver's side rear quarter panel. I tried to stop myself from flying to the right, but the forces were too much. My head cracked the side of the computer. The lights went out.

When I opened my eyes, I was looking at Karri May's face. *"Where'd you come from?"* I wanted to ask. There was this wrinkle between her eyebrows. When she saw I was focused on her, it disappeared, replaced by relief.

"Can you hear me, Cam?"

I tried nodding, but something was around my neck. I blinked. My view of the world seemed to slip towards a long dark tunnel.

"Cam. Stay with me," she said. Her voice was like an anchor, keeping me from drifting. I moved my tongue through my dry mouth. "Waaa-ter." It was more breath than a word.

Karri May shook her head. "Can't have any until we get you to the hospital."

I glanced past her and saw a metal ceiling. I was flat on my back in the ambulance. I swallowed several times, which seemed to work.

"Shit," I whispered. "Lizzie. My prisoner." I tried sitting up and she pushed me back.

"Cam, please. We don't know if you have back or neck injuries. Lay still."

"I need to check on her. She jumped out of the car."

"How is he?" Sergeant Smith stuck his head in the door.

"We're not sure. He's talking, but we don't know what the extent of his . . . " She hesitated. " . . . problems are."

"Oh, I know what he's got for problems. His fucking prisoner's brains are all over the fucking freeway. What the hell happened, Cam?"

"She . . . uhhh . . . she's dead?"

"Get out of here," Karri May said. She suddenly went into that protective mode I liked so much about her — only this time it was for me. She rose from next to me and went close to Smith, then pushed him towards the door.

"Are you deliberately trying to put him in shock?" she asked.

"Get your hands off me," Smith said. "You touch me again and I'll arrest you."

"Oh, really," Karri May said. She looked past Smith's shoulder, then called in a loud voice, "Lieutenant Giles, will you please get this man away from my patient?"

The Ell Tee came to the ambulance. "What's up, Karri May?"

"I think this isn't the time for this sergeant to start questioning my patient. I don't know the extent of Cam's injuries. He's possibly in shock and I don't think he needs anyone making things worse. Do you?"

"Smith," Giles said. "Don't you have things that need doing? If not, maybe I can find some. Like traffic control."

"No, Curtis. I have plenty to do. Like clean up the mess the man you insisted come to my squad made. I'll go see that the fire department gets right to washing that woman's fucking brains off the roadway. How about that?"

"That's enough, Sergeant Smith," Giles said. "When this is over, report to my office."

Smith threw a lackadaisical salute, then left. Giles looked down at me.

"How is he, Karri May?"

"As I said, we don't know," Karri May said. "We need to get him in and do a CAT scan."

He knelt next to the gurney. "Cam, how you doing?"

"Is she dead, Ell Tee?" I said, lifting my head in spite of the neck restraint.

"Yes, Cam." Giles stood up, then sat down. He cupped his hands, staring down into the bowl they made. "I'm afraid so. I'm going to let them take you down to the hospital. I'll be there when I get done here. After the doc checks you out, we'll talk."

I let my head fall back. Karri May closed the back doors and the ambulance began to move. I listened to the siren. Who would have ever guessed that I'd be on this side of that sound? The rig's motion caused me to close my eyes. I must have slept because the next thing I knew, I was in a hospital bed. I noticed the blue light from the TV, then fell back asleep. When I awoke, the room was filled with balloons and flowers. I wondered how long I'd been out. I couldn't see out the window, but the light coming in between the slats told me it was either early morning or late afternoon.

"People have been here all day." The voice was disembodied. I tried turning my head in the direction it came from. "I guess you could say I'm your roommate."

I had to tilt my whole body to see who it was. There was enough light from the monitors to see another bed with a person in it. His leg was in a cast, suspended from some kind of pulley contraption.

"What happened?" I asked.

"Broke my leg."

"I did?" I couldn't feel anything down there and with my neck in a brace, I couldn't look, either.

"Not you, stupid," he said. "Me. I broke my leg. You broke your neck."

"It is?" The ceiling lights came on as he said these words.

"Your neck's not broken. Don't be listening to that old fool." A very large black woman in a nurse's outfit came into my field of view. "I got some pain killers if you want them." She pressed a button on a control by my head and the bed across my back started raising.

"Yes, sireee. I'll take all you got," my roommate told her. When I was up, I saw the man in the other bed was old. If I had to guess, I'd say seventy or better.

"You get nothing, Mr. Carney," she said. "Not till the rest of the stuff gets filtered out by those overworked kidneys of yours."

"I don't need them now," I said. "Can you leave them in case I do?"

"No way, honey. That old codger next to you would cut that leg off to get over here and take your stuff."

"That ain't true, Nurse Damel. I told you, that other nurse made a mistake. She told me those pills were my vitamins. I thought I was getting healthy."

The nurse took my wrist, checking the pulse while she looked at her watch. "Name's Clarrisa or if you're gonna be like him, then its Nurse

Damel. I like taking care of cops, so if you're reasonable, you'll get the royal treatment." She glanced at the other bed with the meanest look I thought I'd ever seen. "Unlike some other people around here."

After she was done making a notation on my chart, she threw another truly evil look at Mr. Carney. "Matter of fact, I think I need to get some more blood, Bill. Lab tests, you know."

"Ya damned vampires," he said. "Ain't no blood left in me. I'd have some if I could get fed around here."

"I'd feed you if you weren't trying to trade the food you hide for people's drugs."

"Mumph." He turned his face away. "That was a misunderstanding, too."

She went to Bill's bedside with a paper cup containing a couple of blue pills. She dumped them in his hand, then watched as he put them in his mouth. After his throat convulsed, she handed him a cup of water. He drank some. As he started to swallow, Clarrisa grabbed his head. With her other hand, she pinched his nose.

"You better swallow them pills," she hissed. It took a few seconds, then his Adam's apple bobbed. She let go and grabbed his lower jaw, forcing his mouth open. She twisted her head around, inspecting the inside of his mouth. He mumbled something incoherently, while she held him.

When she let go, he yelled. "What the hell was that?"

"Found a stash of those under Mr. Bicker's mattress. They looked a little dissolved, like they been in someone's mouth."

"Of all the . . . " I watched his eyes flutter closed. As soon as she was sure he was out, she turned back to me.

"Some people here to see you," Clarrisa said. "If it's my choice, I'd say no. Ain't though. I'll be at the desk. You get tired, push that." She pointed at a button. "I'll be in quick to shoo them away. OK?"

I tried nodding, but the brace wouldn't let me move. Before I could open my mouth to reply, she was at the door, waving. Smith and another man came in as she opened the door.

"Hello, Officer Madden. Cam. Do you mind if I call you Cam?" The other man said. Before I could answer, he went on. "I'm Tom Black, internal affairs. I thought we might talk about what happened two days ago. About…" He opened a notebook. "Elizabeth Ogden's death."

I'd forgotten Lizzie was dead. "Damn," I muttered.

He pulled a chair over, then settled into it. "This is going to be informal, just a little background before I get you in the office for a regular statement."

"Shouldn't I have a rep here?"

"Oh, I don't think we need to do that. I'm not using anything we say today."

"I think I'd prefer a rep being present."

He ignored my protest. "I talked to Officer Adams. He said you insisted on taking her to jail, in spite of his being the first to arrive on the call."

"He was out of his area. It was a Strip call. I was primary."

"He's a Mary unit, too. Are you saying you own the Strip?"

"No, Sergeant Smith's policy as far as the Strip I concerned is . . . "

He cut me off. "I already talked to your sergeant. I have his statement." He nodded at Smith. "Did you know the deceased?"

"You mean Lizzie?" I asked. "Of course. I've dealt with her many times around the hotels and on the street."

"Were you angry with her? Did you bear her any kind of grudge? In spite of policy, you Capstunned her in a closed car. Were you aware that there is a policy against that?"

"What?" I asked. The questions came too fast for me to think about how I needed to answer them. "No. I liked her. Why would I?"

"Cam. I'm asking the questions here. Just try to answer them." I could feel a pressure building behind my eyes, making my brain feel like it would burst. I wished I'd taken the painkillers Clarissa offered earlier.

"Do you think you could have handled the situation that led to her death in another way?"

"Any situation can be handled in a million ways," I said. The door opened and the Lieutenant Giles walked in.

"Hello, Tom," Giles said. "Can I ask what you're doing here?"

"Thought I'd talk to Cam a little before I had him into the office, Curtis."

He looked at me. "Did you want to talk without a rep?"

"I asked for one," I said in a quiet voice, "but they ignored me."

He looked at the two sergeants. "Correct me if I'm wrong, but I think his contract forbids you talking to him if he requests a rep, doesn't it?"

"Depends on how it's read?"

"Far as I'm concerned, there's only one way to read it."

"Far as I'm concerned, Curtis, this is an IAB investigation."

"It's not 'Curtis' anymore. It's Lieutenant Giles. You're out of here and don't make me make that an order. Sergeant Smith, you will be in my office as soon as I get back. I think your buddy here might be doing a little investigating on you when I'm done. Now get the hell out of here."

"Sure thing, Curtis," Smith said. He slouched in his lazy way that indicated insubordination more than anything else a man could do.

"I'd be more than happy to help him leave if he's having a problem," Clarissa's voice came from behind Giles. She stepped around the Ell Tee.

"I have enough right now," Black said.

"I see anything shows up in a report before the date of an official interview and you might find yourself answering to me on an internal investigation I start. I better be making myself clear." Black and Smith started walking towards Clarissa, but when they saw the look on her face, they obviously thought better of getting too close to her. After the door closed, Giles pulled a chair close.

"What'd he ask?" Giles said. I closed my eyes. The headache was back in full force.

"I think he needs those tablets I offered earlier," Clarissa said. She left the room.

"Cam, when you feel up to it, the Department is going to need to talk about what happened. Until then, talk to no one without a rep present. Do you understand?"

"Yes."

"Someone's outside that wants to see you."

"I can't believe I killed her."

"Don't say that. You didn't kill her."

"How do you know?"

"I know, because I know you," he said. "Now, listen to me. Be careful about saying things like that. If someone like Black hears you say it, you're through. You did not kill that woman. She had problems and the system failed her. If anything is to blame, it's not you. Understand?"

I nodded.

"Get some rest." He stood up, started to turn, but stopped. He placed a hand on my shoulder. "This, too, shall pass. Always remember that. It's that way with everything in life."

As he went out, Karri May came in. "Hey, how ya doin'?" I turned towards the window. It was probably late afternoon because it was darker than it had been. "I'm off. I thought I'd stop and see you." She leaned in and kissed me on the cheek, then slid an arm across my back. She pulled me forward, fluffing the pillow under my head. It always surprised me at how strong she was. With her body that close to my face, I smelled her. Even in her uniform, she smelled good. The scent was slightly fruity, making me think of those California fields where the workers would stand out in the sun picking fruit. When the car got close, the smell would grow strong, making me hungry. On top of it was the acrid, mediciny tang of the drugs she must have dispensed while on her shift. There was something else, too. It took me a second to recognize the underlying scent I knew best, that all-too-human odor of sweat. A part of me wanted to let my tongue touch the bare skin at the base of her throat, but the image of Lizzie lying dead on the hot cement of I-15 jumped into my thoughts. My heart started beating faster, as if I'd just seen a snake hidden in some of the foliage that decorated my room. Karri May eased me down. "Better?"

"No."

She picked up my chart. "You need to be on something."

"No. I need to be alone. To think."

"I don't think so. What if I get Doc Sandler to pop up and talk with you? He's the resident psychiatrist."

"No!" I was emphatic. "I don't want to see anyone like that. Enough people know I fucked up."

"Cam, you didn't fuck up. A bad thing happened. People saw you fighting with her in the car. The lady you hit said you practically went out after her. Both of you would have been killed."

"She was my responsibility. I failed at my job."

"This isn't like you. You're feeling sorry for yourself."

"Feeling sorry for myself?" I looked at her in disbelief. "There's a dead woman at the morgue. Did it ever occur to you I might be feeling something for her?"

"Yes, it did."

"You don't know shit about what I'm feeling," I said. "Get out. Leave me alone."

Clarissa took that second to walk in. She looked at the two of us, then handed Karri May the pills and water. "Make sure he takes these."

"I will." She reached into the cup. I saw the two blue tablets between her fingers.

"I don't want them," I said. My head was pounding, but I deserved the pain.

"Take them or I'll have that large woman come in here and make you take them."

Grudgingly, I opened my mouth and swallowed the pills. Karri May sat with me until my mind faded, like the light outside my window.

■ ■ ■

Clothing? None . . .

I t was four in the morning. I had been back in a black-and-white for a couple of days. The doc had cleared me for duty a week before but said he didn't want me on a bike for a while yet. If Sergeant Smith had a say, I'd be kicking cans down the road. The afternoon before, he stopped me in the parking lot.

"Don't get too comfortable in that car. You might not be here at the end of shift."

"Really? I thought the lieutenant had more to say about that than you?"

"Don't be a smart ass, Cam." He tried to make his voice sound official. I ignored the attempt.

"Let me give you a clue, Sarg. It ain't my ass that's smart." I drove away. This was becoming a daily ritual. Twice now, he'd called me into his office in the middle of my shift just to tell me some bullshit thing. The first time I was so mad afterwards that I stopped paying attention to what I was doing. While on a stop, I missed a gun on a suspect, finding it only when it fell out his pants leg at the jail. Things like that got people killed. Added to the distraction of Smith's fucking with me was the knowledge that the investigation was still active on Lizzie's death. I knew Smith wanted me fired and was helping Sergeant Black, his buddy, with anything he could towards that end. There was nothing to be said. The investigation was going to take its course. I'd quit giving a shit.

I heard a siren approaching, so I pulled to the right. It was an ambulance. I stared down towards my lap. If it was Karri May, I didn't want to see her. I'd avoided her calls and the couple of attempts she made to see me. Finally, she backed off. It had been over a week and a half since she visited me in the hospital.

As soon as I hit the street, Dispatch gave me a call right off and it had been going like that since then. By the end of shift, all I wanted was to go home, fill a glass with something stronger than beer and chug it down. That was the magic sleeping potion. I kept a bottle by the bed so that when I woke in the middle of the night, I could medicate myself.

I was heading in, just crossing Industrial Road, the boundary for Mary area, when my MCT beeped. I read the screen and groaned. Dispatch was sending me on an unknown trouble call. A second later, a message flashed across the screen telling me everyone else was logged off and all the grave units were on something. I checked to see what they were on. It was a shooting that had resulted in a homicide. The suspect was holed up in an apartment with an old woman hostage. SWAT was being called out. This was going to take a while. I turned the car around. I had the window down, my arm out. The air was cool. It was nice weather for a change.

The 404A was over on South Maryland Parkway by the Athletic Club. I knew these types of calls could turn into anything, so I typed a message asking for more details. Dispatch sent me a message back that there wasn't anything else. The call originated from a condominium complex in Nora sector, totally out of the bike unit's area. Those condos were pestilential, gone to seed — literally. Tumbleweeds that only needed a little rain to approach gargantuan sizes, and fragrant sage, grew from cracks in the parking lots. Most of the units were owned by out-of-state landlords. They didn't give a shit who they rented to as long as the money came in at the end of the month.

The plants weren't the only weeds. The place had its share of the human sort. We averaged a shooting or knifing call a week from there. The residents were mostly low-class poor or lower middle class, which could be called upper-class poor. They reflected the usual ethnic and racial diversities — south-of-the-border Hispanics, closed-housing-project blacks, and trailer trash whites. Their only saving grace was their young kids. In them, we saw the innocence; the wonder the American Dream could bring if they were given half a chance. The problems, as always, were their derelict parents who didn't give a shit if they went to school, had enough to eat, or what happened to them half the time.

"Bike Thirty, be advised I have no available backup," Dispatch radioed. *Like I didn't know that*, I thought. "I'll get you one as soon as a unit clears." I knew she'd broadcast that on the off chance someone from another channel was screwing off and would cut their call short. Technically, I knew I could hang back because this was a two-man call by policy, but that wouldn't be cool. Smith would think I was milking overtime and besides, if it turned out to be nothing, other cops would talk. I drove straight into the place so I could at least check out the situation. I went through the gate and saw the security shack was dark. It was supposed to be manned twenty-four seven. My guess was that either management had once again run out of money to pay the guard or he was off somewhere getting high.

It was just after 12:30 a.m. I should have had the ride in the barn and been heading home. Instead, I felt like I was back on graves. After the constant hubbub of swing shift — the constant going from call to call, coming into this place with its quiet streets and buildings was like stepping off into another world. The thing I liked about graves was that when there were calls, they happened fast. Just getting to them was a breeze because traffic was just about nonexistent. I remember going from the Sahara Hotel to this complex in seven minutes once. I ran every light and never had to put the lights and siren on. The other great thing about Graveyard calls was that when I got there, the people present were usually the suspects, the victims, or both. That got things sorted out quickly. Those were the advantages.

The disadvantages were just what I was experiencing — there wasn't enough work to justify large squads, so one or two officers patrolled entire areas. Earlier, I'd heard a unit log on as One Nora One. He was the only Nora unit, which meant that this was all his. Nora sector stretched from Paradise Road in the west to the west side of Maryland Parkway, then from Sahara in the north to the airport on the south, an area of about three square miles. I'd heard that most of the graveyard squad had the flu, so only three people showed up for work. What I really thought happened was they'd partied too hard the night before when their sarg was notified he'd made lieutenant. With the squad being undermanned, things could get bad fast, especially if something happened, like an officer-involved shooting or a fire or the hostage situation that was currently unfolding.

Still, graves was good for hiding out. For a second, the thought crossed my mind about transferring back to graves. The problem was I knew Smith would never approve a transfer. His theory was that a good supervisor never let a problem get away until it had been dealt with. Unfortunately, his idea of dealing with me was having me fired.

As soon as I passed the gates, I cut my lights. Before I could find the address, I had to find the street. It didn't help that the streets were dark — what few lights there were in the complex were out. I knew this was because the drug dealers routinely broke the bulbs. They also removed the street signs from the poles and the numbers off the buildings. They wanted to make things harder on us. We had asked management to paint the building and street numbers on the roofs so at least the air unit could find things.

As I drove back and forth trying to figure out where I was going, the computer beeped again. She sent me more details. It seemed another tenant had called in to say two people had been shouting at each other. I stopped the car and got out. One of the other things I hated about the place was that the streets were like narrow canyons, hemmed in by walls of garage doors. Some of the streets also curved, making it hard to see all the way to the end. If this were an ambush, there would be no way to turn the car. I'd have to try to back up, which meant exposing my upper body and head.

Another tactical problem was the way the front of the units faced grassy common areas. During the day, all the kids played out there where the parents kept an eye on them. In the early evening hours, those areas were abandoned. The men sat out on their cars or in the open garages, drinking and making a lot of noise. That led to the Swing cops getting a lot of 416B calls that involved first arguments, then fights, and, finally, the occasional shooting or stabbing. If a cop wanted to make an approach, the only choices were to park a great distance away and try to come on the disturbance with speed, because stealth was out of the question when crossing all that flat grass. Or he could just pull up to the call. That was just what any cop wanted — to drive into unknown trouble.

Right now, all I saw was a ghost town. I rolled the window all the way down, then stepped out of the car. I tried listening for anything that might clue me to what was going on or where to go. Nothing! I got back in. I found Green Street, then one street without a sign, then Hill Street. I was looking for Gray Lane. I turned around and went back to the one without the sign. As I drove down the alley, I came around a curve. There was a white male standing near a pickup truck. Walking down the middle of the alley, right straight towards me, was a naked female. She was oblivious to my presence.

"Not bad," I whispered. She was blond — natural, of course. I guessed five feet two inches tall, a hundred and five pounds, not a pound more, great tits, and mad as hell. You've got to be when you don't notice a ton and a half idling police car fifty feet away. The male's attention was focused on her, but he had seen me. I was thinking they definitely looked as though they knew each other. After all, the guy didn't seem the least bit shocked that he was yelling at a naked woman.

I stopped when I cut the distance in half, shoved the shift into PARK, and pushed the door open. When I got out, I stood with one foot on the ground and the other inside just in case I needed to duck for cover or get the hell out of there. This was just too weird — and what a perfect setup for an ambush. I could see the writeup in one of those training bulletins — dumb cop shot gawking at naked woman. I expected a lot of things when I pulled in, but not this, so I wasn't really sure how to handle the situation. There were obviously no weapons on the female and the threat of physical violence, other than maybe her punching or karate kicking me to death, was all I had to worry about. The male could be a problem, but of the two, he seemed to be the most composed. Maybe more than I was.

"Amy, the police are here," the male called. Before the words were all the way out, she was yelling and cussing at him. She still hadn't noticed me. If she kept going, she was going to walk right into the front of my car. Normally, when I stopped someone, I directed that person to the front of the unit. We called this "step into my office." That was the place we conducted interviews, spread the articles the subject gave up or that were discovered during a search, and prepared the paperwork to take people to jail. So, I guess what I said next made sense.

"Amy, get your ass on the front of my car."

At first, there was no response. She took another step, then her head swiveled. I expected a look of surprise or shock. Blank. She simply stared. I hit the headlight button, catching her in the full glare. *Damn!* I thought. *She's pretty.* As I shifted slightly, I was amazed to see the ground sparkle like it was covered in diamonds. Broken glass. She was barefoot. There should have been a trail of blood coming from where she'd been. I couldn't help wondering what was going on here. She was naked and giving the appearance of being unconcerned with my presence as far as I could see.

"Get over here, please," I ordered. She didn't move. *Did she speak English?* "So, Amy. What's this?" I asked. "Drugs, insanity, or some weird sexual thing?" Still nothing. I tried another tactic.

"Can you come here, please?" I asked. *Maybe she's an idiot,* I thought. "Right there, please." I pointed between the buddy bumpers. Instead, she turned around and walked away.

"Fuck! What next?" I muttered. "Stop!" I yelled. Before I did anything else, I decided I better let Dispatch know what was going on. I reached inside and grabbed the microphone from the seat where I'd left it in case I needed it fast.

"Control, Bike Thirty. I'm arrived. I think this is a four seventeen." I hadn't wanted to call the thing a domestic, but if I went after her, I still had to worry about the male. If I dealt with the male, I lost the female. By telling Dispatch it was a domestic, she knew she needed to find me backup, which meant madly typing a message to the Southeast dispatcher to see if she had a free unit. "It's a male and female and the female's walking away from me." I dropped the mike back in the car and looked at the male. "Raise your hands." I pointed my gun at him. "Don't move. Pretend you're made of ice. Amy, stop!"

"Control, I'll be southbound in the complex," I used the lapel mike to relay this. Now, I felt really dumb. She wasn't running. She was walking.

"Bike Thirty, do you want a code red."

"Not yet, Control." I didn't want to tie up the radio channel for this. "Amy! Will you please stop and come back here?" I called. It felt dumb begging a suspect. I also knew other cops on channel would start paying attention to my call as soon as they heard the words "code red." The word would also go out that a foot pursuit might be brewing. I once thought if we could see radio waves like we did light, the sky would have lit up with all the energy generated by computer messages sent from unit to unit. What I was to learn later was that my dispatcher caught the tension in my voice. She sent the call valley-wide. In Southeast and Southwest, there were no free units due to the shooting. Northeast and Northwest units were clearing up the last swing calls. They read the message or heard the radio traffic from their dispatchers, then checked the status of my call. When they saw what it was they started drifting my way in case things went to shit. That was just a graveyard thing.

"Bike Thirty, Control. Do you have a description?"

"WFA, five feet two, one oh five, long blond hair, middle of the back, approximately twenty-five years of age," I radioed. I knew what was coming next. Amy was still walking away purposefully. I kept my eye on the male, trying to pick up the pace to catch her.

"Do you have a clothing description?"

"Uhhh, yeah," I said. I hesitated, thinking about what I wanted to say next. The best course was just to say it. "There isn't any."

"Clothing?" the dispatcher asked. What always amazed me was how they kept their voices so calm. "None?"

"Affirmative, Control. She's naked," I said. I did my best to sound as professional as she did.

Suddenly, the radio came alive with male officers telling the dispatcher they would be en route. The squeal of units covering each other reminded me of a 444 or 443 call. The thing was, I didn't need assistance now like those calls implied. I just needed another unit to keep an eye on the male.

"Figures," I muttered. One minute, I couldn't get help and now I was going to have more cops here than I needed. "Red lights and sirens for a hundred pound naked woman."

Somewhere in the traffic, I heard a lone female voice, "Control, this is One Henry Thirty-Four. I'm clear four eighty. Disregard those units rolling code, I'll be en route to back that Bike unit."

The dispatcher's voice took on the slightest trace of sarcasm as she did exactly that.

"Henry Thirty-four," I radioed. "I'm in the southeast corner of the complex. Second street west of the guard shack."

"I'll be there in two, Bike Thirty."

I was about five feet behind Amy. She was walking fast, her arms swinging. I should have broken into a run, but I felt foolish enough having a foot pursuit with a naked woman and, the truth was, I didn't know what I was going to do with her if I caught her.

"Amy! Stop!" I called. This wasn't an actual foot pursuit. It was too slow. When I glanced at the guy, he was nonchalantly leaning back on the car. He was watching me with some interest. When he saw me glance at him, he grinned, held his hands up in a shrug and went back to watching. The whole time we walked, Amy hadn't once turned to see where I was. It was like she thought if she ignored me, I'd go away. The whole view was hair, naked back, ass, and legs.

"I just want to find out what's going on." We were at the end of a long section of buildings. There was a breezeway, then another set of condos. She turned right into the breezeway, disappearing from my sight. This would take her in the direction of the condo fronts. She had maintained her five feet lead, or three paces, when she made the turn. In terms of time, I'd guess she was a full second ahead of me.

When I came around the corner, she was gone, vanished — as if into thin air.

I ran a couple of steps forward just in case she had hidden in the bushes that lined the sidewalk. She wasn't there. It really looked as though she'd vanished. I scanned the narrow area. About ten feet in front of me I saw an open door. I couldn't imagine how she'd made it that far before I rounded the corner. It was spooky. I dropped into a crouch, gun up. That really felt stupid — a gun for a naked woman. I made an approach towards the door, crab-walking down the sidewalk. I tried keeping my back far enough away from the bushes so that if she was hiding and had the thought to attack me from behind, I'd have some warning. When I was at the side of the opening, I tried looking in. All I saw was blackness. Quickly, I ducked across the doorway, bracing myself in case she had a gun and shot at me. When I was on the other side, I kept crab-walking towards the front of the condos. I wanted to keep one eye on the door and the other in the direction I was going. When I reached the corner, I checked the grassy area. Nothing. Three or four seconds had passed. No naked running woman could cover that distance, at least seventy feet, in that amount of time. I went back to the condo's open door.

She has to be in there, I thought. I figured there had to be a light switch right inside on the wall. Shifting my gun to my left hand, I flattened myself against the wall. I quickly slipped a hand in and swept it down the wall. My hand hit the switches, changing their positions. Nothing happened. I clicked them several times.

From the alleyway, I heard the guy say, "Your partner went that way."

"Stay right there, sir," a female voice said. It had to be the Henry unit. I was relieved to hear the voice of another cop. I crossed back to the other side of the doorway, then moved to where I could watch the door and be seen by the officer when she came.

"I'm here," I called. When she still hadn't appeared after a dozen seconds, I stepped back and looked around the corner. I saw her talking to the woman's boyfriend. Although I couldn't hear what was going on, I was able to tell she was using her radio. That was because her head was canted over like she was talking to her shoulder. *Probably running him*, I thought. That could have waited.

"Got any guns or stuff on you?" she asked when she was done. I started to get worried. What she was doing was a little ass-backwards. First, you pat people, then you talk to them. When she talked to him, her tone of voice made it clear she wasn't goofing around. I waved to get her attention. She flapped a hand to acknowledge me, but continued talking to him. "Where's Amy?"

"No clue. He was chasing her," the guy said.

"You have her?" she called to me.

"I lost her," I said. "Don't ask me how. She might be inside this place." I pointed at the building. "But the lights aren't working,"

She walked with the guy to where I was standing. "Where is she, Mr. Amstad?" she asked.

"Amy? My wife?"

"Who the fuck else would she be talking about, asshole?" I asked. He shrugged. I looked at the other cop. "We'll be back." I put my hand on his chest and shoved him. "That way." I pointed. When we were close to her car, I asked. "You got warrants?" I put my face close to his so only he could hear me. "Because if you do, on the way to jail we might make a little stop — in some dark alley where we can talk. I'm tired. I should have been off an hour ago."

"Are you threatening me?"

"Turn around," I said.

"Fuck you, asshole. Nobody threatens me."

I grabbed a bunch of shirt and jerked him towards me.

"I'm not *nobody*. I'm the cop that's going to take your stupid ass to jail." Before he could say anything else, I spun him, then pulled an arm to me and fed the wrist into a cuff. He started struggling, but I twisted the cuff edge. The ignition twist raised him to his toes.

"Ow! Ow! Ow," he cried.

"Give me the other hand or you'll be sorry," I said. He couldn't get it around to me fast enough. "Mr. Amstad has decided to sit in my car," I called.

"Sure," she said. She moved back towards me.

"Stay where you can see the door," I said, exasperatedly. "I don't want her coming out and getting away. I want to figure out what is going on."

"I was here last night," she said as she moved to the edge of the building. "Also a four oh four. The details came out a female with a knife threatening a male. When we got here, the female was H-Hank so we cleared. It's the fifth time we've had calls to this address for this kind of thing." A 404 was unknown trouble, and H-Hank meant she was gone when the police got there.

"How long has that been going on?" I asked.

"Month or so."

"So in all that time, you've never seen her or talked to her at all?"

"Like I said, she was Hank."

"Did anybody try coming back by later on any of them?" Before she could answer, I asked, "By the way, what's your name?" I was looking at her, but the guy answered.

"Jason."

I sighed. This was turning into a cluster fuck. "Did it look like I was talking to you?" I moved so my face was an inch from his. It was big dog, little dog. He dropped his eyes. "I don't give a fuck who you are, Mr. Amstad. I'm asking her."

"The 'S' on the nametag is for Sue," she said. Just the way the words came out, I knew it was a little thing she used a lot. I didn't like people who did that.

I turned to Jason. "That your condo?" He didn't say or do anything. "Jason, now I'm talking to you." He continued to ignore me. I tightened my hand on his arm, digging my thumb and fingers into the muscle.

"Ughhh!" He nodded. I wondered if Sue or any of the other cops had gone in the night before or any night for that matter. I hoped so, but it wouldn't surprise me if they just cleared the call on Jason's say-so that his wife was gone. A lot of cops did things like that, not finishing what got started.

"Funny thing from last night, though," Sue said. "Jason here was the boyfriend and now he's the husband." She raised her eyebrows. "The call last night came out that his girlfriend threatened him with a twelve-inch butcher knife. Even after we talked to him for ten minutes, he denied knowing why she'd do that."

Now I knew they hadn't gone in. "I'll be back. I'm gonna put him in my car so we don't have to worry about him running away."

"I won't run. I'm in cuffs, for God's sake."

I pulled him towards the passenger side. As soon as I had him sitting, I took the seatbelt, acting as though I was going to hook it. I hit him in the jaw with my elbow. Before he could yell, I slid my forearm across his throat, cutting off his wind. "You better have something to tell me before you pass out. Otherwise, when you wake up in the hospital, there'll be a bunch of broken stuff." I knew if Sue looked over, it would appear as if my arm was across his chest, keeping him from trying something like head butting or biting me. I remembered when another cop taught me that trick and I said I'd never use it. *Things change*, I thought. When I loosened my arm and stopped choking him, he grabbed a breath like he was going to yell. I immediately applied the pressure again. "Don't yell," I warned. I watched his eyes go wild. "Understand?" He nodded with just a trace of panic.

This time when I let loose, he gasped. "She'll go out the window upstairs and across the roofs."

"Where?"

"I don't know. I think she's seeing someone else in here. That's what we've been fighting about."

"You better be telling me the truth." I looked him in the eye. His fear was like a drug to me. I suddenly understood what other cops had probably figured out long ago.

"I am," he said.

"We'll see, and if you aren't, I'll be back." I slipped out, slamming the car door. I went back to Sue. "She has to be in the house. I was five feet behind her."

"Why don't we get canine," Sue said. "I'm not too thrilled going in there if she has a knife."

"Stay here, then," I replied. "I don't dump shit on other people." I hoped I was making it clear that we wouldn't be here if she had done her job the night before. "If you don't want to go, I'll handle this alone."

"That's fucked up," she said. I heard the tone and it sounded like fear to me. I walked away. After a second, I heard her following. When we got to the door, I yelled a couple of times for Amy to come outside. There was no response. I started getting pissed.

"Let's call for the dog," Sue said.

"I'm not waiting until they get done fucking off with whatever they got going. I should have been off quite a while ago and here I am." To make matters worse, the husband, Jason, had to go to jail because I had a rule that if I had to put my hands on someone, they went.

"Last night," Sue said. She stared at the doorway. This time I saw real fear. "Jason said they hadn't been able to pay the bills so the power is off. He said they have an extension cord plugged into the neighbor's house. It should be laying on the floor somewhere. Let me call canine." Before she said anything else, I slid through the door. I didn't give a fuck if she followed me or not.

I heard Sue tell Dispatch that officers would be entering. The dispatcher asked if we wanted a code red.

"No," I radioed before she could. With my gun ready, I used my flashlight to find the kitchen, checking closets and behind things as I went. Lying on the kitchen counter, there was an unplugged cord. It went out to the garage. I followed it until I saw where someone cut a hole in the wall and stuffed it through. I went back and plugged it in. Nothing happened. "Maybe the neighbor got sick of the moochers and unplugged it from his side," I said. "Let's clear the rest of the house. Please, try not to shoot me in the back."

"Very funny," Sue said. I decided I better keep my mouth shut. From what I had seen so far, it was a possibility. I was a little worried about my flashlight. It was a small rechargeable, the best money could buy. I saw Sue had one, too, which wasn't surprising. It was preferred by most cops — six inches long, an inch in diameter, and bright as heck. The problem was that mine had been used quite a bit all night and it was failing. I wanted to hurry before it gave up. Working as a team, we cleared what was left of the downstairs. When that was done, we headed for the second floor. As we went up the stairs, I thought how, in training, the SWAT guys taught this was the perfect place for an ambush. There were windows, but they had heavy blankets over them. I ripped them down, letting in what poor outside light there was. Just when we got to the top of the stairs, both flashlights simultaneously went from white to yellow. I turned my light off for a second, then back on. The beam came back bright. It was a trick that would work for a short time, and just once.

"Great. Didn't you charge that thing before you came on shift?" I asked.

"Fuck you," she said. Her voice actually quavered. "I'm done with this and I'm calling canine."

"Go wait outside while I finish," I said. I put as much scorn in my voice as I could.

"Fuck yourself! I don't have to take this shit from you. This isn't my job. That's why they have dogs." She turned and walked away. At the bottom of the stairs, she called, "I don't give a shit. Get yourself killed."

"Go watch my prisoner," I said, turning my back. "Pussy," I breathed so she couldn't hear. That was all I needed, her reporting me to IAB. I listened after she left the condo, trying to pick up the least indication that Amy was in here with me. If there was any tactical surprise left in this situation, I wouldn't know where. I moved along the hall until I came to the first bedroom, wondering if my vest would stop a knife long enough to shoot Amy if she jumped out of something. As I went, I pulled the rest of the blankets off the windows. My flashlight was holding out, but I knew how it would fail — all at once. I'd used it on a couple of car stops and the call where someone said they thought they saw a body in an alley. There was a body, but he wasn't dead, just a drunk vagrant lying where he'd run out of steam.

This is fucked up, I thought. Here was the reason I didn't go see scary movies. I had enough of it in real life. I had one room left to clear. As soon as I slipped inside, I pulled the blankets off the window. I was surprised to see how much light this let in until I looked outside, where a streetlight was close by. There must have been a million moths circling the light. It was kind of mesmerizing. I should have kept my attention on the room, since it wasn't cleared.

I heard something, which caused me to spin. The gun was slapped from my hand. I reached out and grabbed the shape, but my fingers slid on the naked flesh. I was expecting the sharp pain I knew would come with a stabbing, if Amy had the knife, or a bullet, if she had my gun. Either way, I wanted her in close. I tried getting a grip on the human shape, but it was like she wore oil. She wasn't waiting for me to find a purchase. She was on me, pushing, hitting, and kicking. My feet became entangled in some of the clothing that covered the floor as I tried stepping back. We fell backwards on the bed. She was nothing but a shape, sharp shadows that were constantly shifting, seeking to hurt or actually causing me pain. Sharp nails raked my face, gouging at my eyes, slapping me, her teeth started to sink into my arm until I jerked away. She ripped the patch off the sleeve. The only thing I knew for sure was I fought Amy.

"Police," I panted. "Stop fighting." There was no response but our grunts and the sound of the blows, most striking my arms and vest. She was slick with sweat, so I couldn't get a grip on her. She hit me with both hands. That let me know she didn't have my gun. I tried throwing a punch, but she was too close. Finally, I wrapped my fingers in her hair, down near the scalp. I was able to pull her in, making it hard to keep hitting me.

"Stop," I said. That was when I felt her teeth sink into my forearm. I yowled like some kind of animal. My fingers slipped from her hair and she literally crawled over me, heading for the window. I tried getting a grip on her leg, but now I was the slick one — partly from her sweat, mainly from my blood.

"Bitch," I yelled.

Sue's voice rose up from outside. "Is everything alright up there?"

I flipped on my stomach, lunging after Amy. She was on her feet, making her escape. Again I went for the hair. I got my finger right down near the scalp again, ripping backwards so her head jerked towards me. This time, I heaved like I was pulling a ship to shore. Her head and upper body came towards me while her legs continued forward. Like a fisherman landing his catch, I landed her on the bed. She screamed. I saw her fingernail reaching for my face, so I used the leverage to flip her on her stomach. I swung a leg across her lower back until I was straddling her. As she flailed around, I pulled her hair so her upper torso arched her back.

"I'll fucking snap you in two if you don't stop it," I said.

"You're hurting me," she cried.

"Then stop resisting." As she tried to rake me with her nails, I bent her backwards even further. I heard bones cracking like I was working my knuckles. She howled. "Stop! Now," I ordered. I kept my voice loud enough that people outside would hear the commands.

"Control, One Henry Thirty-four, Code Red. Code Red!" Sue yelled into the radio. The dispatcher repeated the request.

Amy went limp. "Put your left hand in the center of your back." When she'd complied, I started loosening my grip. That was when Sue came through the door, gun drawn. "Come here and cuff her," I said.

Sue holstered her weapon and moved towards us.

"Give me your hand," Sue said to Amy. When she was slow to react, I gave her a sharp pull. She grunted, but quickly fed her hand to Sue. I heard the cuff ratchet shut. In a second, the other one clicked. I rolled off Amy as Sue pulled her to her feet. Still huffing, I slid across the bed, then got to my feet. Pain flared in my arm. I held it up to the light and saw the blood, looking like black ooze, dripping to the floor.

"You fucking bitch." Without thinking, I backhanded Amy. She slammed into a wall. Sue jerked her away, leading her towards the stairs. I keyed my mike, "Control, Bike Thirty, can you roll medical?"

"Thirty, are you code four?"

"That's affirmative, Control. I'm jiffy. Lift the red."

"Thirty. What's the nature of the medical?"

"Bite, Control. Suspect bit me on the arm." I started searching the floor with my flashlight, but the battery gave up. The room went very dark. I didn't want to leave without my gun. The alley lit up. I looked out the window and I recognized the graveyard sergeant, Jerry Lark, as he got out of an arriving unit. "Hey, sarg," I called. "You got a flashlight?"

"Cam. You OK?"

"I don't know. I can't see. I can't find my gun, either."

"Sue," Sergeant Lark said. "Take your light up there and help him out."

"I can't," she replied. She was out of my field of view, so I couldn't see her.

"Why not?"

"I have the prisoners."

"I'll watch them."

"My flashlight isn't working."

"Did you forget to charge it again?"

"No. I think I dropped it and broke the bulb."

"Fucking liar," I muttered. I saw Amy come into view wearing nothing. I reached back on the bed and pulled a blanket free. I moved to the window. "Heads up." I threw the blanket. "Cover her with that." I saw another unit arrive. When Sergeant Lark saw the officer, he told him to give me a hand. I heard him coming up the stairs, then he was inside the room with me.

"She knocked the gun out of my hand," I explained. "It probably went in that direction."

"You let a naked woman get your gun?" I heard mirth in his voice. I didn't think it was funny.

"Just help me find the gun," I said. "Jesus. This arm is killing me. I probably got rabies or something from that bitch." Far off in the distance, I heard the wail of an approaching siren. "Will you tell Dispatch to disregard medical code?" I didn't want this mess waking everyone in the complex.

The other cop went to where I pointed and played the flashlight's beam across the floor. After a second, the cop held my gun up. I took it from him and started towards the stairs. As I holstered it, I saw a door I hadn't opened. From where it was located, I guessed it was the upstairs bathroom. Without thinking, I opened it. Something launched itself at my face. I guessed later that I knew it was a dog, but that split second, I couldn't have sworn that was the case. Instinctively, I brought the gun up and fired. The flash from the muzzle was like a strobe. I saw the shape, later known to be a Doberman. It actually looked like I saw the bullets destroy its head. I didn't see the body hit me, knocking me to the ground. I lay there stunned for a second.

"Motherfucker!" I yelled, then I heaved the corpse off me. As I stood up, the other cop ran up and shined his light on me. I saw myself in the full-length mirror, starred where one of my rounds had impacted. I was covered in blood. My ears rang from the shots, yet I clearly heard the sound of feet pounding up the stairs.

"Cam! John!" Sergeant Lark came around the corner. He had his gun out.

"We're OK," the other cop called.

"What happened?" the sarg asked. I heard the female officer yelling into the radio that shots had been fired.

"Will you tell her to stop doing that, Sarg?" I asked, wearily.

"OK, everyone. Let's slow things down." He waited until the dispatcher advised everyone that a code red was in effect. He then stated that we were code four and that he needed the watch commander en route. A second later, Lieutenant Giles said to put him on the call.

"Fucking dog never made a noise," I said. "I opened the door and he's airborne. All I saw was teeth."

"Did he bite you? You're covered in blood."

"I don't think so. It's all the dog's. Thank God I had my gun out." When I looked down, I guessed it weighed ninety pounds. I nudged the body with a boot as though I didn't trust the way the bullets had destroyed its body. "Look at it. It's huge."

"OK," Lark said. "Let's get you down and have that other bite looked at before all the shit on you gets it infected."

"Sarg, you better let Smith know. He'll be pissed and I can't afford any more problems with him," I said.

"Giles'll take care of that. Let's just do one thing at a time." He was quiet for a minute. "Cam, Sue said you hit the female suspect after she was in cuffs."

"I did, Sarg," I said. I looked him straight in the eye. "She bit me. I didn't think. I guess I lost my temper."

"That's understandable. Let me see what I can work out."

"I don't want to get Sue in trouble." Lark gave me a strange look. "Man, I'm just having a life lately," I muttered as I walked down the stairs. When I stepped out in the alley, Karri May was pulling a gurney towards me.

"If that's for me, it's a little overkill," I told her. "If it's for the gunshot victim, he's gone to doggie heaven."

"Cam!"

"I'm OK." I saw her eyes start to fill with tears.

I moved closer to her. "Don't cry. I'm sorry. I've been a jerk."

"No," she said. She drew a ragged breath. "You just needed some time."

"You have no clue how happy I am to see you," I said. I quickly bent to kiss her. There was the taste of tears on her lips.

"Me, too. You look horrible. Let me see that bite."

"What are you doing working?" I asked.

"Overtime," she said. We moved to the back of the ambulance, where she went inside to gather supplies. I sat on the bumper. Chris, her driver, came around the corner.

"Cam!" he said. He sat down next to me. "Listen. I want to say this fast. She tried to make me promise I wouldn't say anything if I saw you. You know that guy, John?"

"John?" I was thinking of all the cops I knew by that name.

"The one who hurt Lizzie?"

"Yeah," I said. I scratched at the blood. It was drying. "Dirtbag."

"We had to treat him tonight. He grabbed Karri May."

"Grabbed her?"

Chris looked embarrassed. "In the crotch. I pulled him away." I closed my eyes. It was the only way I could gain a measure of control. Otherwise, I was afraid I'd do something that was going to cause that guy a lot of pain. "He threatened the next time he saw her, he was going to hurt her."

Karri May came back. Chris acted like he was examining the wound.

When things go to shit, they go all the way, I thought.

■ ■ ■

A Case of Beer . . .

The next morning, my arm was sore. When I stripped the dressing away, I saw the teeth marks were red, with pus already forming under the scabs. I picked the tops off, then dumped some peroxide on the wound, wincing as the stuff foamed. Human bites were far worse than anything an animal could inflict. I leaned on the sink, staring into the mirror. The whole thing replayed itself as it had all night long. When the homicide cops showed up, Amy and her significant other said they'd had the dog taken to the vet, where the animal's vocal cords were cut. They said they heard this was a cool thing to do.

I was told not to worry about the shooting, but to take a couple of days off. When Smith showed up, he was pissed. He'd been home having a beer to chase the drinks he'd had at the bar with the other guys when Giles called him. As soon as he got close to me, I knew he was drunk. While I was in the ambulance waiting for my shooting interview, Smith told me I was done being a cop.

I felt woozy, not realizing how everything that had happened that night was affecting me. As Smith's words sank in, I decided I'd had enough of his shit. We ended up in a shouting match with me telling him to go fuck himself.

"You want to fire me, you stupid piece of shit, do it," I yelled. Smith's face turned red.

"Yeah, as a matter of fact, I do." He grabbed me by the front of my shirt and jerked me towards him. I banged my arm on the side of a cabinet and fresh blood began to flow. Giles came around the corner and intervened.

He put his hand on Smith's where he had me by the shirtfront. When Smith let go, I sat down on the gurney. I took a piece of gauze from the counter and staunched the blood trickling from my wound.

"I can't take this anymore," I told Giles. Then I started telling him everything.

"Shut the fuck up," Smith said.

"No. Let him go on," Giles replied. When I got to the part where Smith was telling me every night how I might not have a job by the end of shift, Giles told me it was enough. He moved close to Smith. He smelled the alcohol.

"You been drinking?"

"No. Not really," Smith said.

"You're relieved of duty. Report to UMC with Sergeant Lark." Giles walked away to arrange for a breath test for Smith. Karri May came back inside the ambulance. She saw I was bleeding again. She took my arm and pulled the gauze away. "You're going to need this cleaned and a shot of antibiotics."

She stayed until the homicide detectives were finished interviewing me. She told Chris to take the ambulance back alone, that she was going with me to the hospital in the Ell Tee's car. When we were all inside the vehicle, she asked Giles to stop by the ambulance offices, which were on the way.

"I'll drive him over to UMC, then sit with him while they clean that arm. I can also take him home. In my professional opinion, he's in no shape to be driving." As we pulled away, I saw an animal control officer carrying the dead dog out. He had the animal wrapped in a blanket, which he'd draped across his shoulder. In the spotlights from the units, I saw the dog's head sticking out. It was hard to believe what the bullets had done. The sight made me more depressed than I had been before. It was one thing to hurt a person. People made choices, but an animal's thoughts were only for the people it loved.

After Giles dropped us off, we were alone in her car. I was quiet, thinking about what I had said to Giles and Smith. I'd probably be lucky if I still had a job in a few days. I knew I had to shake off those depressing thoughts. I put my arm across the back of her seat. Being elevated made the pain more bearable.

"Can we get a beer?" I asked.

"I'm taking you to UMC."

"I don't want to go. You can clean this up as well as an ER nurse. I want a beer."

"You shouldn't be drinking."

"Just one," I said. "I won't even drink the whole thing. I promise."

"OK, but only if we can talk. You seem like you need it."

"I won't make that promise. I might want to listen to you instead. But, I do need to chill out for a bit."

I first stripped my uniform shirt off, then the vest, so all I wore was my t-shirt and pants. I dropped my gun down the inside of the shirt so it wasn't so noticeable. She drove until we saw one of the sport bars all the cops and firemen liked. We parked outside, but I made no move to get out. I put my head back and closed my eyes. She left the engine running, the radio softly playing country music in the background.

"Some cops find it necessary to deal with stress by drinking. I'd never wanted to be one of those, so I was careful about doing that after a stressful day or week," I said.

"That's smart." Her voice was non-committal.

"I've tried to be even more careful now that all this has been happening with Smith."

"Understandable." She curled her legs under her, pulled her shoes off, then dropped them to the floor.

"It's one thing to deal with drunk friends," I continued, "or to have my friends deal with me when I'm drinking, but I guess most cops would agree that there's nothing worse than having to deal with a complete stranger who is drunk."

"Is this going somewhere, sweetie?"

"No. Yes. Maybe," I said. "Once I saw what booze does, the way it destroys a person's life and the lives of that person's family — that in itself wasn't the worst part. It was like the time I rolled on this fatal. First responder, you know?"

She nodded. Then she took my hand in hers, tracing the lines on my palm as if she read them.

"There were two cars involved. The guy who caused the whole thing was trapped next to his girlfriend. He was conscious and unhurt except for a small cut on his thigh. The instrument panel was curled around his body, making it impossible for him to move. The girlfriend was another matter. Just before the accident, she had her legs up, feet on top of the dashboard. When he crossed the centerline, maybe passing out from all he drank, he hit the other car head-on. The impact pushed her thighbones out her ass cheeks, then through the seat. It was horrible, watching her die and knowing there was nothing we could do for her. When the firemen pulled the seat out of the car, I watched a traffic cop puke his dinner over the railing at the side of the road. The couple he'd hit were far luckier. They died instantly." I turned my head so I could look at her. Her face was illuminated in a funny way, shadows in the hollows of her eyes, cheeks, and her mouth, which made her look like Death. That scared me until I regained control. I shook it off and continued.

"I have never seen bodies mangled like that. My one thought was that they never had time to know what happened. Later, we learned the other couple was on the way home from the party for their twenty-third wedding anniversary." I stopped as I collected my thought about that incident. "The way we found out was because one of the paramedics heard a cell phone ring. He answered it. I don't know why. I guess no one was thinking straight that night. It was their son." I was quiet as I thought about what had happened next. I suddenly wanted to let the story drop, but I needed to finish it. "When their children arrived, we were told the father was an elder in the Mormon Church. He was a very religious man, well liked and respected by everyone he knew. You know Mormons?" Karri May nodded. "They don't have anything to do with alcohol. Isn't it ironic that this would be the thing to kill them?" There wasn't an answer for that, so she didn't make one. *Smart woman*, I thought. I continued, "For me, that situation and a slew of others took the fun out of being drunk."

"I know what you mean." Her saying this wasn't the same as when a lot of cops said it, as if it was a game of one upmanship. It was the comment of someone who had her own horrible visions. The quiet in the car weighed on me, so I started talking just to fill the silence.

"Did John grab you?"

"Damn, Chris," she muttered, then sighed. "I didn't want Chris being the one to tell you. I should have known when he wouldn't swear he wouldn't."

"What did he say?" I asked.

"Nothing important. He was mad because Chris pushed him into a wall."

"When I catch him, I'll do more than that," I said. I meant it too. When I returned to work, John would become a priority with me. I'd find him and we'd have a serious talk on the way to jail. "I'm not interested in that drink anymore. Can we drive?"

"Sure," Karri May said. She turned the key in the ignition, put the car in reverse, and backed out. She started to reach for the radio. I don't know if she was turning it up or off. I put my hand on hers.

"It's fine where it is," I said. I felt like talking. It was like the pus that would form in my wound, then leak out. "One morning, about dawn." I looked east. The sky might have been getting lighter. "About this time as a matter of fact." I closed my eyes, "I'm driving southbound on Decatur from Sahara. The vehicle in front of me is speeding. That wasn't unusual at that time of the morning. You know, not much traffic."

She uh-huhed to let me know she was listening.

"Normally, I'd just pull the car over and give the driver a warning, but as I tried catching up, I realized the car was going really fast. I positioned the unit behind the vehicle, then started pacing. That's the best way to figure how fast the other car is going in case I was going to cite him."

"I know what pacing is," she said.

"Then you know you have to do it for a distance. That way the driver can't say he was only speeding for a short distance. People always say they have a legitimate reason, like passing someone."

"Yep. I do," she said. "I was married to a cop. Remember?"

"Yeah. I do. Well, it would have been a hard excuse for the guy to use because we were the only two on the road. My speedometer read sixty-five. We were in a thirty-five. So, I'm on the guy."

I opened my eyes and looked out the window. It was getting lighter out. Soon, it would be a full-blown Vegas day, a hundred in the shade if I remembered the weather forecast correctly. It was the same way that morning a year before.

"What surprised me was the other guy made no attempt to slow down. *How the hell can you miss a big black-and-white right behind you,* I thought. Needless to say, but I will anyway, my curiosity was a little piqued. I did the radio traffic." I changed my voice like I was talking on the radio. "Control, One Paul One, copy a four six seven."

We made a left turn on the way to her apartment. I stared inside a convenience store, seeing two guys buying beer. They didn't look old enough. After a minute, I began again.

"It took the dispatcher a minute to respond. Mine must have been the first call in over an hour, so, for a second, I'm wondering if everyone at Metrocomm was asleep. Then she acknowledges me. I tell her the info on the plate. I project where I want the stop to take place and as soon as I finished, I flick on the emergency equipment, both lights and siren. You know, give him a little toot to let him know I'm back there. Nothing happens. In other words, the car just keeps traveling down the road. It doesn't veer, slow, or make any indication that the driver is aware he's being followed by a cop. Now I'm sure the guy must be dead or something." I stopped as I checked the car in front of us. It had no plate on the back. I studied the driver, thinking how I'd pull him over if I were working." *Work, work work*, I thought. To stop those thoughts from distracting me from finishing the story, I closed my eyes again.

"I let my cruiser drift over towards the driver's side. I see an arm resting on the edge of the door. I can also see a head. It's all the way back, but I can't get a look at the guy. I honk. Nothing. You know how Decatur is right there?"

I opened my eyes in time to see her nod, then I put my head back and closed them again. The concentration I needed to tell the story was taking my mind off the pain in my arm and head.

"Arm hurt?"

"A little," I said, then continued, "Straight as an arrow, three travel lanes in either direction. He's in the number one or the fast lane. I can't get a good look at him, so I slow, fall in behind, then jump over on his passenger side. I'm thinking I'm going to see some ninety-year-old geezer at the wheel. Sometimes, old people have a whole different way of driving. They get very focused, like on where they're going and on just getting there. They'll drive with their eyes straight ahead and damn the torpedoes."

"I saw this wasn't the case this time. This guy's young. I say to myself, *He's got to be dead. He looks dead, and if he isn't, then he's really asleep.* It's like the car's on autopilot, the way it's going."

"Now, it might sound like this took a long time, but it didn't. Maybe half a minute. I saw we're approaching the intersection at Desert Inn. If we made that, then Spring Mountain would be next. Either one's a major intersection, which meant even at that time of the morning, there might be cross-traffic. I started honking like crazy. Nothing. The dead-guy-thing was looking more likely every second. The intersection at Desert Inn was approaching fast. If we made that one, Spring Mountain's next. Just when I'm thinking of getting in front of the car and slamming on the brakes, he wakes up." I was quiet for a few minutes, trying to put the look on the guy's face into words.

"What happened?" Karri May asked.

"He jerks awake, swerving into the travel lane occupied by me and my big police car. I have to swerve, too. I almost hit the wall of those condominiums on the northwest corner."

"My friend Bobby lives there," she said. "You might have ended up in her living room."

"Great. I'd have met you under different circumstances then."

"I was still on day shift, so I doubt it."

"What? You trying to get rid of me?" For an answer she took my hand in hers. "Well, OK, then. Back to my story. In the nick of time, I get control of my unit, only to discover the car has outdistanced me. I step on the gas so I can close with him. The red light at the intersection turns red as we approach, but we're going too fast. We both go sailing right through. I don't even want to look as we go right between two cars. As usual, my guardian angel is looking out for me."

"I'd say."

"The driver makes a quick left turn. He crosses the northbound lanes, pulling straight into the corner gas station. There's a lot of cars coming, so I can't do the same thing without hitting one of them. By the time I make the parking lot, which meant driving a few hundred yards down the street, cross all those lanes, and pull into the driveway, I think I've lost the guy. That's when I get back to the gas station in time to see the driver exit his vehicle and go into the store. The dispatcher asks me if I'm code four. I ignored her. I was focused on getting this guy instead of telling her I don't have the car stopped. When I'm in a position where I can get to the store without being seen, the guy comes staggering out. He's carrying a case of beer."

"What?"

"A fucking, excuse my French, case of beer, and he's got one open and drinking it. He isn't even looking at me or my car, either. And speaking of car, there it sits, black-and-white, red lights flashing, and me standing in the door all pissed off and watching him. Before I can even yell, he goes over, climbs in, and starts the engine. He backs right into my car. Hard. The impact moves the unit back at least three feet. I had to jump out of the way to keep the door from hitting me."

She laughed. I gave her that look I reserve for people who sorely try my patience — that only made her laugh harder.

I put my hand over my mouth and acted like I was speaking into the microphone, "Control, can you roll a traffic unit, my supervisor, and an ID tech for pictures. I've been involved in a four oh one. No police liability."

Then in a high-pitched voice that was supposed to be female, I added, "Are you code four, One Paul One?"

"Hell, no, I'm not OK. My uniform is filthy from landing in the parking lot. My pride is crunched along with my car. Now I have to explain to the boss what happened to my car. What can I say? Yeah, I'm *OK* but boy am I pissed and to make matters worse, for the first time all night, I hear some interest in her voice." I was quiet as I remembered the feelings of that morning. What I would have given right then to have that simple time back in my life, working a grave unit, no real bosses bothering me, just handling calls. I continued.

"As I got to my feet, I look at his car. All I see is a set of feet sticking in the air. They are kicking the inside of the roof. The other funny thing is the feet are on the passenger side. I move forward and, when I look inside, I realize the driver has been flung head first under the dashboard. I try opening the passenger door, but the entire side of the car is buckled from a previous accident. I have to go around to the driver door, which I can open."

"Two things hit me right off. The first is how drunk the guy is. The other is he's stuck by the most unlikely thing you can imagine. It's the case of beer. It's wedged between the bottom of the dash and his body. I climb in to see if I can free him, but I can't. In order to free him, I got to take the beers out of the case so the box will collapse. What turns out to be worse than his position is that he shit himself."

She made a disgusted noise. "Do we have to go on with this story?"

"Yes, my sweet," I said. I was feeling better. "We do. I need to get this off my chest. It's been bugging me for a long time."

"In that case, I guess I better let you finish it."

"It's the big Number Two. The hot, nasty, smelly kind. You know, liquid."

"I was thinking of having you buy me a burger," she said, "but I was getting fat anyway."

I looked at her to see where all this fat was. Before I commented on what I was thinking, I decided to finish telling my story. "What makes it really bad is it's already coming out his collar. It's got to be covering his whole body under his clothes. The inside of the car has a stench that would do the sewage treatment plant out south proud. Right then, my sergeant comes up behind me. He sees how pale I am, figuring me for a casualty.

"Are you OK?"

"No," I replied. I didn't realize it, but I was biting my lip to keep from chucking lumps, so when I opened my mouth to speak, all he saw was my teeth all red. Before I can say anything else, he panics. He tells Dispatch to roll medical. Then he glances at the feet kicking spasmodically at the roof and fearing for the citizen, he sticks his head in. Now, you got to understand, Sergeant Bueller came straight from chow. As he tries backing out, I'm guessing he's thinking he shouldn't have had that second helping. Never one for a strong stomach, the smell gets him. He doesn't make it. It's all over the driver seat."

"I hope this is going to end soon," Karri May said.

"Maybe. Anyway, just the thought of climbing across that seat to get the guy out makes me want to hurl too. There's no way. I can't even stand close, 'cause the smell will have me ralphing. I go back to my car."

"'Control,' I say into the radio. 'You better get FD to send an engine with a Jaws-of-Life.' After a second, Dispatch sends me the message on the car computer, *Jeez! You must've had a serious one out there.* And that's the whole moral of my story. Tonight, I had a serious one out there."

She was quiet then. It was supposed to be funny, but like usual, my joke fell flat. I wondered if I had ruined the mood by turning serious. She pulled into her parking lot.

"Can we go in and go to bed?" I asked.

"Sure. You're tired. Sooner or later, you're going to have to see a doctor. If you don't, they won't let you go back to work. I know that's a departmental policy."

Now, it was my turn to be quiet. I really didn't feel up to dealing with anything. "I'll go to Quick Care in a few days. It's my Friday."

"Your choice," Karri May replied. Her voice was emotionless. When she stepped out of the car to come to my side, I felt like I weighed a million pounds. *When had they painted the place this God-awful pink?* I wondered. It was really hard to get the energy to overcome how lethargic I felt. I wanted to stay right there and have her drive me till we ran out of land. I thought how nice it would be to watch the sun sink into the ocean at the end of a hard day at the beach.

"Are you OK?" she asked.

"Yeah. Just tired," I said. A sigh escaped me. I hated people who did that. It was like they wanted free attention.

"Do you want help getting out?"

I thought about it. Like a cop, I analyzed the whole thing, expanding scenarios, one of which went all the way from her having my children to me dying in her arms at some impossible old age. "This thing between us," I started, "is complicated right now. It has the potential to get even more complicated. I can see where things might end up and, right now, I have too many problems."

"Sometimes, problems are easier when they're shared."

I took a deep breath, finding what energy I had left. "They're my problems. I want to fix them myself. I don't need anyone else's help." As soon as the words were out, I saw the hurt in her eyes. I decided to change the subject. "I want you to file a police report against John."

"No," she said. "We all have problems. He was mine. Now, I think it's done."

"Things like that don't just go away," I told her.

"I think he understands what he did was wrong."

"John shot a cop," I said. "Think what it takes to do that."

"If he's out, he paid his price."

I was too tired to argue with her right then, so I climbed from the car. Without looking back, I walked up the stairs to her apartment. I'd hurt her. I'd made her feel pain, which is one of those things that went with life. I was in pain, too, but mine was physical. Hers was in the heart. There was never an easy way around that one.

■ ■ ■

A Couple of Tweekers . . .

When the investigation on the dog shooting was complete, I was finally given the slot on the plain-clothes squad. Getting on was as simple as making my interest known to the sergeant, who happened to like me. I'd wanted the job because I thought it might be a good opportunity to gain experience that might lead to the detective bureau, but what was more important was that I needed to get away from the bike squad. Smith was going through the investigation that Giles initiated. If he kept his sergeant's stripes, it was going to be through a foul-up the Department allowed. The detective bureau test was in two months. I'd talked to a senior detective and he gave me some pointers. He said no one made it the first time, but by testing, I would know what to expect on the second go-around and have a better chance of passing. He also said that being on a plain-clothes squad would help immensely.

The plain-clothes officers worked on squads called PSU or problem solving units. They liked to wear those baseball caps from Pennsylvania State University. It was almost ironic the way I thought being accepted on the problem solving unit would solve my personal problems. What I knew by then was taking a new job meant gaining a lot of others. Each one of the problems was balanced with an incentive, as we were considered street cops, not real detectives. That was because we were still assigned to patrol. This meant we didn't get the eight percent extra pay and other perks that the detectives got. On the other hand, we were a close-knit unit.

Another problem with our positions was that if the area command was short cops to fill a shift roster, we put on uniforms and worked the street, but that didn't happen often because the unit was the captain's baby. The sergeant answered directly to him. Tasks were assigned based on problems that directly impacted our area or as the captain saw fit. Unfortunately, what the captain might consider a problem might be something like his buddy's business, which was an auto-wrecking yard that was having parts stolen off the junkers. That led to my first three days being spent playing security guard for a good part of the night. We finally nabbed a couple of the neighborhood kids, whom the owner knew. He decided not to press charges.

As I settled in, I thought about Karri May a lot. When I left her apartment the morning after I shot the dog, I didn't call her or answer her calls. I thought I'd take a couple days off, but they slid into a week, then a month. Now it had been almost two. The funny thing was that I didn't even see her on calls. Then, the night before, I'd decided I wanted to see her. I tried calling her at work, but the ambulance dispatcher said she was out of town. I couldn't get anything else out of the woman. I tried talking to Chris, but he didn't call me back, either. I figured either he was off or she must have said something to him or he was mad at me and being overly protective. After my attempts failed, I decided to give it a rest.

I threw all my attention into the job. I was happy to be assigned my first case. SWAC was having a huge rash of thefts from business offices. Most of the thefts took place just after midnight. The crime analysis unit ran the stats, which showed a majority of incidents happened between one and two in the morning. The losses had grown to a couple of million dollars in office and computer equipment. The only lead we had was from a janitor who saw a faded red van leaving the area. He jotted down a Nevada plate and gave it to the officer who took the report. That officer passed it on in briefing. I ran the plate through the Department of Motor Vehicles database and got a hit. The name and address of the RO or registered owner was in our area.

When Randy, my new partner, and I went to the address, intent on making contact, then possibly arresting a suspect, we found a mailbox rental business. It was the kind of place that provided one-stop service from shipping boxes to stamps. We talked to the manager and discovered the place hadn't been as scrupulous gathering information on the identity of their customers as they should have been.

As we walked out, I stopped at the car and looked over towards the coffee shop across the way. There were two women sitting outside. They wore shorts and halter-tops. The blonde waved at me. She had bright red streaks in her hair. Randy saw where I was looking.

"Coffee?" he asked.

"Nah!" I said. "Tea."

"Or me," Randy muttered. He wasn't a handsome man by any stretch of the imagination. He was thin, with a face that matched his body, all angles and sharp planes. His hair was curly, tight red coils that clung close to his scalp. What he had was a presence and women noticed. It was as if they also wanted to figure out what it was about him they found attractive.

As we headed for the café, I said, "So much for neatly wrapping up this investigation."

"Get used to it. Nothing goes easy, and if it does, something's wrong."

Randy told me what he wanted and I went inside to order. When I came out, he was sitting at the table with the girls. I brought the drinks over.

"This is Shelly." He pointed at the blonde who'd waved at me.

"I thought you were someone I knew," she said.

"Story of my life," I said. "Some babe waves at me and it's always for something else."

"And this is Heather," he continued. "They work at Odyssey Gardens."

I knew that strip club. I'd been in there a few times. The county had tried banning lap dancing the year before. When the county commission held public hearings on the matter, the club's owner brought in hundreds of hours of videotape. The public watched about twenty minutes of Las Vegas' finest being ministered to by scantily clad females. Those men included police officers, fire fighters, license inspectors, and others. A recess was called when the lawyers offered to show several members of the commissioners' staff, those same fellows sitting at side tables who had drafted the new ordinance, receiving the same treatment. I'd have bet someone, like the club owner, had video of several male commissioners getting the same treatment also, but those businesses would have been stupid to run that out. One thing I knew about dating a stripper was that it was a sure way to stall a career. Thinking that, I quickly lost interest in Shelly and she must have sensed it. We stayed for half an hour. Randy left with a date for later that evening.

When we got back to the station, Randy went to work with the computer. He ran through several databases and, surprisingly, he came up with more information. His next step was to call one of the postal inspectors he knew and ask for some help. The business owner was required by federal law to provide information to the Postal Service on the boxes he rented. An hour later, the inspector called Randy back saying the person who rented the box was definitely not the person who was using it. He gave us a name and we ran it in our system. We immediately ran into another dead end when we discovered the name on the rental documents belonged to a dead guy.

As we investigated the other information from the various boxes on the form, we learned just about everything was fictitious, except the phone number. When Randy called his contact at the phone company, the guy told him the number returned to a beeper. Once again, we were disappointed. The beeper companies wanted subpoenas before they provided a shred of information, whereas Randy's contact would have given us what we wanted and let us send a subpoena later. Another problem with the beeper companies was that Randy said they couldn't be trusted. He told me a story of how they'd arrested a suspect who'd told them the owner of the beeper company called him to say the police were looking for him.

"I have a better idea," Randy said. He opened a drawer and produced an unsigned grand jury subpoena. While I watched, he filled it out. "We're going to see if we can fake this." Randy finished. He held it up so I could see. "Come on."

While he drove, he explained to me that he'd try to make whoever was present at the beeper company think this was the type of subpoena that required the clerk give up information immediately. I was wondering how we were going to use anything we learned through this ploy in court, especially, if the caper turned into a big case. It would be just what I needed — to be under investigation for forgery. When we arrived at the beeper company, Randy told me to wait in the car.

"I'll come in," I said. I figured if he was going to cook, we might as well make it a dual course.

"No. I can do this easier if I don't have to worry about you blowing it."

That pissed me off. "Fine," I said.

"Cam. Chill out." Before I could reply, Randy went in. Through the glass, I watched him talk to the guy. At one point, it looked like things were getting heated. I thought I should go in, but the guy left the counter for the back. Randy walked out a minute later. When he was in the car, he held up the sheet.

"Idiot didn't even make a copy," he said. I glanced over the information we needed, mainly the address the customer's beeper went to. I recognized it as an apartment, not a house. Back at the station, Randy called the postal inspector again. He gave us the occupant's personal information, which we used to search the DMV database. That produced a license plate number. This was the stuff I loved. The DMV file contained information on the make and model of the car that the plate belonged to, which wasn't the red van.

We hopped back in our car and took a run out to the apartment's rental office. Randy sat on the desk while I looked at rental brochures and sweet-talked the agent into letting me have a copy of the lease agreement. In the car, I read the two names, one male and one female, which I assumed were boyfriend and girlfriend, since they didn't have the same last name. They matched what the inspector had given us. While in the office, we checked the names in the computer. There was a criminal history for the male and a work history for the female. The guy's priors included possession of stolen property and burglary. Things were getting better and better.

What amazed me that first day was how Randy did everything without being fancy. It was all basic resources, which any patrol officer had at his disposal. The only exception was Randy's contact with the postal inspector, who was one of Randy's neighbors. I had to admit I was a little disappointed. What I wanted were sophisticated devices — wiretaps, phone traces, and satellite imagery. I couldn't help thinking that if we had those things, we could solve crime in a sixty-minutes episode just as they did on TV. What I'd find out as I worked was that we had other things — six guys who showed lots of imagination, determination, and persistence, men who drove around in a few old, stripped-down police cars and used the same radios as the street cops.

■ ■ ■

By the time all this was done, we called it a night. First, I called Karri May. There was no answer. I went to TJ's Bar with my new squad. We played pool and drank beers. Because the place was a cop bar, they only charged us a buck a draft pint. I was introduced to black-and-tans. I usually didn't drink beer, but these I liked. By the time everyone called it quits, I was blasted. Like a true cop, I staggered out to the oleander bushes at the side of the bar, stuck my fingers down my throat, puked, then drove home. When I got inside my house, I stuck my finger down my throat again, puking up whatever was left in my stomach. For sure, I was going to pay for this in the morning.

The next day, the PSU sergeant sat us down for a briefing. I hoped this wasn't going to take too long. I was fidgety from my hangover. Sergeant Daley said the captain wanted this thing wrapped up. He'd gone to a luncheon where several business leaders and politicians had complained that they didn't think the police were doing enough. Randy explained what we'd learned so far. Everyone was in agreement that we needed to spend a few days following the suspected bad guy to see where he went and what he did. If we were lucky, we might catch him in the act. In order to do this, we needed a few things to happen first. Normally, we worked swings, so the first order of business was to request overtime and barring that, a shift adjustment. We also needed a better way to communicate. Sergeant Daley listened, then went to the Ell Tee's office. A minute later they were in with the captain. An hour later, Daley came back.

"Overtime, no. Shift adjustment, yes. Cell phones, no. Our own radio channel, yes."

"Well," Randy said. "That sucks. The only difference from normal is that we're getting our own time fucked with."

"It didn't hurt to ask," I said.

"Not from where I was sitting," Daley said. "The captain chewed my ass for asking for ridiculous things."

"What else did you ask for?" Randy asked.

"Cars that work, a couple more guys to help."

"My! Weren't you the greedy one? No wonder you got your ass chewed."

"Come on. Let's get to work," Daley said. "You got pictures of the targets?"

I nodded, handing him the copies. The packet included computer printouts, license plate number and vehicle description, and mug shots straight from the photo lab — hers were off her work card and his were booking photos. "Guy's name is Mark Boggs. His girlfriend is Kimberly Wayne," I said. "She's a cocktail waitress and he's a piece of shit."

Daley handed everyone a copy. When everyone knew what we knew, we went out. Randy tossed me the keys.

"You drive," he said. That surprised me. He saw that. "I need to keep notes," he explained.

I drove to the apartment. Daley wanted everyone to get the lay of the land. When everyone reported they had a general idea of where things were, Randy set the cars where he wanted them. Because he was senior and had started this thing, he was the case officer. After an hour, we watched the guy come out. A nagging thought that I knew him crossed my mind. The problem was that there were tons of people I thought I knew. That was because I'd arrested quite a few people since I'd been a cop. He looked like a typical meth-head. He wore a baseball cap on backwards, black heavy metal t-shirt, greasy jeans, and worn work boots.

His hair was brown, long and stringy. He had it pulled back in a ponytail, held with a rubber band. Pimples or meth sores covered all the exposed skin I could see. He had a long goatee that covered a good portion of his lower face. It bothered me that I thought he was familiar.

What was amazing was his girlfriend. She was really pretty, which confirmed the old saying that there was no accounting for taste. We had been waiting for her to come back out in order to point her out to the rest of the squad. If she was doing meth, it was possible her habit was so new she hadn't started the process of changing into a typical tweeker bitch, which would be a shame.

While we watched, we both came to the conclusion Mark was tweeking. If someone had asked me to profile what a young, white burglar looked like, this guy was it. That he used was obvious as soon as he went to the front of his car. He opened the hood and puttered with the oil dipstick. He moved around with choppy, agitated movements, stopping now and then to scrub at the body with a dirty rag. That car said tweeker — a white, late seventies model Camaro. It had seen its best days a long time in the past. The top had once been vinyl covered, but the sun had left only the yellowish-brown glue. In places, there was more rust than paint. The surprise came when we heard the motor start. There was the same deep roar a racing car made, which echoed off the other apartment buildings.

"Reminds me of those moonshine cars my brothers used to build," Randy said. "Looked like shit on the outside, but t'weren't nothing could catch one."

"You don't sound Southern," I remarked.

"Moved north, became a Yankee when I was four. My mama divorced the old man and took only me. Said he could fuck himself and my brothers far as she was concerned. Hear her tell it, he might have. Went back on vacation a couple of years ago and I have to agree with her."

"That's going to be a hard car to follow if he uses it the way tweekers usually do."

"Yep! Let me tell everyone." Randy keyed the mike, notifying the others that the target was getting ready to move. After relaying the info, he muttered, "Low profile. It'll be hard to see in traffic. The only saving grace is the white color."

"Ya know, bro, I think we got a problem," I said. Randy gave me a sharp look. "That guy's familiar."

"Think you know him?"

"Worse," I said. "I think he might know me."

"Then we need to stay back so he doesn't spot you in case he remembers what you might not," Randy said.

Things happened right away as we got ready to follow. Mark left the apartment complex and we fell in behind, staying back far enough we hoped he wouldn't notice us. The ideal method would have been to surround the car with vehicles, placing one in front, and a couple behind, maybe cover side lanes, too, but we didn't have that many cars at our disposal. Another good idea would have been to parallel the target vehicle by using side streets. Again, we didn't have enough cars. We had three, with the sarg's car as a backup in case we needed him. Backup actually meant he was back at the office.

As things got going, we were "the eye." There are responsibilities that went with being the eye. If I thought we were burned, which meant the target driver appeared suspicious or we felt we were in the vicinity of the target vehicle too long, I could direct another car into the eye position. Of course, that was an ideal surveillance. What the PSU squad did was referred to as "modified surveillance," meaning we stayed on longer than we should. Rarely did we have the luxury of calling for another vehicle to replace us.

After we spent a few minutes trying to follow him, he gained an extra block on us. When he made a right turn, I tried speeding up so we wouldn't have him out of sight for long. By the time I made the corner, he was gone.

"Where'd he go?" Randy asked.

"Beats me," I said. I was alternately speeding up to get to the side streets, then slowing down so we could look left and right. "Think he spotted us?"

"Possible, but let's not jump to conclusions. That'll only make us paranoid." Randy pointed at a convenience store. "Pull in there. I'll call the boss and see what he wants us to do. You got a quarter."

I reached in both pockets. Nothing. "No." While Randy was searching through the car for coins to use the pay phone, the target pulled into the driveway. I saw it happen in the rear view mirror. As he parked next to us, I tried to get Randy's attention. He was draped over the seat, searching for something on the back floorboard.

"Hey." I jabbed him.

"You sure you ain't got a quarter?" he asked.

"Randy," I said. I didn't want to seem suspicious, so I was looking straight ahead. The driver looked over at me. The funny thing was I didn't think he recognized me. *Damn*, I thought. *I know him. That's fucking John from the Strip.* I poked Randy harder.

"What!" he pulled his head up and glared at me. As we locked eyes, I nodded sharply to my left. He slid his gaze off me and looked at the passenger, then the driver.

"Shit. Why didn't you warn me?" He muttered.

"What the fuck you think I was trying to do? That's John Simone. I know him from the Strip."

Randy flopped over in the seat. I sat there, trying to look nonchalant, with less than four feet separating the two cars. I watched Simone out of the corner of my eye to see if he recognized me. He seemed to be oblivious of my presence. The passenger slid out the window and went into the store. He returned a few minutes later with a six-pack of beer. They popped the tops and chugged the contents. The passenger finished first, then dropped the can between our cars. He burped happily, smiled at us, and opened another. The car revved and backed quickly out of the spot.

"Wanna get them?" Randy asked. "DUI, open container, might even get lucky and get a possession charge. They look good for it." I guessed he was worried about letting them drive away drunk. It was in the back of my mind, too. It was all the shit the Department fed us about liability — what if they drove down the street and crashed, killing some poor family of ten? It would probably come out in court that we sat there and watched them drive away drunk.

"You know the sarg would have our asses if we burn the cars," I offered up as an excuse, then thought, *The guy goes in with a doctored grand jury subpoena and he's worried about the driver drinking a can of beer.*

Randy was quiet for a second. "If they haven't already."

"Yeah. Its my luck," I said. As soon as the car was out of the parking lot, Randy was busy talking on the car-to-car channel. Jeff and Smitty had taken the eye.

"I wonder who the other guy was?" I muttered out loud.

Randy shrugged. As I drove, he jotted descriptions and times, made notes. He took out a cell and called the sarg. When he was off, Randy told me to drive to Southeast Area Command. When we went to their PSU office, we had a lengthy negotiating session where we ended up trading our car for one of theirs. Randy must have told them ten times that this was only a temporary deal.

"What was that about?" I asked. The question was supposed to be about the transaction we'd just gone through with the other area command PSU team. Instead, he was looking at a flatbed tow truck taking a black-and-white away.

"I don't understand what someone could be thinking to miss that." He pointed at the car on the truck. The whole side was riddled with bullet holes. While we were in briefing, the story everyone was buzzing about was that a day shift officer went out to take the car out on patrol and found the damage. They called the grave officer back to work, as he never reported it. When the guy returned to work, he was clueless. The closest he came to an explanation was that someone must have shot the car during his shift while he was in an apartment dealing with a domestic. The call came out in the Sierra Vista and Cambridge area, a real shithole. It was a place things like that happened often. I bet the cop who missed the damage would get hours for failing to inspect his vehicle at the end of shift as policy dictated.

We headed back to the area in the lent car. I drove while Randy dug through a bag he kept in the back seat. In a second, he produced two baseball caps and a couple of t-shirts. He stripped off the shirt he'd been wearing and put on one from the bag.

"Here's one for you." I could smell the sweat, even with the windows open.

"You didn't get that off a vagrant did you?" I asked.

"Not unless you consider Jeff to be homeless. His wife caught him cheating and he's sleeping on the sarg's couch," he replied. "Just put it on. We can't afford to be recognized by these guys."

"OK. But only because it has cop cooties on it." Randy held the wheel as I made the change. While I had the shirt over my head, I stepped on the gas. The car sped up. Instead of getting scared as I thought he would, he trapped the shirt so I couldn't see, putting a hand on my leg so I couldn't get my foot off the gas.

"Wanna play games, motherfucker? See if I care," he said. The thought of the car hurtling down the road without me being in control scared the bejesus out of me. I struggled until I was able to wrench free. As I regained my vision, we approached a long line of cars at a high rate of speed. He let me go. I slammed my foot on the brake, arching my body for the impact. The car screeched to a stop, less than a foot from the bumper of the car in front of us. The driver, an older woman, had eyes as big as saucers as she looked back.

"You fuck," I yelled. As soon as the light changed, she hurriedly changed lanes. Randy was laughing so hard, I thought he'd pee himself.

"Don't fuck around if you don't want to pay the piper," he said.

"Oh, I can pay. Believe that. I just don't want anyone else to pay along with me."

"That's cool. Now get us back to where we're supposed to be."

Things got boring on surveillances, which made cops tend to lose focus. Sometimes, that resulted in discovering the people you were supposed to be watching were gone. I dozed and Randy watched. I figured that was fair after my near-death experience. An hour later, Simone and his buddy came out.

"How do you know that guy?" Randy asked.

"I should have arrested him when I worked bikes on the Strip. He threatened a friend of mine."

"He didn't seem to know you," Randy said.

"Weird, wasn't it?"

"Not really. It's amazing how when you get out of a uniform, people see you differently. It's like they see it — not you.

"Hope you're right."

"I am. Who'd he threaten?"

"Woman I like."

"Chippy?"

"No. A while ago," I said, quietly, "I thought I might marry her."

"That's serious. You gonna be able to keep cool around him?"

I nodded, but I wondered. I watched Simone walking to the car. The passenger slipped through the window again. It seemed to be his trademark. They both looked high as kites. The Camaro backed out and took off east. They drove down Flamingo, which had a lot of traffic. It was easy to stay close without being noticed. When we neared the Interstate, the car turned towards downtown. While we were trying to play keep-up, the sarg, who had replaced us while we traded cars, was called back to the station. That put us back to two cars, which was not enough to follow someone on the freeway. We lost him pretty quickly. To add insult to injury, not only did we lose the Camaro, but we got stuck in traffic.

"Why do you suppose they call this the fast lane?" Randy asked. "Nothing's moving."

I pushed the lever for the air conditioning over to COLD. Nothing came out except hot air. "It's worse," I muttered, then groaned. "I think the air conditioner's giving up the ghost."

He grabbed the microphone, "Jeff, where are you guys?"

"Six cars behind you. We're stuck too," Jeff radioed back.

The air conditioner made a loud squealing noise. The hot air turned hotter.

"I think the things stuck in the heater position," I said. "Well, that explains why those guys at Southeast were so quick to give us this car."

The cars in front of us moved a few hundred feet, then stopped. For the next thirty minutes, that was the manner of our progress. When we were further along, I saw the reason the traffic wasn't moving. There was a series of accidents. As things went, the first one wasn't even a bad fender bender, but people who had been gawking ran into each other. That caused the Highway Patrol to close down all the lanes and leave only the emergency lane open. They were letting through only a few cars at a time. As we sat there waiting, I happened to glance at the oncoming lanes. The Camaro came towards us. I was sure it was the right one. After all, how many could be in that condition? As it passed, I tried to see through the line of light deflectors installed on the top of the three-foot barricades that separated the northbound lanes from the southbound. I thought there might have been two people in the car. The barricades meant there was no getting turned around unless we reached the off-ramp, which was directly to our right. Since we were in the fast lane, Randy would either have to lean out the window to indicate to people we wanted to change lanes or actually get out and stop traffic. I was thinking this would work well if he showed his badge to people. He opted to lean out, yell at people to quit being butt-heads and let us in.

As we started the process of moving to the number four lane, I saw a black-and-white also going in the other direction. I turned my head fast enough to catch the vehicle number. I had also seen the letters "SW" in front of the number. That meant it was one from our area. The unit was maybe six cars behind the target. I guessed he was just coming from the jail, heading back to the station. I changed from car-to-car to southwest patrol channel, asking what unit had passed us. When he identified himself, I requested he follow the car until we could extricate ourselves. He first asked Dispatch what was holding in his area and when she told him it was slow, he agreed.

"Want me to follow or stop him?" he asked.

"Follow. Nothing else, Sam Four," I radioed. "We should be out of this mess in a few minutes."

"Okay," he said. Just as we exited the freeway, the unit came back with the information that the Camaro went into the apartment complex. The officer asked if we wanted him to follow the guy in. Randy told him not to bother.

A half hour later, we were back where we started. We sat in the car listening to the radio, hoping the temperature would drop. I tried beating on the control panel, but all that did was bruise my hand. Finally, around ten, they came out and left in their car again. We were able to keep a loose surveillance all the way to Sahara Avenue, where the traffic started getting heavy again. We lost them. I thought about what came after the Sahara exit. There were three directions that could be taken — east to downtown Las Vegas, north to North Las Vegas, or west to the residential areas along Charleston. The fact that we kept losing them was getting frustrating.

"What'd you want to do?" I asked.

"Find them before the sarg thinks we're idiots."

"I know we need to find them, fool," I guessed the words came out harsher than I intended. I softened my voice. "I meant which way."

"Let's check the downtown area. It's a hunch."

"Anything sounds good right now. Especially a cold beer." My personal cell rang. When I answered it, I heard Karri May's voice call my name. I felt as if the breath left me.

"Hey," I replied. This was the last person I expected on the phone and I didn't have time to talk. What was it with that feeling when someone twisted a knife in your guts?

"I was thinking about you," she said.

"Yeah. I've been doing the same lately."

"What? Thinking about yourself only?" She laughed.

"No. Thinking about you." I glanced at Randy. He was staring straight ahead, but I sensed his interest. "You take vacation?"

"No. My father died." I heard the catch in her voice. There was silence as I negotiated the interchange between I-15 and U.S. 95. A car almost hit us when the woman driver changed lanes without looking.

"Bitch," I muttered.

"What?"

"Not you. The shithead that almost hit us."

"You're busy. I'll call you later."

"No. Wait." But, the phone went dead.

"Nice going, Sherlock," Randy said.

"Fuck you. Next time I'll just pull over and finish my business. The way we're going, this bullshit could've waited anyway."

"Wow! I was kidding. Chill out, bro." Randy's face showed nothing but concern.

"I'm sorry. Chick problem. I'm making a mess of it and I don't know if I want to keep from doing that."

"Understandable. If it don't feel right, fuck her. There's a million fish in the sea."

That wasn't what I wanted to hear, but knowing Randy as well as I did, I understood it was just his attitude where women were concerned. I turned off at the Third Street exit and started making my way south. There were taxis double-parked all along the street picking people up and dropping them off. Along one wall, six vagrants sat, passing a bottle back and forth. As we waited for a break in the traffic, an argument broke out. I listened as they yelled at a scummy woman in layers of rags for drinking too long. One of the men called her a whore and another man stood up.

He said something slurred, which I translated to, "You don't call my woman a whore. Only I call her a whore. You got me?" He stood there swaying as if he were a stalk of grass in a breeze. The man who called her the whore laboriously climbed to his feet.

"Your woman?" the bigger vagrant asked. "Since when is she your woman? She slept with me last night. I'll call her anything I want!" He put his hand on the other vag and pushed.

"Shit," Randy muttered. "We don't have time for this." As he reached for the door handle, the side doors of the casino opened and six very large security officers filed out.

"They'll get it." I pointed at the guards. Before they got to the vags, traffic started moving.

We drove around with the hopes of seeing Simone's car, figuring downtown wasn't very large, so we might get lucky. The problem was that, since the closing of Fremont Street, which had been turned into a walking mall, people had to move about. Since Fremont was one of America's most famous streets, the tourists chose to walk. That meant something had to be done with all their cars. That was the reason for the proliferation of all the parking garages downtown.

When we had no luck finding the car, Randy called Jeff and told him to go to the detective bureau parking lot at the City Hall complex. Jeff had called Randy to suggest an idea that the bad guys might be parking the Camaro in one of the garages, then taking the van out to caper. It was brilliant, but maybe too brilliant for a couple of tweekers. I had to admit it wouldn't be a bad way to commit crime. The downtown area had a lot of freeway access, was centrally located and the garages were secure because of the security patrols and all the cameras. Also, during the day, there was a lot of traffic to hide in if they wanted to move the property to a fence. The Horseshoe Casino alone owned five complexes, all connected to each other and the casino. Randy suggested putting out a bulletin and having security do the looking for them. The down side would be if a security officer was involved, the crooks might get tipped off. I'd heard of things like that happening.

We split up and canvassed the area one more time. After half an hour, when nothing was found, we returned to the apartment. There was an hour left on shift and by the time that was up, the Camaro still hadn't shown up. We called it a night. I tried four times to get hold of Karri May. I fell asleep on the couch with the phone at my feet.

The next morning at ten, Randy called me and said a construction company was hit the night before. All the office equipment and computers were stolen. The coincidence made it seem like we were on the right track with these two guys. For the next three nights, we sat on the place, watching as John bought beer, picked up friends, and drove north on the freeway. I wanted to put up the helicopter, but the time he left each day was the busiest time for air unit calls.

While following them into a grocery store on the second day, I discovered the guy who was in the car the first day was John's brother, Bob. He had a criminal history that included grand larceny auto, burglary, and possession of controlled substances, which just happened to be meth.

By the end of our first week, we knew a lot about the other people Simone visited. Those peoples' criminal histories led to other associates that had been arrested with them. The amount of information that could be put together from sources available to the police was amazing. Before I knew it, we had a tight circle of people we were looking at. This included the vehicles they drove, where they lived, and how they were connected criminally. I even knew who some of their girlfriends, wives, and children were. This led me to reflect on that old adage: "Birds of a feather flock together," was true.

I liked to think of how I felt as if I was one of those ancient gods the Greeks wrote about. I watched these people either from behind the tinted windows of the car or through a pair of binoculars. I saw them at their most intimate, picking their noses or scratching their asses. I was among them, but not the reverse. I spent the boring moments creating mental stories about what went on in those people's heads. It was slow going, though. What frustrated us and really pissed the brass off was how we couldn't seem to stay on John long enough to prove he was the guy we wanted. We didn't know where he went at night. And every night, it was the same old story — just as we hit the freeway, we lost him. It didn't matter what we did, whether it was putting a car out front, or trying to stay on his ass. He just disappeared. Randy wanted to get so close, people would think the cars were glued together, but the sarg nixed the idea.

"Patience, you guys," he'd say. We'd glower at him, sulk even, but we kept our distance, following just close enough to keep John from suspecting we were on his ass. It was as if John had gotten some kind of spell or juju cast on his car. It never got caught in traffic and couldn't be followed. The other alternative was believing he'd made us from the first day and was now playing with us.

One day, at the end of the second workweek, we watched John leave the apartment. There were two other people in the car besides him. We had our usual three cars, including the original one just back from the other PSU team. It had taken the captain's involvement to get it back from Southeast. Because they had refused to return ours, we decided to have some fun at their expense. A few days before, we dropped their car off at the shop. What we hoped was to get it fixed, then keep it longer. When we dropped the car off, the mechanic was at lunch. An hour later, he called and told us that the Southeast guys had brought it in a few weeks before, but had taken it back when they found out that before he could fix it. The parts would have to be ordered. That meant he'd have the vehicle out of service for a couple of weeks once he started tearing it apart.

Like them, we needed the car, so we first decided to let the work slide. But as soon as we got back to the station, we called the SEAC guys to ask about getting our car back. They told us it was being used. Over the course of that day, they started playing games with us. They first told Randy it was on a call, then it was being used for something else and couldn't be released. Only then did we get our captain involved. He called their captain and they were told to give it up. We made arrangements as if we were going to give them back theirs.

The trick was to keep the transaction from looking as if it was one of those cold war hostage swaps. After a fashion, we worked that out. On the way over, we stopped at the shop and Randy told the mechanic to begin the work for the new air conditioner. We waited long enough to see them get started pulling the radiator and hoses and assure ourselves that in another hour their car would be in too many pieces to stop the process. The thought of how pissed the other squad would be when they discovered they were down a vehicle, which meant they would be three to a car for a month or so, delighted the shit out of us. We had Jeff drive our car away before we went in and told them we'd dropped theirs off at the shop. When Randy innocently explained how we'd done them a favor, I had a hard time keeping a straight face. One of their guys raced for the phone. Randy handed his buddy the invoice showing how he ordered an oil change, brake check, tire rotation, and full detail of both the interior and the exterior. I was amazed we made it out of there intact.

An hour later, we were back to the serious business of following John. I thought about how many burglaries had happened over the last two weeks. They were adding up. Those thoughts were all that kept my mind off Randy's driving as he stayed with the target vehicle. Twice Randy cut people off, making me think that if obscenities were birds, there'd be a flock behind us. When we hit the freeway, the traffic was jammed, as usual. We closed on Sahara, the place we usually lost him. It was then John made one of his moves that we never could duplicate. This time, it didn't work. The car he cut off clipped his back bumper. I watched in disbelief as he lost control of the Camaro and it slammed into two other cars. Randy barely had time to get us stopped before we could become part of the mess.

I immediately got on the radio and told Dispatch what had occurred and told her to notify Highway Patrol. When I got out, there was the smell of gas in the air. I was afraid some fool would come by and drop a cigarette out the window, then things would get ugly. Randy ran to a small Toyota, where I saw an old woman hunched over the steering wheel. When she looked up, her mouth was a bloody mess. When I got closer, I saw she wasn't wearing a seat belt. Her teeth were imbedded in the steering wheel's plastic.

I went straight to John's car. The front seat was empty. I looked towards the side of the road, where I saw him sitting with his back to the wall. He was holding his leg near the ankle. The car was still running, so I reached inside and shut off the engine. Bob, John's brother, was slumped against the passenger door. He had a dazed look on his face. When he tried to move, I saw his neck.

I approached him, closely. "Bob. Stay still." He grimaced when I said his first name. If the circumstances had been different, I would have relished that he'd be wondering how I knew it. "If you move, you might hurt yourself badly. Stay still!" The collision with the other two cars had ripped the hood off, crumpled the fender, and caused the occupants to catapult forward into the windshield. Bob looked at me, but there was no comprehension in his eyes. "Stay still," I repeated again. "Help's on the way."

I started around the car when I saw John trying to climb over the wall.

"Hey!" I yelled. He looked at me and for the first time, I saw recognition.

"I'm going to get help for my brother," he yelled.

"We already called, John. Medical's on the way."

Slowly, he pulled the leg back over the wall. "I know you," he said.

"Officer Madden," I said. "Yeah. You know me."

"Strip bikes?" he asked. "I didn't recognize you without the uniform."

"I get that all the time. Are you OK?"

"My foot hurts."

"Like I said, Medical's coming." He glanced at his car. There was an extremely worried look on his face. "Everything's going to be fine." Saying the words was supposed to alleviate some of his concern. "Sit tight. They'll be here as soon as they get through traffic."

"Cool, man," he said. He placed his palms on the retaining wall, then lowered himself to the ground until he was sitting. Far to the south, I saw the ambulance coming. It wasn't fast, but that was because it had to come in the emergency lane, waiting for the cars to pull left so that its bulk could lumber towards us. I went back to Randy.

He opened a first aid kit a motorist had brought up to him. Randy found a package containing a compression dressing. He reached into a front pants pocket, taking out rubber gloves. That was what experience did for a cop because I'd never thought to stuff a pair in my pocket. He pulled them on, then ripped the package open. The old woman's mouth was bleeding as only a head wound can.

"This is going to hurt a little," Randy said. "OK?"

She nodded. Randy had her open her mouth and bite down on the bandage. I glanced to where Bob lay. I wanted to check on him again. There wasn't a lot I could do because he wasn't bleeding, which I knew how to treat. He appeared to have a broken neck, which I knew very little about other than he wasn't supposed to be moved.

"Cam, did you check the people in the other car?"

"Jeff and Dave are over there. I think they have it."

They watched the old woman press the dressing to her wound. She winced, but he had his other hand on the back of her head, holding her steady.

"Careful ma'am. You're going to be fine. Let's just get this bleeding to stop."

The ambulance pulled up. I saw Karri May get out. Chris went into the back, then came towards us with a bag. When he got to Randy, he had the old woman pull the dressing away for a second. The wound showed itself to be deep before a fresh flow of blood obscured it.

"Keep that in place until I can get a new dressing out," Chris ordered.

I went to where Karri May was talking to John. I didn't like the grin on his face.

"Hey," I called.

"Cam." She glanced at the cars. "You weren't in this were you?"

"Not this time," I said. I liked the look of relief on her face. For a second, there was a flickering interest in John's eyes. That I didn't like. "His brother's inside the Camaro. He needs to be looked at."

A Clark County paramedic unit pulled up. Karri May reached for her bag, but the two firemen went to John's car. One crawled into the driver's side, the other waited while he rolled the passenger window down. I noticed the smell of gas was stronger.

"We need to stop traffic before someone comes along with a cigarette," one of them called. I felt like saying I had already thought of that.

"I'll be right back," I said. "You gonna be OK?"

"Go," she said. "I'm fine. His foot might be broken."

I moved away, but I couldn't help looking back. I headed for the one lane of traffic that was still moving. As I looked south, I saw the cars were building up. It was like a giant blood vessel, suddenly constricted. I picked a car that was a few lengths back.

At the driver's window, I called, "I need you to stop."

"I've got to get to Cashman Center," the driver said.

"I don't care. There's gasoline spilled up there, it could…"

"Listen, Buddy, stop the guy behind me. I'm late and I'll miss the game," he said.

I pulled the badge I kept on the string around my neck so it hung inside my shirt. "Turn off the car, sir." He glanced at the badge and sighed. The guy behind him stuck his head out the window. "It's going to be a while,"

I called. People were already pissed, which meant they weren't as likely to listen to a plain clothes officer. I looked for a Patrol officer when one of the firemen ran up.

"You better get back there!" he said.

"What's up?"

"Hurry!"

I ran with him. As I got closer, I saw Jeff, Dave, and Randy pointing their guns at someone in the back of the ambulance. A bad feeling swept over me as I drew my Glock from under my shirt.

"Get back, fuckers." I recognized the voice. It was John. I moved around the ambulance where I could get a look inside. He held a buck knife to Karri May's throat.

"Put it down. Put the knife down!" Jeff ordered.

"So help me God, I'll cut her motherfucking throat," he screamed. I couldn't imagine how things went from cops and firemen saving people, to this, so quickly.

With my partners already pointing guns at John, there wasn't room for one more. I moved towards the front of the ambulance. When I got there, I tried a door. It was locked. I moved to where I could see John through the windshield. He had his back to me. I had the shot, but I wasn't sure what the forty-caliber round would do. The glass was angled, which meant it might go in a direction other than what I intended. Still, if I kept the sights centered on his back, the first round would penetrate the glass. The rest should hit him. The question was whether my shots would kill him instantly. I decided to take the chance. Just as I was ready to squeeze the trigger, he took a step to the right, as if he sensed I was there. Behind the driver's seat of the ambulance was a metal wall. That was what came between us. My chance was gone. I tried moving around to the passenger side, thinking I could get a shot from that angle. John saw me.

"Get your fucking ass away, Madden," he screamed. Bright blood welled from where the knife was pressed into her flesh. Karri May raised her head slightly. I moved to where the other cops were.

"John. Don't hurt her," I said. I kept my voice calm in spite of what I really felt. "What's the matter? What do you want?"

"I'll tell you what's the matter," Jeff said. "His brother's sitting on a shitload of meth. There's got to be five pounds."

"I'm not going back to prison," John said. "And what I want is the keys to this thing."

"No," Randy said. "Put the knife down and come out."

"Fuck you. I'll die first."

"Cam," Randy said. "Call a supervisor. Tell him what we got."

"Have Jeff do it," I said quietly. "That's my girlfriend he's got in there."

"Jeff?" Randy redirected his voice.

"Yeah?"

"Call the sarg."

"He's on the way already."

"We need to slow things down," Randy said quietly. "Cam, see if you can get him to talk."

I lowered my gun and moved closer. John jerked the knife, cutting deeper into Karri May's neck. She moaned.

"Get back, dickhead."

"Listen, John," I said. "If you hurt her any more than you have, you'll never work this out."

"Call the airport. Tell them I want a plane to Mexico, Cuba, some shit like that."

"They only do that in the movies," I said.

"Oh, yeah?" John jabbed the knife into Karri May's shoulder. She screamed, lunging forward from the pain. The knife slid into her flesh as if it were butter.

"So help me God," John screamed. "I'll fucking kill her."

Karri May grabbed the hand holding the blade and twisted her body. I jumped on the back of the ambulance, but my heel caught the metal edge. I started to fall back, which spoiled Randy's aim. Before I fell, Jeff stepped in and caught me. When I got up, Randy and a Highway Patrolman were kneeling on John, struggling to get cuffs on. I scuttled across the floor of the ambulance towards Karri May. When I rolled her over, I saw just the handle of the buck knife protruding from where he'd stuck her.

"MEDICAL," I screamed. "Jeff, get one of the firemen."

She opened her mouth to say something to me, but all that came out was blood.

"Hold on. It's going to be OK."

She closed her eyes. The way her body shuddered, I felt my heart skip beats. She whispered something. I leaned closer.

"I knew why I was afraid of knives," she said.

"Out of the way. Get out of the way." A hand pushed me to the side. One of the firemen knelt next to her. He checked her vital signs. "Chris, get your gurney. We need to get her on it."

In front of me the two firemen worked on her, while behind me, John was being dragged to the patrol car.

"She made me do it," he screamed.

I began to tremble — as if I'd suddenly come down with a fever.

"You OK?" Randy asked.

"I should have . . . I mean . . . " The words started, froze on my lips like I didn't know how to use them anymore. "I could have . . . " But nothing came to mind.

"There was nothing you could have done," he said. "Nothing!" He grabbed my chin and turned my face until I was looking him in the eyes.

"Did you see the fear on her face?" Before he could answer, I continued, "I shouldn't have left her alone with him. We knew he was up to something." I was quiet because the shock was wearing off and everything was coming apart inside me.

"You're right, Randy." The words sounded as if they were coming out of a dream. "There was nothing I could have done. There is nothing any of us can do. How do we protect people? How do we do anything?" I asked.

"You can't do everything, just what you can. It's life and fate and their karma. It's their burden to bear."

"Then why do we do this?"

"What?"

"This job," I said. "Why bother?"

"Bro, if I have to explain it to you, then you're truly lost."

I was. Everything I cared about was lost to me right then. That was when I went after John, who was seated in the back of a unit, waiting to go to jail. I had to be pulled back before I got to him. I figured if he could do what he'd just done and still live, then something was terribly wrong.

■ ■ ■

Who Can You Trust . . .

something changed in me that day that I didn't understand and still barely do. If I had to explain anything now, I doubt I could — other than to say I realized the only person I could take care of was myself. That was hard to reconcile with what I did for a living. For a while, I believed some crazy things — like they ought to give all the kids in America a gun, teach them how to use it, and make them carry it for life. That way, all those pedophiles, kidnappers, and truly evil people wouldn't stand anywhere near the chances they currently did. Another idea I came to believe wholeheartedly was that the system sucked and I was a part of what made it that way. After shift and with a couple of beers in me, I'd bring my ideas up, debate them to their bitter conclusion, and watch the looks people gave me.

I saw Chris. He told me about Karri May. I hadn't been able to go to the hospital. I felt as if I'd failed to keep her safe. Chris said the knife had missed anything vital, but she had bitten her tongue, which resulted in a serious set of stitches. Chris said she asked him to find me and bring me to the hospital. I stayed away. If this was what I could expect when all I was trying to do was bring a little safety and sanity to the world, then all I wanted was to take care of myself and not have anyone close to me be dependent. With that came the realization that anything I felt for Karri May or anything I imagined I could have had with her had ended.

The next two months were a quiet time, a healing time. But that healing was unlike the good process it was supposed to be. I let it grow an ugly scar that lurked inside me, made life hard. We solved our series, then worked small crimes that were easily put to rest. I spent a shift on ride-along with Peter Harvey, the senior general assignment detective who had suggested I test. He walked me through a mock oral board, suggesting ways to answer the questions that would impress the raters. I studied as hard as I had in the Academy. I wanted that slot. I wanted to be off the street, behind a desk where all I dealt with was paperwork instead of people.

The day of the oral board, I was the second person called into the interview room. When I walked out, I felt I'd done well. The major reason for the feeling was the trick I'd used with the raters. It was something a staff sergeant had cued me to. The advice was to act like I didn't know the answer to one fairly hard question, finish the test, get up and start for the door, suddenly stop and get the board's attention.

"Excuse me. Concerning that question I missed," I'd said. "I've been giving that question some thought. The answer is . . . " I gave it to them. I watched them change the score on the work sheet. The sergeant who was conducting the board even gave me a smile and nod. When I used the trick in the military, it earned me a perfect score on the promotion board — the first time that had happened in my unit. And now, I realized it had obviously worked, again. I was sixth on the list. That left me one last month as a street officer, then I would be a detective. The funny thing was that when Randy found out, he was mad.

"Damn, Cam! Why would you want to go to the land of laydowns?" he asked. "We're making lots of overtime. The hours are flexible and we're getting things done out here."

"I'm going to be different," I explained.

"Let me tell you something. I was up there. The way the system works, you can't," he said.

"I didn't know you were in the bureau."

"Yep," he said. "Hated it. Hated the sitting behind a desk with all those old fossils who are retired on duty." We were in an unmarked car watching two people do a drug deal. I couldn't help thinking that if I sold drugs I'd stay off street corners. "People can't help being laydowns up there. The bureau is where old cops go to get the extra four percent so they can retire as alcoholics." He started the car.

"Aren't we going to get them?" I asked. When he looked at me, I jutted my chin at the two guys. Randy hit the siren. Their heads jerked our way. I thought they might be feeling like people caught in rifle sights. As Randy cut the sound, it was like the spell was broken. The one on the left started running. The other shrugged and walked away. That told me who was holding.

"Get used to not catching people doing shit if you're going to be a detective," he said. Randy put the car in gear. "Those guys up there are a worthless bunch of idiots. It's like someone removes part of their brains when they get there."

"Same thing happen to you?"

"No," he said. "I wanted to work. I tried to work, but after my third talk with the Ell Tee, I saw the writing on the wall, as they say. I quit. Came back here," he was quiet for a while. "Does this have anything to do with the girl?"

He hit the gas, causing the car to accelerate until we rocketed down the street. This was Union area and people didn't drive like that.

"No," I answered. "If you didn't want me testing, why didn't you say something before I tested?"

"Would it have done any good?" he asked. I shook my head. "You sure about the girl?"

"Yep." It had everything to do with her, but I wasn't explaining that to him or anyone else — no matter how close we became as partners. As far as I was concerned, there were certain things people shouldn't know about each other — like what really went on down there at the bottoms of our souls. For instance, there was this thing Randy had about minorities. He always seemed to skirt that issue, especially where Blacks and Mexicans were concerned. He was downright mean to them.

I hadn't bothered to ask him why he acted like he did and he wasn't volunteering the answer. He had to know I didn't like it — I'd dropped enough hints. Maybe, I'd think, his problem was that he thought I'd say something to someone else if he told me, so he never could be sure. I knew I was afraid Randy would question my ability to act under stress if my doubts got in the way. He had to be able to believe he could trust me. What I came to realize was that we cops acted like we were tough, put on a good face. It was the way we fooled each other and the public into believing in us.

I changed the subject. "What're we doing?" I asked.

"We're looking for a street that a snitch described," he said. "The info is a corner house with lots of cactus." He kept his face away from me, looking out the side window. I was afraid we were going to road-kill someone's kid. "Once we find it, we look for the third house to the right. The guy living there is supposed to be into kiddy porn. I hate child pornographers. I once found out my brother-in-law was doing my niece. Took the whole family to keep me from killing him."

"I bet." It was almost six o'clock and ninety degrees, which for Vegas was considered a cool summer evening. I liked the feeling of being two cops riding, as though we were on routine patrol, but without the uniforms and calls for service. As Randy navigated through the neighborhood, I thought how funny it was to hear cops refer to patrol as routine. No citizen would ever think that. We passed street after street of middle class houses, which is what Union area was made of. We called these people "John Q. Citizen" because they were mainly average, law-abiding, blue-collar worker bees, that I was happy I never worked much. Patrolling the areas where they lived was boring and I figured it rotted a cop's brain. If there was anything good to be said for working areas like Union, it was that it was difficult getting a bunch of IAB complaints unless a cop really went out of his way. That was because these people liked the police.

Personally, I preferred tougher places, like Sierra Vista and Cambridge or Pennwood and Arville. When you drove in those areas, the drug traffickers and prostitutes were obvious. They were like dirty laundry that was hung out for everyone to see. The Union area citizens had to be dealt with in a far different way than those who lived along Pennwood or Sierra Vista. In those neighborhoods, the slime treated each other badly and expected the police to do the same.

"Remember some of the instructors in the Academy?" I asked. "Always telling you things like never, ever curse at anyone. Treat people like you want to be treated."

"Yeah," Randy said. He was checking out a pickup truck without plates. "When I was a rookie, I bought that shit. Like it was gospel. Then I woke up in the real world."

"I know. Remember that one female instructor? The one that always brags how she brought that other cop down?"

"Yeah. What's her name?" he asked.

"I can't remember," I said. "If I was forced into that position, you know, making a case against a brother officer, I wouldn't be proud I'd done it and I sure wouldn't go around bragging about it." I hesitated. The truck's driver was acting very suspiciously or what we referred to as four twenty-five. It was like my other train of thought was derailed. The first prickles of something that had been missing from my diet — adrenaline, surged up. I was cranky for it. We were westbound on Washington, just passing Jones. It was a brand new Ford pickup with three black kids inside. Trucks without plates were common up here. What wasn't, though, was one that cut in front of us without using a turn signal.

"Anyway . . . " I tried starting the story again.

"They look young," he cut me off.

"No shit. Too young and too banger looking to be driving that truck."

"Now, Cam," Randy said. His voice took on an admonishing tone. "We can't be racial profiling those fine examples of ethnic diversity."

"Racial profiling?" I asked. "Me? I would never say anything derogatory about those pieces of shit except for comments about the way they're driving. My comments are meant strictly in the sense that it's a far too expensive ride for their demographic."

"Then, there was the way they cut us off," Randy remarked. "They almost hit the front of this police vehicle. What would the sarg say? I think he'd be pissed if he knew we allowed them to almost damage this fine car he's entrusted to our care." He reached for the radio but I stopped him.

"I'll be the one to notify Dispatch that we wish to make a traffic stop in a block or so."

"That sounds like a fine idea," he agreed. I busied myself with the details concerning the vehicle description since there was no back plate. That also required I gave Dispatch the number and description of the occupants, then the projected stop location.

When I was done, Randy remarked, "There is a front plate, you know." and he gave me the number. I was impressed; it reminded me just how smart a really dedicated cop could become.

I updated Dispatch with the plate number. While we waited for them to run it, Randy remarked, "That's a white man's truck if I ever saw one."

"Think so? You're saying a brother would never be driving a truck like that? Let's see if I can articulate what you mean in case it comes up," I said.

"No. Allow me. I am the senior officer after all." I slipped off my seatbelt, pulled my shirt over the butt of my gun so I could get to it easier. This was because I had taken to sticking my gun in my pants, Mexican style. I took out my badge and left it where it could be seen.

"No tint on the windows so you can do illegal things without people seeing in," Randy said. "It's not booming, because I'm sure it ain't got a ghetto blaster in it and it doesn't have all that lift shit on it that is bought with the proceeds of dealing dope in the hood."

"Sounds about right to me," I said. Just to be sure about the stereo, I stuck my ear out the window in an exaggerated manner. "Nope. Not booming." He glanced at me, then grinned.

"What?" he asked. "Not a sound of 'nigger this' or 'nigger that'. Yes, I would say I was right. Definitely a white man's truck, but we'll never be able to put any of what I just said in a report."

I was ready to hit the lights and siren when the dispatcher told us the truck was stolen.

"I knew it," I said. "Bitch is four eleven."

"Yep," Randy said. "I was, too. Here we go." He sat up straight and put both hands on the steering wheel like he was getting ready to do the race track at driver's training. I asked Dispatch to confirm it stolen. That was a strict requirement. Nothing like making the owner lie out in the street on his stomach while a bunch of cops point guns at him.

As other units started clearing calls so they could join in, I said, "Bet they run."

"Goes without saying, partner." Maybe it was my imagination, but I thought the driver was acting agitated. That led me to believe he might have recognized us slipping into cop mode. His head swiveled back and forth like it was on gimbals. At one point, he said something to the passengers. The one riding bitch turned around in the seat to look directly at us. Randy nodded and I hit the emergency equipment.

"The dogs are barking," he said. As soon as I activated the lights and the siren, the truck accelerated. First, I told Dispatch they weren't stopping. I waited half a minute, then said we were in pursuit. That made it official. Using the word "pursuit" on the air was considered the same as cursing. We referred to it as the "P" word, like people said "fuck" was the "F" word. It started a process when a pursuit was called. First, the Dispatch supervisor was required to notify the area lieutenant and the watch commander. Either one had the authority to cancel the chase for any reason — for example if an undercover car occupied by two plain clothed officers did the chasing. Policy said that if the higher-ups decided to let it run its course, the pursuit became their responsibility.

■ ■ ■

As we traveled westbound, we closed the distance until we were less than a dozen feet off the back bumper. I'd guess from the way the driver jerked the steering wheel hard to the right, he didn't like us that close. We went around a corner. The truck went up on two wheels, making me think it would flip. It didn't. The turn took us off the main street into a residential area. I called out the names from the street signs as we passed them. I didn't know the area, so I was lost, meaning I couldn't anticipate where we were heading. Like those people who drive in California fog, my only reference was the vehicle in front of us. My biggest fear was that we would round a corner and find the street filled with kids playing.

Randy might have been thinking the same thing. He let off on the gas pedal, slowing our car. What they taught in driver training was that this might cause the other driver to do the same. It worked a little this time.

Units kept breaking in on my radio traffic, asking where we were. This was a bad thing — not only were they tying up the channel, but if it kept up, we weren't going to get backup soon. In between their cutting in and my direction-of-travel broadcasts, the dispatcher tried repeating the street names in a calm voice. At one point, she advised that she was trying to get an air unit up. I hoped that happened so everyone could back all the way off. It was like driving through a ghost town with no one on the streets. For once, I was glad it was still kind of hot out and around dinnertime. Still, I was surprised the area lieutenant hadn't canceled the pursuit.

I was totally lost and nothing was straight. The neighborhood was laid out as if the builder used a rattlesnake's spoor to plot the streets. Because of the curves, all I could see was four or five houses at a time. Randy put all his skill to use, trying to keep us in a straight line. This meant taking the turns close to the sidewalks, which is called apexing. That way he kept our speed down, yet stayed close enough to not lose sight of the truck. Still, the pursuit was traveling at sixty miles per hour, which would make a mess of someone's house if either Randy or the other driver lost control.

"I think if this gets much faster, we'll call it," Randy said. He glanced over.

"You OK? You're pale." I wiped sweat from my forehead. The way I was being slung about the cab made me feel like puking.

"I'm glad you're calling the pursuit. Listen how calm you are," he said. I groaned as he pulled some serious "Gs" going around a corner. "Did you get that last street sign?" I shook my head. It was getting dark and at this speed, I couldn't read them. "I hope they get the helicopter up. I don't know where we are." As we took another corner, I made an effort to read the sign by swiveling my head. There were tree branches in front of it. The quick motion was almost my undoing. The dispatcher asked where we were.

"Eastbound," I guessed. "I can't see any signs."

"Control, I'm calling the pursuit," the watch commander said over the air. Before the words were all the way out, we saw the truck's brake lights come on as it skidded around a corner. When we made the turn we saw he'd driven into a cul-de-sac.

"Control, we've got them boxed in. They're gonna bail," I radioed. The truck slowed. I made sure my seat belt was off. When the truck slowed, the doors flew open and everyone piled out. The driver ran east. The two passengers went in the opposite direction. The truck was still rolling down the street. Randy slammed on the brakes, then threw the transmission into park. As I exited my door, I saw a black-and-white pass the cul-de-sac entrance. Randy left the driver's seat. He stayed in a crouch as he went for the truck. There was the sound of squealing tires as the patrol officer realized he'd just passed us. I made the driver my target. If anyone was going to have a charge stick to him for the stolen truck, it was going to be the driver. As I ran to cut him off, I threw a quick glance back. The truck jumped the curb at the end of the street, heading for the front of a house. Randy threw his body across the seat, using his hand to slam on the emergency brake. It jerked to a stop.

The driver headed for the block wall between two houses. I was close, but he was fast. I reached for the radio, only then realizing that I didn't have one with me. *It won't matter,* I thought. *I don't know where I am anyway.*

As I ran, I yelled, "You better keep running. When I catch you I'm going to kick your ass."

I heard him curse. He jumped and caught the top of the wall. Being close, I saw the sweat on him. The light was failing fast as the sun dropped. We were through the backyard. He went over a wall just as I caught the top. It felt as though I were wearing springs as I left the ground. I knew I was going to catch him. As I came to the top of the wall, there was the sound of him hitting the ground. I looked down as I fell. I hadn't realized how far it was. When I landed and my feet were solidly under me, I drew my gun. He was about ten feet away and picking up speed. My intention was to have the shortest foot pursuit ever.

"Drop the gun," I yelled as loud as I could. "Drop the gun or I'll shoot." He glanced back, seeing that I had a good bead on him. It was as though he ran into a wall of Jell-O. He slowed, then put his hands up. "I'll shoot, so help me God if you don't drop the weapon."

"No gun," he screamed. His eyes were almost white all the way around. "I ain't got no gun." I gave a quick glance around. It was like we were in a canyon. There was a sidewalk, the roadway, another sidewalk, and twelve-foot-high walls on either side. The street extended east and west for blocks. The street lights had come on, filling the air with pale yellow. We were the only people.

"Police!" I screamed. "I said drop the gun."

His eyes got big. I knew he thought I was going to shoot him and I actually wanted him thinking it. He took a wobbly step away from me. His ankle turned and he fell to the ground. Instantly, he was back on his feet, but now he was limping. That cut his speed significantly. I jogged after him.

"You better keep running," I called, softly. "When I catch you, I'm going to kill you," I noticed the echo, so I made my voice even quieter. He panted while he ran another fifty feet. I wasn't even winded. "You better keep going 'cause you're dead as soon as you stop."

Within half a block, he started sobbing. The sound of sirens filled the space between the walls. I knew they hadn't caught the other two or else they would be looking for me. I stayed ten feet behind him, letting my threats push him along. Finally, he'd had it. He dropped to his knees, sitting back on his haunches. I slowed as I approached, making sure I kept my gun trained on him.

"Put your hands up," I ordered. When he didn't, I put my finger on the trigger and extended my arms in the classic Weaver stance. "I will shoot you dead, so help me God!"

He covered his face with his hands like he didn't want to see what I was going to do to him or his flesh would stop a bullet. I thought how shooting him in the face would produce what homicide detectives referred to as "defensive wounds."

"Just you and me, asshole." I moved closer until the gun was an inch from his nose. I knew he was looking down that black hole because his eyes were crossed. "Who you claiming?"

"I ain't . . ."

Before he finished the sentence, I kicked him in the lower stomach. He cried out. "Who you claiming?"

The breath went out of him. "Fuck you," he whispered.

"No," I said evenly. "Fuck you." I drew my foot back.

"Bloods," he said, hurriedly.

I figured that was true because he wore a lot of red — like the rag that bound his hair, the large blood ruby set in an earring, the shoelaces in his three-hundred-dollar sneakers, and his belt.

"Open your mouth."

"W-w-what?" he said.

"Open your mouth or I'll kill you right here."

He opened his mouth and I stuck the end of the gun inside. "I think I'll kill you anyway," I said. "The same as you'd kill a Crip. You're not part of my set, so no one would say a word but your poor mama. I'd say you got my gun in a fight because I was tired of chasing you. They'd believe it." His color had turned a sickly gray. I tightened my arms so he could feel the tension in his teeth. I made my eyes into slits. I knew he thought I'd do it because he couldn't see my finger wasn't on the trigger. Suddenly, I jerked the gun and screamed, "Bang!"

He fell over backwards, covering his eyes. Piss made a dark stain across the front of his pants. I started laughing so hard I thought I'd piss myself, too. As he struggled to his knees, I booted him in the ribs, which flopped him on his stomach. I holstered my gun and hooked him just as a black-and-white slowly turned the corner at the far end of the street. As soon as the driver saw me, he sped up until he was right in front of me.

Before the cop was out, I nudged the suspect on the thigh with my toe. When I had his attention, I said, "I know where you live, motherfucker. I'll come find you one night and do a drive-by. Get me?"

He studied my face for a second, then nodded. When the unit stopped, Randy jumped out of the passenger seat. "I knew you'd get him."

"Me, too."

"There ain't a bruise on him. Bro, you're breaking the rules," Randy said. He put his face close to the guy. "You lucky. If I'd chased you, your ass would be beat."

The guy looked at me. I saw the fear. "I wished you'd chased me," he muttered.

"Dude!" Randy exclaimed, stepping back away from him. "You pissed yourself." He said it loud enough for the officer who'd driven him and the two climbing out of another arriving unit to hear. The kid put his head down. "That's fucking disgusting," Randy complained. "You're man enough to steal a car but not hold your piss. Jeeee-sus. Get this piece of shit out of here."

As they loaded my prisoner, Randy put his hand on my shoulder. "You OK?"

"Sure. Why wouldn't I be?"

"You looked like something's bothering you."

"Nah. I was thinking how much I'm going to miss this once I'm a big, bad detective."

Randy smiled at me, then turned to the cops. "We're going to walk back." As soon as they started pulling away, he went to the block wall. He made a stirrup with his two hands. "Go on. Get up there."

"I thought we're walking back," I said.

"You think I'm walking six blocks back to our car, you out of your mind."

"We could've rode in the back of one of the units," I complained as I gauged the height of the wall.

"Fuck that," Randy said. "This might be the last exercise you get since you're going to be riding a desk soon." I put my foot in his hands and he catapulted me to the top. I lay on my stomach with the back leg hooked on the opposite side. Randy stepped back from the wall. He made a short run, jumped, and caught my hand. I dropped some weight off the other side, pulling him up. In a second, he sat beside me. We were looking at the Spring Mountain Range. It was desert three quarters of the way up, tans and browns, then green from the pine trees at the high altitudes. In a few months, there would be snow.

"Nice view," he said. We climbed to our feet.

"Hear that?" I asked.

"Yeah," he replied. "I think it's our siren." We ran along the top until we were back where I had started chasing the kid over the wall. As soon as we dropped in the front yard, we both noticed it — the truck was gone. A couple of citizens were in our car. When one old guy saw us, he yelled, "I was trying to attract some attention. I guess I hit a switch but I don't know which one."

"Let me in there," Randy yelled. When he deactivated the siren, the silence was almost palpable. "Where's the truck?"

"Exactly," I seconded. A second later, three units turned the corner, coming to a stop near us. I recognized the watch commander as he got out.

"Where's my truck?" he asked as he approached us.

"You mean the stolen one?" Randy asked.

"No. I mean *where's my truck?*"

We looked confused. "We just got here," Randy said. He looked at the old guys who were looking at all of us. "Where's the truck?" Randy asked.

The watch commander looked at me. "Is he stupid?"

"No, sir. He's confused and so am I," I said.

"Then let me make this clear. That stolen truck was my mutherfucking truck. Why the fuck did you think I let this thing go on for so long? That was my brand new truck, taken from over at the substation. Where, I might add, I parked it two hours ago. Do either one of you have an idea where it went?"

Randy and I looked blankly at each other.

The old guy stepped up. "It went that way," he said. His arm pointed back the way we'd come and the opposite way the units had pulled into the street. "Couple of kids took it. White boys."

"Holy shit!" I muttered.

"Control," the lieutenant said into the radio. "This is Three Thirteen. Where is that air unit?"

Before she gave the answer, Randy and I started for our car.

"Hey, Ell Tee, we have to book our prisoner," Randy called. I was wondering if we could do that without the evidence, which was the stolen truck.

That night, Randy asked me if I wanted to get a beer after work. I said I was going straight home for some sleep. I didn't. Instead, I went to the hills south of town. On the way, I stopped at a convenience store to pick up a twelve-pack of beer. My truck barely made it to the top of the dirt road that ended at the hill's crest. After I parked, I sat on the still hot hood. The whole town was laid out before me, as though one of those model train collectors had designed and built it. I traced streets that I knew and thought about things that had happened — such as the naked girl, Amy; or Lizzie, or the guy who'd shot himself in the room. I avoided thinking about Karri May as much as I could and when the thoughts managed to intrude, I drank whole beers.

Far off across the valley, I saw our helicopter, Metro's, circling over a neighborhood. The spotlight illuminated something the grave or swing units were obviously trying to deal with. I had my radio in the car and I could have turned it on and found out what it was. Instead, I just tagged it with the thought, *Just another situation that isn't going to mean anything to anybody.* It was a bad thought. Another came to me. *Just like sticking a gun in a suspect's mouth and putting the fear of God into him.* The alcohol in the beer was working slowly. I just felt swollen, like I was going to burst. I realized I should have brought something stronger. For a second, I closed my eyes and I let my thoughts wander down every imaginable path I could conceive of. The ideas just got too big for me. I shook each one off, then let another take me somewhere else. It occurred to me that my thoughts were no more real than what was happening under that spotlight. They were nothing, like the nothing inside me. I guess I was looking for some pity or shame.

"What is it you want?" I asked out loud. I looked at a nearby bush, waiting for just a split second for an answer. I wanted a voice to speak to me from out of it, but there was only silence. I held my breath as I listened — nothing but the wind and the car's engine cooling. Nothing. I listened carefully. Nothing. I was alone with my thoughts. Above me a few clouds reflected the lights from the city, a billion stars noting their silent passage.

■ ■ ■

Ambulance Chatter

It was my first day as a detective in the bureau. I got up, got myself ready, and put on a suit. I only had two, which was made me consider getting a couple more. I stood in front of the mirror as I hooked my badge holder to my belt, stuck the Glock in the new holster I'd bought, and held my jacket open by sliding a hand in my pocket.

"Detective Cam Madden, burglary," I said to the image in the mirror. I laughed, let the jacket go, and after pouring a cup of coffee, drove to work.

When I walked in, I knew who the new guys were — we were the only two men wearing suits and ties. The first person I was introduced to was Norman Smart. He was one of those crusty old detectives — tall, thin, a head of silver hair, and those stupid-looking half glasses that sat towards the end of his nose. He was forever pushing them back after they slipped down.

"That's your desk." He used his chin to point. I looked. It was the usual government gray monster. The top was neat, which was the last time as long as I had it. Someone had set out new supplies — a centered calendar blotter, a magnetic paperclip holder, a gray stapler, and several different types of notepads. There were a document tray, a phone, a computer, and a stack of case files a foot high. It all looked antiseptically neat. I took off my jacket, hung it on a coat rack, then sat down.

"What'm I doing?" I asked.

"Solving crime. There it is." Norman pointed at the stack of files. I pulled the first one towards me and began reading the burglary crime report. It was a shit case. The officer who took the report had done a poor job. He hadn't requested ID to come out or interviewed the neighbors, which meant there were no leads. I set it aside and read the next one.

Over the next hour, I read through the stack. They were all about the same. I knew the desk had belonged to a detective who probably moved on to another detail. He was required to clear as much of his caseload as possible prior to my taking over. This meant most cases should have been closed out, submitted for prosecution, or clearly marked with what was required for further investigation. Instead, he had left me sitting there reading bullshit, which pissed me off.

I caught Norman's eye. "I'd like to have a talk with Detective Johns about this shit," I said.

"That would be hard." Norman's face became very still.

"Why? He go to narcs or something?"

"No. He's buried over at Palm Memorial Gardens on Eastern."

"Oh," I was quiet. Just like me to stick my foot in my mouth on my first day. Of course, once Norman said that, I knew who Detective Johns was. I just hadn't put the name Keith Johns with Detective Johns, since there were at least eight Johns on the Department.

Norman picked up a file from his desk. Then, looking down at it like he was reading, he said, "About two weeks ago, he put his Department-issued semiautomatic pistol in his mouth and pulled the trigger. For a couple of days afterward, all kinds of rumors circulated. Some people said his life was shit after his wife left him. His doctor diagnosed him with a major medical problem, cancer I'd heard, and Lieutenant McMahan threatened to suspend him for drinking on duty. They wanted him to retire but he had nothing except this job. That afternoon, the Ell Tee gave him a good dressing down. Right in there." He pointed at the small, open office area. Everyone in this place heard it. Keith was sent home. Billy in homicide told me he put on his Mickey Mouse pajamas, ate a bowl of ice cream while he watched the History Channel, then created a Rorschach on the ceiling."

"That so?" I asked.

"Yep," Norman said.

"Then he'll appreciate this." I pulled my gunmetal gray garbage can from around the desk's corner, then shoved the whole pile of folders off my desk into its maw. "I guess he won't be too upset with me for doing that." Norman started laughing. When three of his cronies looked over to see why, he pointed. They all howled as I got up to get another cup of coffee.

"Shit, boy," Robby McCoy said. "You'll do around this place. You'll do just fine."

That was how I ended up under their wings. It was a good thing, too. Sergeant Smith could have taken ball busting lessons from Lieutenant McMahan. The first two days, he left me alone other than commenting about my attire. Then on the third day, he called me into his office. It was to be my in-processing interview. As I sat squirming in the wood bottom chair, wondering where the hell he'd found it, he quietly absorbed the contents of my blue file.

"You got a lot of commendations in here," he said. He picked at each one like they were covered in something he didn't want to touch.

I thought I'd try a touch of humor. "I got a knack for getting into shit, sir."

He gave me a serious look. "Is that right, Madden?" His eyes went back to the file. "Well, don't be getting into shit while you work for me." He closed the file with a snap. "I got less than a year and I'm off to the islands. I want it to be smooth sailing. Sit at your desk and handle your case load. Answer the phone, tell people nice things, and make this the last time we talk unless it's 'Hi' at the start of the day and 'Bye' at the end. Clear?"

"Like glass, sir."

"Good! Dismissed. Send Detective Smart over here when you go back."

"Yes, sir." I got up as he tossed my file in a pile on the corner of his desk. When I got to Smart, he was on the phone. I excused myself, "He wants to see you."

Norman ignored me. I went to my desk. A minute later, McMahan appeared.

"Did you tell him?" He directed the question at me.

"Yes, sir."

"I said I wanted to see you," the lieutenant said.

"I'm on the phone," Smart said, then went back to his conversation.

McMahan walked over and snatched the phone from his hand. He put it to his ear. "This is Lieutenant McMahan. Detective Smart will call you back." He slammed the receiver in the cradle. "Get over to my office."

Norman smiled at him. He pushed to his feet with the most insolence I had ever seen. McMahan turned a bright red. They went towards his office area. Just before they went in, Norman looked back and winked at his buddies. They grinned and as soon as the two were around the corner, they crowded towards the office. Kyle Simms motioned for me to follow. The four senior detectives simply stood next to the door where they could eavesdrop without being seen. I felt that I wouldn't be immune in the same way they seemed to be, so I stood by the file cabinets, acting like I was looking for something. McMahan roared, "When I tell you . . . " His secretary's phone rang. I heard her say, "Yes, sir. He's in a . . . Right away, sir." McMahan's phone rang. He yelled.

"Dorothy, you know better than to bother me," he yelled.

"Sir, you better . . . " she started.

I heard McMahan grab up the phone and yell, "What!" There was a moment of silence, then, "Yes, sir. He's right here."

I chose a file at random, then went towards my desk. As I went by the door, I glanced inside. McMahan was holding the phone out to Norman. "It's the sheriff."

Norman took it and without covering the mouthpiece, he said, "I know it's the sheriff, Telly." His voice dripped sarcasm. "Who do you think I was talking to? We were discussing our weekend golfing trip when you hung up on him." He placed the phone to his ear. "Jim. Let me get back to my desk." He listened, then looked at McMahan. "He wants you in his office. Two minutes." He pointed at the office door. "Close it on the way out." Through the glass, I watched him take the lieutenant's seat to continue his call. All the old guys started laughing, not even bothering to hide their glee. McMahan went to the vehicle board, took a set of keys, and left. That was my first indication how badly the Ell Tee was disliked.

After a couple more days, things settled into boredom as I learned the things I needed to know to do my job. The detectives stayed glued to their desks, working cases through their phones. When they went out, it was to lunch or on personal business. After a month, I was dying for something else to do.

Finally, the chance to work undercover was presented to me. It happened while McMahan took a month off to go to Hawaii. He had an offer out on a house there, which he was going to buy for his retirement. The situation involved me playing the part of a booster and was part of an ongoing investigation. It developed when the intel unit targeted a couple of crews who were supposed to be ripping off area businesses. The individual thieves, called boosters, made their livings stealing items from retail stores and then selling the stuff to fences. It was exactly like something out of the movies. When I got called into intel to get a briefing, I learned a lot of things I didn't know.

"Some of these guys steal five grand a day," Detective Simms said. "When Smart talks to groups about boosting, he tells them that if they figure a booster spends about ten months or three hundred days on the street, and if the suspect steals only a thousand a day, this averages out to three hundred thousand dollars a year. That's not even a good booster. The good ones average five grand a day. That comes to one point five million a year. Smart gets their attention with that. Invariably, someone will ask what the booster does with those other days. Any idea?"

I shook my head.

"People have this impression the booster is off on some exotic vacation, spending that money. The truth is they spend the time in county lock-up."

"Wow! That's a lot of money," I said. "I had no idea, either. I've had my share of booster arrests when I worked patrol, too."

"Well, that's the impression," he continued as he set up the body wire I was going to wear. "There's also the impression that shoplifters are small-time criminals. Some are and some aren't. The kid that goes in and steals a candy bar or a CD he's been wanting, is. The guy who steals thirty CDs every chance he gets, isn't. That kind of crime gets the owners all fired up about putting those people in jail. Smart likes to tell them at the meetings that the individual boosters aren't where the focus needs to be. It needs to be on the fences. They are the ones who buy the shit, paying ten cents on the dollar, repackaging everything, and selling it to legitimate businesses. That's where the real money is, with the fences. What little money the booster gets ends up going for food, a room, and his biggest expense, drugs."

As I listened, I thought how I'd been brought into Sergeant Durant's office and asked if I was interested in working as the undercover.

"Holy cow, Sarg. Are you kidding? Of course I want to do it," I said.

"Thought you might. The old guys said shit around the office was killing you. I guess Norm mentioned it to the sheriff and now you're in here. When McMahan gets back, he won't be too happy, but the sheriff will make sure it'll be OK." The next thing he did was explain how I had a week to get ready.

"What's there to do to get ready?" I asked.

"Lots. For instance, this morning you took your last shower. From now on, you wear the same clothes every day. Friday, you'll go to the North Las Vegas swap meet where you'll be working. Walk around. Let people see you."

"Wait. No showers?" I asked. "Boss! It's August. Do you have any idea what I'll smell like in two days, much less a week?"

"It'll be longer than a week. Want me to find someone else?"

I shook my head. That night, when I went home, I stuffed a pair of jeans and two t-shirts from the laundry into a plastic bag. I took them out to the trunk of the car they gave me. The next morning, I didn't shower. Before I went to work each morning, I stood in the entryway, where I'd put the clothes on. At first, the smell was like a physical assault, but within ten minutes, I grew used to it. I did learn one thing; I had to stop drinking. After a night out, I had the worst hangover. When I took the clothes out, the smell had me at the sink dry heaving.

The swap meet was across town. The Department-issued car they gave me was a beat-to-shit Ford. When I first saw it, I thought it had more dings and dents than a demolition derby car. The radio was under the seat where I couldn't see what it was tuned to, thus I couldn't change the channel. Within a week, they gave me a partner. Technically, I'd be working alone, but they figured I needed someone to cover me. Another new detective, Gary Burls, met me at the parking garage of the bureau one morning before the sun rose. When we first got in the car, he quickly rolled the window down and stuck his head out.

"What the hell's that funk?" he said. "Smells like vagrant feet."

"It's me," I said.

"You!"

"Yep. Me. Your new partner."

"Jesus, Mary and Joseph!" We rode together until I was a block away, then I dropped him so he could walk in. He was out of the car the second it slowed down enough so that he wouldn't go rolling down the street. By the third day I smelled so bad, he refused to get back in my car.

On the second day, I'd made contact with my first target. His name was Joe. While I showed him a bag of batteries, video movies, razors, and aspirin, all supposedly stolen, he told me that people said there were undercover police in the area.

"Really?" I slowly turned so I could survey the crowd. Right then the wind shifted and he got a whiff of me. When I turned back, he had moved away a short distance. I almost grinned. Joe waved me into the back of his booth.

"Ya ever hear of water?" he asked. "People take baths and shit like that in it."

I lifted an arm and smelled my armpit. "I guess I could consider it."

"Anyone smells as bad as you can't be the police." He sorted through the stuff. "What else can you get?"

"Anything you want." This was true. We'd made deals with certain businesses that were getting hit the hardest. They agreed to give us whatever we wanted after we offered them a deal, which was that whatever money we collected, was theirs as well. Then, when we made the arrests and recovered property we thought belonged to them, the owners received their cut. Those items would go back to the stores. When the cases went to court, the Deputy DAs were instructed to ask for restitution, which they would also get. I referred to this as the triple whammy and it was what caused every business we approached to decide to participate in the sting.

"These don't sell well," Joe said, holding up a bottle of Bayer aspirin. "It's the small ones people want. Maybe you can steal only those. You can carry more of them. They're easier to hide. I sell them faster."

"I'll keep that in mind, but right now I have those. Do you want them, or do I take them to Arnie?"

"That thief, he won't give you near as much as I will."

"He did all right yesterday," I said.

"What'd he buy?" Joe asked. He looked mad. "I thought you were giving me first choice at everything you had." This was one of those times when I was sure I'd made a mistake. "I told you I'd take everything you had." It became obvious he was trying to make me feel guilty.

"I've got to keep my options open," I said. "What happens when I need money and you ain't here? You know I can't wait a day."

"True. True. Just don't sell him nothing too good."

"Joe, you know I come to you first." I actually liked Joe and I was going to be sorry when we arrested him. The first night I'd dealt with him, I knew I was going to like him. That made me decide I wouldn't make the mistake some cops did of getting too close.

"I'll bring you the smaller bottles next time."

Joe removed a wad of bills from a front pocket. He carefully counted what I'd asked for, then shoved the money in my pocket. I patted it, gave him a wave to let my cover team know I was done, and moved on. Each day was the same. Gary and I started together, then later in the morning after I had a feel for the place, the rest of my team showed up, which was Norman, Simms, McCoy, and the sarg. That day, we had a fifth member who was an FBI agent. His name was Tyler Smith and he'd come to the FBI as an attorney.

A week before, the Febbies heard we were doing something and approached us, asking if we'd let Tyler tag along. Their special agent in charge promised to pitch in with some funds, equipment, and property if they liked what they saw. While Tyler sat in on our briefing the day before, Norman said they wanted to buy in for a minimum, then take all the credit when the thing went down.

"That's pretty common with you feds," McCoy said.

"I'm not going to deny it. We got money to spend and Congress wants to see us spend it. What better way than to give it to you for what you need and we get our credit?" In a way, I couldn't blame them. They were dependent on Congress, just as we were on the city and county governments. They had to produce the same as we did.

After Tyler was gone, Norman told me fed stories. He said they usually did their own operations by themselves, but fucked them up so badly, they needed the local ones now and then to look good. Actually, I was happy to have Tyler along. Twice in the past week my team had gotten distracted when they were supposed to be watching me. I had walked away from the booth with no cover. That caused problems because I either had no idea I was alone or if I did, I just couldn't go back there and say, "Hey, I'm over here."

Still, things were going well. I'd sold quite a bit of property to the crooks I identified. The cases we built were going to be strong. And, best of all, I was out of the office.

When I got to Arnie's booth, I had to wait while he dealt with another booster. While I lurked around, I got a good description of the booster, went to meet Gary, and passed him the information, which he gave to the team. Sarg had a Northtown unit wait down the street. They watched the guy leave, then picked him up as a routine pedestrian stop. The Northtown cops were told to grab the guy if he so much as spit on the sidewalk. He did and they did. Thank the powers that be for stupid laws. When they searched him, we got really lucky because he was carrying a bindle of dope, which I guessed came from the Mexicans. That put a felony on him. It was all about eliminating the competition so I had a clear path to the fences.

As I headed back to Arnie's booth, I was happy to see a couple of my team moving through the already growing crowd. I thought about Arnie as I waited for him to finish with a customer. When I first made contact, he gave me a business card that said he'd been around for nine years. He was short, my height, thin with thinning hair. He could talk a mile a minute and I'd watched him sell people things they didn't need. He'd been a hard sell when I first approached him. Now that he knew me, we'd come to the stage where he'd buy everything I brought, including electronic devices, over-the-counter health and beauty aids, vitamins, make-up, medicines, and videotape movies or music cassette tapes. There were days he had boosters waiting like jets in a holding pattern. As I'd leave his booth, I was astounded at what I saw in back. There was sheer product volume there and he was moving it. I knew that because it disappeared some time between my visits. We hadn't been able to determine where the stuff was going. We had tried, taking an hour here and there to do nothing but following Arnie. Recently, I had pushed for an entire day where all we would do was concentrate on him, but the bosses wanted to build all the cases before concentrating on any one individual.

Today, as whenever I came around, Arnie's wife, Maria, acted both nervous and angry that I was there. She made no effort to hide her dislike of me. She constantly told Arnie she didn't want him dealing with me. He was a greedy man, though, and all I could say was, "Thank God for greed." The really funny part was that whatever I showed him, he'd take and hold up so Maria could see it. Automatically, she looked at it and quoted him the price they were to pay. I never got more than she said, no mater how I argued.

When I decided he had ignored me enough, I called, "Hey. I'm here."

"I tell you, Arnie, he's a cop," Maria said. The morning breeze became noticeable as I started sweating. No matter how hard I tried, if someone accused me of being a cop that was my reaction, causing thin streams of sweat to run down my ribs or into my eyes from my hairline. Within seconds, my sides would be drenched and that made me shiver. I wished I was one of those cops who were so chilly, it was like they were ice sculptures.

"Come here, Maria," Arnie called. "Get a whiff of him. No cop smells like this, baby."

I took a newly released movie from inside the bag. These had come from the vault at a local retailer because they weren't set to be released for two days. Arnie's eyes lit up.

"Look, honey. See what he brought?" She wouldn't budge from where she stood looking at me. "She'd be happier if you proved you're not a cop."

"That's bullshit, Arnie," I said. "I'll take my business to Stan or Joe. I don't have this shit with them."

"OK. But can they buy as much as I do?" he asked. "All I'm asking and all she wants is for me to make sure you're not wearing a wire. The way you're acting, maybe you are. Only a cop wouldn't want to prove she was wrong."

"She thinks I'm wearing a what? A wire?" I asked. I wasn't, but there was a small recorder hidden inside a pack of Marlboros, the microcassette tape reels spinning.

"She thinks you'll have a thing like a tape recorder taped to your body somewhere."

"What do you want me to do, take off all my clothes? I asked.

He leaned in close and whispered. "No. If you have one of those things, there'll be a wire thing with a microphone. It'll be taped on your chest. Maria watches a lot of movies so she thinks she knows this stuff." He raised both hands apologetically. Normally, I'd have no problem lifting my shirt to show I wasn't wearing anything, but the problem was that I had a gun stuck in my waistband. If I raised my shirt, he'd see the .38 caliber revolver. If a wire was going to blow this, a gun definitely might.

"I should walk my ass out of here," I said.

"Go ahead," he said. "Now, you're making me nervous."

"I don't mean to," I said stalling for time. The only thought in my head right then was that I'd get Joe and Stan, but my gut instinct said Arnie was big, so I had no intention of walking and letting all the work we'd done go to waste. Later, I'd learn I was getting ready to make a classic mistake, which was putting my life at risk for property. "I don't want to make you nervous, Maria," I called, "And to prove it, look."

I turned so I faced away from the crowd, which meant I also faced away from Arnie. I figured, after all, this show was for Maria. I raised the back of my t-shirt. I dropped the back, turned toward Arnie, and lifted the front. Maria moved around in front of me so she could see, too. As soon as the material was up, they both saw the gun.

"Mother of God," Maria said. She moaned like she was in pain, then turned pale. I thought she'd faint. Before I'd let go of the shirt, Arnie snatched the gun out of my waistband. I was staring over their shoulders at my five cover team members, who were starting to draw their weapons. With Arnie and Maria's backs to the crowd, they didn't see this.

"Cool gun. You wanna to sell it?" Arnie asked. His eyes were down, looking down at the weapon in his hands. Before the team's guns were all the way clear, I met Sergeant Durant's eye and shook my head. I had this terrible picture in mind of my team firing at Arnie and hitting me. I actually tensed for the impact of the rounds. Sarg stepped forward and shook his head. Everyone left their guns in hiding. As I looked around, I realized what was really amazing was that no one in the crowd had seen a thing.

"Come here, honey," Arnie said. "Take a look at this." Maria didn't move. He flipped the cylinder and inspected it. When he saw it was loaded, he snapped it closed, then sighted along the ground so people in the crowd wouldn't see. I fully expected him to pull the trigger.

"Whatdaya want for it?" he asked.

This wasn't a Department issue weapon. I'd paid hard currency from my own pocket for it. Besides, there was no circumstance I could imagine where we would let a weapon slip into the hands of a criminal, even if it wasn't mine. I knew my boss would step in and arrest the fence before he'd let a gun walk.

"Give me that." I grabbed the gun. It was probably stupid. If his finger slipped, it could have gone off. I made a big deal of sticking it back in my pants. "Man, you should know better than to touch a man's gun without asking his permission. You trying to dis me?"

"Nah. It ain't like that," Arnie said. He rubbed his finger where I'd almost removed skin.

"I need this gun. How'm I gonna protect myself? You know where I live, man?" When Arnie shook his head, I continued, "I live in a shithole motel down on the south end of the Strip. You ever been down there?" Again he shook his head. His eyes were on the front of my shirt where I stuffed the gun. "I don't have a gun, I get killed. Then who's gonna take care of my lady?" This was part of the cover story I'd built with all the fences. I'd told them I had a strung-out girl I was living with, who I was trying to get off heroin. I constantly complained about how hard life was by making up stupid shit she had done — like getting us kicked out of one motel after another because she went on crying jags that involved a lot of screaming when I couldn't score dope.

"Well! I know that neighborhood," Arnie said. "You could get another gun down there. Sell me this one. I'll give you enough to buy two. Then if you need more money, I could buy one. This one stolen?"

"Do I ask you questions? This is shit," I said. I grabbed the bag I'd dropped. "I'm taking my business to someone else, back to Joe."

"Chill out, man," Arnie said. He began talking really fast. That was how I knew he intended selling me a sob story. The whole time, his eyes stayed where the gun was hidden. I didn't like that. "What you need is a semiautomatic, instead of that old wheel gun. Come over here." Arnie took me by the elbow. I shook him off. He gave me an apologetic look, then held a hand palm up towards the front of his truck.

"Arnie," Maria called. I heard the warning in her voice.

"Later," he called.

"Arnie, I need to talk to you," she insisted.

"Not right now. We got a customer." I glanced at one of the front tables. There was a little old Spanish-looking woman standing there holding up a bottle of vitamins. She must have weighed ninety-five pounds, yet her hair was black as a raven's feather. As soon as she spoke, I recognized the Italian. Maria looked surprised for a second, then went over and they fell into a deep conversation. While I went to the front of the truck, the two women's heads came within a few inches of each other. *It's like they're on the same wavelength,* I thought.

Arnie opened the door of his truck. He leaned in, reached under the seat and pulled out a rag-wrapped object. He folded back the material like he was showing me an expensive piece of jewelry. Lying in his hand was a crummy semiautomatic Saturday night special. *Be still my beating heart,* I thought. Arnie was an ex-felon, which meant he was now guilty of the crime ex-felon in possession of a firearm. He was screwed. He held the gun up.

"I'll trade this gun," he said. Arnie pointed at the gun in my waistband with the barrel of the one he held. "For this gun." If I didn't know better, I'd thought he was trying to get himself killed. Again, things were moving fast.

"Don't point that thing at me, asshole" I said. I kept any anger out of my voice. "What if it went off?"

"I got the safety on."

"There's no way I'm going to trade this gun for that piece of shit. Let me see it." This time, I snatched the gun away from him. I looked it over. Up close, it was even worse than I had thought. If the thing had ever been cleaned, I'd be surprised. There was rust on some of the parts. The slide was pitted. "This is a piece of shit, but I'll buy it off you."

"I want yours."

"Not for this." I turned so my body was clear of Arnie's, then hefted the gun. If he wouldn't sell it to me, I wanted my team seeing it so they could testify in court.

"How about a 1911 Colt?" he asked. I raised my eyebrows. He must have taken it as a negative. "Complete with silencer."

"Really?" I let my voice ooze doubt.

"The gun's supposed to be delivered in a day or two. It's hot, came out of someone's house," Arnie said.

"A burglary?" I asked.

He nodded. "So, you'll have to be careful with it." Arnie took the pistol back. "Whatdaya offer me for this?"

"Thirty," I said.

"Fifty," Maria said from over my shoulder.

"I got thirty and I'll throw in two of the new movies."

Arnie hesitated a minute. "Done."

I counted the money into Maria's palm. I slipped the pistol into my pocket, then left the booth. I thought I had never been so happy.

"I think that took two years off my life," the sarg said as he came even with me. "Were you trying to give Norman a heart attack?"

"No. It just went down that way."

"That's not what I mean. He's down the street. His heart went crazy."

"Really? Holy shit! Get me over there." I hurried through the crowd. Over the course of the last couple of months, Norman had become one of my favorite people. He was teaching me a lot about what police work used to be like and what a detective should be. He was also my guardian angel where Lieutenant McMahan was concerned. As I went through the front gate of the swap meet, I broke into a jog. When I got to the sidewalk, Gary picked me up.

"Holy shit," he said. "Don't do anything that makes you sweat, it only makes it worse."

"Sorry." I hit the button that opened the window and pointed two air conditioner vents in my direction. He turned the knob to full ON. "How's Norman?" I asked.

"Medical's with him," Gary said. "He's worried about you and doesn't want to go."

I was quiet as we drove to the alley where the ambulance was parked. The fire department's para-rescue team stood around talking to the rest of my team. As I walked up, I heard everyone talking shit because the annual police/fireman football game was coming up and there was a lot of rivalry between our two departments. As we parked, I saw Karri May in the back of the ambulance. Suddenly, I was concerned with my appearance. Gary parked. I took a deep breath. I couldn't seem to move.

"I'm not shutting this car off until you're out. The smell might not come out of the seats as it is."

I opened the door. It was hot in the alley, making me feel as if I'd just stepped into a blast furnace. Karri May was bent over the gurney. She looked up just as I raised a foot to step up into the ambulance. Her eyes got big as she glanced past me. I turned to see what she was looking at.

"Will I see you tonight?" The fireman who stood there was taller than me by an inch. I studied him surreptitiously, seeing the way his body was layered in muscle. *What else did they do all day but work out, polish fire engines, and draw equal pay with us cops?* I thought.

"I'll call you later, Jim. Don't plan anything," she said. "I might be too tired when I get off."

"OK. If I don't hear from you by six, I'll be at the gym."

I watched him go. "Muscully, isn't he?" I remarked, using something I'd heard at the gym. "Does it have a brain?"

"Yeah," she replied. "I think it's . . . he's . . . getting a master's in fire science."

"Wow! I'm impressed. If he sees one, he'll know what it is," I remarked. "You know? A fire?"

"I knew what you meant."

"Oh, I see you two already know each other," Norman called from the gurney. "I was just telling her I could introduce her to a nice cop."

I moved past her, going to Norman. "How you doing, buddy?"

His eyes went past me to Karri May. When I glanced back, I saw her looking at Norman with concern. The side door was open, so I turned my eyes to the outside world. There was a block wall next to the ambulance. A blue-belly lizard ran along the surface, seemingly able to defy gravity. He crossed the joint lines and the cracks like a creature on a mission. I searched the wall ahead of it. There was a large blue bottle fly buzzing near a brown stain on the wall's surface. It looked like human shit. The fly landed and took off, in constant motion. When the lizard was close, it sprang into space and caught the fly in its jaws, then landed back on the wall, as if its feet were made of Velcro. I heard the insect's exoskeleton crunch.

"We know each other," she continued. "Unfortunately, Cam must have had an accident with his fingers."

"Really?" Norman asked.

"Either that or he forgot how to use a phone," she said.

"I called," I said. The words came out sullenly.

"Once. Then nothing for the last few months," she said. She took a deep breath as though trying to get control of something. "What is that God-awful smell?"

"That be me," I said. My face felt like I'd gotten too much sun.

"He's undercover," Norman said. "He cleans up well. Like if someone wanted to go to dinner with him."

I was quiet. I wasn't sure what Norman was trying to do. I'd made up my mind about any relationship with her, but my emotions were still trying to settle out from the exchange I'd witnessed between Jim the fireman and Karri May.

"I can't break my cover," I said.

"And I can't break my date with Jim tonight."

"Nonsense. You two people are acting like a couple of fools. Even an old geezer like me, laying here dying, can see that. Young lady, this idiot will call you by five. He will be freshly showered, that thing he thinks of as a beard will either be trimmed or gone, and his hair will be clean." Norman pushed the half-glasses back up his face. "And he *will* be on time."

"I can't . . . " My words came out softly, almost uninteligible.

"If he calls before five, I'll break my date with Jim. I've only been seeing him for a week anyway."

"He will," Norman said. He pushed himself to a sitting position. Karri May put a hand on his shoulder as if to make him stay. Norman pointed at his chest. "Did you hear anything wrong in there?"

"No, sir. Your heart sounds OK. They want to take you down for a few more tests."

"It was indigestion. I told that idiot Simms that. He never listens to me. The man's a hypochondriac and he thinks if he has a pain or twitch, real things are wrong with him. He went all crazy and called you guys without telling me what he was doing. Let me get back to work." Norman grabbed his jacket and exited the ambulance. He stopped and looked at me. "You two make some plans." He walked over and stuck a finger in my chest. "Fuck this up and you'll wish you'd never become a big, bad detective. Hear me, boy?"

I nodded. Peculiarly, I was suddenly very happy.

"My dear, if I was only a few years younger." He winked at Karri May. As he walked away, he muttered, "And not so afraid of my wife."

■ ■ ■

What's My Name? . . .

broke the promise to call. I had to do it. When I stood in the back of the ambulance looking at her, I'd gotten weak. All the things that happened between us rushed back into my head. And, as always, they were balanced by the smell of her perfume, the soft brush of her touch and the kindness she showed Norman while he lay on the gurney. It was those things ganging up on me that made me forget why I'd stopped seeing her. But when I was away, back on the street where things were their normal shit, I remembered what my worries were. At five o'clock, the phone rang. I wanted to answer it so badly my hand shook. I waited until it stopped, then called the sarg. He wanted to stand down the operation for a while so we could get some paperwork caught up. I figured I'd make him a gift of sorts.

"Hey, Sergeant Durant."

"Cam," he said. His speech was slurred like I'd either woken him or he was drunk. "Something wrong?"

"Could I take a week's vacation?"

"Someone die?" he asked.

"No," I said. "I just need some time. Some personal things are getting me down. I thought I'd go somewhere before they affect the operation."

"Yeah. That would fit in with me wanting to get caught up. Take a week. Call me if you need anything."

I hung up. As soon as I did, the phone rang, again. I went into the bedroom and packed my things as if the cops were coming to get me. I wanted to drive down to the beach by Santa Monica. I wasn't even in trouble, either.

The week there passed quickly, like they always did. I met a couple of Santa Monica cops and they had me drinking with them. When I got back, I did a whole bunch of things such as look for a new house to rent, get a new phone number, and put a restriction on who PBX put through to the new number. Then, I jumped right back into work. In the meantime, the boss wanted me to start at the swap meet the following weekend. Just as something to do, he said.

Before that happened, I picked up a series of hot prowl cases at the Bellagio Hotel. The security people thought an employee was helping the burglar get into the rooms, because there was no sign of forced entry. Norman gave me a long spiel about his best hot prowl cases. He explained some of the psychology that went into the mind of a person who entered a place where he knew the victim was present. The scariest thing was that the crimes could turn into rapes or murder. When they had another break-in, I went. While I looked around, security detained an old guy for shoplifting in the gift shop. They asked if I'd handle it while I was there. This wasn't unusual. Detectives sometimes opted to complete the paperwork for patrol before they arrived. That way, the only thing they had to do was haul the guy off.

When I sat down in the security room, the shoplifter raised his head. I was surprised to see he looked like he was a hundred. He raised one arm, then the other. They were covered in tattoos.

"What's your name?" I asked.

"Freddy Miser," he replied.

"Where at?" I pointed at his arms.

"Attica. I did four dimes for burglary," he said.

I imagined the bulb turning on over my head. I had burglaries and I had a burglar.

"Wow," I muttered as I pulled up a chair and sat down.

"Take the cuffs off," I told a security officer. When he looked uncertain, I said with a little mockery in my voice, "You guys can take care of him if he gets out of line."

"Too old for that shit," he said. "Now if I was twenty years younger . . . "
I thought about Norman saying that in the back of an ambulance. It
made me smile while the sadness lurked in the background. I started
questioning him, but before I got far, he admitted everything.

"It's this modern world we live in," he said. "I can't make ends meet.
I'm sick of being broke." We ended up talking for a while. His excuse was
that he needed new clothes so he could mix with the crowds and not look
like such a vagrant. A security officer came in and told me patrol was
going to be a while.

When the conversation drifted to the specifics of his prison sentence,
he said he'd been a damned good cat burglar and that resulted in the
forty-year stint. I found that hard to believe until he told me about the $8
million dollar jewelry heist. I realized this guy was the real deal, the stuff
of legends as far as I was concerned.

Cops no longer saw burglars who actually planned and executed
jobs. These days, crooks did door-kicks, home invasions, or just smashed
windows — no finesse in any of that. Freddy knew all the old ways, such
as picking locks, defeating alarms, opening safes without dynamite.
When he was in, he took all the valuables, fenced them, and lived the life
of James Bond. Freddy had been places I couldn't imagine.

When I asked Freddy what he did with the stuff he'd taken in the
upstairs rooms, he said he'd sold everything on the street because he
couldn't find a fence worth dealing with. He lamented the fact that
the old fences, those with balls, were gone. That left only those cheap
bastards that'd rip an old man off sooner than look at him. I felt sorry for
him, which was the old Cam. The new one did the booking paperwork,
adding every charge for the rooms Freddy admitted to.

"You're not much for cutting a man a break, are you?" he asked.

"Nope. Had my share of cutting people breaks. They don't use 'em," I
said. "You had your chance when you got out of prison. Now you're going
back. I know your type. You're going to end up dying in prison."

Two days later, I was back in the swap meet. I sold quite a bit of
property to each of the fences I'd been dealing with. Each one bitched
the whole first time about me being gone a week as I sold them my stuff.

I told them the truth — I was in California. I told them a lie — stealing from the stores down there.

When I got back to the office, I discovered the team had finished getting the case ready for prosecution. I was in time to help get the rest of our evidence packaged for the DA. Now, all there was to do was wait for the warrants to be signed for all the suspects we wanted to arrest. With those in hand, we'd pick a day and serve them along with search warrants on their storage sheds, houses, and businesses. The Department decided it was to be a big operation.

I was on down time again. I spun my wheels investigating a string of firearm thefts from different gun stores. A street cop called to say he heard on the street that some of the guns were showing up in the area of Pennwood and Arville. Since this was one of those places where guns were bound to show up, I decided to seriously work the info.

I knew Pennwood-Arville from my days in Southwest. It was a Hispanic barrio of sorts, but it hadn't always been that way. When the neighborhood was first built, the housing covered the economic spectrum, lower, middle and upper class. The Clark County School District built a high school, junior high school, and an elementary school in the area. As I drove through with Sergeant Durant, I thought that if I were a county commissioner, I'd make it my job to never allow apartments to be built anywhere I didn't want things to slide into poverty. Invariably, apartments were like festers on the flesh. I didn't care what people said about the lower classes needing places to live. The apartments along Pennwood were the reason the neighborhood had fallen into seediness. They didn't even have the remotest echo of their former glory. Illegal aliens filled them. Then there were the houses, filled with old people now afraid to walk the streets at night, and the schools with a bunch of kids whose only interest was acting as if their stupid gangs were more important than human life.

The area sergeants, bending to the community's concerns, had initiated a plan to slow some of the crime. What they proposed was a heavy police presence, which translated into a lot of citizen contacts. People who seemed to be loitering or up to no good were the primary focus. When

Durant and I went to the supervisor's briefing, we were asked to help out by stopping people who looked suspicious if we had time. Durant decided that might meet with our plans perfectly because we needed to develop a source, a snitch, who could get us to the gun location. Once I had verification on the guns, I could get a search warrant.

My main desire was to recover some of the weapons that had been taken. I wanted this in the worst way. The main theft had happened from a gun store around the corner on Sahara Avenue. I was able to piece together the crime. First, the suspects stole a truck. They took it to the business, where they disabled the alarm. They backed the truck through the front plate glass window, attached a chain to the security grate, and ripped it out. That was taking a huge chance because Sahara was a very busy street, even at two in the morning. With the truck inside, they loaded everything they could. As far as we knew, they took over a hundred rifles, tens of thousands of rounds of ammunition, and an unknown number of handguns. The reason the number was unknown was because the owner had not kept reliable records. In fact, he was now in trouble with the ATF for this failure.

With this in mind, I'd been driving up and down the street in a plain car looking at people. The plain car didn't seem to matter. It was as if the people knew we were the police anyway. Some got really nervous and walked north between the apartment buildings, while others just stayed where they were, figuring with so many targets, they were safe.

We had no interest in stopping illegals. As far as I was concerned, those people were doing society's shit labor. The things these people did were nothing anyone else wanted and it wasn't going to change. I didn't need a policy to say that said I shouldn't fuck with them; I had long ago decided I wasn't on this earth to make their lives harder. That garbage people said about them coming here and taking good American jobs was crap.

On the other hand, there were the other groups that came here. They were the tatted-up assholes who stood at the convenience store, drank beers, and caused trouble. They were the ones I intended making my own trouble for. I wanted to harass the shit out of them, send them back to wherever they came from, and, maybe, once they were there, some third world death squad would do us all a favor. On our third pass, we knew which guy we were going to stop. He was walking up and down the street without any noticeable purpose. It was seven o'clock and still over a hundred.

"Let's see what his story is," I suggested.

"Yeah," Sergeant Durant said. "I'd already decided that. White boy in this neighborhood. Can't be up to any good."

This was supposed to be a consensual stop. Normally, they started out with words like, "Hello, sir. How are you? Can we talk to you for a second?" Instead, as soon as Durant stopped, I stepped out the passenger door.

"Police. Come here," I ordered. He walked right to the front of the car, spread his feet and placed his hands gingerly on the hood. In bygone days, the hoods of black-and-whites had been painted black. In the summer, those surfaces became very hot, what with the engine putting out all that heat and the sun baking the metal. When cops had slammed struggling suspects on those surfaces and held them there, the result was often serious burns.

"I knew you were the police," he replied.

"What you doing out here?" I asked

"Nothing."

"Where you live?"

"Across town."

"Where exactly?"

"Well, I'm kinda between places right now. I was waiting for a friend ta pick me up so I could stay with him for a few days."

"What's his name?"

"Who?" he asked. I sighed. I hated these kinds of interviews.

I stepped in close. "Listen, motherfucker. You're going to piss me off in a minute and I'm either going to kick your ass, take you to jail or both."

"For what?"

"For being stupid." I poked him in the chest with a finger. I did it so no one saw, except maybe Durant. "What you been arrested for?"

"I never been arrested." I thought about the way he'd walked right to the front of the car and stood with his shins against the bumper. Only crooks knew to do that.

"Do you have ID?" I moved behind him. He immediately put his hands behind his back. Here it was again, something only a bad guy could know. I grasped the fingers while I patted him for weapons.

"No, officer," he said.

"Detective," I corrected. "I'm not an officer. I'm a detective."

"I'm sorry. I didn't know," he said. I saw what I wanted, which was the light of uncertainty in his eyes. "Detective, I don't have any ID on me. It was stolen."

"And you never been arrested? How about stopped by the police?"

"No. Never. I'm just a righteous citizen."

I needed a second to get calm so I looked across the street at the apartments. In one of those, I was sure I'd find a whole lot of the guns. I wondered if this lowlife would be the one to tell me which apartment held them. I looked at the high block walls, which were covered with multicolored graffiti. Their meaning was as obscure to me as if I were reading hieroglyphics off an ancient Egyptian temple. I hadn't hooked the guy and I was considering whether I should. He was starting to shift his weight from one foot to the other. That usually meant people were getting ready to run so we called it "happy feet."

"You wouldn't be thinking of running would you?" Durant asked. He pointed at me. "That guy has greyhound genes in him. Not only will he catch you, he'll probably bite you to boot." The guy settled down.

"What's your name?" I asked. Durant reached into the car and pulled the radio mike close to his mouth. He told Dispatch to put us on a 468. The street officers believed this myth that sergeants or detectives didn't know what they were doing. As soon as Sergeant Durant put us out, a unit cleared and said he'd be en route to back us. I let him do it because he'd have a computer in his car, which meant we'd be able to run the guy easier than on a cell phone.

"I guess that patrol cop believes the shit about them taking out part of your brain when they sewed those stripes on you," I remarked to Durant.

I kept my voice low enough that the suspect wouldn't hear. I didn't want him thinking he could play the two of us against each other. Durant gave me a sour look, then grinned. He turned his attention to the suspect.

"So what'd you say your name was?" Durant asked this time.

It was funny how sometimes you could swear you saw the gears working in people's heads. "My name is Thomas Stevens," he said.

"Well, Mr. Thompson. Do you have a date of birth?" Our prospective snitch didn't catch the mistake. I acted like my pen wasn't working. "Give me that name again."

"Steven Thompson. My birthday is one two seventy."

"Wow! That's an easy one to remember. And you said you never been arrested before."

"No, sir. Never. What do I look like? A criminal?"

"Why, as a matter of fact . . . " I hesitated. I needed to not push the guy into lawyering up. "Nah, you look like everybody else around here. Got a sosh?" he closed his eyes for a second as if he was trying to remember something, then recited the social security number. I wrote it down. When he turned to give the page to Durant, there was the sound of an arriving car. I glanced back and saw the unit pull in. The officer who got out looked to be sixteen. At first, I thought a cadet had responded. Then I noted the gun on the hip. "Jesus," I muttered. "They sure are looking young these days."

"How do you do, sir?" The cop said when he was even with me. "I'm Toby Stevens."

"You related to him?" I asked.

Toby took a hard look at the guy, then said, "No, sir. I don't think so."

"First," I said. "Knock off the 'sir.' He's the sergeant so you can call him that." I pointed at Durant. "I work for a living, just like you."

"Yes, sir."

I sighed in an exaggerated way. He looked at me apologetically. If this night kept going in this vein, it was going to be miserable.

"Here's Mr. I'm-Lying-to-the-Police's information. Can you run it for us?"

"Yes, sir."

"Call me *sir* one more time and I'm going to take your baton away and beat you with it. Understand?"

"Yes, si . . . " he stopped with a confused look on his face.

"How long you been out on your own?" I asked.

"Two days."

"OK. Never mind about the sir crap. Can you run that?" I pointed at the paper.

"I'd be happy to, Detective." He went towards his car but before he got there, he leaned into ours and said to Durant, "How you doing, sir? Toby Stevens." He stuck out his hand, but Durant ignored it. Durant was on the phone. I guessed it was to his wife again. He'd been caught cheating and he was trying to convince her it was nothing. He nodded at Toby. I knew he wasn't being rude, just preoccupied.

"I'll bet he's Mormon," I muttered. He had that clean-cut look and enthusiasm a lot of those guys brought to the job.

"Sarg, can you watch him while I walk back with Officer Stevens?" I called. He nodded at me. I saw the distracted look in his eyes. I walked over to the suspect.

"Turn around and put your hands behind your back."

"Why?"

"It will make me a lot more comfortable if you were in handcuffs."

"I ain't done nothing."

I came really close to him and dropped my voice. "You can either put your hands behind your back or, by God, I'll make you wish you had. Now, do it."

His hands went quickly behind his back. A second later, there was that satisfying sound as the handcuff bars ratcheted closed.

"Don't run off with these. Ya hear?" I said.

He nodded. Toby ran the information on the computer. After a second, the machine beeped and I read there was no such person. Toby tried DMV records next. I went back to our car and brought the guy back to stand between Toby's buddy bumpers. Durant followed me back, muttering in what sounded like a pleading voice. He went to the passenger seat and motioned for Toby to get out.

"Hey, Mr. Stevens-Thompson-Thomas, there is no record of you. Any idea why not?" I asked.

He shook his head.

"I know why there isn't. It's 'cause you're a fucking liar. You better come up with something in this computer or I'll do you as a John Doe for jaywalking," I said.

"I was never in the street," he called.

"That's funny, I saw you step off the curb back there." I pointed at a place where the oleanders came almost to the street.

"I was never there," he said. "That ain't fair."

"Neither is lying to the police," I yelled back. "Will you go talk to him?" I asked Toby.

A few minutes later, he came back with new information written in his notebook. After he handed it to me, I gave it to the sarg to run. Toby went back to the front of his car and talked with the suspect. While Durant finished talking with his wife or, as I thought more appropriate, soon-to-be-ex-wife, if the look on his face was any indication, he typed new information into the computer using the index finger of his right hand. This was a cop multitasking at his best, I thought. He hit a button, a second later, the computer beeped. Durant caught my eye and shook his head. *Nothing again*, I thought. This was starting to really piss me off.

"Hey, sarg," I called. "What now? That's three times at least."

"OK," Durant said. "Watch this. Hey, Officer Stevens. Bring him here." He pointed at the side of the Patrol car.

"Thomas, if that's your real name. I need you to tell me the truth," Durant said. "If you have a warrant, we might be able to work something out." This was technically true, but not in the way it sounded, which was that the statement implied the guy might walk, but he wasn't going to. He had simply lied too much, so I had already decided he was going.

A dejected look passed across the guy's face. "My name is Jason Simon. I think I have one for child support." He provided another birthday and social security number. When I checked it, the information produced descriptors, but there was no way they fit the guy standing in front of us. Durant leaned in and looked at the computer screen.

After a second, Durant straightened. "Jason, you've got a murder warrant out of a place back East for murdering a cop." He said this with a perfectly straight face. Then, when Toby jerked his gun from his holster and slammed the muzzle into the back of the guy's head, I wasn't as surprised as I thought I should be. That it didn't go off, blowing brains all over us, did surprise me, though. The force of the blow and the pressure Toby followed it with pushed the guy's body all the way down to the hood.

"You fucking murdering . . . " Toby started yelling.

Durant was instantly by his side, hand on Toby's shoulder, pulling him back. "Easy, boy," Durant said. He put a finger under the barrel of the gun and lifted it towards the sky. "Put your gun away. Give him a chance to talk."

The guy was pale as he hyperventilated. "My . . . my . . . my name is Keith Stephens, with a 'p' and an 'h.' I'm twenty seven years old, my birthday . . . " The words came so fast, I had a hard time writing them down. When I ran the new information, the computer showed he had a bunch of warrants for drugs, traffic offences, and possession of narco paraphernalia.

"He's four-forty," I called. "He's got six or seven warrants." Dispatch came on the air a second later and asked if Three Paul was clear wanted person. I answered that we were code four and had the suspect in custody. I didn't want her sending anyone else to our location until we had things straightened out. Durant had a hand on Toby's shoulder. He muttered something to him while he kept the suspect pinned to the hood with a hand in the middle of his back. The guy's face was towards me, so I could see him quietly sobbing. A pool of blood gathered, then ran towards the front of the car.

"Control, can you roll medical?" I radioed, then quickly added, "Head wound," before she asked.

"I never killed any cop," the guy cried. "I was using my step brother's stuff that last time."

"Don't worry about it," I said. Sarg let go and I took the guy back to the front of the car. "Let me see your head." I pulled on the pair of rubber gloves I now routinely kept in my pocket. When I parted the guy's hair, I saw a perfectly round wound where the muzzle had caught him. It was probably going to take stitches.

"Turn around and sit here." I pointed at the push bar between the uprights. *That's going to be hard to explain,* I thought. Toby got a sheepish look on his face when Durant finished whispering to him.

"I'm sorry, sarg," he said. "You should have told me what you were doing."

"Yeah. I guess so. He peed his pants, so you get to drive him."

"OK," Toby said. He had holstered his gun and was playing with the snap. "Hey, sarg, can I use that trick sometime?"

"Toby, I think you better leave it for us professionals," he said. Sarg saw the hurt on Toby's face. He added, "You know? The detectives?"

"Oh, yeah. Right." He nodded with a really serious look on his face.

"Besides," Durant continued, "without someone like you around, I don't think it works as well." He ran his finger around the collar of his shirt. By the time I had a pressure bandage out of the first aid kit, Stevens' blood had turned brown and crusty on the hood of the car.

"Yeah." Toby's voice relayed disappointment. "Maybe that's a good idea. I want to be a detective someday."

"God help us," I muttered as I listened to the far off sounds of the ambulance coming. I took a cuff off one of the guy's hands. After I moved the cuffs to the bumper, I let him apply pressure to his wound with the bandage.

"You know I'm going to have to take you to jail? You have a lot of warrants," I said.

"Hey, you want to make a deal, Detective?" he asked.

"Probably not."

"Too bad. I know where you can get some dope. Not some either, but a lot. We'd have to visit four apartments. How about a stolen car? It's less than a block away. There's a guy who lives in the apartments on Decatur. He's into breaking the locks on Coke machines and taking all the money out. Or I know an apartment where this Mexican guy is running girls. You know, prostitution?"

"How about this for a trade?" I said. "You wouldn't know anything about some guy who's supposed to be selling guns or the guy who might have bought them, would you?"

The suspect shook his head. That disappointed me. From what he just said, he would be the one who would know. Far off, I heard the sound of the ambulance coming, which suddenly made me feel apprehensive.

"Hey, Sarg," I called.

"Yeah, Cam?"

"I'm going to walk down to the convenience store and get a Coke. You want anything and can you pick me up there?"

"Wait until medical gets here," Durant said to me before he turned back to Toby. "Can you take this?" Durant asked him. I started walking towards the convenience store, keeping my head down. "Wait, Cam. We'll go together."

The sound of the siren was getting closer. "Listen, Sarg. I need to pee."

"Jesus! I'm ready." He stepped back into the car. "Toby, you have any problems because of the injury, call me. When I get a minute, I'll straighten it out with your boss."

"It'll be fine, sir."

"OK. Cam, for God's sake. I know you got to pee, but it'll be faster getting there in the car."

I walked back and climbed in. I was afraid he was going to linger until medical arrived. When Durant was back in the driver seat and the car was moving, he looked at me. "What's the big deal?"

"I just had to go pee," I said, but even to my ears the words sounded as if the suspect had said them. *I'm supposed to be a better liar than the crooks*, I thought.

"Is it that girl, the one in the ambulance Norman was telling me about?"

"Jesus. That man has a big mouth," I muttered. "Am I asking you about your wife?"

"Easy there, Cam. OK?" He grinned. "I should make you stay just so I can see this woman. She must be something."

Maybe the look I gave him was imploring, because he stepped on the gas.

"Sorry," I muttered, keeping my eyes on the road. He drove up the street, made a u-turn, and passed the ambulance on the way back. Karri May sat in the passenger seat. Just seeing her caused my heart to feel like it skipped a couple of beats. It also caused me to sink low in the seat — like one of my mopes did when I ran him past a house he was giving up. Somehow, I vowed, this wasn't going to keep happening. There had to be a way to get one's emotions under control.

■ ■ ■

Everything's Solved . . .

"**B**eing a property crimes detective is one of the hardest and most thankless jobs in the Department," McMahon said. He held the microphone in his left hand, while he shook Norman's hand. He let go of Norman's hand, reached under the podium and took out a plaque.

"In line with that, I'd like to tell you that Norman has given . . . " McMahan put on his glasses, leaned his head back so he could see, then read, " . . . the Department sixty-six thousand, three hundred and four hours of free time. That equated to five million, five hundred and sixty-two-thousand, nine hundred and five dollars and sixty cents when I figure that Norman makes eighty-three dollars and ninety cents at time-and-a-half."

McMahan beamed as he presented the plaque to Norman. He held up a fake check. The amount astounded me. I refused to believe it. That was until I caught Norman staring pensively at the award he held. Five minutes after Norman stepped down from the raised platform, I moved close to him.

"Tell me it ain't so," I said. I picked up his beer. It was warm, so I took another plastic cup off the bar and replaced it.

"No," he said. "I imagine he's got it pretty much correct."

"Damn, buddy. That's a lot of moola you didn't get paid."

"Get used to it if you want to be good at this," he said. He set the plaque on the bar like he didn't care who stole it. "You know, Cam. When you've been here a while, you'll see that government looks like it takes a lot of people to function, but it's not true. If I had to put a number on what it took to run the whole shebang, for that matter, any shebang from the federal system to the City of Las Vegas, I'd say you could keep ten percent of all the employees and that other ninety percent — you could fire. All they do is hold down a desk and drain the public coffers."

I'd heard this theory a few times from him. Still, I paid attention as though it were all brand new. He was an impressive man. He'd lived through a tough time in the world when people settled things with their fists, not guns. He'd been stabbed twice and shot once. None of that was on a plaque. He'd been a cop for forty years, ten as a deputy up in Idaho, the last thirty with Metro. He started when he was eighteen years old, which meant he'd done nothing but be a cop. For a second, I thought about the term "lawman" and how it fit people like him. I also wondered if I'd ever be able to live up to that title.

"Where's that girl of yours?" Norman asked.

"There is no girl. I'm not seeing anyone."

"Then you're a fool." He studied my face for a second, then grinned. "You got it bad. Don't wait too long for her."

"I heard she's engaged to that fireman," I said. It was surprising the amount of pain that still lurked in my mind whenever I thought of her.

"Then you waited too long." He looked sad. "People need a place to go to be safe, someone to hold them in their arms when they've seen horrible things." He looked at the table where his wife, Gene, sat talking to the other guests.

"Norman!" she called when she saw him looking at her. "This is your party. Get your ass up here and accept some of those pathetic things that worthless crew of whoring drunks you call poker buddies claimed to have bought but are really stolen." She fixed a stern eye on me. "Cam, did you do an inventory on the evidence vault. I thought I saw red stickers on some of that stuff."

I walked over to hug Gene. McCoy pulled Norman up to the stage after he stuck a finger in his beer.

"Getting warm. You need to drink faster," McCoy said. While the presentations were being made, I stood in the back of The Briefing

Room. Our union, the Police Protective Association, owned the bar. It was here that many of these types of functions, retirements, graduations, and wakes, were held. It was also here that a lot of lonely old guys came to drink at the end of their shifts. The bartenders were carefully trained to take the keys away from those who were too drunk to drive, sending them home in cabs that the PPA paid for. As I played with the change in my pocket, I thought how I wasn't going to be one of those guys. There were several of them lurking in the crowd or pushed way over by the other end of the bar. They only left when it was time to sleep a little or head for their shift.

I surveyed the rest of the crowd from the shadows at my end. I figured about a quarter were Norman's family, another quarter from the DA's office, and the rest cops. Three of the DAs I disliked intensely. It was bad enough when cops milked the public, but when the prosecutors did it too, it made the system more prone to breakdowns. That was because there were a lot of cops and someone might get one that actually worked, but there were few deputy district attorneys, so the chances went way down that someone got a good one. I wondered who thought up those television shows where the police and the DA's office worked so well together. It was all a dream world that was a near-total myth. This knowledge was based on my own experiences and what other cops said.

Sometimes, it seemed the DAs worked harder dumping perfectly good cases than they did prosecuting them. They filled the requests-for-further-investigation forms with impossible tasks. A week before, I caught a burglar stealing mail boxes off people's houses. He'd hit four places. The same DA who sent me the request asking for statements from all four victims was standing at the bar drinking free booze we cops paid for. In the request, he instructed me to include a sentence that these people hadn't given the guy permission to destroy their property in the middle of the night, which meant I needed the statements to back that up. After I went to the victim's houses, sat while they wrote the voluntaries, which took a whole afternoon of my time, the DA negotiated the case to a misdemeanor destruction of private property charge.

When the case disposition came through, I sat at my desk staring at it. The file sat open, with his criminal history on top. I leafed through the crook's criminal history. He had five arrests for burglary, pled to drug court, then dismissed; two for possession of stolen property, for which he did three months in county, and a malicious destruction. Each charge started as a felony and all had ended as misdemeanors or, in other words, he'd walked on every bad thing he'd ever done. This only made it clear the type of crimes I'd been assigned was a hard area in which to make any kind of positive impact. I remembered one day when Norman was in a particularly bad mood and I was railing about the system not doing enough.

"If you think they'll put up a statue for you, Cam, think about this. Clark County had approximately thirty five thousand burglaries last year. There are twelve people sitting here working them. We're swamped. We all know it. After the last election, the sheriff went on record as saying crime was down. His logic was that over the decade, burglaries went from twenty-seven to thirty-five thousand, but during the same period, the population went from half a million to a million. The sheriff, who I'll remind you is my good golf buddy, says it's a matter of math — that anyone can see the percentages are down. Unfortunately, we don't work percentages. We work crimes and thirty-five thousand is bigger than twenty-seven thousand — a fact of life that all the fancy talk isn't going to change. It also isn't going to change the fact that ten years ago there were twelve detectives working burglary detail and, today, there are still twelve detectives working burglary detail."

As he finished, my beeper went off. It was Dispatch. A phone call and a half hour later, I sat looking at Mr. Malloy's house. He was a pain in the ass. He was also my first call out of the office my first day as a detective. His garage had been burglarized and I told him, three times so far and soon to be four, we were doing everything we could to catch the guy, return what was taken, and make everything right.

What I was really doing was nothing. That was because there was nothing I could do. What happened was that Mr. Malloy left his garage door open. Some opportunistic soul stole the lawnmower right out from under his nose, which wasn't hard, considering the guy was seventy years old. Mr. Malloy lived in a nice neighborhood located next to a bad neighborhood. It wasn't like the old guy didn't know he lived next to the bad place — Pennwood and Arville. He'd told me about every crack dealer, meth head, car thief, and prostitute that lived over there. That being true, I couldn't imagine why he left his garage door open.

After a week of answering the calls from the old man, then avoiding more of them, then having the calls answered by Durant, then being told to answer the calls the sarg was getting, Durant's patience ran out. I was told to do something. I considered going to the swap meet and getting Arnie or Joe to supply me with a stolen lawnmower before we finished with them. Now, it was all a moot point. Mr. Malloy had decided to take matters into his own hands. He called the sheriff at home. How the fuck he got the private number was a mystery.

Right then, two things came to my mind. The first was that I was witnessing the old adage, "Shit rolls downhill" first hand. The shit-rolled-downhill part came when the sheriff called his assistant who called the assistant sheriff who called the deputy chief who called the captain who called Lieutenant McMahan who called Sergeant Durant who had Dispatch call me when he didn't see me standing among the crowd of those who were wishing Norman good luck on his retirement. The second thing was that I needed a transfer now that Norman was going. He was the only saving grace around burglary detail. Either way, things were back to where they started, which was me sitting outside Mr. Malloy's house.

So, as the very hot afternoon sun beat down on the metal body of the unmarked car, the one where the air conditioner was losing the battle with the heat, I tried to get up the spunk to go knock on his door — again. I stared at the house where the garage door was open, showing other tools, lawn furniture, and boxes of unknown items that looked as though they'd been searched through.

What else have they stolen? I wondered. From what I saw, many items in there would fetch some dope addict another bag of junk and a lot more work for me. I decided I better let Dispatch know what I was doing. That way, there'd be a record of me being here when the old man said I hadn't been doing anything with his case.

After I locked the car door, I turned. He was a foot away from me, which almost made me jump out of my skin. How the hell he'd been able to sneak up on me was scary.

"You here to take fingerprints?" he yelled.

"Jesus, Mr. Malloy. I'm a cop for Christ's sake. You shouldn't be sneaking up on me like that."

"I was a scout in the Army. World War Two. You know about that war? The whole damned world was fighting. They said my life expectancy was seventeen seconds. Look at me. I'm still here and some asshole came to my house and stole my lawnmower. You get it back yet?"

"No, sir. I been looking." I studied the man for a moment. There was no way I'd look like this when I was old. Mr. Malloy's tan Dockers were pulled up high on his stomach. If he let them down, they'd cover his bony ankles that were exposed where his black socks had slipped, making them look like oozed wax around the tops of his shoes. The old man wore a shirt made of heavy material. I was sure it was the same one he'd been wearing the last three times I saw him, red and black plaid, buttoned all the way to the top. Just looking at him made me sweat. He was bald, with those big liver spots covering his pate. The afternoon sun had moved closer to the western mountains, so it glinted painfully from his glasses, making the large square lenses look as though they were windowpanes in a building. I thought if I moved just right, I'd see planes banking away from the glare's reflection. "Can I ask where you got the sheriff's home number?"

"I told you. I was a scout in the Army," he yelled.

"Sir. I'm standing right here. You don't have to yell at me."

"I'm not yelling . . ." He stopped talking, then pulled a hearing aid from a shirt pocket and played with a control. He shook it at me. "Batteries dying, I guess. Don't like to replace them until they're dead. Waste of money. What about those fingerprints?"

"I thought we agreed looking for fingerprints is useless."

"I saw the TV cops solve a murder that way. Last night. On one of those new shows."

"Yeah. They do that a lot on TV. Rarely works for us."

"Why?"

"Do you always yell? I'm not deaf, you know?" I pointed at the garage. "I thought I asked you to keep that closed."

"How are you going to catch the thief if I don't put out bait? Now about those fingerprints."

"Mr. Malloy. I told you, the garage door is metal. Metal gets hot. Heat dries the oils from fingerprints. Makes it impossible to lift."

"Then why are you here? How about if I call that asshole I voted for, tell him I want me one of them TV detective types?"

I sighed. "No. There's no need for that." I pulled out my cell and requested ID. I knew they were going to be pissed when they got there. I didn't care. I was at the point of running over to the shitbag part of the neighborhood, looking for the first burglar I knew, and beating a confession out of him right in front of the old guy just to make him happy.

In the meantime, I thought I might get some more information from him. When I first took the report, I did it hurriedly, knowing this wasn't a high priority and he'd probably just be happy with any report. Now I thought I should make things look like I'd done a better job in the beginning. I took out a small notebook and flipped pages until I found a blank one. I poised my pen and looked at Mr. Malloy expectantly, hoping I looked like one of the TV detectives he so badly wanted.

"Make and model?" I asked.

"Why didn't you do this in the first place?"

"Please, sir. Can I just get the info?"

"OK. Sears Roebuck or Monkey Wards," he replied. "I think."

"Whatdoya mean you think?" I caught myself in the nick of time. With a deep breath, I went on. "You don't know?" I watched as Mr. Malloy bent closer to me. He looked like he was examining some weird form of fungus. He shook his head.

"Serial number?" I asked.

"How the hell am I supposed to know that? I bought it ten, fifteen years ago."

"Color?" I tried putting some hope in my voice.

"Red or green or something like that. I don't remember since I don't use it anymore. I had all the grass from the yard taken out." He pointed. "Put that damned green rock in."

"What about the back yard?"

"Dirt. No grass back there," he said.

I drew a shaky breath. If the guy had been a crook, I'd take him to jail. I closed my eyes and imagined being home later.

"Well, sir, you don't have a lot I can go on here. I can't flag your mower in pawn detail without a serial number or a description. And without that same description, I can't tell the area officers what to look for while they're out patrolling."

"I'll tell you what to do," he says.

"What's that, sir?"

"Go down to that Winchell's Donut House and get a bunch of those lard-assed motorcycle cops I see sitting around down there and get them to go look for it. Yeah! Those idiots who wrote me that speeding ticket the other day. I tell you I looked and there weren't no children in that school zone. It's a damned speed trap, just so the city can collect more money so they can sit around there and drink coffee and eat donuts and get fatter. I'm an honest man and they're taking money from my pocket. The sons of bitches. I want you to make them go door to door and search the houses around here until you find my lawn mower."

"I'm not sure I can ask them to do that, sir." Mr. Malloy was turning red. I watched as a vein in his temple throbbed. His hand went to the side of his chest.

"If those cops took care of the school zone by busting all those little shits who hang out there and sent them back to California or Mexico, where they belong, I'd still have my lawn mower. I could feel safe in my own home. Instead, you guys ride around on motorcycles writing decent people like me tickets and eating donuts."

The next sound out of his mouth reminded me of something I'd once heard a zoo animal make. He gasped, grabbed the left side of his chest. *Heart attack*, I thought with clinical detachment. *I should have brought my handheld.* It was either run for the car or call 911. My experience with the emergency system and cops calling in on it was all bad. The call takers were sometimes confused, trying to figure out why an on duty officer was calling on a phone instead of just radioing. That time delay was frustrating for us when we were used to getting things done quickly. Without thinking, I stepped forward and lifted the little man like he was a child. I carried him over to the side of my car.

"Hold on," I said. I fumbled the key in the lock, opened the door, and as he started to turn that peculiar gray of dying people, I got the car started. "Control, Baker Fifty-Five Thirty-Two, I need medical to my location. My victim appears to be having a heart attack."

Her calm voice came back, asking if I was at the address I'd gone out at. I replied in the affirmative. As Mr. Malloy slumped, I jumped out of the car and pulled him to the front seat. Putting the seat back, I sat him down, then adjusted all the air conditioning controls so they blew on him. Sweat ran off my forehead in streams. With his mouth opening and closing, he looked like a fish out of water.

"They have people coming," I told him. His eyes kept rolling upwards in the sockets and I saw the first tinges of blue appearing. "Control Baker Fifty-Five Thirty-Two. Tell them to expedite."

"They're on their way, Thirty-two."

"Copy," I replied.

There seemed like nothing I could do except stand there and watch the old man die. In that eventuality, I knew what to do. Far off, I heard the sound of the approaching medical unit. I glanced up and saw a neighbor looking at me from the front window of her house. She had a fat face and a bright pink housecoat. Her hair was dyed bright red, almost orange. The fear on her face transmitted itself across the several dozen feet between us, amplifying what I felt. I wondered why. I had been on a hundred calls like this as a patrol officer, usually after the fact, though. When she saw I had noticed her, she quickly closed the shades. I wondered what would happen if I wasn't here and he fell down in his yard? Would some passing motorist be the first one to call someone for him?

As soon as I saw the ambulance turn the corner, Mr. Malloy became very still, not even seeming to breathe. I was sure he was dead. I knelt, reached in and cradled him in my arms. It was going to be hard for them to work on him in my car and the sidewalk was so hot, I felt it through the cloth as I knelt. As the ambulance stopped, I hurried towards the back doors. I recognized Chris as he got out the driver door. I nodded my head towards the back. He moved in front of me. When I came around, Karri May was there with the Med kit on her back.

"I got him," I said.

"Put him on the gurney, Cam." She was all business. I saw the ring on her finger. *So*, I thought, *it's true. She was married.*

"He was talking to me," I said. "Then he just started wheezing. He turned this color. Gotta be a heart attack." He weighed so little I had no problem stepping up into the ambulance. I laid Mr. Malloy on the gurney and stepped back. Chris grabbed his heavy shirt and tried ripping it open. The buttons refused to pop. I couldn't help thinking the old man must have used extra-thick thread on them. While Karri May handed Chris scissors, they ignored me, fully involved with their actions while they traded medical phrases that described what was happening. Outside, a fire engine pulled up. In a second, I was pushed out as two county paramedics entered and started hooking up sensors and oxygen lines.

I didn't wait to see what was going to happen. Instead, I went to my car so I could get out of there. If Karri May hadn't been there, I'd have nothing to do with a medical emergency and with her there, I wanted nothing to do with how I was feeling. I watched a black-and-white as it turned down the street. By now, all the neighbors were out by the side of the road watching. They were an ancient crowd, appearing to be from the same era as Malloy. They mingled, coming together, then breaking apart in new groups. I did notice one guy who looked a few years younger.

"Is he going to make it?" one old man called. I shrugged. He frowned. "Well? What do you think?"

"I don't know. I'm a cop, not a doctor," I called back. The guy pulled at a bushy white eyebrow. Some of the individual hairs must have been an inch and a half long. He was wearing cut-off military cargo pants that were bunched at the waist with a leather belt. I glanced at his flip-flops, fixed with duct tape. His skin was tanned so brown it looked like the belt.

"He's an asshole," the man called. Several other neighbors nodded. "He lent me his lawnmower so I could cut my grass. Damned thing wouldn't start. When I came over to give it back, said he'd call the police if I didn't get it fixed. Is that why you're here? Come to take me to jail?"

I walked closer. "When was this?"

"Day before yesterday," he replied, trying to see past me. I glanced back and saw a fireman come out of the ambulance. He didn't look happy.

"What color is the lawnmower?"

"Red. Sears model. I used to have one like it. Got stolen. Actually thought this one was it, but I couldn't remember 'cause the thing was missing for so long."

"So, let me get this straight. He gave you the lawnmower the day before yesterday?"

"No! No! No! He gave it to me a few months ago. I came over to give it back the day before yesterday. That's when we had the big yelling match. He's an asshole and he gets whatever God gives him in there."

"That's mean, Pete," the woman with the red hair said. Now that I was close, I noticed how the beautician had botched the job. She turned to me. "I wouldn't wish anything bad on anyone. We should say a prayer for him."

"Fuck him," Pete said. "I'm going to get that lawnmower and stick it back in his garage. If he lives, maybe he won't remember."

Pete walked back towards a house with knee-high grass. A cicada flew off the tree, almost hitting him in the face. He ducked, windmilling his arms as though he were swimming. I went back to the ambulance. When I looked inside, they had Mr. Malloy strapped down with an oxygen mask hiding the lower part of his face. He looked like a geriatric fighter pilot.

His watery blue eyes were open. He kept blinking them. As if he couldn't believe what was happening to him.

"He wants to say something to you," Karri May said. She injected a clear liquid into the IV tube that ran down from the sack. The tube snaked towards him, disappeared next to the gurney, reappeared along his arm, and ended in a needle that was shoved through the skin at the back of his right hand. I turned to Karri May.

"You married, now?"

She lifted her left hand an inch off the sheet and stared at the big stone like she was as surprised as me. "I waited."

"The fireman?"

"Yes," she replied. She wouldn't lift her eyes as far as she lifted her hand.

"What was his name?"

She ignored the question. It didn't matter anyway. It wasn't my last name she used. "He wants to say something." She nodded at Mr. Malloy. I came close. His lips moved, but I couldn't make out the words. His fingers flexed like he wanted to touch me. The straps kept him from raising the hand. I bent closer.

"Fingerprints. I want fingerprints. Compare them to Pete, my neighbor. I know it was him."

I nodded. "I'll get right on that, Mr. Malloy." I stepped back where Karri May was. "Take care of him." I put my hand on my throat like I'd strangle myself and made a face. For the first time she looked me in the face. I saw her eyes and knew what was coming next.

"I got calls to answer," I lied.

"Get out of here," she whispered fiercely.

I went, but I stopped at the door. "Good luck," I whispered back. I knew she didn't hear me. When I was inside the car, I stretched the mike to me so I could stand in the heat.

"Control, Baker Fifty Five Thirty Two, cancel ID to my location. I think everything's solved."

■ ■ ■

Joey Armpits . . .

Being lonely was something cops got used to. We saw things, and sometimes had no words to tell the stories. Even when we were great storytellers, and I had met a few, we couldn't relate exactly what we'd seen. Pain was supposed to be like butter on bread — spread a little over as much surface as possible, so it was shared by many people. That was because there was never in the telling the same effect as when you were standing there in the puddle of blood or watching a mother who had been told her child drowned in the family pool.

At night, we were either in a car working or trying to sleep around the memories or dreams those things produced. I took the lesson I learned from work, which was to stay detached, and applied it to how I dealt with my feeling for Karri May. Each day, the hurt grew less, I grew used to being lonely and the idea that I might always be that way — until it didn't matter anymore.

What mattered was that everything came back to people — whether it was those who would not die when they were shot in my dreams or the real people that did get wounded and sometimes died.

Now that I was a detective, I also was expected to use people. They became tools that provided the names of those who committed crimes we weren't able to solve through other means. These people were referred to by different names — confidential informants, CIs, sources or snitches, depending if the conversation took place in the street or the DA's office.

"Developing sources is a cop's best way to solve crime," Norman had taught me. "We can't go out there and do drugs or hang out in really seedy places or commit crime or watch other people commit crime without being arrested, so we use people who can. We use those people — snitches and they are the most important people in police work, other than you."

After he said this to me, I signed up for the CI class so I understood how to use them. There were all kinds of tricks that had to be considered when snitches were used. I had to know what their motivation was for working and how they could play the police and what happened if you got caught sleeping with one. The instructors made their points by telling stories about cops who had done anything anyone could imagine with a snitch, all bad things.

"Today's snitch, tomorrow's suspect," Norman constantly reminded me.

Within months of going to the bureau, I had a stable of eighteen regular, full-on heroin addicts who were ready to sell out everyone they knew, including their mothers. One did it for revenge, which was just another motive. Some worked off charges, and some I paid. These were the best. That was because I understood what it meant working for money. In my book, a man who took money had a very clear motivation, a very old, time-honored tradition. On the other hand, a man who had something hanging over his head was living in fear, which could make a person do or say anything. It was the same with revenge. People did anything for revenge.

Any way you cut it, the trap to be avoided was trusting these two groups. The other thing a cop wanted to avoid was calling a CI a snitch to his face. Snitches knew they were snitches and they didn't want it rubbed in. The great thing about snitches was that they could be the scum of the earth, which meant they provided the best lessons anyone could ever learn.

One of my snitches had been working for me for a few months. He was a small-time criminal, which was a thing I constantly found myself being reminded of. The reminding came in the form of suspect descriptions, written into reports that crossed my desk that could only have been from Joe. There were calls, late at night, from patrol officers who had Joe stopped in areas of high drug trafficking or where a series of burglaries had occurred. Most of the time, his being stopped was enough to rein him in, but in other situations, he became too brave. Then, I had to leave off whatever I was doing or get my ass out of bed, drive to where they had him, and take Joe aside for a little talk. Because of him, I learned there was an art to running snitches. Half of the process was being able to change an incident from a true crime to a minor "transgression." The other part was my "little talks." I had them with all my snitches, including Joe. It came in the form of a story that had been told to me by another detective, but was now claimed as my own.

"Joe," I said, "I had this guy, Fred, who was working for me. One night, Fred decides he'd steal from a Wal-Mart. He plans it for two a.m. because he's sure that if he gets caught, I wouldn't get out of bed and deal with him. He was sure I'd be like every other detective and tell the street cops to release him because of what he was currently working on for me. Instead, I climbed out of bed, went to the shithole location where he was in custody, and took him to county. I did it on my own time, without charging the Department a penny of overtime. It took me four hours, so I booked him for things even I didn't know were crimes."

When I finished, I saw the look of doubt in Joe's eyes. He didn't believe me. I didn't care. I'd said it and, when he stepped over the line, I'd prove it to him. That's all that mattered, except that no matter how hard cops tried not to have relationships with snitches, they developed. CIs were people and it was hard not to feel sorry for them. Some snitches knew this and used it to exploit every ounce of compassion they could. Constantly, I had to remind myself to be careful, but it was difficult. It was a major reason the Department came up with the rule that, under most circumstances, there had to be two officers present when dealing with a snitch, especially if the CI was a "she" and the cop was a "he." Another point concerned the ideal partner, who was one that hated snitches. That kept things in perspective.

Being new, I was still a little leery of my snitches. What I did appreciate was their ability, especially Joe's, to do things, like get close to the street slime. Joe tried hard to make me trust him, which actually had the opposite effect. He brought me things without me asking for them, he did things I didn't ask him to, and he tried to compliment me on how I ran things. I couldn't help feeling he was playing me.

That feeling always reminded me of the story I'd heard from an Intel sergeant. It was supposed to be true and about a friend of his, who was on the LAPD Intel Unit. This snitch's wife threw him out for cheating. So, that night, he went to the bar where he and the detective routinely met. They had drinks. This was supposed to be a debriefing for information the snitch had gathered, but quickly turned into a bitch session, much like two friends might share. When the snitch laid out his troubles, the cop took him home. The cop gave the snitch a key and free reign over the entire pad when the cop wasn't there. The next morning, the cop went to work. That night, when he came home, the house was empty — guns, furniture, police equipment, and silverware. The story's happy ending was that the cop got to keep his job.

Of all my snitches, Joe was the best. I could take him to a house, point it out, and tell him the information I needed. He got out of the car, walked right up, knocked, got invited in, then came out with what I wanted. It was absolutely, downright fucking amazing to me.

That ability was what put me in a situation where Joe was to get us into a small bar, where I suspected the owner, who was also the bartender, happened to be buying everything and anything stolen. That made the guy the biggest fence on the street. I had tried two other snitches against the guy, but neither made any headway. Using Joe, I already had written a couple of misdemeanors, but those were write-you-a-ticket crimes. I wanted the put-you-in-prison-for-a-felony crimes. Ultimately, my desire was to seize everything — the guy's business, money in his savings and checking accounts, cars, and his home. The reality was that even Joe was having problems getting me there because the guy just wouldn't deal on anything major.

After two weeks of trying everything I could think of, I was stalled. Then, two ATF cops, Jerry and Fred, approached me. I knew these guys from the gun store burglaries that had happened months before. For the first two weeks while I chased those guns, the agents kept in constant touch with me by phone. They sounded so alike, I actually thought they were the same person playing a practical joke. Then I met them. They were the two most nondescript people I knew. I just couldn't get their names straight. To avoid looking like a fool by mistakenly calling one the other's name, I skipped using names altogether. When I mentioned to Norman that I couldn't get them straight, even after meeting them, he looked at me strangely. Fred was short, fat, and had curly red hair, while Jerry was muscular, shaved his head every day, and looked out of eyes as cold and blue as Antarctic sea water. *Or was it the other way around?* I thought as I described them. We had a meeting, the four of us, ending up in our bureau conference room drinking stale, burnt smelling coffee from the pot we had going down the hall.

"Hey, Cam," the muscular one said. "We heard you have something going with the bar over on Bonanza and Eastern."

"If you wanna call it *going*," I said. "I'd call it *trying* to get something going. The guy's bought some batteries from my snitch. Misdemeanor quantities for personal use."

"We hear he's buying guns."

"I hear the guy's buying everything," I said. "I just can't prove it."

"The guy supposedly has a burglary crew hitting houses," the other one said. "When they get the merchandise, especially guns, they bring 'em to the bar. We'd like to catch him with the guns, but we don't have time to sit on the place for twenty four seven."

"Me either, Jerry. I've . . . "

"I'm Fred." He interrupted, then pointed. "He's Jerry."

"I thought the taller one . . . " I muttered, letting my voice trail off as I gave them both a hard look. They had those stupid mirrored sunglasses on, so there was no reading emotion on their faces to see if they were fucking with me. "Never mind." I sighed. "I don't have time to sit on the place. I've got something else brewing, which I think might be big. I wanted to get the bar thing done and over with before I start that. I do know what'll solve this thing with the bar quick, though."

"What's that?" Fred asked.

"Money. If I had some money, I could get my snitch to buy something. Like, maybe a gun."

"We got money. We're rolling in money." That was an understatement. I liked to tell people the feds had all the money. After all, God let them put his name on it.

"If you got the money, I got the snitch," I said.

"We want all the credit for the case," Jerry said.

"I don't care. If it's a federal seizure, the Department will still get a cut."

"True," the one I thought was Fred said. "You guys'll get half."

I liked this bartering for dollars. It was haggling at its best. I wanted something, they wanted the same thing, and I wasn't the type to care how it got done, as long as it got done.

"We want to run the snitch."

"Nope. He's mine," I said as I examined my fingernails. This was something Norman had beat into my head. I had to let anybody with the PD use the snitch because he was considered a Department asset, but the feds could be told to go to hell.

"Emphatically. No!" Norman told them.

They looked at each other, then nodded. "OK." It came out in unison.

"It comes down to sending Joe, who is also called Armpits, into the bar. I have a recorder he can wear, but if you got a wire, that would be better."

"We have a wire."

"You'll give Joe the money. He'll buy the gun and give it to you. From that point on, I'll help any way you want with the case. Fair enough?"

"We'll do the paper on the business and we'll serve it," the muscular one said.

I almost laughed. I knew something about the way the feds did search warrants. They didn't move fast, so we might be waiting a couple of months.

I shrugged. "Fine." All I had to do was keep them from fucking over my snitch, let them bask in the glory of the news release, and have one less problem business to deal with. It sounded simple, which told me something was wrong — nothing the feds did was simple. They had the ability to fuck up anything simple. I pulled my cell out and called Joe. Right off, just by hearing his voice, I knew he was high.

"He's fucked up," I said to them. "Listen, Joe. Call me when you're straight." I started to close the phone.

"No. Let me talk to him," Jerry said.

"OK. But I'm telling you he's fucked up." I handed him my phone. The agent walked away so I couldn't hear what was said. That pissed me off, but Fred grabbed me by the elbow when I tried to follow.

"Let him talk. We're not going to steal your guy. Jeez, have a little faith in us." I did and it was all bad.

"He hung up on me," Jerry said when he handed me my phone back. That pissed me off even more, although I can't say who all the anger was for, the ATF agents or Joe.

"There are three places we can go look," I said. I counted them off on my fingers. "The first will be somewhere along Fremont, where he'll be in a casino — probably planning or doing a bucket theft. The second might be over in Naked City, where he would be buying dope. The last place would be his mother's house, which is not likely as he's fucked up and she won't put up with that. That means mom's out. Naked City is the closest, so let's start there." I looked at Norman. "Wanna come?"

"Nope. I retire next week. I'm cleaning out my desk. Fifteen years worth of shit in there."

We went down to our cars. They offered to drive, but I declined for two reasons. I knew where we were going and their car looked like a cop car.

Surprisingly enough, I found him fast. When I turned on Boston Avenue, he stood on the corner with two guys, one black and the other white. Joe was on the nod, which meant he'd just done some dope. His head lolled on his neck like one of those dog toys people put in the back of their cars. I didn't want to walk up on him, so we parked down the street in a parking lot. I pulled in at an angle. Fred parked facing the other way so the driver windows were next to each other.

"Think he's up to no good?" the tall one asked.

"What do you think, Jerry?" I got a blank stare.

He pointed at his partner. "He's Jerry." I squinted my eyes at him, then decided once again I wasn't going to make an issue of it.

"He's an addict before he's anything else. That's his motivation. Either to get high or stay that way."

"Are we going to pick him up?"

"Not yet. We'll see if we can get you a twist."

They traded looks.

"Paying him isn't going to be enough?"

"No." I was going to leave it at that one word, but Jerry, the passenger, looked like he had his doubts, so I elaborated. "When Joe's high, money's a means to an end and I didn't trust that end. Jail is a good incentive. Jail means he'll be jonesing in a cell." I was referring to the way county dealt with addicts. They threw them in a cell and let them go cold turkey. It was an ugly sight. "Circle around where that red house is. I'll drive closer and get out. Wait till I'm close, then get ready to run, because he's going to. Please try not to let him get away. Otherwise, we'll have a really hard time finding him again."

When I saw they were in position, I drove slowly up the street. When I was a few houses away, I stopped and opened the car door quietly. The heat hit me like a bat. When I came up with this plan, I noticed the way the two agents wore the faces of people happy to be staying in their car. It worried me seeing that, because I doubted they were going to get out and chase Joe when he ran. When I was twenty-five feet from Joe, I noticed their car roll slowly forward. That wasn't part of the plan.

Just as I opened my mouth to call Joe over, a beater car pulled to the curb. Joe leaned in. He appeared to be negotiating with the driver. As he finished speaking, he happened to glance towards the agent's car. I was still a house distance away. Fred hit the gas, squealing the tires. Joe looked in my direction, probably intending to run that way. Instant recognition appeared on his face. I grinned so he knew I knew. Before any of us could do anything, Joe grabbed whatever the driver held, which was probably dope, and ran. In his other hand, I saw what looked like money. I guessed then that he'd forgotten to pay.

The dealer wasted no time. He cut the front wheels, gassed the car, and made a u-turn in the street. In a second, he was chasing Joe. The only one to notice me was Joe. The feds tried to follow, but the direction their car faced meant they had to back up and get turned around. Joe's sights were on me, so he wasn't thinking about the dealer. He stayed to the front yards, running west. Surprisingly, he put some distance between us. We came to what I thought was his getaway but turned out to be a one-way-in-one-way-out alley. The dealer's car accelerated past me. He skidded around the corner, right behind Joe. I had no idea what happened to the ATF guys. They should have been right behind everybody.

When Joe heard the sound of the engine, he turned his head to look back. His eyes got huge. Maybe it was then he realized he'd forgotten to pay. He came to the wall at the end of the alley. There was nowhere to go. Joe turned. For sure, he faced certain death. He threw his forearm across his face. The small four-door Toyota bore down on him like it was bent on taking him through the wall with it. At the last minute, the driver slammed on the brakes. There was the sound of locked tires on gravel. I didn't think it would stop, but it did — an inch from Joe's kneecaps.

The door flew open and the driver, a Hispanic, jumped out with a tire iron. The funny thing was that it was red, which made me think we'd have a hard time discerning paint from blood if he hit Joe with it. The driver was screaming in Spanish. Joe dropped the arm when he realized he wasn't going to be squished, but immediately raised it again when he saw he was about to get clobbered. Joe didn't speak Spanish and the guy wouldn't have cared if he did. That was obvious from the way the driver swung his arm all the way back for the mother of all strikes. I was five feet away.

There was no time to yell silly things, like, "POLICE!" or shoot him without being sure of not hitting Joe. So, I did what I could, which was leap in the air, hitting the top of the Toyota's hood on my right hip. My forward momentum carried me across the hot metal, straight at the driver. I pulled my legs back to my chest so I looked as though I was doing a cannonball. When I was in striking distance, I kicked out with both feet. The blow landed in the center of the dealer's back. I hit him so hard I thought his back would break. He was driven forward off his feet, his body arched like a bow. His stomach slammed into the wall, causing the breath to go out of him. I knew there wasn't going to be much of a fight from that point on. What happened next was a bonus, which was that his hand, still holding the tire iron, slammed into the wall, too. The force knocked it loose, bouncing it off the bricks. It flew back towards me, barely missing my head, and hit the windshield. The glass shattered. I was still on the hood of the car.

After the driver's torso rebounded off the wall, the next thing to happen was a prime example of an opposite-and-equal reaction. His butt landed on the car's hood like he was going to sit there. The hood was thin metal, which acted like a trampoline. He bounced forward so his face went right into the wall. There was a sound like a hollow melon hitting something hard. His head bounced back, but instead of falling over, he caught himself. At that point, he was probably still conscious. He turned towards me like he'd walk away,. His nose was mashed flat, blood already covering the lower half of his face. His eyes rolled up into his head and he dropped like he'd been shot, right in front of his car. I looked at Joe to see if he was alright. His face showed pure terror. He darted away. I should have known why.

There was the same sound of tires locking up on gravel that the Mexican's car had made, now the feds ran their car into the back of the dealer's. The force of the collision threw me forward like I'd been launched from a catapult. I barely had time to get my arms up, thus keeping my face from connecting in the same spot that the dealer's had. After I bounced off the wall, I landed back on the hood with enough force to permanently dent the metal.

I couldn't move. Slowly, I flexed body parts in an attempt to discover what was broken. When I was sure nothing was, I rolled to the ground. I stood up, looking for Joe. He lay on the ground. The passenger door had sprung open at the impact and caught him square across the front of his body. As I stood there, wondering if he was alive, I heard groaning. It came from under the car. To say I was surprised was an understatement. I figured the dealer was dead.

I painfully went to all fours, feeling like an old man. Once I was down and my eyes adjusted to the shadows, I saw the guy was pinned beneath the car. There was a lot of blood.

Hopefully his nose, I thought. He opened his mouth to cry for help. *And he's going to need a new set of front teeth.* One thing was sure, he wasn't coming out of there easily. As I climbed back to my feet, I looked in his car. The front driver-side floorboard was covered with small balloons. There was also a paper cup that had been filled with brown liquid, which I assumed was Coca-Cola or Pepsi. He probably had the balloons hidden in the cup in case he was stopped — a pretty common trick.

"Jesus," Fred said from on the other side. He was trying to help Joe to his feet. "Have you ever heard of deodorant?" Fred asked.

"I can't use it. I get a rash. I bled once," Joe mumbled.

"Fuck his BO," I said. "Look at this car."

"Hey. Check it out. Not even a dent," Jerry called. His hands were on his hips like he was surveying something he'd made. I hobbled back and was absolutely amazed. The Fed's car looked as good as new. When Jerry backed the two cars apart, the dealer's back bumper fell off. The front end was totaled. I pulled the cell from my pants and called Dispatch.

"I need medical, a traffic cop, and my supervisor," I told the call taker.

"Where are you?"

"Wait a minute. I need to walk out and figure that out."

"Hey, Armpits," Fred called. "You drop something?" He held up a small balloon. The fed looked at me. "He's high."

Like he's telling me something I don't know, I thought. Joe started puking. Right then, I knew what he was feeling. After all, I'd just been the equivalent of a human rubber ball, too.

"How much you doing, Joe?" Fred asked.

"Only a little," Joe said. "Who are you?"

"Can this wait?" I asked. "We have this other guy under the car, I don't feel well, and where the hell is medical?"

"Strike while the iron's hot I always say," Jerry said. He winked at me. They were treating this as normal. That made things feel a little surreal.

"I'll ask the questions," Jerry said. "I'm Fred. He's Jerry."

I turned at the sound of a marked unit pulling up at the end of the alley. "Tell Dispatch," I yelled, "We need the fire department here." The officer waved. I wondered if that meant he'd heard me.

"Listen, Cam," the one I thought was Jerry said. "While you get this straightened out." He gestured at the mess. "I thought we might borrow this guy."

"You need to stay," I said. "I need you guys to explain what happened here."

"We're feds. We don't get involved in local situations. Have your boss call us if there are any problems." He turned to Joe. "Let's go."

"You gonna throw me in jail?" Joe asked.

"I ought to, but . . . no . . . you're going to do us a favor."

"Wait." This was out of control. "Do I need to remind you there's a guy stuck under this car? And that you guys are the ones who killed him?"

"It's cool," Jerry said. "We'll fill out a report and fax it over."

"But . . . " they were already loading Joe in their car. I could see there wasn't much I could do other than pull a gun on them. They backed the car up to the black-and-white, Fred leaned out, flashed a badge and honked, actually tooted the horn, as he was on his way out. I hobbled over to the car where the guy was trapped. We were the only two in the alley.

"Hey. You speak English?"

"A little," he moaned.

"I have medical coming. The fire department, too."

"*Qué?*" he asked.

I didn't have the energy to give him an explanation to his question. "Just hang in there. We'll get you out as fast as we can."

The word came again. I stood up, but didn't move away so he could see I stayed close. I thought I'd like a human presence if I were in his position. A monarch butterfly dropping into the alley caught my eye. It was the size of my palm. It dropped through the air, floating down the vertical surface of the wall as though it were a leaf. Before it reached the level of my head, it fluttered around. For a few seconds, it looked lost, then with quickening wing beats, pushed up and over the wall. I tried following its flight, but it went straight into the sun, causing me to blink furiously. That made me dizzy. I looked down and saw the man under the car had seen it, too. The butterfly must have had the same effect on him as it had first had on me, which was to make him calm. The dizziness grew, making me feel as if I'd faint, so I leaned on the front of the car. The guy underneath yelled and I backed towards the wall to lean on the warm brick.

Ten minutes later, the alley filled with firemen, supervisors, and traffic officers. A fireman pulled out a brand new Jaws-of-Life, then started discussing the best way to cut the front end off the car. I couldn't stand it. I went to the Toyota and opened the trunk, where I found the jack.

"Here," I told one of them. "This is a time-honored method for raising cars."

The traffic sergeant came over. He wanted to know what happened. I explained the best I could.

"You let them leave?" he asked.

"Let?" I asked. Before we got into it, Sergeant Durant came walking towards us.

"You OK?" he asked.

"Banged up, but nothing's broken. They already looked at me," I said as I nodded at the paramedics.

"You look like someone who shouldn't be standing." He touched the side of my face and I winced. "Go to the hospital. I'll get a uniform to take care of him when they get him out."

"There's a lot of dope in that car," I said.

"Yeah. Looks to be about an ounce of black tar. Good bust. That'll make things a little easier with the captain. I want a medical professional to look at you. Make sure you get the occupational injury forms on my desk tomorrow."

I grimaced. What would I write in the "How could this accident have been prevented" part?

My phone rang. "Yeah?" I listened. After a minute, I looked at Durant. "The feds just lost Joe and their wire. He went in the front door and out the back."

"Yeah?"

"Just so you know," I said. "I told them he was fucked up. I saw him on the nod when we first pulled up. They want me to help track him down."

"No way. Tell them it'll wait. Go get yourself looked at. You're limping. What if something's broken in there?" I made a face at him. "It's an order, Cam."

"OK, Sarg. I'll get on it."

"Get your car and go home." He gave me a push, then turned to the traffic sergeant.

"I need the name of the other driver," he said to Durant.

"I don't know the feds other than by first names. They're ATF." I needed to sit down. The alley was hot and I was dizzy.

"Billy, you can talk to him tomorrow," Durant said, speaking to the traffic sergeant. "OK?"

"I'll follow him down to the hospital and take a statement."

"No," Durant replied. "And if I have to call the lieutenant to make sure that doesn't happen, I will. Tomorrow. Understand?"

"Buddy, you know that's not procedure." From the look on Durant's face, I saw what he thought about procedure and so did the traffic sergeant. "Sure," he said. "I guess I can do that." He gave me a look like I was the suspect who'd been let off. I didn't like it, but there was no use getting into a pissing contest with him. I walked away.

When I was in my car, I pulled the cell from my pocket. I winced when I put it to the side of my face. I looked in the mirror and imagined what I was going to look like the next day. As the line rang, I switched it to the other ear. I moved my face close to the air conditioner. The dispatcher came on and I told her to clear me and log me off. I clicked the phone shut.

When I looked outside, I saw people up and down the street looking at the sky. I leaned forward, looking through the windshield, trying to spot what it was. There was a man parachuting down. He was probably an illegal jumper because I didn't remember hearing anything about the Stratosphere putting on any kind of show. Normally, it would be fun to drive to where he landed, put the habis grabbis on him, then haul his body off to jail, but right then, I had other concerns. That made this the guy's lucky day unless the area units got to him first. If they did, he'd be sorry. The cops would first handcuff him, then cut the parachute off his back because he was handcuffed. I didn't know what one of those things cost, but I'd bet it was a lot.

I cracked the window and listened. I didn't hear the sound of sirens, so I doubted that he had anything to worry about. I watched him until he drifted so low he disappeared from sight. In his circle, he'd be a legend — the one that got away. Then again, seeing where the wind blew him, right into the heart of Naked City, he might be calling if the shitheads got to him first. They'd probably steal his parachute and whatever else he possessed.

"Screw the hospital," I muttered. I was going to go to a bar, get a drink, get a bunch of drinks, get drunk, go home, take a hot bath, and sleep. In the morning, I'd get up, go to work, and hobble around looking for Joe. When I found him, I was going to make sure he knew I'd told him the truth about his becoming a personal project if he screwed me over. Technically, he'd screwed the feds over, but I'd been there.

I smiled. Joe would probably run, which would give me a reason to beat his ass, then book him for everything I could think of. With that thought in mind, I put the car in gear, and drove to the bar.

■ ■ ■

The El Tees Bike . . .

"I found him," I said. Gary raised his eyebrows as if he didn't believe me.

"Where?" he asked.

"Motel on Fremont."

"He run?"

I held out my hand. The knuckles were skinned. "We visited UMC first."

"Get the feds their money back?"

I gave him the you-have-got-to-be-kidding look. Actually, Joe told me after we arrived at the hospital that he'd bought a bunch of dope only to get rolled by a couple of blacks over by the Atomic Bar.

"Served you right," I'd said. When I asked where the wire was, Joe said he'd pawned it. That was good. It meant the pawn shop was required to hold it for thirty days before it was sold. I thought I'd wait a bit before I told Jerry and Fred where they'd have to go and pay to get their equipment back. When I repeated this to Gary, he laughed.

"Did you know they'll get in more trouble for losing that wire than they would for wrecking the car?" Gary remarked. He had his feet on the desk and was cleaning his fingernails.

Then again, I thought, *Maybe I won't let them know where their equipment is.*

"Well, Joe's in jail," I said. "That's what counts."

"Can I make a comment?" Before I could reply, he continued, "You look like shit."

I rubbed a hand across my ribs. They hurt. "Whatever," I said.

Durant came in. "Cam, you qualify this quarter?"

"Nope, Sarg. Thought I'd go to the range next week."

"Go today. Get it done. I'll have the new guy, Mike O'Brien, meet you out there."

"He Norman's replacement?" I asked.

"Yep. Be gentle with him," Durant said. He gave me the once over. "On second thought, maybe I should keep you two apart. He's new. I don't want him thinking I send people out to end up looking like you."

"Hmmmm. Virgin meat," I said. Durant just smiled at me, but it was one of those smiles that was ugly.

When Mike and I got back from the range, I was the one in shock. I went straight into Durant's office.

"Holy shit, Sarg. How the hell has he kept this job?"

"Mike has people in high places who like him."

"Got to be," I said. He was second generation Irish with the foulest mouth I'd ever heard. The first words out of his mouth were, "Glad to fuckin' make your acquaintance, Cam." Then it was, "Won't this fuckin' car go any fuckin' faster?" When he missed the target, which wasn't often, it was, "Fuck this and fuck that." Half the guys out there knew him and laughed good naturedly when the sound of his cursing reached them. Mandy Baker, a female officer from my Academy, came over while we reloaded.

"Do you think you can keep a lid on that toilet you call a mouth?" she asked.

"Fuck you." He smiled, looking her straight in the eye.

"I don't appreciate having to hear that kind of language."

"Then go the fuck somewhere else," he said. His eyes narrowed and I could see the trouble coming. "It's a big range and I didn't ask you to come all the way the fuck down here where I'm trying to hit that fucking little piece-of-shit fucking target." He moved closer and dropped his voice as the sentence progressed. I could tell he was deliberately trying to goad her. She started forward. I stepped between them.

"Go away, Mandy," I said.

"Who do you think . . . " she started.

"I said go away, Mandy."

"No, Cam. I intend to make sure he gets what's coming to him for speaking to me that way."

"Hey, wasn't that Tommy from Southeast Area Command I saw you with at that bar the other night? You and Eddie divorced now?" I asked.

"Bastard," she whispered.

"Life's a bitch . . . "

"Then you fuckin' marry one," Mike finished.

After she walked away, I turned to him. "I don't mind a beef," I said. "But I do mind a hassle. Can you make an effort to draw less attention to us if we have to work together?"

"Fuckin' A," he said. "I didn't like that fuckin' cunt anyway."

"When was the last time you were in Ireland?" I asked.

"Never fuckin' been there."

That was how things were left. As I drove down off Sunrise Mountain, my eyes drifted across the valley. I followed streets with my eyes, not paying attention to my driving. I had to jerk the steering wheel when I almost drove off the road, causing the car to swerve.

A few minutes after I walked out of his office, Durant came over and sat on the edge of my desk. "We have a search warrant to serve pretty quick. This'll be the second time in four months that construction theft detail is hitting the same guy's house. The cops are at the guy's place so often, people might be thinking we have a Metro substation inside."

"Then what's the problem?" I asked.

"The problem is the owner fills it up with stolen property as fast as we can empty it out."

"Ever wonder why that is?"

"Are you looking for a philosophical discussion on this or would you like to hear what we're going to do?"

"Sarg, I know what we're going to do. We're going over there, kick in his door, arrest him, watch the court let his dumb ass go. Did I miss anything?"

"Basically, you got it right, but he's already arrested. Specifically, I need you to listen to the story of the patrol cluster that happened last night."

"We hitting fuckin' Jamie Watkins' house?" Mike asked as he walked into the office from the bathroom.

"How'd you know?" Durant asked.

"Fuckin' figures," Mike said. The Sarg lifted an eyebrow at him. I figured they'd had the discussion about his mouth. "Last fuckin' night I was on the fuckin' squad that caught the fuckin' shithead. He was fuckin' leaving a construction site in a fuckin' jeep loaded with fuckin' tools. We had a merry fuckin' vehicle pursuit, which was fuckin' not exactly a vehicle pursuit."

"First," Durant said. "I just counted eight *fuckings* out of that mouth. Try not using the word in a sentence. Second, how can you not exactly have a vehicle pursuit?" Durant asked.

"The fuc... Sorry, Sarg. The guy sped away, but later stopped. Claimed he couldn't see the unit for all the shit in the jeep. We asked him what he'd thought about the sirens following him. Said the stereo was up too loud. When we asked what he was doing on a job site at two in the morning, he said he fuckin' worked there."

"Not bad. Only one and a half times with the bad word. Work on it. Did he?" Durant said. Mike looked at him stupidly. "Did he work there?" Durant asked again.

"Jamie never worked a fuckin' legitimate day in his life," Mike said. Durant's face registered exasperation.

"So, how'd he get in?" I asked, hoping to deflect the lecture that was brewing.

"Said he used a pair of bolt cutters because the boss told him to get some stuff from the yard, but he forgot his key. Said he'd get fired if he took too long bringing it back."

"You patrol guys buy this?" I asked. I could see a cop doing that. Heck, I could see me doing it.

"Almost. There was that little look on Jamie's face, though."

"Little look? What little look?" I asked.

"The little I'm-a-fuckin'-lying-dirtbag-motherfucker look," Mike said with the most innocent expression I'd ever seen.

"I seen that one before," Durant said with a laugh.

"Me, too," I added.

"Well, right after he gave us the look, he decides to go out the passenger door. The foot pursuit was short and painful, but only for him. The official version is Jamie fell over a wall, into a backyard, and met the owner's pit bull."

The Sarg looked interested. "Did he?"

"He did meet the pit bull. As for falling over the wall, well . . . The dog was well trained. He did stop eating Jamie when his master called him off."

"That's fucking too bad, dude," I said. He had me saying it now. "I mean, that they didn't let the mutt finish him."

"I fuckin' know," Mike said. "Anyway, the dog's owner says she knows Jamie. We asked how. She said he lived up the street. I took him out front where it would be easier for the ambulance to find us. While they looked at him, I took a walk. While I was out front, I smelled something fuckin' funny. The garage door was open and in plain view was a working meth lab."

"In plain view? My ass," Durant snorted.

"Honest to Jesus."

"Then why are we doing a search warrant on the place?" I asked. An active lab fell under one of the exceptions to the search warrant rules because it was considered a danger to the community. That meant a narcotics lab team could go in and take it apart and dispose of it first. Only after they were done or while they were neutralizing the threat did they have to obtain a warrant if they later wanted to prosecute.

"They called out narcs," Mike said. "Jamie denied knowledge of anything, including living there. He went to jail anyway because the neighbors all said he did. The lab team came out and dismantled the lab. I was starting here this morning, so I left to go home and get a few hours sleep."

"While I was taking a fuckin' piss, Jeff called," Mike continued. "He told me the rest of the story. After narcs carted everything off as the sun came up they told patrol they might want to look inside. They thought the house was full of stolen property. Patrol did."

Durant cut in, "They called us and I've been waiting for you. Type me a warrant, Cam."

"Ah, Sarg. Why isn't construction theft doing it?"

"They're sitting on the house and have been for a couple of hours while I waited for you to shoot."

"Why didn't you have me come straight in?"

"You needed to qual before you missed the quarter and I had to deal with the captain. You know around here admin things take priority over police work." He threw a stack of pages in front of me. "Here's the reports. Get typing."

I groaned. It was hard enough doing my own warrants without trying to make sense of someone else's story. When I glanced at the address, I knew where it was. I'd been on the last one. I felt dread just thinking about how much shit we took out of there the last time. If this was anything close to that, it was going to be a long day tagging, recording, then impounding all the shit we'd find. Then there was going to be all the carrying out to our cars for transport to the vault.

When I finished, I took the warrant to a DA, then a judge. She read it and signed it. I called Durant, telling him we were signed, before I drove out. That way, they could get started and save me some grunt labor. When I arrived, I learned my dread was justified. For the next five hours, we carried things outside until the front yard was covered with large tools — drill presses, welding rigs, and compressors — microwave ovens, televisions, VCRs, cable boxes, and furniture. By the time the temperature was in the triple digits, every square inch of the dirt yard had something sitting on it.

At ten, the press showed up to do a live feed for the Ten Thirty Show. It was a slow day, so this was the most exciting thing happening in the valley. Ten minutes later, the first victim called in. He said his wife recognized some property that was taken from his house. It didn't take him long to get there. The reporter was excited. This had the potential to make her story more interesting by adding the human element. She decided to put him on live from the scene. Right after that story went on, two reporters from the other TV stations showed up and we suddenly had more press than a typical murder scene.

"That's my shit," the victim said. The reporter winced. "I'd recognize that god awful orange f . . . " She quickly covered the microphone with her hand. He seemed to realize what he was about to say. " . . . couch my wife bought anywhere."

From behind the scene, Durant turned to Mike. "Relative of yours?"

"Fuck no. If he was related to me, he'd a said, 'Fucking shit.'"

For the next seven hours, victims showed up steadily. They took things that were theirs and some stuff they said looked like their stuff. We'd had the news stations tell people to bring crime reports if they had them or we wouldn't release the property. That wasn't necessarily true. I knew that the more stuff I got rid of, the less I had to impound. It wasn't long before the yard looked like a garage sale.

As far as the return process was concerned, it was simple. Once we'd *verified* the item belonged to a victim, we had ID photograph it, figured what the value was for later prosecution, and helped carry anything the victim needed help with to their car or truck. If they needed the help, we considered our part done.

About nine that night, I was sorting through power tools when I noticed one with a Henderson telephone number on it. Flipping it over, I saw the name of the business engraved in the side. I took out my cell and called. Someone answered.

"Hi, this is the police," I said.

"Holy shit, Rodney," the voice on the other end said. "It's the police."

"Why'd you answer, fool?" a second voice asked.

"I don't know man, it was ringing," the first voice replied.

"Well, hang up, dude. Get the stuff together."

The phone went dead. "That's weird," I said.

"Get a wrong number?" Gary asked.

"Don't think so." I checked my caller ID, where I saw it was the same number as on the tool. I took out my radio.

"Control, Baker Fifty Five Thirty Two, I think I have a Four Oh Six in progress. Can you have a Henderson unit check it out?"

"You think you called a burglar?" Gary said.

"Two," I replied.

"Affirm, Thirty-Two. Where?" Dispatch asked. I told her I didn't know where, but I did have the number. She said she'd have them check it in their directory.

A half hour later, she called back on Durant's cell. "The Henderson cops got lucky. As they pulled in, they caught two guys leaving. Dispatch says they were impressed and wanted to know how we knew. I told her to tell them we have a crystal ball. I'll call the Henderson sergeant later and tell him the whole story."

The lieutenant showed up at ten. He walked around in his uniform, acting like he was the one who typed the warrant and served it single handedly.

"Probably fuckin' wants to know why he's paying all this fuckin' overtime," Mike said as he wiped sweat from his brow. I watched McMahan as he smiled and shook hands with the reporters. He seemed to be on a first name basis with many of them.

The front yard was still covered with property. It was as though we couldn't give it away as fast as we found it. There were still items that were very noticeable, like the eighteen almost-new BMX bicycles. When I pulled the first one out, I discovered it had a company sticker on the bottom of the crank. The sticker had a phone number for a place in Reno. Durant called but it was out of service. Next, he called Reno police He asked their dispatch if she could provide a better number. She had the same one we did. She did a search of their system for old reports, but there was nothing for the bikes. She said she would have a unit respond to the business on the off chance they had a new phone number posted or someone was there. When she called back, she reported the company had gone out of business. That part of the investigation looked like it had dead-ended.

When no one else had showed up by the finish of the eleven o'clock news, the media packed up. I grabbed a bike and wheeled it towards a truck.

"Where you going with that?" the El Tee asked

"I'm going to impound them," I said.

"Negative. Metro has an entire yard full of bikes. We don't need more. Leave them."

"But, sir," Durant said. "Who has eighteen bikes like that? Not that tweeker, for sure."

"He does as far as I'm concerned. We're not taking them. That's an order."

"Yes, sir," Durant said.

I felt a stab of anger. This wasn't the way things should be done, but then I thought, *What the fuck? Ain't my bikes.* As we finished, I thought about going home for some rest. It had been a long day. Then, a mental image of my empty place and the picture of me and Karri May I'd found a couple days before came to mind. That picture, dredged from the bottom of a drawer, showed the two of us — smiling, happy, and content. I remembered how I'd been thinking of asking her to marry me. If that had happened, we wouldn't be living in an apartment in the ghetto. I'd have done what normal people did — bought a house, planted flowers, built a white picket fence. Instead, I slept alone and wished I didn't. Now, I had to go back to pushing the pain, like dirt, under the imaginary rug I'd woven in my mind.

This crime scene made me realize what Norman said about how all we did was keep the lid on. It was no more, no less. It was like the people who came down to reclaim their property. They had much more taken than we'd recovered. One victim had his entire shop cleaned out. He told me he couldn't afford insurance because he had only a small business, which meant he was forced into bankruptcy.

Another woman had lost everything in her storage shed, including all her daughter's things. We found the empty boxes next to the fireplace. Jamie had burned everything — the family pictures, her grandchildren's school work, old letters, and postcards from trips they'd taken together.

His probable intention was to destroy anything that would link him to the crime. What made that particular victim's story worse than the others was that several months before, her entire family had been killed in a car accident as they came back from California. Those were all the things she had left of her daughter, son-in-law, and grandkids. I watched a neighbor lead her away to his car and thought, *Well, that wasn't exactly true, she has her memories. Just like the rest of us.*

As I walked around the yard with people, I also realized how much stuff there was. Jamie had been a very active burglar. His criminal history, which I'd become intimate with while I typed the information into the search warrant affidavit, was long. He had been arrested seven times for burglary, possession stolen property, receiving, and grand larceny. Each charge was a separate incident. Each time the police got him, we always recovered at least this much. It wasn't the things. It was all the sheer pain and misery that those things represented for the victims. I couldn't figure it. Jamie didn't look like he was coated in Vaseline, but the system sure had a way of making it look like he was.

"When we're done, ya wanna go get a fuckin' drink, Cam?"

"Nah, Mike," I said. "I sure hate putting those bikes back."

"I know. But what the fuck ya gonna do? At least we don't have to load our cars."

I had to smile at that. The evidence vault sent their truck out. We loaded everything on it and all we had to do now was lock the house so Jamie had a safe place to come back to when he got out of jail.

"I'm tired," I said. "I'm going back to the office, then home, and then I'm going to crash."

"My fucking da says that enough alcohol can make life easier."

"Been there, tried that. I threw up a lot. There ain't enough booze if they filled the sea," I said.

"Yeah. But I'd try drinking it anyway."

"We done?" I asked.

"Fuckin' aye. It's off to the bar for me. Sure ya don't want to join me?"

I clapped him on the shoulder. "It's home for me, a couple of cold beers, and a warm bed."

"A warm fookin' body to fill it I hope, laddie."

I didn't feel like telling him there was no warm body in my bed because that might lead to a discussion that there had almost been one. Instead, I said, "I hate that fookin' accent, laddie." All he did was grin at me.

"Practicing," he replied. "I want to fit in if I ever make it to Ireland."

Before I went home, I drove to the station and went to my office. On the corner of my desk was a pile of case files. As I rested my hand on them, I asked myself, *What would it take to put all this in order?* I glanced at the garbage can but knew I'd already gotten away with that once. I sat down and wrote the arrest report for the additional charges I intended putting on Jamie. If the court did nothing, people couldn't say I didn't try. Afterwards, I got up and left without looking back.

Forty-five minutes later, I stood in my living room with a cold Coors. The phone rang. I picked it up.

"What?" I said, not bothering with any politeness.

"Remember those bikes?" the El Tee's voice asked. That stopped me for an instant.

"Yes, sir."

"Go back in the morning and get them."

"You said to leave them," I said.

"Now I'm telling you to go back and get them," he yelled. I didn't move. His voice came back, quieter this time. "My wife watched the eleven o'clock news. Those bikes belong to her school." I knew McMahan's wife was an elementary school principal somewhere. "When she saw them, she was very happy. I didn't have the heart to tell her you guys left them there."

I wanted to ask, *We left them there?*

"Tomorrow morning, those bikes will show up at her school. Tomorrow afternoon, her kids will be happily riding them around the playground. We, the police, will be the heroes. Do I make myself clear?"

"Yes, sir."

"After all that's taken care of, you will go down to the jail and you rebook that asshole for everything we found at his house but especially those bikes. I'll call the DA, not some deputy, and make sure he doesn't get a deal."

"OK." That was what it took — piss off someone important. Now, Jamie was in trouble. Steal an old woman's last memories and get nothing. Steal some used bikes and get hammered.

"Good," he said. There was satisfaction in his voice. "Just take care of this, Cam."

"You can count on me, Ell Tee." He could, too. I didn't like him, but I was it. I was a cop — just one of the people who stood between people like Jamie and people like the old woman or the shop owner.

The phone went dead. I tilted the beer and took long swallows until it was gone. I popped another, then looked around. I wondered if taking out the trash, washing some dishes, sweeping, and dusting would make life a little more livable. But meanwhile, I had to get out of there. I picked up a jacket and went out.

I took my car and headed for Sunrise Mountain. The night was cool, but I left the car window down. There was very little traffic on the road. Twice, I passed patrol units going the other way. The insides were dark so I couldn't see if I knew who was driving. I came to Lake Mead Boulevard and made a right. The ground began to elevate as I drove for the pass. When I was at the place where the road dropped away in both directions, I turned around. I drove off into the desert about fifty feet, turned the key in the ignition so the engine stopped and sat in the silence. I wanted to get out and sit on the hood, but I was too tired to move. I loved this spot with its view of the city — lights glistening and shiny in the distance. There were people down there who changed little over the course of their life and that was because age made that happen.

I pulled the handle and pushed the door open. When I got to the front of the car, I stared at the valley. Without the dirty windshield to dull them, the lights shone in a beautiful kaleidoscope of color. What took place under them was another matter. There were murderers and robbers loose and burglars stealing a lifetime of memories. Then, I thought of my mother, my sister, and a woman who tried to love me. That made me realize that there were other things down there — such as love and joy and happiness. I opened a beer and took a sip. It tasted good and I wanted to get drunk. I held the can up so it blocked some of the view, then I dropped it. That wasn't the answer. Being up here by myself wasn't the answer either. It was time to go home and put my life in order.

■ ■ ■